WHEN EVIL WALKS AMONGST US

Chrissie Yates

WandS Books

To Vanessa,
Enjoy!

The characters and events portrayed in this book are fictitious. Any similarity to real persons, living or dead, is coincidental and not intended by the author.

ISBN-13: 9781914243080

Cover design by: More Visual

For my Lola & Luna

For the joy you both bring every day.

PROLOGUE

HOW IT BEGAN

In contrast to the normally pristine, stratospherically expensive Italian porcelain tiles, the spattered and smeared crimson blood now looked almost like a grotesque Jackson Pollock work of art. Hard to believe that life's essence could so easily resemble spilt paint. There was so much of it.

Later when it was all done with, it was the sounds of anguish that stayed the longest with them, not the blood. An almost unworldly sound that came from a place of utter despair, utter desolation and from a heart so wounded that it would almost certainly break to never recover again. Finally, one of them spoke.

"How many times?"

"How many times what?"

"Could she have stabbed him?"

Silence then, "A lot. Not the once but … a lot."

The full horror of what was before them began to form and take shape opening another chasm of silence yawning before them. Only the normal household sounds could be heard as they competed with the sounds of utter despair and regret.

"So we now have to decide on the best way to get rid of the body. Any suggestions?"

CHAPTER 1

Earlier that day, the day life changed forever for all of them, Imogen Holt was driving a large white van stuffed with food and not for the first time Imogen wondered why anyone thought grey concrete pebble -dashed walls was ever a good look? June 2020 was a year like no other when instead of looking forward to the summer break, most pupils had barely been to school and instead of doing the normal duties of a Deputy Head, she was delivering food to vulnerable families. Driving through the grey streets she passed a poster on one of the lamp posts stating the bleak reality for some saying how 'Abusers enjoy working from home'. She knew like many on the front line that Covid had created more than one sort of victim and she felt the familiar knot of despair tighten further.

Finding her first address Imogen stopped the school van. She heard excited squeals as soon as she vacated the vehicle as the front door opened to reveal thirteen years old Molly balancing her baby brother on her hip, with her two other younger siblings crowding behind her. Molly looked exhausted and Imogen experienced the day's first heartbreak.

"Morning Molly. Bad night?"

"Yes, bless him. He's teething aren't you Freddy?" The child looked at Imogen with that look all babies have, as if they already know the answers to questions yet to be thought of, yet it was the gaze of complete trust and adoration he gave his older than her years' sister that was basically ... well, wonderful. Imogen's constant ache of loss hit her mercilessly once again.

"How's mum today?"

"She's not so good Miss. They've had to stop her chemo because of the flu thing. We don't know when she'll be called again and I think she's scared," which was code for Molly telling Imogen how terrified this young Carer was. Not for the first time Imogen found herself silently railing against the fates or whatever, that would send such an awful burden to one so young. Molly's mum had been diagnosed with breast cancer directly after the birth of baby Freddy and just before Molly's father had been sent to prison for dealing in stolen goods. The family had been kept together due to Molly's maternal grandparents moving in but they too were in their seventies with health issues who now needed to shield. This family needed support but frighteningly it was left to schools, the church and an overworked social worker to keep it functioning and more importantly together.

"I've not managed to do any of my homework Miss. Sorry, but I will try to catch up."

"Don't worry, we'll sort all of that out when this is over. Now you lot! Plenty of goodies today but remember I want to know that the fruit and vegetables will have been eaten first before the…," Imogen paused for dramatic effect, "chocolate biscuits or yoghurts! Is that a deal?" Molly's younger siblings nodded excitedly as Imogen placed the bags on the doorstep.

"Thanks Miss."

"Take care Molly and remember you can ring the school any time. Ok?"

Nodding, Molly instructed the children to carry the bags inside as she closed the door to the world and began the hard process of coping for another day.

Sighing heavily, she knew the next stop would be very different and it was. Pulling the van outside a particularly ill- kempt property with the rubbish strewn garden of old bicycles and discarded toys giving an insight into what probably lay inside the four walls, Imogen braced herself. Before she was able to knock on the rotting front door it was flung open and standing in all of his unwashed beer bellied glory was, George Cowden, a notoriously difficult to deal with individual who was the undisputed small time drug supplier for the immediate area. Some of his drug activities had spilled into school and therefore into Imogen's jurisdiction and she disliked his kind with an intensity that was palpable. Cowden was a bully, a chancer and a man without any real moral compass. They had had more than one run in and she knew there would be more in the future particularly as his teenage sons were becoming clones of their father and bringing into her school his drug activities too. The eldest son who had been asked to leave Grove South school a number of years previously, due to his bringing on to school premises a BB gun and summarily firing it at an unsuspecting crowd of year sevens, was now in prison for drug related offences combined with grievous bodily harm. A real 'chip off the old block' indeed with a no doubt very proud father. Imogen was so on their case and Cowden and his sons knew it.

Pointing to the food bags Cowden growled, "What's that rubbish you're leaving and who gave you permission to be on my doorstep? Sticking your bloody stuck up nose in my business again?"

Swallowing down what she really wanted to reply Imogen simply said, "You're on our list Mr Cowden, as neither you or Mrs Cowden have been in paid employment for quite some time and the fact that you have three children here, or should have," she added, "you meet the Government criteria for support via the meals your children should expect from school. Ok?"

"Rather 'ave cash!"

"Not going to happen." The staring stand- off lasted a few seconds until an enormous crash followed by screams made him turn his back on Imogen, slamming the door in her face.

Sighing Imogen turned to leave but not before noting the brand new Series Five BMW four - wheel drive standing proudly on the small drive come front lawn, small time drug dealing obviously immune to the global pandemic. The door opened again and Imogen turned to see Katie Cowden standing there. "Hello Miss. Can I come to school with you please?" Imogen looked at her sweet earnest little face and wanted to weep.

Smiling she replied, "I'd love you to come to school Katie, but your dad thinks you'll be safer at home." The lie was a harmless one as no child deserves to know the truth about their parents until they have no choice as Imogen knew only too well from her own difficult childhood.

"Katie! In. Now!" bellowed George Cowden and it was a very sad little girl who now waved goodbye and closed the front door leaving Imogen with an impotent fury that she realised was never far away these days.

Imogen knew there should be only three siblings of school age living in this house. Colleagues had requested that Year Seven Katie be allowed to attend school due to her very unique special needs status and the fact she had a full Statement giving her access to so much well needed support. Her parents had predictably refused. Katie Cowden's Dyspraxia, a form of autism compromised her motor function but little Katie was as bright as a button and very different from her siblings as she loved school and was doing well. Imogen knew cycles could be broken, hadn't she herself done just that, so she hoped upon hope that the hidden gem in the Cowden household such as little Katie would one day do so. The odds were stacked against her though and Imogen knew it. Sighing heavily whilst getting back in her white van, Imogen also acknowledged that there were more people currently in the house than should be and as always she was again, put in a difficult position where this particular family was concerned.

Rounding the corner onto the Red Rec Imogen slammed on her brakes as she took in the scene before her. Football! Again! The multitude of young boys gathered together seemed oblivious to everything except their game. Donning her mask Imogen got out of her van the same time a police car screeched to a halt and on seeing both vehicles it took precisely twenty seconds for the group of budding football stars to scatter in a cacophony of shrieks of "Pigs" and "Run for it".

"Little buggers! How many bloody times do they need telling?" fumed the huge bear of the man in uniform, who was heaving his considerable bulk out of the police vehicle. His significantly smaller, in comparison anorexic looking partner also alighted the vehicle grinning his hello to Imogen. Brad 'the bear' as he was known, was recently separated from his wife Beth who was part of Imogen's close knit friendship group, a group of four women who had grown up together from the age of five and were as close as any four people could be, blood relatives included: Imogen, Beth, Harriet aka Harry and Sarah.

"How's it going Brad?"

"Same shit, different day. You?"

"Same shit my friend," grinned back Imogen. She was inordinately fond of Brad and had had more than one 'chat' with her friend about whatever issues they had going on. She knew Beth had and was having a tough time for all manner of reasons, but still, Imogen knew you didn't walk away from something so precious and so rare.

Brad looking uncomfortable but clearly desperate for information casually asked, "So have you girls managed to have a socially distant out door meet up recently? Everyone ok? Sarah? I know you girls are worried about her and that arsehole she's married to!"

"We're meant to meet up at Hawthorne Park for a walk at the weekend. We've cancelled the last two recently for one reason or another though so who knows," shrugged Imogen. Sensing Brad's total sadness she offered, "Do you want me to try talking to her again?"

"Thanks but she's got to want to talk to me and only me," shaking his head adding, "and it's not just the balls up at work, it's her mum as well and lets not even think about the baby business. The results we had were just too much for her."

"And you my friend." Recent fertility tests had revealed that not only did Beth have a 'Hostile' uterus but Brad also had a low sperm count which was making a natural pregnancy very hard and which was one of the reasons they were having this 'break'.

Brad's frustration was palpable. "I see such shit every single day but for Christ's sake, why is it those who can give a child a good home can't while there are those who shouldn't be allowed anywhere near a bloody guinea pig to look after...," he abruptly stopped. "Sorry..." Imogen held up her hand.

"No it's ok and you've every right to feel as you do. There's nothing right or fair in any of it."

They were gratefully interrupted by the return of his partner Will who had made sure the group of boys had sufficiently dispersed. “If anyone else today tells me to go and arrest Dominic Cummings first I swear I’ll bloody arrest them for just mentioning his sodding name!”

Grateful for the interruption Imogen smiled, “They really could have said a lot worse, trust me. Actually I’ve just done a delivery at the Cowden household. There should only be three children of school age there but it sounds like many more so God knows what he’s up to but he has a brand new BMW on the drive. Fancy paying him a visit? I’m actually worried about the youngest daughter who has dyspraxia. I worry that she may be exposed to real risk of infection.”

“Like I said, some shouldn’t be allowed to look after a bloody guinea pig and it would be our pleasure to drop by to upset our George on this fine sunny day wouldn’t it Will?”

“Can’t think of a better way to pass the time.”

Several pleasantries later Imogen found herself back in her vehicle, emotionally and mentally trying hard not to go where she was never far from if she was honest.

CHAPTER 2

Imogen and her husband Neil had spent Christmas with Neil's parents who lived in Stamford near Cambridge. It had been a lovely, traditional family time with Neil's parents, two sisters and partners and their assortment of fabulously bright, precocious children. A wonderful chaotic melee of laughter, party games, overindulgence, tears and tantrums and Imogen had loved every single second of it.

It was a stark contrast to her own experience of a family Christmas. Her mother had tried her best as she did every single day, but her father was... a brute...no other word for him. The adult Imogen now realised that he clearly had been a deeply troubled, complex man who should have never married and who most definitely should have never fathered a child, particularly a daughter. He may have had time for a son, but Imogen was a clone of her Anglo French mother, inheriting her dark hair, olive skin and clear pale green eyes and for reasons only he knew, her father seemed to despise Imogen and her mother more and more as the years went by.

As a little girl Imogen use to see other fathers with their daughters, holding their hands, hoisting them up onto their shoulders, buying ice scream or playing chase in the park. Children brought up in such bleakness would automatically think they were at fault, must be unworthy of love. Not Imogen. From a very young age she knew where the fault lay and her father saw that she knew every time he looked at her.

Her mother Arlette did her best to protect her daughter as she too had been brought up in a similarly dismal brutal household. The day she was swept off her feet by the blonde haired charismatic Jake Taylor, Arlette felt all her prayers had been answered. So desperate was she to escape the hovel she called home, she silenced that inner voice that told her if it was too good to be true, it probably was.

The day he first slapped her, she was already six months pregnant with Imogen and the blow came completely out of the blue. He was of course sorry vowing to never do it again and Arlette remembered forgiving him, shrugging off the idea that she knew deep down that it really would happen again, just like her own mother had years before her. Arlette also foolishly believed a baby would make a difference but it seemed to make him worse.

Later he would tell her how she had made him to do it because the baby was making her neglect him. "I have needs," he had screamed one day, "but all you're bothered about is that brat." She had scooped Imogen up there and then and left, hoping to find a sanctuary somewhere although returning to her own parents had been out of the question. Jake's sick smile said it all the day they returned because she literally had nowhere else to go. Arlette had come to the conclusion that a homeless shelter for her but particularly for her baby Imogen could not be the solution. So she eventually had to return, making Jake feel even more all-powerful where she and their daughter were concerned.

"Glad you've finally realised when you're well off Arlette. You're where you belong and you belong to me!" as he grabbed her face hard in his hand before pushing her away.

So Arlette and Imogen learned to live with this cold, moody, quick to anger, completely vain man, who spent most of his wages on himself because womanizing and looking dapper did not come cheap, whilst Arlette worked two sometimes three jobs to make sure Imogen did not go without. She secretly opened a savings account in Imogen's name too, as she was determined that her bright, beautiful kind child would get away, would break the cycle. If Imogen was able to go to University, Arlette was determined she would do so and Jake Taylor would have to kill her to prevent it.

Imogen's three friends from school, Beth, Harriet and Sarah, even in those bleak days were often a sanctuary for them both. Arlette would never stop being grateful to Beth's father, a hard working no nonsense quietly strong, typical Yorkshire man, who having seen unexplained bruises on seven-year old Imogen's arms and legs had called to see Jake, on the pretense of making sure Imogen got home safely from their home only two streets away. Arlette could remember so clearly looking up from the sink as Imogen opened the door and walked in followed by Beth's father Terry Fletcher.

"How do Arlette. Thought I'd bring young 'un home with it getting dark so early now."

"Thank you Terry, that's really thoughtful of you." Imogen's father looked up then and smiled affably. He was always very affable when anyone called not that many did.

"How do Jake. Wondered if I could 'ave a word in private like?"

"Course mate," as rising from his seat Jake moved to just outside the front doorstep. Through the window, Arlette could tell that Terry Fletcher was saying something to her husband that made him first very very red, then very very pale, then very very afraid. The finger now jabbing

Jake Taylor's chest was firmly pushing whatever point being made, home.

Taking a final look back at Imogen and Arlette who were now silently standing close together, Terry Fletcher nodded his goodbyes and left. When Jake reentered the house, the look he gave them both was one of pure hatred and for one breathless moment, Arlette thought Terry had unwittingly made everything worse. Then his shoulders slumped, looked defeated and yes bizarrely full of self- pity, as if he was somehow the wronged one.

For a while things got a little better, not totally but better because Jake Taylor was quintessentially a bullying coward with a strong sense of self preservation. As the years passed though, his inner demons would find their way to his fists and usually to Arlette's torso where the bruises could not be so easily seen. Young Imogen though was now spared and for that Arlette would always be grateful to Terry Fletcher and take all Jake Taylor wished to lash out.

So Christmas days were like most other days except for more food and small gifts that would not instigate one of his rages that often came without warning.

The day he was found dead brought nothing but relief to both of them.

How different life was now. From the day she met Neil Holt, Imogen finally understood what had been missing, to finally feel that being in someone's arms was like coming home.

They'd both met whilst studying at Imperial College London, in the University cafeteria in Fresher's Week but it took them another eight months to actually become an item. Not looking where he was going Neil had unceremoniously knocked Imogen as she was balancing her food and coffee whilst collecting cutlery.

"I'm so sorry, I'm such an idiot. Please let me go and get you something else."

"Honestly it's really fine, no harm done," smiled Imogen. Mortified though, he had insisted on buying her another lunch despite Imogen's protests as she had in fact been pretty pleased the incident had occurred as she had been drawn to this quiet, hopelessly shy young man who clearly had no idea how utterly gorgeous he was. Neil for his part was completely overwhelmed by the beauty that was Imogen as he hurried away.

So Imogen noticed Neil and Neil was very aware of Imogen for quite some time with neither making a move to get to know each other better. Neil also witnessed how seriously clever Imogen was and the double fact that she was seriously scary too made him completely smitten and terrified in equal measure, so approaching her for a date was for him out of the question.

Smiling as she drove, Imogen was now recalling that first afternoon on the Campus green. Neil was sunning himself and had fallen asleep as Imogen, passing by, saw how burnt the fair skinned Neil was going to be if not warned. Imogen sat beside his prone shape and gently nudged him. Neil opened his eyes and thought he was still dreaming until he heard, "The burnt to a crisp look has never been a good one. You need to get some sunscreen or shade pretty sharpish."

Neil startled, sat up quickly colliding with Imogen's forehead as he did so. "Ouch. That hurt!"

"God I'm so sorry. I swear I am never this clumsy except near you. Are you ok?"

"I've had worse believe me," laughed Imogen then as seconds ticked by, they both realised they couldn't stop really looking at each other. Seriously looking until finally Neil asked, "Fancy a coffee?"

"I thought you'd never ask," and that was all it took. Within a month they had moved in together, sharing their tiny hovel of a three bedroom rented flat with four others. They were good days, student days and all that means like mooching round Petticoat Lane on Sunday mornings looking for a bargain, coffee in the parks and the obligatory student March against the government of the day.

They had their moments like all couples do, spectacular rows usually instigated by Imogen just in case Neil was like her father, followed by intense make ups, all the norms. Imogen had experienced two sexual partners before Neil and up until their meeting had yet to really get what all the fuss was about and Neil was as inexperienced as she was but together their natural connection made them realise how extraordinary being together actually was.

Imogen was now recalling the first time Neil had invited her home to meet his parents. She had guessed he came from well- heeled stock. For a start he didn't have to work part time to pay his way like she did but it was that quiet confidence people who have never really gone without that showed itself so often, such as in restaurants or just in the way he dealt with everything. Standing on the doorstep of the most gorgeous original Georgian stone house with its graveled drive and landscaped gardens made Imogen want to turn and run.

The door had swung open and she was engulfed immediately by the warmth of the welcome perpetuated by Neil's wonderful parents. "So this is the girl who has smitten my boy!" boomed a fifty something clone of Neil, "definitely punching way above your weight my boy!"

"For goodness sake Henry," smiled his mother, "let the poor girl get in before you start. Well

Neil, you did say she was a beauty but you're simply gorgeous," and just like that she was held in strong, warm arms and accepted for who she was.

Imogen loved Neil's family, loved their charm, their honesty and pride at what they had achieved. Henry had built his law firm from nothing; a former scholarship boy from a low paid farm worker's family who by sheer determination and hard graft had succeeded where others had failed. He was proud of his roots though and never forgot them and didn't allow his children to do so either whilst his mother Ruth was equally as grounded. Yet it was their kindness and huge devotion to each other and their family that made Imogen grieve for what she and her mother had endured.

She could still remember the day she told Neil about her dead father and about her life before his death. They were sitting on the Embankment overlooking the Thames. Imogen knew how she felt, knew she was falling in love and knew total honesty was now important to them both. So she told him everything about growing up in her difficult abusive home…almost everything.

When she had finished, she turned to look at him expecting to see pity which she really didn't want. Instead she saw tears of anger streaming down his face. "Well I'm glad the bastard is dead because I'd fucking tear his miserable black heart out!" He was holding her then and both were quietly crying, she for a lost childhood and he because he hated to think of his Imogen as a small child, living in such a hell.

Yes, they had enjoyed wonderful carefree days before the business of finals and the prospect of work and becoming proper grown-ups came into view on life's horizon. Neil intended to follow in his father's footsteps and enter Law, specializing in Criminal Law. Imogen knew she wanted to teach English but she also knew that she wanted to return home to the small really very insular Market town of Penton lying at the foothills of the Pennines. Neil had been expected to work in his father's firm in Stamford but knowing how strong the pull for home was for Imogen, he found a post in Sheffield and although disappointed, Neil's parents understood.

Her mother Arlette was beyond happy, clearly relieved that her daughter was not drawn to men like her father and would be coming home. The small intimate wedding, tastefully done and celebrated in the marquee situated in the grounds of Neil's parents' home was without question the happiest day of Arlette's life and finally she felt the ghosts of the past were finally buried deep. If only.

Four years, seven months, three weeks and two days ago. Chris Rea's 'Driving Home for Christmas' was on the radio and in her mind's eye she could still hear Neil's voice laughing at little Milly's antics particularly the 'attitude' comment. Their four- year old, seriously beautiful niece had proudly explained to them how her mummy had informed her how she had "Real attitude already." Stroking her ever growing baby bump, Imogen was already dreaming of the wonderful days ahead, when the son they were due to meet in less than three months, would finally arrive and would undoubtedly have some 'real attitude' too.

It happened so fast. Without warning. Neil was an excellent driver but even Neil wouldn't be able to negotiate the erratic, drug induced speed of the stolen car with its thieving scumbag of a driver at the wheel, which without mercy ploughed into them as it pulled out of one of the many T junctions.

She was now remembering a beam, a light. She'd heard noises. She remembered looking at her Neil and he was reaching for her hand and saying something but she couldn't hear him and she so badly wanted to hear him, to take his hand.

She knew.

No one had to tell her that her baby was gone, that her Neil was gone.

She knew it. Could feel it.

It's as if she had blinked and then…nothing. No more love, no more beauty, no more hope, no more future. Nothing but a bleak empty abyss that threatened to consume her...should have consumed her.

How she had wanted to die in those first few days. All she wanted was to be with her family, her boys as she had already begun to think of them. She even began to formulate plans to do it which she knew now she would have never have gone through with, but in those bleak early days, she really felt she could not live with the agony of such loss.

Imogen could vaguely remember familiar faces and voices arriving at her bedside. Her mother's face of relief she still had her daughter and devastation knowing what her daughter had lost, but it was Neil's parents that she couldn't face because she knew that their pain would be equaling hers if that was possible. Like her they had lost their child, their only son.

Imogen had no recollection of the ritual that follows death. Neil's funeral was well attended by all accounts as he was well loved by all who knew him, from his fellow lawyers, friends old and new, neighbours, his clients, even the very dodgy ones. For if you knew Neil then you would love him for his gentleness, his consideration of others, his wicked practical joke sense of humour, his innate kindness, his intellect, his strong sense of justice, his hatred of cheats and his profound sense of loyalty. All gone in the blink of an eye.

It was her friends who got her through the hard part, the decision to live part. The three arrived at the hospital like the force of nature they were when one of them was threatened: Beth, Sarah and Harriet simply took over.

With Arlette they listened carefully to the doctor in charge of Imogen's injuries. Medically she was lucky to be alive as her left leg was shattered and had to be pinned together, her spleen removed and when the impact had killed her baby, it also took away the prospect of future children too.

For weeks Imogen was never left alone, even when she screamed at them to do so. She would wake to one of them sleeping in bed with her, or cooking for her, or forcing her to take a shower or a bath or bullying her to do the daily exercises prescribed by the Physiotherapist who as Imogen often screamed at the poor woman, was "Nothing better than a fucking sadist". For months they were there, her safety blanket and her protection whether she wanted them or not, until the morning she woke up as if from the longest nightmare and began the hard process of living again.

Death and loss brought together a great deal of surprises too as Imogen suddenly found herself very wealthy. To begin with her mortgage insurance kicked in so the large five bedroomed house with its crippling payments was suddenly paid for. Neil's life insurance paid up handsomely and then Neil's place of work handed her a six figure cheque due to Neil's death in service. It felt bizarre, unclean somehow because all she wanted was him back. It was again her friends who made sure she did not do something she'd later regret such as giving all the money to the local food bank or Cancer Research because that was indeed her first instinct.

Imogen was now remembering sitting in a courtroom later that year to face the guilty ones, little more than boys really, but old enough to know what the consequences of their actions could be. Of course the four of them had walked, no had run, away from the scene of the carnage they had caused without a scratch. In court their bravado came across as a lack of guilt too, laughing when they came in, waving to their families and friends who vociferously shouted their support until the threat of removal by the judge was issued.

Before sentencing Imogen was surprised to see Henry, Neil's father being invited by the judge to address the guilty boys before sentence was issued. As Henry took his place next to the Prosecution Counsel Imogen was again struck at the resemblance between father and now dead son. It wasn't just the features and height but the manner in which Henry carried himself and his voice sounding so very familiar. This was her Neil in thirty years ... if he had not been stolen from her.

She would remember his words for the rest of her life:

"May I thank the court for giving me this opportunity to speak today and to address my son's killers, because you are all to blame for his death. Neil was a remarkable young man with much to offer the world. He was a lawyer who passionately believed in defending those who couldn't defend themselves. He believed in fairness and he also believed that people were basically good, that good people often found themselves doing unforgiveable actions. I know he would have found a way to somehow forgive you for the decisions you all made the night you took drugs and stole the car which took not only his life but also the life of his unborn child, his son, my grandson. So do what is right from now on. Pay your penance society will demand but also make a choice today that when society allows you back, that you will begin the process of making my son Neil proud of the futures you will then begin. Work, learn and contribute but never forget what you have stolen from me, Neil's mother, Neil's wife, his siblings, his friends. One day when you're holding your own child, remember your actions, your decisions, your choices on the night of 28th December and quietly remember and mourn for our loss as we will do now every day, for the rest of our lives. Promise us all today that you will treasure and protect who is in your arms with everything you have because the thoughtless and cruel actions of others can so easily snatch them away from you forever." Imogen saw how his words came not from a script but from his heart, how dignified in grief he was and how utterly bereft.

The silence in the few seconds that followed Henry's powerful words was deafening, except for the muffled sobs of the mothers of the boys, or at least the ones who had bothered to turn up. The belligerence of the rest of the supporters had completely dissipated to be replaced by a defeated form of shame as the custodial sentence was issued, the boys now looking down, smiles gone. All would be free by their twenty first birthdays. It was so very sad and so very pointless.

As they were leaving the Court building a man unknown to Imogen approached her. "Excuse Mrs Holt but could I have a word in private please? I won't take much of your time." Moving into a small alcove just off the main corridor the man introduced himself. "My name is Malcolm Speight. Your husband was my lawyer when the Sheffield Constabulary tried to fit me up, unsuccessfully I might add thanks to your husband's due diligence."

"Ah yes I remember that case. I also remember how unpopular that made him in certain quarters," smiled Imogen, now looking closely at this very rough diamond standing before her. A balding, stockily built man who wasn't particularly tall but had that menacing stance that made you instinctively want to give him a wide berth. His very loud pin striped suit was clearly expensive and in the most appalling bad taste too; the epitome of what a modern day gangster would look like without really trying.

"I'm no angel Mrs Holt. I've done bad things I can justify because they were done to bad people who had it coming. Your husband believed me and defended me because it was the right thing to do. People like me don't often meet men like him, a good incorruptible man and well I came to think of him as less as my lawyer but more as someone I could trust and that is a rare thing for a man like me." He was blinking now and Imogen realised he was close to tears. "It was proper good what Neil's dad said in there, but I'm telling you now it was a waste of good oxygen because I will guarantee they will come out worse than they're going in. Now my reach is long and I would like your permission to sort it for you properly." Malcolm Speight was now looking at Imogen expectantly and as seconds ticked by, it dawned on Imogen what he was actually suggesting. Shaking her head she responded, "You know that's not what he would want and I'm not even sure it's what I want now but thank you though, for being here."

"I attended the funeral too."

"I'm told I attended it also," she smiled. Sensing the odd looks coming from the girls and others she began to take her leave of this physically intimidating but perversely honourable man. Gently taking her arm he leaned towards her and whispered, "If you ever need anything or if anyone tries to mess with you, you call me right? Here's my contact because your bloke was a good'un and didn't deserve this. I'll never forget what he did for me... so remember. Please promise me?" Taking the card, she nodded then joined her friends.

Pulling back into the school gates Imogen came back to reality realising she had driven across the city and back to school. Sighing heavily, she mentally told herself to 'Get a grip'. She had come to terms with her past a long time ago so dwelling on 'if onlys' was less than pointless.

Hours later, Imogen eventually entered her smart converted loft apartment she now called her home, thanking God it was Friday, with the wall clock telling her it was 7.05pm. It had taken a while but finally she had the place just as she wanted and it did indeed look like something out of an Interior Design magazine. The space was magnificent and very large. The whole building had been redeveloped from an old disused mill, dating back to the 1800s. With clever design and planning, the old dark monstrosity now housed a collection of beautiful dwellings, from apartments such as Imogen's, to houses of varied shapes, sizes and prices, all set within a private gated communal area with panoramic views across the Pennines.

Imogen knew about style and elegance and she did it with ease. Various shades of grey and white with beautiful original art work carefully chosen, brought life, light and colour to what could easily have been stark, unfriendly walls. Money being no object did help though, so she had gone to the ridiculously overpriced Design Centre in nearby Wakefield and got the look she had always dreamed of, paying ridiculous prices for lamps, rugs and sofas. However, it was the magnificent view of the Pennines from the huge bi-folded doors onto the balconied terrace that made her home so special.

The decision to leave Neil and hers home in the prestigious Lodge Park, Sheffield's super affluent area had been an easy one. Although beautiful, it was too big, too far from work, too far from her mother, too far from her friends and held too many memories. Also being surrounded by footballers and their families, business men and their vacuous wives who appeared to make going out to lunch as their life's work was just something she really didn't get. Neil had been coming to the same conclusion too so selling it was very easy as the area was very sought after and it allowed Imogen to cash purchase her new build apartment and also to buy her mother the cottage of her dreams, both in the small market town of Penton of her birth. Imogen remembered how as a little girl she had promised that she would buy her mum that very home when she had grown up and become very rich. "When I grow up mummy you and me are going to live there," she used to say whenever they walked past it, qualifying with, "but just us two mummy, no one else."

Sighing, Imogen kicked off her shoes and walked over to the fridge where she found an already opened bottle of cold Rose de Provence. She poured herself a large measure then wandered over to the large double glass doors opening on to the large terrace overlooking the stunning panoramic views she'd always known. Neil's smiling face beamed up at her from the picture situated on the small side table placed just beside the bi-fold doors.

"Been thinking a lot about you today my darling, not that I don't think about you every day but today I seemed to be more in the past than the present." Settling into her comfortable chair, she realized how tired she was, acknowledging it had been a bit of a day and seeing Brad hadn't helped to be honest. Beth wasn't herself at all. Out of the four, Beth was the brave, naturally gregarious 'in-your-face' one who took no prisoners. Smiling to herself Imogen was now remembering the day the four of them cemented their friendship nearly three decades ago.

They had been pupils at St James Infant School and in Class Two with the very wonderful Mrs Barnet as their teacher of all things. They had been put on the same table and sharing the same box of crayons which Billy Boyle had tried to take from them. Beth had told him no so he had pushed Sarah hard, as she was so tiny, making her cry. Harry comforted Sarah, whilst Imogen and Beth got Billy Boyle behind the 'tuck' shop making sure he never bothered any of them again. Yes, they had become one entity from then on and if you took one of them on, you had the rest on your case.

Recently though Beth seemed reticent to talk or meet up and Imogen was beginning to really worry about her. Sure she'd had a rocky few years with one thing and another but still, she certainly wasn't herself.

The ringing of her phone made her jump and looking at the screen she saw it was Harriet.

"Hi Harry, is everything ok?"

"Imogen. I'm at Sarah's. Get over here now!"

"What do you mean? We're not allowed to..."

"Just... just get over here now. I've already rung Beth. It's...bad Gen. Really bad!

Imogen stared at her phone as Harriet had already disconnected.

CHAPTER 3

Earlier that day, the same day life changed forever for all of them, like Imogen, Beth was also negotiating an early start. She felt like death but knew it was completely self –inflicted and she hated herself more and more. Taking a deep breath, she adjusted the regulation clip on tie, closed her locker and proceeded to make her way to where her partner would be waiting. Deep in thought she did not see her estranged husband Brad until she collided with his massive frame. "Whoa steady there. You okay?" then closely looking at her shook his head.

"What?"

"You look like shit that's all. So are you okay?

"I will be thanks but I am now running late so if you'll excuse me…"

Still holding her gently by her arms he said, "I just worry about you, how can I not?" Beth now found she wouldn't look at this man whom she cared so deeply for and instead reacted as she always did when cornered.

"I'm fine ok? Now just back off 'cos I've a job to get to and last time I looked, so do you!" Putting his hands up as if in surrender Brad allowed her to pass but she could still feel his eyes boring into her retreating back.

Getting in their designated squad car, her partner Police Constable Asif Khan and all round 'good egg' handed her the Styrofoam cup of a much needed coffee and then grinning knowingly at her said, "Is that a hangover I see before me?"

"Please God, do not tell me you're auditioning for bloody Macbeth this time?" groaned Beth, gratefully receiving her coffee as her headache continued to pound with uncontrolled vigour.

Asif, a keen am dram enthusiast, smiled good naturedly at her. "No just an observation."

"You should be a bloody detective."

"I should be an Oscar winning actor with a pad in LA and my own Caribbean Island but instead I'm here with my partner about to dispel wisdom and justice to the nation's great unwashed and often ungrateful."

"So where to first?"

"Well most people are working from home but our friendly neighbourhood burglars are not following the rules of lockdown, that's for sure. Two break- ins down Limes Road, one a nurse who had just finished a fifteen hour shift for

God's sake, plus a stolen car at the other address as well as the burglary, then onto a neighbour reporting multiple households meeting and then a complaint about a mysterious gathering just outside Penton, your neck of the woods. Strange lights appearing which has led the complainant to suggest there may be a Satanic cult at work which may, according to said complainant be the cause of the Pandemic, summoning up evil spirits to spread it. That should just about take us to lunch," Asif grinning now as Beth choked on her coffee.

"Bloody hell fire, not in the mood for the bloody Nutters today," muttered Beth as Asif put the car into gear before driving them out of the station.

Giving her a sidelong glance whilst negotiating the traffic, Asif, taking a deep breath knew he had to address Beth's current state saying, "Don't like to think you going home and drinking on your own Beth. Come and have dinner with me and Robena tonight."

"I'm not a bloody alcho Asif, just had a couple more than I should that's all."

"For the third time this week. Now, I'm not having a go but we just worry about you that's all. Worry about Brad too if I'm honest," Asif added tentatively not wanting to interfere but finding it hard not to such was his and his wife's concern for his partner and joint friend.

Beth smiled at Asif and was genuinely touched by his concern. She'd had similar conversations with Imogen and Harry too, but she knew it was something she just had to work through. She alone knew a Beth and Brad reconciliation was looking increasingly unlikely particularly since...no she wasn't going there again. Beth knew she was on a downward spiral of self-destruction too and at the moment couldn't seem to stop. She also felt such a sense of self – hatred that she was genuinely scared how far she would stoop. Hence the drinking.

"Others are noticing too Beth. The Sarge was asking how you were doing too so...just start taking care of yourself love. Alright?"

Beth looked straight ahead and swallowed hard, trying not to allow the fury that was always so close to the edge these days, to erupt and spill all over this kind man who was merely trying to be her friend.

Eventually, before the silence became unbearably uncomfortable she responded with, "So who do you think you're calling 'love' you patronising chauvinistic pillock!"

Asif, breathing a silent sigh of relief replied, "There she is! There's my girl!" only to receive a very hard thump on his arm. "Ouch, that bloody hurt that did!"

Being a Police Officer in the time of Covid had its challenges to say the least, particularly with the weather being so good. Uniformed officers spent a good deal of their days patrolling areas and asking groups of people to disperse, often receiving a good deal of belligerence in the process. Victims of crime too were vociferous about the lack of police presence where they believed it mattered with burglaries and car theft still happening but also dog theft too had really taken off. Desperate times certainly made people do desperate things.

Asif and Beth went about their duties, taking statements and offering nuggets of comfort where they could. The nurse who had just done a fifteen hour shift and who had come home to a ransacked house was particularly distressed. "What is wrong with people?" she sobbed, the marks of the PPE still visible on her tear streaked face, "it's not as if I have 'owt worth stealing for God's sake!"

"I know how hard it is, knowing strangers have been in your home but occasionally we do get lucky and catch them," offered Beth, "but here's your Victim of Crime Reference for your insurance purposes. Please tell me you are insured?"

"Oh yeah, dad insisted when I first decided to leave home."

"That's good because you wouldn't believe how

many people aren't these days. Can I also just thank you for all you do? You're the last people who deserve this rubbish," offered Beth as she and Asif took their leave. Back in their squad car, Asif turned to his partner and smiled. "Ok, now you're really scaring me. What?"

"You're just really brilliant with people, knowing exactly what to say when someone needs just a bit of comfort." Batting away the well- meant compliment, Beth replied, "Let's see how brilliant you think I am after our next stop, because my friend, I know where we're going and who you are going to meet!"

As they drove across the city towards Penton, it was easy to feel the stress of the urban bleakness begin to briefly recede. Dark, badly kempt high rise flats were being replaced by better housing with larger gardens, interspersed with fields, then onto open country with views of the Pennines and the wind turbines in the distance. Beth could feel herself relax as she felt the pull of home and being on familiar turf.

She directed Asif off the main roads down a barely used track which led to a collection of almost derelict outbuildings and a collection of old discarded scrap metal objects. Standing in the middle of the yard was a diminutive, very thin woman with waist length white hair, who must have been at least eighty years old. As Asif and Beth walked towards her, she backed away looking confused and afraid.

"Hello Miss Nicklethwaite, my name's PC Beth Fairchild and this is my colleague PC Khan. We've come to investigate your complaint?"

Hazel Nicklethwaite staring wildly merely nodded then pointed across to the open fields. "They're there," she whispered.

"Who Miss Nicklethwaite?"

"Them that worship the Devil. Them that's brought the plague." Hazel Nicklethwaite moved a little closer, squinting at Beth as she did so before declaring, "I know you!"

Smiling kindly Beth replied, "I live in Penton too, have done all of my life. I used to be called Beth Fletcher and I think you might know my dad Terry. Most Penton people do to be fair."

Nodding now as the long past memories returned she replied, "Yes, I remember you and your three friends! Right little buggers, always up to mischief. Needed good hidings, all of you!"

Smiling Beth replied, "A long time ago but you're not wrong. Now who exactly should we arrest?"

"Him over there!" pointing over to the next field where her farming next door neighbour resided and who for years had made sure this eccentric elderly neighbour always had plenty to eat, helping any way possible to keep her safe. It must have been exhausting thought Beth particularly in the present circumstances.

Beth knew that this always lonely old lady had forever had issues with all of her neighbours. As children they would scare themselves silly with stories about who lived at the Nicklethwaite farm and Beth had no doubt that if this poor soul had lived four centuries earlier, she would have been dubbed a witch and burnt accordingly. As children they were convinced she actually was. Beth now knew what the real problem had always been and with the mental health issues that come with old age, quietly felt her heart breaking for this former figure of childhood fun and games.

"Let me take a full statement, then we will take action. Is that ok?" Nodding she beckoned for them to follow her inside the old farm house. Beth saw that Asif was clearly shocked as Beth grinned sadly at him and followed accordingly.

Later, back in their squad car, Asif turned to his partner and smiled sadly saying, "Poor old bugger. It's certainly no way to live particularly at her age," then trying to lighten the mood asked, "So how naughty were you and your mates then? Spill."

"She was our resident witch, 'looney', always alone, just her and her dad stuck up here in all weathers. We used to dare each other to walk past her house and scream blue murder and run like mad if she saw us, convinced she would put a spell on us. There were rumours that she had a baby but it had been born dead but it turns out she was being sexually abused... no more than that, raped by her father for years and years and years but in those days nothing was said or done to stop it."

They were both silent, lost in their own thoughts, wondering how it was possible to survive such a horrific existence. Asif finally broke the silence asking, "How do you want to proceed?"

"We should have a word with next door then onto to Social Services and possibly Age UK, need to get involved if they're not already I should say?"

"Agreed. Poor love eh?" then because he had to, Asif brusquely attempted to normalise the atmosphere of hopelessness now pervading them, "Now for some snap I think!"

"Yep get your priorities right my friend," smiled Beth, grateful to change the subject as she began to peel away her sandwich wrapper, wishing she was elsewhere.

Later that day as they neared the end of their long shift they were radioed to assist in dispersing an illegal lock in at one of the pubs around the Attercliffe area; a rough, run down, former steel works area in the back streets of Sheffield. In the ensuing struggle Beth received a very bloody nose, mainly because she took particular issue at a couple of the racist names directed at Asif which she was not having.

"Look what we've got 'ere," one particular had Neanderthal jeered, "a bloody towel head and a Barbie bimbo." Red mist descending Beth launched herself at the said Neanderthal, twisting his arms behind his back, handcuffing him only for him to back head butt her hard. This meant a visit to the local Accident & Emergency Department.

"Really hope it's not broken mate. Bloody pillocks!"

"Just clock me out then bugger off home mate. I'll get a taxi to the station to pick up my car when they let me out. Go on bugger off!"

"Ok if you're sure? See you tomorrow then and leave off the booze tonight eh Beth?"

Nodding her assent, Asif left, leaving Beth to her own demons and thoughts and memories and not for the first time she wondered how she had got to this place in her life.

CHAPTER 4

Beth had left school straight after her 'A' levels, unlike the other three friends, and had done a variety of office based admin jobs until, at the age of twenty-six had an epiphany to join the Police Force, much to the complete and utter outrage and despair of her father Terry.

Terry Fletcher was a child of the fifties and like most of his male peers had followed his male ancestors to work in the then thriving coal industry. Sixteen-year old Terry left school on a bright July Friday and with pride and trepidation had entered the gates of Walkley Colliery the following Monday. There he was to work for the next twenty- one years until 1984.

Although decades had passed, some memories are difficult to erase, some emotional scars difficult to overcome. For Terry and many others who had been striking miners in what historically became the bitterest of industrial disputes, he had developed an almost illogical distrust of the police.

He still remembered vividly the militarized

marching of the boys in blue, the 'Zulu' rattling of their riot shields, the waving of the wads of cash earned in overtime in front of hungry desperate working men who were fighting for the very survival of their families, their communities, their way of life and right to work. He still remembered the horror of Orgreave, the violence and how unfair the whole business had been reported and the long walk back to work that had ended their hopes of survival, of a future they could count on.

So when the 'apple of his eye', his Beth, his beautiful, clever, sassy, brave Beth sits him down to tell him she intended to become a Police Officer, he felt completely devastated and illogically betrayed.

"You want to do what?" he had roared, "after everything I have tried to teach you about our lost heritage? After everything you know those buggers did to good honest working men?"

"Yes dad over three bloody decades ago!"

"Some things can't be forgiven or forgotten!"

"Well dad I'm living in the twenty first century and I suggest you join me," said Beth as she had flounced out of the room.

Several more rows of a similar rhetoric had ensued but Beth had remained firm, with Gill her mother being pragmatic about the whole situation. "Do you want to keep your daughter in your life Terry?" she had asked one day after a particularly vitriolic exchange.

"What sort of a bloody question is that?" scowled Terry.

"The only one that matters. She's her father's daughter Terry and like him, she is bloody minded and as immoveable as a bloody lump of coal!" Sighing, he knew she was right of course, when was Gill ever wrong when it came to their children?

The question was, did he accept that life was now very different? The police now a very different force to the one he encountered in those dark days of the eighties when good people suffered immeasurably and accept her choice? Or lose her. The outcome was never in any doubt.

The day she passed out at Hendon, Terry Fletcher felt a tremendous surge of pride. His Beth would make a difference, would be one of the good ones and of this he was in no doubt.

Beth had really loved her job. She enjoyed the prestige of now being regarded as a professional, feeling useful and she loved feeling needed. She also knew she looked 'smoking hot' in her uniform too which was a real bonus. Beth was Amazonian, towering over her friends particularly petite Sarah as she was broad shouldered and strong whilst remaining incredibly feminine and downright sexy. The long blonde hair and pale blue eyes undoubtedly helped too and even the most belligerent drunks often acquiesced at the sight of Beth, happily being escorted to wherever they were being put. She also had a natural empathy with victims of crime, particularly the very young and the very old but it was with the brutes and the bullies that her infamous temper had to be reined in. Probably because of what she knew Imogen had endured growing up, Beth dreaded the Domestic Violence call outs for a variety of reasons. She just hated seeing the fear in the eyes of the children, the utter defeat in the eyes of the women and sometimes men too.

It was also where she had met Brad Fairchild, her husband, her 'great bear' of a man who she really did still love very much indeed. They had officially met whilst on football duty, officially because she had seen him from afar in the station and also watched him represent their station at the Inter-league Police Rugby matches. "Who's that?" she had asked another WPC.

"Brad Fairchild," answered her colleague Sharon who she was later to find out had also had a crush and a bit of a fling with the object of their scrutiny.

"Do you know him?"

Sighing Sharon replied, "Yes. Well it's common knowledge that we've hooked up a couple of times, usually after one of the matches but it hasn't led to anything, more's the pity. He's seriously very nice in all aspects if you know what I mean," she added giving Beth a knowing nod and wink.

"So I wouldn't be treading on your toes if I gave it a shot myself?" asked Beth.

"No," replied her colleague sighing heavily, "more's the pity!"

The following Saturday afternoon, Sheffield Wednesday was actually playing its city rivals Sheffield United in a rare meeting as they were leagues apart but this was the FA cup. The city was at fever pitch, family and friends were divided and battle lines drawn. It could have been a long ninety minutes but the match was incident free in the end, possibly because the football itself was so utterly awful. So when Wednesday scored in injury time it was a relief to everyone that they would not have to endure a replay or Extra Time.

Beth and Brad 'officially' met whilst they were escorting a couple of 'wannabee' hooligans to the Police Van. Both boys had tried hard to instigate some sort of riotous affray between the fans only to be met with a certain apathy so they and their mates decided to try their luck by causing a rumpus with the police instead.

Professionally ignoring the personal jibes that were being flung their way, both Beth and Brad were glad when both boys were firmly secured in the Police Van. "Well, I'm sure their mothers must be very proud," smiled Brad.

Looking up at this gentle giant of a man, Beth took a deep breath and said, "Fancy a drink later?"

"Pardon?"

"A drink, preferably alcohol... with me, unless you're busy? Attached? Oh please tell me you're not secretly married?"

Brad really smiling now answered, "No and yes."

"No and yes to what?"

"Oh sorry. No I'm not married and yes to the alcoholic drink... er later."

Smiling, Beth turned to take her leave, "Later then."

"Hang on what about our contact details?"

"Already sorted. I'll ring you," and off she went.

Later that evening in Beth's local pub in Penton, the love and affection that was to epitomise Brad and Beth began. "So," began Brad, "how did you get my number?"

Grinning Beth replied, "Sharon Summers. You and she I believe went on a couple of dates."

Blushing Brad confessed, "Well I wouldn't exactly call them dates."

"Neither would she, but she did say you were a

really nice guy. I think she would like to be your girlfriend," Beth teasingly replied whilst fake fluttering her eyelashes, "my round I think."

As he and every other red blooded male watched her make her way towards the bar, Brad couldn't quite believe that this gorgeous feisty, 'in your face' woman had gone to so much trouble to meet him and soon realised that he basically hadn't stood a chance. Having learnt what a well-respected officer and downright nice guy he was, she was determined that he was to be hers because that was what Beth did. She made up her mind and that was usually that. For Brad's part, he realised too, there and then, as he watched her laughing with the pub's regulars, that he was and always would be hers from then on too.

Beth had been a Police Constable for four years when she began the process of becoming a detective, joining CID. As much as she loved her daily interaction with the public, Beth found herself becoming increasingly frustrated with the constraints of her role as a uniformed Police Constable. A natural problem solver by nature, she began to resent handing over cases and information gleaned by her own tenacity, to the station's detectives, so she decided to become one of them, taking the necessary qualifications to do so. Brad and she were already happily married and confident that the babies would eventually be forthcoming. There was no reason to think otherwise as they were both young and frighteningly fit, so until they decided to appear, Beth continued making progress in the job she was loving more and more.

She was a particularly effective Family Liaison Officer as it is a sad fact that many serious crimes and unexplained deaths are often perpetrated by members of a victim's family. A FLO is vital in forging positive relationships, gaining trust whilst being alert and fastidious in the information that would often be inadvertently given. In this role she excelled and along with her partner Detective Constable Lydia Smith, who were predictably referred to as 'Cagney and Lacey' were accredited in being responsible for a good many guilty men and women currently serving at Her Majesty's pleasure such was their collation of confessions and other incontrovertible evidence.

She and Lydia made a good team because they were so very different. Beth was naturally gregarious, someone you knew was in the room such was her magnetism. Lydia was her opposite, quietly studious, a natural rule follower unlike Beth, so it was an excellent pairing that kept Beth on the straight and narrow and made Lydia take necessary risks. Lydia knew she was always in Beth's shadow but didn't seem to mind as their results were becoming legendary.

The case of Richard Black was to change all of that

Although part of CID, Beth and Lydia had been asked to assist in a fire arms offence allegedly perpetrated by Richard Black. Beth had been given the lead and called in to take her statement and with Lydia, to oversee the psychological assessment that would be required due to the nature of the alleged offence. Richard Black, according to his married daughter Helen Spencer, was now a danger to himself and particularly a danger to her mother who was in the process of ending their marriage of thirty-one years.

"My father isn't a bad man, but he's beside himself. He doesn't understand why mum wants to leave him although to be fair, she should have done so years ago." Helen continued to explain how very selfish her father had always behaved, putting himself first before his wife and children.

"I can't tell you how many times mum would plead for us all to go on holiday together but all he wanted to do was be with his golf club or Lodge cronies. When he was persuaded to be with us, he would be miserable and moody so mum stopped even trying. Now we're all married she's had enough and I can't in all honesty blame her because quite frankly she's downright lonely and wants a life whilst she's young enough. So she's told him that she wants a divorce and he hasn't stopped drinking and threatening her since." Taking a sip of water, Helen looked at Beth, "Detective, my father terrified me today."

"Take me through what happened, leaving out no detail, however unpleasant," prompted Beth as she switched on the recording device as Helen Spencer went on to describe what she had walked into. How drunk her father had been and how terrified her mother was, with the half- cocked rifle lying between them on the carpet. How her father had picked up the gun at the moment her husband had entered the room successfully removing it from his drunken grasp.

"I can honestly say that I have never been more terrified and so grateful when the police arrived as quickly as you did and took his guns away. He's just not fit to have them," she continued.

Nodding sympathetically Beth assured her, "We're letting your dad sleep it off then we will have him assessed whether he is psychologically fit to continue to hold a gun licence as he has quite a collection. We will speak with your mum to see if she is prepared to press any charges and then we will take it from there." Leaning across the table, Beth added, "I know it is easy for me to say, but try not to worry. This could be the best thing that could have happened. Maybe now your father will meet your mum half way and try and see a way through this."

"I do hope so. It was so frightening though Detective ..."

"Beth. I'm Beth. We have it in hand now so let's hope the worse is over." And it should have been.

After meeting with the duty medical officer and the Head of the Firearms Unit, Sergeant Hardy, who had been called to the incident earlier that day, it was agreed by all concerned that the gun license currently held by Richard Black would be revoked, with all firearms permanently confiscated until further notice.

"He needs some real psychiatric help," agreed Lydia as the meeting drew to a close.

"Let's hope he can get it. Such a shame for the family that it's come to this but at least no one has been hurt this time." They knew of such cases when fatalities had occurred in similar circumstances though thankfully they had not been the ones to deal with such misery.

Having finished her report with the necessary recommendations, Beth was surprised to be summoned by Superintendent Giles Baker. Entering his office, she knew instinctively that something wasn't quite right. Giles Baker was an officious looking man, who was infinitely more politician that policeman. Looking up he nodded at her to sit. "Thanking you for joining me Detective Constable. I'm just reviewing the incident regarding Mr Black and although I admire your rigour and attention to detail, I think in this instance you may be a little over zealous. I would like you to amend this report and allow Mr Black home with his license and guns as they were. Thank you Detective that will be all."

Stunned, Beth had remained seated. Giles Baker looked at her over his glasses and said, "I said that will be all Detective?"

"I'm sorry Sir but there is no way I can in all conscience revoke the decision regarding Mr Black. He is currently under tremendous duress and needs ..." Giles Baker held up his hand interrupting.

"You've made your findings very clear so now let me be clear. Mr Black is to be released with his property with no further action to be taken."

"You are suggesting we give his guns back to him? With respect Sir, are you being serious? Have you interviewed Mr Black? Spoken to Sergeant Hardy who arrested him and my colleague DC Smith..."

"Am I being serious? Are you questioning who is in charge here Detective?" The low menace in Giles Baker's voice was very obvious and Beth now realised she was on the cusp of making a very important decision.

"Of course not Sir, it's just having met the family

we have very real concerns about their safety."

"Which are duly noted. To be clear your colleague DC Smith concurs with my findings too so now do your job which last time I looked was to follow orders issued by your superior officer. You are dismissed Detective Constable!"

Completely baffled, Beth walked back to her desk she shared with Lydia only to find out that Mr Black was already on his way home "What the fuck?"

"Would appear Richard Black and our esteemed Superintendent are members of the same funny handshake club. Black demanded to see him as soon as he reached the desk today and our Giles came running. C'est la vie my friend, c'est la vie!"

Head in hands, Beth was shocked to the core. She knew the old stories of what policing used to be like, the sexism, the chauvinism verging on misogyny, the corruption. She could not believe that a potentially dangerous man was being released because he had a high ranking police officer for a mate! Looking at her partner with real concern, Lydia said quietly, "Let it go mate."

"No! You sat in the interview so you fucking well know this is not right!"

"Yes but an order is an order and we don't actually have a choice unless we opt for career suicide."

"Actually we do. Why didn't you stand by the

initial report and support me? He says you agree that I've been 'over- zealous' I mean are you for fucking real?"

"Perhaps I'm the one who lives in the real world here for Christ's sake! Let it bloody go!"

Incandescent with a barely concealed rage, Beth logged off her computer, picked up her bag and prepared to leave. She did have one final statement for Lydia and for the rest of the Detectives in the CID base who were trying to appear busy and not listening to every word of the exchange between the two female detectives.

"You look after your own back then Lydia but I for one will never be ok with such a blatant abuse of power and position. It's 2018 for Christ's sake not 1918! It's a fucking disgrace!" and with that she stormed out.

Lydia looked around the CID base and saw that almost all would not meet her eye and she suddenly felt very much on her own. Detective Sergeant Eddie Sinclair looked on with quiet disgust, shaking his head.

"Something to say Sarge?" asked Lydia, looking at him with a challenge in her eyes.

"Plenty Detective Constable if I thought it would do any good to say it, except to say we should all know who we can rely on to watch our backs in this job and I'm telling you now, it won't be the ones who occupy the offices upstairs!" and with that he turned his back towards his own desk and problems. Looking at her Sergeant's back Lydia at that moment, and to her credit, did wonder if she had actually made the biggest mistake of her career so far.

It was another two days before Richard Black shot his daughter Helen before turning the gun on himself.

For as long as she lived Beth would never forget the ensuing few days. The recriminations from the family, particularly Mrs Black and Helen's husband who was now looking down the abyss of single parenthood of three young children, all under the age of five years old, were very hard to take. That in itself was heartbreaking enough but what was so infinitely worse, was how those occupying the upper echelons of the station were now closing ranks, discussing damage limitation and firmly focusing the blame onto no other than Beth.

Bob Smeaton, her Police Federation Representative was a sympathetic, curmudgeonly man, who had seen it all before. "We can play it two ways. We can go head to head with the Super and nothing would give me greater pleasure but you will be saying goodbye to a very promising career, or you can take it on the chin and suck up the crap that is coming, so I suggest you go home and sleep on it. Discuss it with Brad and we will do whatever you feel you have to do."

Curled up on their sofa they discussed their options. Brad was all for them both resigning, telling the powers that be to "Stuff their fucking jobs where the proverbial sun don't shine," being beside himself with the sheer unfairness of what his Beth was dealing with stating more than once, "I can't in all honesty feel I can continue working for that bunch of Tossers!"

Beth at one point was actually the more reasonable one saying, "So what else would we do? You've been a copper since you were nineteen years old and a bloody good one at that and I love my job. Admittedly I'll hate going back to being in uniform but it will do until the babies come along. Okay?"

"Aye you can become a kept woman when the bambinos arrive," Brad uttered as he nuzzled her neck, hating what his hard working, totally committed wife was unjustly dealing with.

Sighing heavily with frustration Beth decided there and then, "Yes I'll take the rap because that bastard Giles Baker isn't driving me out. I was just doing my job and I did it well but I still can't bloody believe it though. How much worse would it be if I went and punched the Super's lights out as well?"

Smiling Brad replied, "It would be beyond bad and the scumbag isn't worth it my love."

"I'd really enjoy it though," she mused "and we'd make a fortune selling tickets. Nobody likes the sanctimonious little prick!"

In that moment, Brad felt such a surge of love and pride for his wife as he knew how hard this was for her, but here she was making a joke whilst in reality being completely devastated. So Beth took her written reprimand and was demoted back into the uniform division but with a fury and bitterness that was never far from the surface.

The worse part of this episode however was having to sit in the Coroner's Court at the Inquest that took place six months later. There Beth had to sit and listen to a representative of the IPCC, the Independent Police Complaints Commission, relay "the litany of errors and lack of the clear following of given protocols" to the court, whilst Beth sat there staring straight ahead, knowing that the relatives of the dead hated her, blamed her, and those who were to blame, were allowing it to happen. That day Beth swore she would have her revenge.

Leaving the court, Beth was approached by Lydia, her former partner in CID. "So sorry you've had to deal with this Beth."

"Really? Sorry enough to do what was right?"

"That wasn't an option for me Beth."

"Actually, Lydia it was. So now why don't you

just go and fuck off," and with that Beth turned on her heel and walked away with her head held high. Lydia started towards Beth when Imogen grabbed her arm and said, "I think you've done enough damage here don't you?" Lydia stared into Imogen's face and saw nothing but complete contempt. With a face burning with embarrassment and something akin to shame, she nodded before walking in the opposite direction.

Beth and her friends got spectacularly drunk that evening. "I don't think I'm being sexist here," slurred Imogen, "but I did expect more from Lydia. I expect men to be low-lives but for another woman to shaft her partner? Well it's so disappointing!" announcing the proclamation louder than she intended drawing looks from other tables.

"Absolutely," agreed an equally inebriated Harry, "where are our next Tequila shots? Barman! Tequila now please!"

"Well not all women are like us," bemoaned Beth, "just my luck to have such a prissy bloody 'good girl' as a partner. You know she's even proud to be have been her school's Head Girl!"

"Says it all!" slurred Sarah, "We need more tequila! Barman it's now an emergency!" as she banged on the table drawing even more looks from the other tables. Their collective hangovers were spectacular and lasted for days.

That was the time when the need to have a baby really took over, becoming almost an obsession. It was also when her mother Gill became ill with terminal breast cancer at only sixty -two years old.

Lying on the hospital bed waiting for her nose to be examined, Beth was now remembering why she hated hospitals so much and those last few months with her mother.

Gill admitted she'd had the lump for a while but didn't want to know until it was too late. She'd been with her Terry since she was an eighteen -year old girl working for Slazenger's down in Barnsley town centre. She'd met Terry at Barnsley Bus Station one Saturday night when she and her girlfriends were waiting for the Darfield bus whilst Terry and his mates were making their way to catch the last train to Penton. Terry heard Gill's laugh before he saw her then took one look at her golden hair and bright smile and that was that. Forty- four years later, after giving birth to two sons and one daughter, Gill was now making her peace with what was to come.

Beth was now remembering her mother reaching for her hand. "You know you've always been the apple of your dad's eye so he's going to really need you now more than ever. Make sure he doesn't pine and shut himself away love, promise me that. He's got years left and he shouldn't be alone and you will be the only one he'll take any notice of."

Biting back the tears Beth promised and attempted at humour, "You know I'll always look after him, even though the old bugger will be a bloody nightmare. Thanks for this mum, as if I haven't got enough on!"

Smiling Gill squeezed her hand tightly. "I've always been so proud of you, but this last few months have made me realise how very special you are. My beautiful girl, my brave Beth."

Openly crying now, Beth admitted, "I don't feel brave or special mam. I'm so furious all the time and I can't bear the thought of you not being here anymore."

Gill now stroking her daughter's hair and making those soothing noises all mothers do when wanting to take away the pain their child is feeling whispered, "I'll not be far away my Beth. All you have to do is look in the mirror and there'll I be my Beth, in your eyes because you have my eyes. When your babies arrive, there I'll be, in their eyes too."

The day Gill died, Beth saw her father die a little too and she couldn't bear it. The girls were there of course, helping with the arrangements, rallying around, getting drunk with her, crying with her, just being there with her. It was months later that the cracks in her marriage started to appear and widen. Sex was now all about getting pregnant, more so now for her father who needed something to live for too and a baby had to be the answer as far as Beth was concerned. That was when the medics also now stepped in to deliver the news that they were unlikely to normally conceive although they still had hope. “It could still happen, probably when you least expect it,” one well -meaning specialist had said but after three attempts and eighteen thousand pounds of IVF it was proving to be more and more unlikely. It was when Brad mentioned the idea of using a surrogate, Beth really and truly lost it.

“You want another woman to have our baby? Well why not ‘do the deed’ properly and find someone else to fuck then?! I hear Sharon Summers is still available. I bet she’ll happily drop her knickers for you again so let’s give her a call shall we? Bet she can get here in…”

“For pity’s sake Beth stop it,” raking his hand through his hair looking at her with tired, bleak eyes muttering, “honestly I don’t know how much more of this I can take!”

“Then go! Go! Get the fuck out of this house and my life because the last thing I need is another fucking man making me feel like I’ve done something wrong! That somehow I’m to blame. Again!”

Lying in the A & E bed she now couldn’t bear to

remember the rest of the things she had said, the things she had accused him of. Words can never be unsaid or unheard, so a heartbroken Brad had moved out, leaving Beth alone and embittered.

Now back in her home, Beth picked up her mail as if on autopilot. As she passed the mirror in the hallway she looked at her reflection quietly saying, "Can't see much of you at all these days Mam. Where have you gone?"

Beth began peeling off her blood splattered clothes when she was startled by the ringing of her phone.

It was Harriet. "Beth its Harry. Get over to Sarah's now. It's really bad. Beth are you there?"

Staring at her reflection and seeing only a ghost of herself, Beth replied, "I'm on my way Harry."

Finding clean sweat pants and hoodie, Beth proceeded to get in her car and as if on auto pilot drove the short distance to Sarah's.

CHAPTER 5

Harriet aka Harry had just finished the night shift at Sheffield's Hallamshire General Hospital, the morning of the day life changed forever for all of them.

Although Harry had not worked as a nurse for a number of years, the call to arms from the NHS due to the Covid crisis was something she couldn't ignore. The kids were at an age where they could just about fend for themselves, particularly with her mother offering to move in and take over home- schooling too.

"It will be such fun to spend quality time with my grandchildren," her mother had gushed. Harry was wondering if she was still thinking like this after trying to make their nine-s year old twins do the online lessons, particularly the lessons they perceived as pointless and boring as they often vociferously voiced. Harry also knew her mother's fallback position was now bribery and the twins were making a fortune out of her.

Driving home now from another gruelling shift, Harry's head was full of what she had dealt with and seen in the last few hours and was so grateful she still had a mother. So many had lost theirs in such a cruel way too.

The lack of PPE was a constant source of anger and worry but it was the sheer volume of infected patients that at times seemed overwhelming. The loss of each one was like a physical dagger to the heart with so many dying with only strangers to hold their hands and that too with plastic gloves as a barrier. The distress of the families and the sheer exhaustion all of them felt was like nothing she had ever known or imagined. Just earlier that day Harry had come across a colleague in a store room sobbing her heart out through sheer exhaustion, both physically and mentally. The thirty minute drive home gave Harry time to breath, to think and often her mind went all over the place with worries about the future but reflections about the past too.

Harry knew how charmed her life was and had always been. Her dad had worked in Insurance whilst her mother worked as a teaching assistant in her old Primary school. They were comfortably well off and life went by at a gentle pace. Even her parents' divorce when she was thirteen couldn't have been more civilized or amicable. Harry remembered Imogen's horror when she told the girls her parents were separating. They were on the school field eating their packed lunches and Imogen was beside herself. "But your dad is lovely. What is your mum thinking?"

"Well she still loves him," explained Harry, "but she's just not 'in love' with him anymore."

"That's the most ridiculous thing I've ever heard!" exclaimed Imogen, ignoring the elbows now digging into her from both Sarah and Beth. "Does he beat her if the carrots are hard and tell her she's stupid all day and every day?"

"Of course not."

"Then she should be bloody well grateful," and with that a tearful Imogen had stomped off.

Later, walking home, Imogen turned to Harry, "Sorry for earlier."

Smiling as always, good natured Harry merely shrugged, "S'ok. I get how weird it is. It's just mum wants more and dad just wants her to be happy because he loves her so much, so he's willing to let her go. They'll still be best friends though."

"Really. Wow."

"Wow what?"

"For someone to actually love someone that much." Imogen's wistful expression told Harry that although the girls knew Imogen's dad was not a nice man and very different from their own, they really had no idea what their friend's life was really like once she stepped through the door of her home and Harry felt a sadness for her friend like never before.

Harry had met her GP husband Alan Wood at Sheffield's Northern General hospital when he was a Junior Registrar and she a Student Nurse. The first time she had clapped eyes on Alan, he was covered in vomit that had spectacularly ejected from a feverish three -year old girl. The poorly little one had held her arms out to Alan, who despite the mess he was in, scooped her up to quiet her distress and Harry had fallen for him there and then.

"Can I help at all?" Harry had ventured.

"If you wouldn't mind getting this little one some fresh bedding please Nurse, that will be great won't it Alice? Get you nice and clean and better shall we?"

Harry was remembering Alan looking up and smiling at her and she had smiled back. He was such a 'geek' to look at with black rimmed glasses and unruly Albert Einstein hair and he really had no idea how attractive his lack of ego made him. He was also an exceptional talent in the medical sense but also someone who genuinely cared for all around him which was so unlike some of his colleagues who had egos the size of the building and who were in the job for self- gain and the money to be earned. Not her Alan. He had been offered so many specialisms which potentially could have brought him fame and fortune but all he wanted to do was be in General Practice and work in a community and preferably one where he was needed. Their fourteen years of marriage was a strong and very happy one, blessed with three fabulous children, Olivia twelve and nine-year old twins Will and Jasper. They lived in a huge old converted vicarage in the centre of Penton with her husband's Surgery a short walk away on Penton's High Street and yes, Harry knew she was indeed blessed.

Harry was also thinking how her world was in sharp contrast to that of her three best friends and how it always had been that way. Imogen's accident and loss of Neil and her unborn baby had been devastating and Harry often wondered how on earth Imogen had come through it. Beth was such a mess at the moment too but it was Sarah that was currently causing Harry to lose sleep.

The last time they had met for a walk, one of the only allowed activities to do together these days, Sarah was wearing a scarf, even though it had been a very warm spring day and they had all seen the bruises and finger marks that the scarf had not fully hidden. None of them liked or trusted Sarah's husband Grant but getting her to talk about whatever was going on was proving difficult. The fact they were unable to meet as they used to, didn't help matters either.

Harry was remembering their last conversation. "What's wrong with your neck Sarah?" this from Beth as blunt as ever.

"Nothing."

"It looks like you're covering bruises. Has someone hurt you?" ventured Imogen.

"Because if that someone is your husband, I will go to where he can be found and arrest him now," said Beth barely concealing her rage, "just say the word."

Near to tears now Sarah's response was, "Just leave it! It's nothing, nothing I don't deserve anyway," and with that she had turned and walked back to her car, leaving her friends angry, sad, afraid and worried in equal measures.

"Do you think she will ever forgive herself?" asked Imogen as she watched Sarah walk away.

"Perhaps she shouldn't!" muttered Beth.

Rounding on her friend Imogen angrily retorted, "Bloody hell! A bit harsh even for you!"

Before things really got out of hand Harry had intervened, "Don't you two. All this is hard enough without us having words as well."

After a moment, but still furious, a calmer Imogen said, "He's hurting her, that much is obvious and he needs to be stopped." Remembering this altercation Harry realised she was now driving past the gates of Sarah's remote barn conversion on the outskirts of their small market town. Harry was tempted to call in there and then but decided she would do so after she had got some sleep, perhaps just before her next shift later that evening.

Later, Harry would always regret that she hadn't called and in that instant had possibly made the worse decision which would ultimately affect all of them for the rest of their lives.

Walking through her back door Harry made her way to their utility come shower room where she put all her clothes including her shoes in the wash then thoroughly showered before being greeted by the usual chaos of her home and she wouldn't have had it any other way. The twins were glued to a computer game, their treat before school work whilst her daughter Olivia was having a very serious conversation with her father about the virtues of becoming a vegan which was her latest passion.

"But dad, animal husbandry is a very real threat to the planet's survival. We must do our bit!"

"I know Liv but I don't believe it is as simple as not eating any animal product," argued Alan, "as a medic I would advise caution, that's all I'm saying."

"Morning. Wow, such a heavy conversation already and it's not even eight thirty," smiled Harry kissing Alan on the top of his head as he sat at the breakfast island placed in the centre of their large living kitchen. Olivia looked up and smiled making Harry's heart swell. Her little girl, now practically a teenager was going to be a real heartbreaker. How would her dad cope?

"Liv here is considering veganism," said Alan, returning her kiss and surreptitiously winking at her.

"It's an informed life choice and environmentally critical," announced her daughter.

"Well it is certainly something to consider these days although it won't just be food that will be the issue will it?" Olivia looked questioningly at her mother as Harry continued, "Clothes and make up, shampoos, soap, the list is endless. Is that coffee fresh?" Olivia was in the process of discovering clothes and make up so this was now a whole new ball game for her to consider. Rising from the bar she announced, "Need to log on. Got History first thing," and with that she left for the sanctuary of her room and no doubt FaceTime with her friends.

"Nicely done Mrs Wood."

"It's a gift!" joked Harry as Alan gave her the much needed coffee. Now looking closely at her with concern he reached for her hand.

"Tough night?"

Nodding Harry looked down at her drink as her lips began to tremble. "It's never ending.

Remember Dr Scott?"

"Annie Scott?" asked Alan with real concern in his eyes.

"Found her in a crumpled heap crying her eyes out in the scrub room. She's exhausted and she can't remember when she was last home or with her kids."

"Lose many last night?"

"Too many, too many heartbroken families to deal with too but it is less than it was so all good except we have had three nurses come down with it so they're having to self- isolate leaving us really short- handed." She then asked the question she asked regularly, "Should I stay away from home Alan? I'm risking bringing it here?"

"We've discussed this Harry and you know we'd rather have you here at home some of the time and so far so good. You are being incredibly careful and I have it on good authority that a vaccine will be available in record time. We just need to keep doing what we're doing."

Pulling herself together she looked at her concerned husband, who like she was dealing with so much. "Thank you my love, you always know what to say don't you but be careful too Alan. You've got plenty on too despite what everyone is thinking but this nightmare will end eventually, one day."

"But not today," he smiled. "Promise me you'll get

some proper rest before you return tonight?"

Nodding Harry blew her husband a kiss then took her drink and made her way to the isolation of their room. Looking around their spacious home, she wished she could shut the door to the world and just keep everyone she loved safe. If only.

CHAPTER 6

The morning of the day when everything changed forever for all of them Sarah did not actually experience. The clock said it was 12.15pm when she finally managed to wake from a drug induced sleep. Still feeling groggy she managed to drag herself out of bed, wincing with pain but it was the stench that made her want to gag. Now looking at the blood, urine and soiled stained sheets she was so confused. Dragging herself to the bathroom she began to retch, then vomited violently. Everywhere hurt and she didn't know why? What had happened?

Stripping off her nightclothes she saw the bruises, the bite marks. What the? How did they…? Then as the fog in her head began to clear Sarah put her head in her hands as the events came flooding back into her consciousness. Touching her rectum she winced at the pain and gasped at the blood from the open wound and was now remembering the excruciating brutality her husband Grant had forced on her. She was also remembering how she had begged him to stop but how it seemed to make him be even more brutal. "Stop! I've not even started yet. You have no idea what's coming your way," as he whispered images of pain and degradation, as he took his time, extending her agony whilst seemingly enhancing his own pleasure. But it was the look of sheer joy and pleasure on his 'movie star' handsome sadistic face that was now etched in her mind, making her vomit again. Unbelievably she'd been relentlessly raped by a man who had stood before others promising to love and honour her.

Sarah now was feeling the shame which all victims of abuse, violence and rape feel, predictably wondering, as all victims do, what she had done to make Grant do what he had done the previous evening.

Stripping the bedsheets from the bed, intending to burn them, she tentatively and slowly made her way to the kitchen, very badly needing coffee and pain relief. She did not understand why she was feeling so completely spaced out these days, had even discussed it with Harry who in turn had asked Alan. Maybe she was just going mad? Maybe it was her mind trying to protect her? Maybe she should just lay down and die and do everyone a favour?

As she watched the disgusting bed sheets burn, she wished what she had in her head could burn away too. She thought not for the first time how those decisions you make, the ones you know deep in your soul are wrong, will always come back to haunt you. Perhaps wickedness has to be paid for because she had done a very wicked and unforgiveable thing. Perhaps mused Sarah, she deserved every cruel shitty thing the monster she lived with wanted to do to her. Life could have been so very different. If only.

*

Sarah had been seventeen the first time she had met John Hilton. She and Harry had called into her family's small construction business, Greens Builders of Penton, which was next to Penton railway station. The firm had been started by her grandfather back in the day but was still a thriving concern. Sarah had forgotten her house key so had gone there to borrow one and John had just secured a brick layer apprenticeship at Greens and had been there around six months. Neither Sarah nor Harry had been looking where they were going, when they heard someone yelling for them to get out of the way, both avoiding colliding with John's loaded forklift.

Jumping from his seat he'd rushed over shouting, "Are you ok?"

"Sorry. That was so our fault," stuttered Harry whilst Sarah appeared to have be struck dumb.

"As long as you're both ok," replied John who

was now looking as if he'd just discovered the meaning of life in the shape of pretty, petite, auburn haired Sarah.

"Well no harm done eh, Sarah?" this from Harry who was still trying to snap Sarah out of the obvious lightning strike that had just occurred, dragging her into the office building where they were supposedly going. Rounding the corner, they stopped, looked at each other, and then shrieked like only seventeen -year old girls can. "Oh my God! Have you ever seen anyone more gorgeous in your whole life?" shrieked Sarah. That chance meeting was the beginning of John and Sarah but Sarah's parents had plans for their daughter and getting involved with a brickie and a trainee one at that even, wasn't part of those plans. "You know he's only after your money, my money. Well he can think again, because you'll not get a penny..." and on it went.

John was summarily dismissed from his job and Sarah practically put under house arrest until she had completed her 'A' levels and secured a place at Veterinary College in Leeds where she and John resumed their relationship but this time openly because they had never given each other up. She and the girls had become adept at the subterfuge required for Sarah and John to regularly meet. Arlette used to discreetly leave Sarah and Imogen alone to allegedly study, then John would be snuck in and Imogen really did study alone. The girls even spent many wet rainy days in Cleethorpes so they could be together. Beth had been particularly fed up one such day when it incessantly rained as it invariably did. “This is above and beyond being best friends! Bloody Cleethorpes in the bloody rain.”

“We’d do it for you,” smiled Harry, “and it’s not so bad.”

“Why are you always so bloody cheerful?”

Harry had merely smiled unable to take offence at Beth’s bad temper. It was the way they were, still were.

It was at college that Sarah became pregnant at only nineteen. John was convinced they would manage but it was the sheer ferocity of her parents’ venom that made Sarah falter and make the choice that was to ultimately destroy them. Her mother had been particularly vicious. “Have this baby and go and live in that grubby little council house in grubby little GrimsDales but no decent mother would wish that on their child. I’ve been poor, you haven’t! I suggest you think about someone other than yourself for once Sarah Green. You’re still a child! What sort of mother could you possibly hope to be? Do you think lover boy will stick around when you get fat? When you’re stuck in with no money?” and on and on and on it went.

John was beside himself declaring, “Who cares

what your parents and their stuck up friends will say or do? We can't not have our baby?"

"What would we live on? How would we manage?"

"Others do every day. We can go and live with my parents until I have enough money to pay for a rental bond for a place of our own," John reasoned.

Sarah now was ashamed of her horror at such an idea. To live in a small cramped council house in GrimsDales with John's kind well- meaning parents with a baby was something at that time to Sarah, seemed unimaginable as her mother's words echoed in her head. And so it went on until the day she found herself with her mother at the private clinic in York, making the hardest decision and the biggest mistake of her young life.

John did not forgive her and had walked away, joining the army in his own bid to get as far from her and the abortion as he possibly could. She was now remembering their last meeting, their last words. John was standing there, his face a mask of stone as Sarah pleaded with him. "Please John, you can't go. Please, I love you so much."

"You don't love me enough, or you wouldn't have done it and to be honest at this moment in time, I can't bear to bloody look at you. It's as if I never knew you."

"I have a right to choose," she had angrily retorted, "I'm not ready to have a baby and live in..." but then had snapped her mouth shut knowing her next words would really hurt.

"Some grotty council house in GrimsDales? Eh? Is that what you're about to say? So your mum was right all along. No, you go back to your kind and I'll go back to mine." Then he was gone and Sarah's parents had finally got exactly what they had always wanted. So she left college and returned home, damaged and broken. Imogen, Beth and Harry as always were there to pick up the pieces of Sarah that weren't broken beyond repair.

"You'll get through this," Harry had said whilst both Imogen and Beth were pretty upset with both Sarah's parents and John. "It's your bloody body for God's sake, who does John Hilton think he is? What bloody century is he living in?" was Beth's reaction.

"They should never have bullied you like this," Imogen had declared, "and I'm so sorry you've had to deal with all this awful crap alone. We should have bloody well been here for you."

"You were all so far away and for once I should have been strong enough."

"Well we're here now," Harry had said as they encircled her in their collective embrace, willing the hurt to leave her.

So Sarah with the help of her friends packed her things, left college and returned to the home of her birth, feeling like she was now living with cold, unfeeling strangers such was the relationship she now had with her parents. Sarah began a half- life from then on, resuming her part time job at the local vets, something she'd done since the age of fifteen. Taking part time courses she eventually qualified as a veterinary nurse then moved out of the family home to rent a place of her own. On her thirtieth birthday she came into the Trust money her grandfather had set up for her which then enabled her to buy the converted barn just outside of Penton on the hill looking down on the place she had grown up. The girls loved it. "Wow look at the view," Harry had exclaimed.

"Don't you think it may be a little isolated here on your own?" Imogen had worried.

"Not going to be alone," Sarah explained now showing them the area she was having converted into a selection of dog kennels. "I've been accepted by the Dog Rescue Service to provide shelter to dogs who have been abandoned or rescued from abusive homes.

"That's bloody fantastic!" Beth declared, "who better than 'Man's' or should I say 'Woman's' best friends for company and protection!"

Sarah's life began to have meaning again often having up to eleven dogs at any one time, loving them back to health and only allowing them to leave her sanctuary if the people wanting her charges passed a variety of tests. These were her children now and only the best people would have any access to them. Two remained with her though, a Staffordshire bull terrier called Scooby Doo and Cyril the Pug. She would never be able to part with these two and on their part, they would have pined away if they were ever to be parted from her and would protect her with their lives if needed.

It was at one of the infamous Lodge dinners that she had reluctantly attended with her parents, that she had first met Grant Downs. Her father George Green was the Lodge Master that year and he had asked, no begged her to attend the dinner that would celebrate his year of office. It was her father who had actually introduced them to each other for Grant was everything George and Elaine Green wanted for their daughter and a key reason they wanted their daughter to attend that evening.

"Sarah may I introduce you to one of our newest members. This is Grant Downs, Grant this is my daughter and only child Sarah."

Grant was the archetypal tall, dark and handsome with a natural athleticism that made him move well and with confidence, attracting attention whenever he entered a room from both men and women alike. Women wanted him and men wanted to be him. Now looking down at pretty petite Sarah, Grant began his charm offensive, “Wow George, but you never told me what a beauty you had stashed away. Pleasure to meet you Sarah,” replied Grant extending his hand out in greeting and holding on just that fraction too long, thus indicating his obvious interest in her.

Even on that first encounter, Sarah recognised the smooth operator that epitomised Grant Downs and wasn’t particularly attracted or impressed by him. However, both Grant and her father George had other plans. Grant was the sort of man George Green wanted on his daughter’s arm and he believed he had found in Grant a man from ‘good stock’. Public school educated, an entrepreneur, a business man, a man who had acumen and who was probably already on his way to being a multi- millionaire in his own right and who would help him diversify his small local building business into the multinational conglomerate he had always dreamed of it becoming. George Green couldn’t have been more wrong because Grant Downs was nothing better than a con man who had already got a criminal record, had been thrown out of his state comprehensive school and was worth absolutely nothing. Grant now had Sarah in his sights and he was ruthless in the execution of his campaign to woo and ultimately win her and all that would bring for him. For Grant Downs had plans, huge plans.

Sarah for her part did recognise what was happening but she was lonely and tired of being the spare wheel when she met up with the girls and their partners. Imogen and Neil, Beth and Brad, Harry and Alan were all happily married with Harriet busy having numerous babies too. Lucky, lucky Harry and to be honest, she was very flattered by his attention. Everywhere they went women were practically throwing themselves at him but he only appeared to have eyes for Sarah.

She remembered the day Grant had tearfully told her about how his parents had died, on a boating accident on the Cote D'Azur, when he was away at boarding school when he was only twelve years old. How he now craved to have a family of his own to give them all the love he felt had been taken from him at such a tender age. Sarah had been deeply moved.

"That's such a dreadful thing to deal with," she had sympathised.

"So I guess you can now see how I feel like I've been waiting for you all my life," he had tearfully said, "and I believe we can make each other so complete, so happy. I've been alone for so long."

Sarah nodded replying, "So have I."

"Let me make you happy then? I swear on my

life you will never regret it and just think of our future babies," he had promised.

So knowing deep down she would never love anyone or be loved by anyone the way she and John Hilton had loved each other, Sarah allowed herself to be wooed and won by Grant Downs believing that she could and would learn to love this man and find some form of happiness again with a family of her own to love and nurture. Her friends were not happy.

All of them including their men neither liked Grant or trusted him. Sarah was aware how different he was to the other men that constituted her friends' partners and Grant was particularly uncomfortable around Beth, Brad and Neil as all three were part of either judiciary, or law enforcement and this did not go unnoticed.

"So how much does Sarah actually know about him then?" Neil had asked Imogen one night.

"He's wealthy in his own right, no family, all tragically killed. Why?"

"Something off about him," replied Neil and Imogen had agreed.

Beth and Brad were having similar conversations. "So which one is going to do a surreptitious background check on him?" asked Brad one evening.

"I can't tomorrow so? Please my bear?" Beth had

pleaded and of course he did.

Grant Downs however was more than a match for Sarah's friends. He had not been born Grant Downs but Samuel Thornton but he had known a Grant Downs and in effect had stolen his identity when the real Grant had met an untimely end. When you knew certain people, getting a fake passport or National Insurance details could be arranged, so Brad actually verified all that Grant had said, including the death of his family in France.

It was three months after first meeting Grant when Sarah and her friends were in their favourite wine bar in Penton, a beautiful, plush place that had once been Penton's one and only bank. They were meeting to celebrate Sarah's recent engagement and for three of them, to do some straight talking as only friends who were in effect more like family could.

"Are you absolutely sure he's what you want?" asked Imogen.

"What do you really know about him?" asked Beth.

"Don't you think it's all a bit quick?" ventured Harry.

Taking a huge breath, because this is what she had expected, Sarah silenced them all with, "Yes I am sure he's what I want and I know as much as I need to know about him and yes it's quick but why wait? What else have I to do with my life?"

"Oh honey," whispered Harry with tears now in her eyes, "why are you just settling for this?

"Easy to say when you have such a perfect life so listen to me all of you. He's the man I'm going to marry and it's up to all of you if you wish to come to my wedding, so speak now or... whatever comes next!"

Sarah took a huge gulp of wine, then looked up defiantly at her friends, the ones who she would do anything for and who she knew were only worried for her. After what seemed like an age Imogen was the first to speak, "Well, that's that then. Are we bridesmaids?"

"Of course!"

"Are you going to make us wear something truly hideous?" this from Beth.

"Might," replied Sarah now smiling and just like that the awkwardness had passed but not their real concerns.

"So to Sarah and Grant," said Harry, raising her glass.

"Sarah and Grant," said her friends in unison. They really weren't happy at all.

Her wedding day took place three months later at the ridiculously over- priced hotel in Harrogate and it was like something out of 'Hello' magazine. The setting was magnificent, the food excellent and her dress a sensation as it should be mused Sarah when she thought how much it had cost. Her friends were stunning in their lilac gowns, particularly a newly pregnant Imogen who was radiant and Sarah's groom Grant, looked like he could audition for the next James Bond in his equally expensive tuxedo. Her parents looked on as if all their dreams had come true and for Sarah it felt like it was happening to someone else.

Now drinking her second cup of coffee, still trying to shake the awful 'Mind fog' she was constantly in, Sarah not for the first time wondered how she could have been so stupid and how right her friends had been. Grant Downs had played her and her parents for the pathetic fools they were.

Thinking now, Sarah was trying to remember when it all had changed between her and Grant and she realised it was when her father had died suddenly and Grant took over the complete running of the building business. It was also around the time she met someone Grant told her he would be doing a great deal of business with, a man called Cameron something or other.

Occasionally in life you meet someone who you know instantly is a 'Wrong Un' as her dearly departed Grandpa would say. This Cameron had a smile designed to charm with the dead eyes of a killer shark and he had immediately made her flesh crawl. "Well my friend, she's as pretty as a picture," he had crooned and she'd felt her blood run cold. Yet looking at her relaxed, smiling husband she saw he was finally in his comfort zone. Grant was with his kind, his tribe and she'd never seen him happier and more at home.

Practically overnight he became authoritative, positively aggressive particularly when it came to having sex. She had always felt he was very controlled, holding back but in the past few months he was demanding more, wanting things from her she felt uncomfortable trying. He had bruised her badly only a few weeks ago when he had squeezed her throat so hard whilst they were having intercourse she thought she would actually stop breathing and die. Her panic and distress had merely amused Grant as he made his contempt for her very clear. "You're so uptight, can't let yourself go for a minute can you? Perhaps if you did you'd begin to enjoy sex instead of enduring it."

The girls had seen the bruises and had wanted an explanation and now she was wishing she had reached out to them. If she had done so, last night may never had happened. Sarah now closed her eyes remembering what she was certain he had done to her dog Scooby and how that should have really made her take action. Why she should have then shouted for help.

She had been to the Rescue Charity shop helping

out as a volunteer as Grant had been particularly bad tempered that morning and she was glad to get out of his way. She was now remembering entering the house waiting for Scooby Doo and Cyril to come and greet her with their usual over the top exuberance but they were nowhere to be found. This was so odd. Where were they? So she had ventured outside to the kennels where all seemed to be normal except that lying in a pool of his blood was her beloved Scooby Doo with Cyril the pug shaking and crying next to his prone body. Sarah remembered screaming, then checked he was still breathing which he thankfully was, scooping him up, racing to her car and taking the poor damaged creature to the vet's where she now worked.

Charlie, the vet looked grim. "Looks like someone has taken a baseball bat to him. Poor lad. Come on Sarah, let's see what damage there is and how we can fix him."

They worked on Scooby Doo for the next few hours and eventually Charlie said, "We've fixed his internal bleeding and his skull is gratefully still intact and his broken ribs will heal but they'll take a while. How did it happen?"

Shaking her head Sarah replied, "I don't know but I intend to find out!"

She was now remembering how Grant appeared as equally shocked, or so he pretended to be but Sarah knew, sensed he was lying to her. "Sorry to hear that but I thought with it being so warm today that they would be better outside. I suspect someone must have climbed over the wall possibly to steal the dogs, I mean I've heard dog stealing is rife and Scooby probably tried to protect them. Will he be ok?" Sarah nodded.

Grant smiled, "No harm done then so what's for dinner?" Stunned by his lack of real sympathy Sarah had looked him squarely in the eyes and asked, "Promise me you didn't hurt him?"

Grant looked at her and his eyes narrowed and suddenly she was frightened. "What are you accusing me of?" he asked her in such a way that she instinctively backed away from him.

"I'm just asking because I need to inform the police and ..." but she was unable to finish as suddenly he had her by the throat.

"The police have better things to do and I for one will not be happy with them asking me some pointless questions about some god ugly mutt. Comprender?" As Sarah nodded her assent, he then let her go, then as if nothing had just occurred he smiled at her and said, "Fancy cooking one of your famous Spaghetti Bolognese for dinner? I'm starving." And just like that she cooked his dinner, didn't contact the police and just pretended she wasn't living in a nightmare.

Well that was then but this was now and never again would he hurt her or anyone or thing she loved. Because quiet, kind, shy Sarah had come to a decision, one she should have come to a long time ago. That monster was never going to touch or hurt her or anyone else again. She'd kill him first. Or she would die trying.

CHAPTER 7

On the morning of the last day of Grant Downs' life, he woke up in the huge bespoke bed that resided in the house of his latest business partner Cameron Sheldon and he was not alone. There were two other bodies in the bed with him, both female and both under the age of sixteen years old.

Smiling now Grant was remembering the previous night's activities, what these girls were prepared to do unlike his pathetic stupid bitch of a wife Sarah. The biggest turn on for Grant had always been having absolute power over another human being. It was what had made him the playground bully from the youngest age and it was what had made his parents and siblings realise that he was not made like the rest of them. From an early age they had become afraid of what he was prepared to do, what he was capable of. The classic sign of his psychopathy occurred with the killing of the family pet, a cat, by strangulation when he was only ten years old. No one saw it happen but they all knew who had done it. He often remembered, often reminisced over that first kill, the thrill of being all powerful, feeling the life drain out of another living creature. He also remembered how distraught his younger sister had been when she had made the grisly discovery and how that had made him feel even more powerful.

“Sammy,” his mother had begun, “please tell me you had nothing to do with this?”

Grant aka Sammy had turned his huge sorrowful eyes at her and with a trembling lip had said, “Honest mum.” She had then pulled him into her arms apologising for even thinking it but his sister had seen the smirk on his face as he buried himself into his mother’s embrace. She knew and eventually all who knew him would know and fear what he was becoming. So he discovered then at that tender age, how easy it was to manipulate others and how having power to do as he pleased over other living beings was a turn on like no other.

Grant loved nothing more than putting his hands around a woman’s neck and slowly squeezing whilst penetrating her as roughly as he wanted, loving the panic and fear he was generating, knowing that he could snap a neck or windpipe on a whim if he so chose and had indeed done so more than once. He had needlessly panicked the first time he had gone too far in Cameron’s London flat in Camden

Town where they had been partying for some time with friends, with many young women and boys available for them all to do with as they pleased. When Grant had realised the young woman he had been having very rough sex with had stopped breathing he had rushed to find his friend. "So? Nothing to worry about. She'll just disappear, won't even be missed. She's a nothing, she's nobody," his friend had said, dismissing the incident as if it were a daily occurrence.

Cameron had assured him that these women, these girls and in some cases mere children were not only disposable but also untraceable. They were young runaways from abusive homes or human trafficked young women and boys from places around the world that offered only poverty and despair. Now only degradation, addiction, misery and death at a too young age were their collective fates.

Looking at the sleeping forms, he saw with satisfaction the bruising and bite marks plus the cigarette burns that were already forming on their young bodies and once flawless skins. He'd left his mark on them alright and he hadn't finished. No they would never be able to forget him so kicking them awake he indicated what he now wanted again and without any reluctance or hesitation they proceeded to service this monster they had the misfortune to be with, making him hard whilst they wished they were dead. Closing his eyes he smiled as he loved nothing more that the smell of someone else's fear and his own orgasm in the morning.

After he had showered, he proceeded downstairs to the breakfast room of the huge mansion. Passing the numerous rooms, he saw the remnants of last night's activities where absolutely anything could and did happen, thinking he could have been looking at a scene from the old movie 'Caligula' at one point in the evening's proceedings, where local men and the occasional woman of standing, had uninhibited sex with young women and boys often young enough to be their grandchildren whilst snorting cocaine and consuming alcohol, all together in the same room. It had been hard at one point to see where one body began and another ended such was the depravity. The contrast between the flawless bodies of the young, trafficked by Sheldon for such purposes, contrasted grotesquely with those using them without pity but merely as a receptacle for their own pleasures.

Grant acknowledged as he made his way to find his host, that Cameron Sheldon was without doubt very clever, even gifted in his own perverse way. His specialism was reading people, understanding how they ticked and what they needed. Last night his house had been full of well- connected men and women from every walk of life, including the judiciary, the police, a couple of semi well- known actors, even an MP thrown in. All their secret desires, some darker than others, were made available and enjoyed and secretly filmed by Sheldon and his people. When the time came, he would make them do as he wished and they invariably did because to do otherwise would result in a number of unthinkable options such as public humiliation, public disgrace, bankruptcy, real threat to the well- being of family, or all of the above. He found his host in the breakfast room eating a hearty meal. “Morning. I take it you enjoyed our little get together last night?” greeted Cameron.

“And this morning,” grinned Grant.

Cameron grinned back. He had a lot of time for Grant Downs and their association was proving to be mutually beneficial. Both of them were psychopaths for a start, neither had any concept of empathy or remorse and both enjoyed similar perversions. One of the best nights of Grant’s life had been the first time he and Cameron had shared the same young woman; ‘roasted’ her as Cameron called it. A very common past time amongst footballers he had reliably informed Grant and he had loved the shared roughness, the slapping, the humiliation, the not having to care about the fact that the poor girl was someone’s daughter, someone’s sister, a human being.

“You played a blinder with our esteemed member of the Constabulary,” reflected Cameron.

“I’m constantly amazed at the stupidity of men in public positions of power,” smiled Grant shaking his head as he helped himself to coffee.

“He really thought he was winning all of your ‘hard earned’ cash, believing he was the next great poker player this side of the Atlantic. What a fucking Muppet!” laughed Cameron now, remembering how easy it had been to ‘play’ his ‘guest’.

Cameron was the son of a single parent, a known drug addict who earned her living by prostitution in London’s East End. From his earliest memories he had known nothing but violence, poverty and deprivation and in truth, his formative years had been devoid of any real kindness and as such had grown up angry and determined to have his turn, his share. He of course had done time in various prisons which had been the best education he could have had, collecting contacts, learnt from the best and was now flying high. It was where he and Grant (aka Sam Thornton in those days) had first met.

Now for men like Grant and Cameron, Covid and lockdown had been gifts from the gods. The authorities had no choice but to protect the public from themselves whilst Cameron and his ilk, which included Grant, continued to traffic in drugs, money laundering and human misery where there was always a market demand even in a global pandemic.

"So is all in place for Thursday's delivery?" queried Cameron.

"Yep, there will be no problems at my end as long as they get through the customs at Hull."

"The lorries have the best hidden compartments with decent fucking airflow. Won't be having another Dover debacle. Lessons truly learnt my friend."

Cameron had come to Yorkshire not because he had wanted to but because he'd had to leave London pretty quickly. He had been responsible for the death of over forty people, including women and children, who had slowly suffocated to death in a hidden compartment in one of the fleet of lorries Cameron owned and used to ferry those desperate to get to the UK. They had paid with all they had including their lives. The driver had taken the blame, refusing to implicate Cameron because he was too afraid for his own family's survival not to.

That had been four years ago. Grant had encouraged him to relocate to Sheffield and he had been very pleasantly surprised how easy he had found it to inveigle himself within the circles he needed to continue his business interests. It would appear that all you needed was a plush office, a good suit, a driver, a Mercedes, a large house and people saw a successful man who must be good at his job and who could therefore make money for them too. Cameron couldn't believe the prices too; what you could buy 'up North'! He should have done it years ago. Grant then made sure that his father in law George sponsored Cameron to join the Lodge and having met the naive buffoon that was George Green, Cameron instinctively knew that his friend Grant had done well for he had found a sure fired solution to his storage and distribution problems. He and Grant were going to have more 'gold' than Midas and have a ball in the process.

George Green had long realised that Grant Downs was not the man he thought, had hoped he was but had died of a heart attack before he could actually do anything about it. That had left Elaine and Sarah as joint owners but with Elaine being the majority Shareholder. Elaine had decided that she would rather spend her time in their villa situated in picturesque Moraira, the small Spanish coastal town in the Marina Alta and about sixty miles from Alicante airport. She had friends, she had sunshine and she and Sarah were barely on speaking terms, not after York which if Elaine was honest with herself, she regretted nearly as much as Sarah did. That had left the door wide open for Grant to slowly but methodically take total control, dismissing most of the workforce, some who had only ever worked for Greens, replacing them with his own people and eventually Cameron's.

Penton was well placed to disguise criminal activities as it was set in a beautiful rural location with a population that had endured for generations and it is fair to say that the general public don't expect criminal activities and exploitation to take place in areas of such beauty. Strategically however, when it came to logistics, Penton could not have been better placed.

Grant had already set up a network of juveniles who had become adept at crossing county lines, carrying drugs. The railway network was an excellent and efficient method of travel and Penton station was directly next door to Greens. Juveniles would carry their illegal contraband in their childlike rucksacks which they would place on a seat for the next one of their gang to collect then take across the county. It was genius in its simplicity. Money laundering was also fairly easy to do when building and selling new houses. A house valued at one hundred and fifty thousand would be sold to those who needed to hide illegal earnings for double the price. So very simple with few questions asked. However, when he had gone in to business with Cameron, Grant discovered just how well placed the canal network in Penton was as well as the areas excellent motorway infrastructure. They could get their human cargo or drugs from Hull or Goole to wherever in the country in mere hours either by lorry, barge or train. It was again quite simple and therefore quite brilliant.

Cameron and Grant had also systematically taken care of the local competition who were no match for the viciousness of these London boys. They just needed to be careful with their preparations and up to date with their intelligence because they of course had 'friends', who were rewarded handsomely in the police who kept them as well informed as possible. Hence the poker game last night would become very useful, particularly the position the said officer had in the force. It would not cost them a penny either as he was in debt to them for an eye watering amount of money such were his losses the night before. He would pay his debt by being their eyes and ears.

Driving home to Penton later that day, Grant smugly felt that he had it all. He and Cameron had a very lucrative few months coming their way if all went to plan and quite frankly what could go wrong? It wouldn't be long now before he would have absolute control and freedom to live his life as he had always dreamed of doing. No strings, no attachments, no answering to anyone. Sarah would soon be dead as the drugs he was systematically putting in the filtered water jug found in the fridge was making her so spaced out that when she is found at the bottom of their very steep stairs or drowned in the bath, no one would be able to prove foul play from him. Suspect maybe, but proving it would be very difficult, even those bitches she called her friends, her family. He wouldn't be surprised to find she may have already done so after what he had enjoyed doing to her last night, before he had left to really have his fun with those who actually knew how to please a man. Actually a repeat performance tonight probably would tip her over the edge. He was relishing the thought as he pulled into his driveway.

The house was very quiet and very still as he entered the front door. Walking up the stairs into the main bedroom he saw Sarah's prone body in the bed and for one elated moment thought she was already dead but on closer inspection he saw she wasn't. Nudging her he realised too that she wasn't going to wake up easily and he wasn't the type to have sex with a woman when she was drugged or out of it. No, they had to feel every ounce of pain coming their way. Hearing a car pulling up onto their drive he looked through the window and smiled when he saw who was getting out of it. Well, well, well he thought, could this day get any better?

CHAPTER 8

Pulling into Sarah's drive Harry was surprised to see Grant's car there and nearly turned around but thought they may have already seen her. She'd only be a minute and speak from the doorway anyway so, taking a deep breath, she made her way to the front door. After ringing the doorbell a while, she then tried the door to find it unlocked.

Harry called out, "Hi there. Sarah? It's me Harry. Just checking to see that all's well with you both? Sarah?"

Nothing. The hairs were started to stand on the back of her neck as she began to slowly move into the home of her friend. She sensed that something was wrong and then she began to smell it. Only blood smelt like that, like copper, so strong that you could taste it. She'd dealt with enough of it in her time.

She first saw Sarah before she saw the still body of Grant. Sarah was sitting on the sofa just staring at what was before her, the bloodied knife still in Grant's body. Harry's first instinct was to turn and run, her second, to reach for her phone and alert the others.

Upon arriving they took in the scene before them in a collective silence. In contrast to the normally pristine and stratospherically expensive Italian porcelain tiles, the spattered and smeared crimson blood now looked almost like a grotesque Jackson Pollock work of art. Hard to believe that life's essence could so easily resemble spilt paint. There was so much of it.

Later when it was all done with, it was the sounds of anguish that stayed the longest with them all not the blood. An almost unworldly sound that came from a place of utter despair, utter desolation and from a heart so wounded that it would almost certainly break to never recover again.

"How many times?"

"How many times what?"

"Could she have stabbed him?"

"A lot. Not the once but … a lot."

The full horror of what was before them began to form and take shape opening a chasm of silence yawning before them. Only the normal household sounds could be heard and as they competed with the sounds of despair and regret as Sarah began to crumble before their eyes.

"So we now have to decide what will be the best way to get rid of the body. Any suggestions?" asked Imogen.

Harry and Beth were now looking at Imogen as if she had truly gone mad. "What are you talking about?" whispered Harry.

"I'm talking about making sure Sarah doesn't end up in prison for doing something to that piece of shit that he probably had coming."

"You're being ridiculous," barked out Beth, still not be able to take her eyes from the blood stained corpse before them.

"So why haven't you arrested her already Officer Fairchild? And while you're at it, you'd better arrest me too."

All eyes were now staring uncomprehendingly at Imogen when Beth looking completely baffled asked, "What the bloody hell for?"

Imogen hesitated then looking at them with something close to defiance in her eyes quietly said, "For killing the bastard who was my father!"

All, even Sarah were now looking at Imogen, their friend whom they had thought they had known and loved for more years than they could remember. Imogen[N1] continued, "So you think we, that is Mum and me, just got lucky that night all those years ago? When had we ever had any luck where that bastard was concerned? No that night I'd had enough..." Imogen walked over to Grant's lifeless body and began to speak, the words now spilling out as if they'd been trapped inside an overfull bottle just waiting to be emptied.

"It was the usual. He'd come home from the pub, stinking of beer and some other woman's cheap perfume spoiling for a fight, any excuse to use mum as his favourite punch bag. I was in my bedroom when I heard the front door bang and I knew what was to come. I heard his shouts, I heard her trying to reason with him, I heard her cry out and I heard something hard clatter to the floor. I remember walking down the stairs and I remember I didn't rush. I went to the living room, to the fireplace and picked up the poker. I walked into the kitchen and there was mum, curled up like a foetus, trying to make herself as small as possible whilst he, the monster who called himself a man, was kicking her so hard I thought she's die this time. I remember striking him on the head as hard as I could and I remember the absolute disbelief on his face, how he touched his head looking at the blood on his hand as if he couldn't believe he could actually bleed. I hit him again, and again and again and would have never stopped if mum hadn't snatched the poker from me."

Imogen was now lost in the memory of that night over twenty years ago. She was remembering how it was snowing hard and how difficult it had been dragging her father's dead body down Dark Lane before leaving him there on the side of the road like the piece of rubbish he was. She was remembering how they cleaned up the blood, got into bed together, holding each other so tight, just waiting for the police to come and take them away, separating them forever. How when the police did arrive it was to inform that he had been hit by a car on his way home from The Red Lion, had obviously been drinking and the car had most likely skidded into him due to the awful weather and how the driver hadn't stopped but had dragged his body causing even more injuries. She was now remembering the policeman's kindness when he mistakenly thought their tears of relief were tears of grief and devastation.

Imogen now looking at her friends as she continued, "So…if you're going to arrest Sarah, then you'd better arrest me too because we've both done what was necessary to survive."

It was Sarah that eventually moved towards Imogen first, holding out her arms which Imogen walked into. It was then that Beth and Harry saw the blood seeping from Sarah's rectum on to the sofa through her pyjamas.

The gasps and look of horror from the others made Imogen look at them questioningly. Sarah turned and looked at her friends, Harry now silently crying, then looked down at the trail of blood she was leaving. “Don’t make me tell you. Please… I can’t…” as her sense of shame took over, consuming her.

At that point Sarah simply dissolved with noises of such anguish that could only have come from a place of such pain and darkness which were awful to hear or comprehend. Cradling their friend Imogen turned to them. She had made the decision. She could do this… again. “Beth you need to leave, you too Harry. You both need to let me take care of this.”

“No!” stated Beth. “I know I’m the police but you’re right, no one is taking her from us and they would. If not prison, she’d end up somewhere and she’d have to tell the world what that scum has done to her too. Harry?”

Looking at her friends Harry slowly nodded her agreement.

“You two still need to go because the less you know the better. Grant Downs will disappear and we will be here to support our friend like we’ve always done for each other.”

“Ok, but I need to look at the wound first, she may need medical attention, even a Doctor,” said Harry.

“No,” said Beth, “this has to remain just with us. Do what you can but if not then I’ll have no choice but to ring this in.”

Nodding they proceeded to move to the

bathroom where Beth ran the bath whilst Imogen and Harry gingerly undressed Sarah. What they saw shocked them all, the bruises, the bite marks on nearly every inch of her which was so much less than usual. Why hadn't they seen how thin and frail she was becoming? No one said a word as a silently crying Harry gently bathed, dried and soothed their damaged friend, dressing the visible wounds as best she could. The ones they couldn't see would be the hardest to heal.

"I think the damage is superficial but if the bleeding persists by morning she'll have to go to hospital," said Harry as Imogen and Beth nodded their agreement. It was therefore with reluctance and with more debate but finally Beth and Harry left. Imogen then took Sarah into the spare room where she lay with her until she finally sobbed herself to sleep.

Back downstairs Imogen took out her phone and in her contacts rang the one person she knew who could help them. The person on the other end of the phone answered on the second ring.

Taking a deep breath Imogen said, "Mr Speight? Malcolm Speight? Imogen Holt here. It would appear I need your help."

CHAPTER 9

After looking at what was once Grant Downs, Malcolm Speight was now looking at Imogen. "Well this is somewhat unexpected."

"If you can't help me Mr Speight then may I ask you to leave, but please keep this between us?"

"On the contrary this is what I do, what people pay me for?"

"Money won't be an issue. I can pay...."

"No I owe you, remember?"

"I know that's how you see this but you really don't."

"Well let's agree to differ shall we Mrs Holt?"

"Imogen."

Nodding he continued, "Imogen, I need to know what's happened for the purpose of what happens next."

"That piece of garbage is or should I say was, married to my friend who lives and owns this house."

"I take it this is something your friend has done?"

"It looks that way yes."

"Does the piece of garbage have a name?"

"Grant Downs," came the reply from the open hall doorway. They both turned to see Sarah standing at the entrance to the kitchen. Imogen saw Malcolm Speight take in what was before him, a tiny, small framed, frail looking, badly bruised Sarah and she saw his gaze harden as he turned to look back at the dead body.

"So this is THE Grant Downs is it? Or what's left of him."

"You know him?" asked Imogen.

"Of him and nothing good."

The three of them were now silent until Sarah asked, "Will you help us?"

Nodding Malcolm replied, "Yes but you both need to understand that there will be no going back. What happens here next will impact on you both for the rest of your lives so decide now to call the police or if not I'll do what I do best."

Sarah looked at her friend and nodded then Imogen turned to the man before them and said, "I rang you for a reason Malcolm."

Knowing their decision had already been made Malcolm began. "We have a lot to do, decisions to make to ensure your safety because I'm afraid your husband had some very unpleasant friends who will miss him very much not to mention the law."

"I knew he was dodgy," muttered Imogen.

"Oh he was that alright," shaking his head then muttering, "you have no idea." Taking his phone from his pocket Malcolm summoned his colleagues who had been waiting in the car outside. Two of the biggest men they had ever seen in their lives, were now standing in the kitchen which seemed to diminish in size, such were their bulks.

"Right lads you know the drill, so start by emptying his pockets." The men approached the body and roughly searched the dead man's pockets finding a phone, keys and the illegal drugs Grant had been slowly poisoning Sarah with. "Looks like Spice," muttered the man called Eddie, "I'd say K2 as well."

"Spice? The "Zombie" drug?" asked Imogen, "what's he doing with…Oh my God Sarah. Has he been drugging you as well as …oh my God!"

Sarah was just staring at the contents that looked minuscule in the hands of Eddie. "So I'm not going mad? I'm not ill?"

"No lass, you're not," said Eddie.

"How did he give it to me though? He never made dinner or a drink? I don't understand?"

Looking in the fridge Albert, Eddie's equally enormous colleague said, "I'm betting it's this jug thing with the water in it. Or t'orange juice.

Sugar perhaps? 'Owt if he dissolved them or crumbled them. Easy enough to do."

"Right then, get the stuff and we'll get this piece of shit out of sight. Then empty all liquids out of the fridge and anything else you can find that's got a broken seal. Ok? Right? Pronto then!" Malcolm barked out his orders as he and his team went to work, removing the remains of Grant Downs and his means of hurting Sarah once and for all

It was around midnight by the time Eddie and Albert had disposed of the offending body, cleaned thoroughly the blood from the floor and had emptied all drinks that could be contaminated by the cruel street drug that started out as a legal high but which now accounted for so many drug related deaths and the destruction of so many families. For the first time in a long time Sarah felt she had had a lucky escape as Malcolm was now explaining their crucial next steps. "We need to buy you some time before it becomes apparent that Downs has disappeared and we have to then make sure that it looks like he's done a runner to somewhere like the Cayman Islands."

"Why there?" asked Sarah.

"It's where you can have dodgy bank accounts without anyone asking questions?" replied Malcolm, "and that's what we want the authorities to think for a while. Before that though, he needs to go somewhere else. Any suggestions?"

"My mother lives in Spain, Moraira near Alicante. She's part owner of the firm, the main shareholder."

"So he could feasibly go there on business?"

"Yes I guess so."

"Right then ladies, I think we should book a couple of flights, so the Computer is where?"

It was around four am when Malcolm and his colleagues finally left. The plan was very simple. They had booked a single flight to Alicante for the next day, a Sunday. Then he would be scheduled a flight to George Town in the Cayman Islands the following Tuesday from Barcelona. One of Malcolm's men, someone, who from the CCTV cameras at Doncaster airport, would look like Grant Downs, have the same hair, build, height as Downs and would park his car and proceed to check in. Before security though he would nip to the toilet, change his clothes, don a baseball cap and proceed to the exit where he would be picked up by another of Malcolm's men and return home.

"That will buy you time Sarah to do a number of things. First you will need to replace the floor tiles where the blood was spilt. If the police suspect foul play you will be their main suspect and they will use Luminal to see if blood was spilt here. It looks clean but it will still be detectable."

"How can we do that? Only essential shops are open," asked Imogen.

"I know a man," said Malcolm, "he'll be here later on today so I'll just take a photo to send to him. The other thing, well they will look into the money. You may need to have a good lawyer Sarah because I'm telling you now your firm, the one you part own is not the firm that was once your family business and the police will suspect you're involved."

"Involved in what?" Malcolm now looked away thinking because he really didn't want to say more.

Imogen urged, "She needs to know what she's dealing with here, we both do."

Taking a big breath and a huge leap of faith where these two relative strangers were concerned, he finally opted for honesty. "Your husband was in bed so to speak with Cameron Sheldon, correct?"

Sarah nodded, "Yes I've met him and he made my flesh crawl!"

"Putting it mildly I'm afraid. Your small family business will now be the front for money laundering at the very least with drugs and human trafficking thrown in too most likely, if the rumours are true. Millions will be going through your books and the police will find it." Sarah was now staring ahead, seeing nothing. Getting up on shaky legs she began the hard process of leaving the room, stopping only when the pain of her injuries took over. Malcolm and Imogen watched feeling impotent to really help her as she finally managed to reach the stairs.

Imogen was shaking her head, tired and tearful. "If the bastard wasn't dead I'd stab him myself!"

"Get in the queue. You do know she's also got withdrawal to deal with too? That's another reason we need to buy her time so she can get her head and her story straight. She's got some very hard days ahead I'm afraid."

"How long?"

"Depends. Two possibly three, could go into four."

Getting up to leave, he turned to Imogen. "Make sure you're ok too. Promise."

"Promise but I don't know how to thank..." he put his hand up to stop her.

"Listen. I'm not a good man by any stretch of the imagination. I know what I am, what I've done, what I do but I am glad to be able to help you and that poor lass but be careful. The coppers aren't stupid and they will be looking at her hard and I'd hate for you to be implicated too. Perverting the Course of Justice is a serious offence, I hope you know this."

Swallowing hard Imogen replied, "I hadn't thought of it like that, just... well just wanted to protect Sarah."

Malcolm nodded his understanding whilst looking immeasurably sad as he replied, "And we will and I will also protect you Imogen, if it's the last thing I do. I owe it to your husband but I have to say..." now embarrassed Malcolm stopped and turned to walk away.

"Please Malcolm, what were you about to say," urged Imogen.

Smiling with something akin to sadness, he continued, "That I am wondering what a man like him would have made of all this." Shaking his head and sighing heavily, Malcolm nodded his goodbye as Imogen watched him get into his car and drive away.

Watching his retreating car Imogen realized dawn was breaking with the mists across the Pennines making the majestic peaks look like they were shrouded in mystery and secrets of their own. Imogen shivered and realised she was now on a journey that would mean her life would never be the same again and she also realised that she was very afraid and already full of regret.

CHAPTER 10

That weekend resembled the days after Imogen's accident. The girls formed a rota ensuring Sarah was never alone whilst she dealt with her withdrawal from K2, her injuries and the absolute horror of the situation she and her friends were in. It was decided that Imogen would move in for the foreseeable future too so she had rung the Head to tell him she had Covid symptoms and would be self- isolating and working remotely for the next two weeks. It would appear the 'plague' had its uses.

They listened quietly as she relayed the plan of action to them as Sarah finally slept, after experiencing a terrible night of sweats and nightmares. Beth was clearly impressed and said so. "Bloody hell. Dare I ask who the brains behind this is? No don't tell me, but wow, it's good."

"Let's hope it works," nodded Harry.

Imogen took a deep breath and said, "It's not just him being missing though. It seems Greens is now a front for money laundering, possibly drugs and human trafficking too."

No one said a thing but just stared then Harry burst into hysterical laughter, “You cannot be bloody serious? Have I just entered the Twilight Zone?”

“It appears the dead scumbag was in league with someone called Cameron Sheldon.”

Beth staring wide eyed at them said, “If human trafficking is involved the MCIS will be all over this,” then when the others looked blankly at her, “Major Crimes Investigative Support and probably the NCA, which is the National Crime Agency, our equivalent of the FB1. Oh my God! We are in such deep shit! I don’t bloody believe this!” Beth was now pacing around the room, running her hands through her hair.

Seconds ticked by and no one spoke until finally Imogen said, “I got us into this so I have no choice but to get through this with Sarah, to see it to the end but I get it that you guys will now need to bail.”

Silence then, “Never going to happen,” said Beth shaking her head.

Harry was biting her bottom lip looking very close to tears. “But this is where you bail Harry,” said Imogen softly and was pleased that Beth was nodding her agreement. “You’re working on a Covid ward, you have three kids and you’re married to the local GP, so there’s no way you can be involved in any of this and Sarah agrees. Ok?”

Harry looked at her friends and nodded because they knew her so well. Harry, the one with the charmed life could definitely not do this.

By Tuesday Sarah had come through the worse and although she still felt terrible, the vomiting and shakes had stopped and she was managing to finally eat something that remained in her system. It was now time to implement the plan.

This started with a text to Grant's phone then a rare telephone call to her mother Elaine, all eminently visible for the Police to see. Taking a deep breath Sarah dialed the number and waited for the connection, being more than relieved when the answer phone kicked in. "Mum it's me Sarah. Just wondering if Grant has left for home yet? I haven't been able to get hold of him and I thought he was due home today. Let me know ok? Oh and I hope you're well."

Breaking the connection Imogen squeezed her hand, "Good job, as we will notify the police that Grant never materialized in Spain when she rings back, ok?"

Nodding Sarah sat back into the chair, thinking how insane her life had become. "Why can I not remember doing it? You'd think a person would remember stabbing someone?"

"You were drugged and traumatised so your mind has probably just switched off."

"You remember though."

"It was different because I needed to protect mum and we'd had years of it. I didn't do it in the heat of the moment, it was with, well cold fury I guess."

"I hope I can be as brave as you."

"You will be, you already are."

It was several hours later when Sarah's mother rang and left the message that was to be crucial to what happened next. "Sarah it's your mother. I have no idea what you're talking about as Grant has not been in touch for months and has certainly not been here so ring me back. Oh and I hope you're ok and not catching this bloody flu thing. Bye then."

Listening Sarah smiled wryly. "I know you had the father from hell but at least you had Arlette. You know, I don't think I can remember either of my parents ever saying that they loved me. Ever. Disappointed in me? Absobloodylutely!"

Taking her friend's hand Imogen just smiled sadly at her. "So? Ready?"

"Let's get it done," said Sarah as she reached for her phone to inform the police her husband Grant Downs was missing.

CHAPTER 11

Detective Chief Inspector Max Stainmore was not a happy man. The drive from London had been a nightmare; he thought the M25 was bad but the M1 was in another league. Now he was sitting in a room with a group of men that for him epitomised everything that was wrong with the world at large and definitely the police force of which he had served for many years. He could not stand the political side of the Force and here before him were men, only men, he noted who had not walked the beat in a while if ever.

He was introduced to the power house of South Yorkshire's key police personnel in the office of South Yorkshire's Chief Constable Jim Haggerty. Present were the Chief Constable, his Deputy Chief Constable Ralph Jones, Superintendent Giles Baker and his immediate boss, the one he would answer to first, Detective Chief Superintendent Tom Blakely.

"We of course will do everything to support the ongoing work of the NCA but so far we have no reason to suspect this Mr Sheldon of anything other than being a successful business man," this from Superintendent Giles Baker.

"Oh he's remarkably good at covering his tracks, but if he's here in your neck of the woods, I'm telling you now his activities will be immense."

Sighing dramatically Giles Baker replied, "But why here?" Max leaned forward and looked at this career police man in the eye. "Where better than to come to a place where the systematic abuse of approximately fourteen hundred young girls of a certain social and economic group by a certain group of men was allowed to continue for sixteen years despite so much evidence presented? Where better than to come to a place where the police hierarchy here in Sheffield were responsible for, and I quote, "extraordinarily bad failures that were a substantial cause that killed ninety-six people." This force actually made it harder for the public to trust any of us to even police a football match? Why wouldn't a certain criminal element look at this force and think easy pickings?!"

The outrage on the faces of everyone in the room, some very proud Yorkshire men, gave Max a certain satisfaction but he was being deliberately provocative for a reason. He needed them to be so fired up at his suggestion of their lack of vigilance that they would do everything to show this arrogant bloody London 'upstart' bastard how good they were! How different their people were from past mistakes made!

It was South Yorkshire's Chief Constable Jim Haggerty who eventually replied first, in a measured but clearly authoritative tone that badly concealed how very angry he was, "We are aware of the reputation we have had for past mistakes made by some of our predecessors Chief Inspector but I assure you, we are a very different force today."

Smiling now Max leaned back in his chair and replied, "Good. Now let me be very clear. Sheldon will be bringing in his human cargo and I intend to find when and where. I also intend that Sheldon is stopped and pays for what happened in Dover because gentleman this man is a monster of the first order. He pedals in human misery and what's more he loves doing it."

The collective nods told Max he now had their full attention. Now for the hard part as Max looked at each man before him before he began his well- rehearsed speech.

"A man like Sheldon cannot get a grip on a place without help. Gentlemen, he will own people on this force who will be his eyes and ears therefore keeping him at least one step ahead of us and they need flushing out as soon as possible before we can really have any chance of stopping him."

The silence in the Chief Constable's office was deafening as Max looked at each of the men of position before him. And there it was, the flick of the eye, the insignificant twitch barely detectable unless you knew when to look, the guilty give- away. "Well, well, well," thought Max, "and there it is."

*

Max had been a police officer for over twenty years, from the age of nineteen. He had come up through the ranks, first uniform, then CID, even doing a stint undercover for the Major Crimes Team. He was known to be methodical, ruthless too but also a Maverick, often putting himself at risk of disciplinary although as yet he had avoided anything major. He just had no time for the 'bull shitters', the ones in positions of authority who were more concerned with pleasing the politicians and the readers of the more salacious tabloids. As far as Max Stainmore was concerned they just got in his way of doing his job. Those who worked with Max however had huge respect for him as a man as well as his methods. He was fair, rarely pulled rank and worked harder than any of them. When the NCA came calling it seemed a natural progression for him particularly now he had Cameron Sheldon in his sights.

Max had been at Dover when the bodies had been found and would never for as long as he lived forget what he had seen that dark, dismal, cruel night. He vowed there and then that he would get the bastard responsible, no matter who it was, no matter how long it would take because those poor souls deserved so much better, particularly the children, the babies. Max had his own demons to live with too and he sometimes had walked too fine a line stepping over it more than once. He did believe in the Justice system though but there were times when it was really hard to keep seeing the real criminals walk away.

Yes, Max Stainmore was driven in his quest for justice and he made no apologies for it. It was the reason he had a failed marriage and numerous failed relationships behind him, why he was so spectacularly bad at sustaining one for the long haul. Why he knew he was destined to probably die alone despite being handsome and charm personified when he chose to use it.

Just over six feet with dark hair going prematurely grey which only added to Max's attractiveness, he had very blue, almost ice blue eyes, but with a complexion that tanned easily. His sister had traced their ancestry and had discovered Norwegian and German ancestry on their father's side, which accounted for their looks. He was prone to weight if not careful so exercised daily to keep trim without the gauntness that some have. His first trip to the Police Canteen in Sheffield Central had caused more than a few hearts to flutter and a few interested glances from both sexes.

Standing in the designated Conference room he had been allocated, he surveyed his team of four detectives and one uniformed officer. They were an eclectic bunch that was for sure, four men and one woman of various age, shapes and ethnicity, the powers that be clearly highlighting to Max that they were as diversified as the rest of the country.

So before him stood, sat or lounged his team all openly scrutinizing him. To break the ice Max began, "So … name, rank and serial number then?" pointing to the younger man who was sitting to attention with folded arms. Clearly the youngest amongst them Max recognized the gleam in the eyes and the energy of only the young and ambitious.

"Detective Constable Daniel Devon Sir."

"Or Desperate Dan or Daredevil Dan depending what bloody scrape he's got himself into," remarked the older man sitting next to him.

"Or depending what bloody hole I have to dig you out of Sarge!" remarked Dan who was taking no offence as the comment was said with affection and respect.

Turning to 'Sarge', Max asked, "And you are?"

"Detective Sergeant Eddie Sinclair" replied the Sergeant in his rough Barnsley accent and it was not lost on any of them that the obligatory 'Sir' was not forthcoming.

Max turned to the only female who responded quickly "Detective Constable Lydia Smith Sir." That left two of them, one being the recently promoted Brad Fairchild who was the uniformed officer attached to Max for the duration of his stay. "Sergeant Brad Fairchild Sir."

"Which leaves..?" asked Max turning to the final member of his team.

"Detective Constable Isaiah Heath Sir," replied the man before him who quite frankly would not have looked out of place as a linebacker for an all American Football team being huge, black and very proud.

"So you will all know who I am by now. DCI Max Stainmore currently working for the NCA and trust me, it isn't as sexy as it sounds. I'm here because I believe you have a very dangerous man who is actively using your patch to continue his trade in human trafficking. You will all have heard about Dover and the deaths in the lorry fiasco?" Acknowledging their nods, Max turned to his laptop and clicked to reveal the face of Cameron Sheldon on the screen in front of them.

"This is Cameron Sheldon, and I believe he is responsible for the deaths of those forty three men, women and children found in that lorry. That won't be all he's responsible for either so catching him, stopping him, incarcerating him will be our lives work until it has happened. I'll expect long hours, drudge work, total commitment. I'll also expect loyalty but I'll earn it first. Any questions so far?"

Eddie Sinclair was the first to speak. A bit of a parody Eddie was the quintessential grizzled detective who had seen it all before, was not easily convinced about anything unless he actually witnessed it and quite frankly was showing septicism now. "May I ask why you're so convinced he's responsible? Isn't there somebody already banged up for that Dover business?"

Max, anticipating this now showed another picture of another man. "Here Sergeant is Anthony Dolan, the lorry driver and the man currently incarcerated and who would not give up Sheldon. You want to know why?" Max now clicked to another image, one that chilled the room and made even the grizzled Eddie Sinclair sit up and take note because before them was a photograph of a child's, a toddler's little finger, one that had been expertly severed at the knuckle.

"This was sent to Anthony Dolan whilst in custody along with a picture of his grandson Oliver who at three years old must now live without his finger with the promise of more to follow if he didn't do as he was told."

Max scanned the now silent room, looked at their faces, then turned to Eddie Sinclair. "As for the Dover 'business'! It was a business alright, a business in human misery the likes that is unimaginable for any decent human being to even think of. Never refer to what this scum does as a 'business' Sergeant or get the hell out of this room and off my team now."

To say that no one knew where to look would be an understatement until Sergeant Eddie Sinclair of nearly thirty years' experience, stood up and walked towards Detective Chief Inspector Max Stainmore. All held their collective breaths until Eddie then extended his right hand and said, "I will be pleased to be of service Sir. Welcome to Yorkshire."

Clasping his hand Max looked at the man before him and instinctively knew that here was a man he could trust.

CHAPTER 12

Unlike Max Stainmore, Cameron Sheldon trusted no one except to a point Grant Downs, so it was with frustration and a real sense that something was wrong when he couldn't contact him. The Thursday shipment and distribution had gone to plan as Grant's hand- picked workforce operated as a well- oiled machine but Grant was unusually MIA – missing in action.

At the same time Cameron Sheldon was beginning to worry, Sarah had contacted the Police to report her missing husband. Brad was in the call base when he spotted Beth. She looked terrible and that made him sad and angry in equal measures and he still didn't really understand how it had come to this. Going over to her he said, "So how are you this fine morning PC Fairchild?"

Startled Beth jumped round then visibly relaxed when she saw who it was, replying, "Same old Sergeant Fairchild, same old." Then it came, the awkwardness, the not knowing what to say or how to act and they both hated it, missing their ease and neither knowing how to fix it.

"Better not keep Asif waiting," was Beth's eventual fallback position and Brad sadly nodded as he turned away to attend to a query but being aware when she was no longer in his vicinity. It was then that Sarah's call came through and he had accidentally over heard it.

"May I ask how long he has been missing? You are sure of these details? Thank you Mrs Downs. Someone will be in contact." His first thought was to call back Beth but was at that moment he had been summoned to meet Max and the other team members.

Max and his team had compiled a list of all of Cameron Sheldon's known associates and business interests no matter how small and tenuous. This was the brunt of good police work which was arduous and time consuming.

Walking into the conference room Max was speaking to the team, "So we need to establish who may have relocated to the area prior to Sheldon. We have three names known to the NCA. David Richmond, Stephen Richardson and Grant Downs."

"Grant!" this from Brad as he entered the room. "Bloody hell fire!"

"Something to add Sergeant," smiled Max.

"Grant Downs is married to a friend of my wife's who has just reported him missing Sir!"

"Really? How well do you know him Sergeant?"

"Not really to be honest. Never liked him, a bit too full of it for my liking Sir."

"Right so let's go and talk to his wife then. Could be a good way in so probably need a female here to help things, so Lydia you'd better join us........."

"Sorry Sir," said Brad interrupting, "but Detective Constable Smith won't be welcome at Mrs Downs so her presence could be counter-productive."

Lydia Smith was now looking daggers at Brad and scarlet in the process and said, "That isn't your call to make Sergeant Fairchild!"

"No but it's mine so Brad and Eddie, let's pay Mrs Downs a visit and later we'd better sit down and have a chat people because I'm thinking we may have internal issues that I can well do without," and with that Max got his coat, leaving Lydia practically apoplectic with fury. Isiah openly grinned at her whilst Dan merely shrugged and said, "Well what did you expect Lydia?" The two fingered gesture was the response he got back.

*

As they approached Penton, Max was silently appreciating the beauty that was South Yorkshire's countryside. He had also been appraised of the circumstances of Beth's demotion from CID with Detective Sergeant

Eddie Sinclair being very vociferous regarding the utter unfairness whilst Brad had just quietly given Max the facts.

"Lydia should have stood with her partner that's for sure. Beth's a bloody good copper in uniform and out of it, not that I've seen her out of her uniform. You know what I mean, Brad, no offence meant."

"None taken Sarge."

Max then asked Brad, "So what do you know about Downs and how come he's married to a friend of your wife's?"

"I regard Sarah as my friend too Chief Inspector as I do with the rest of the girls. None of us liked or trusted Downs and I know the girls tried to talk Sarah out of marrying him. It was all too quick and he was just that bit too smooth but I did a covert background check on him but found that his story checked out," shrugged Brad in way of explanation.

"That's because he is actually Samuel Thornton and has a rap sheet as long as your arm," replied Max.

"I bloody knew it!" Brad now angrily slapping the steering wheel as he drove, "and here we are," as he turned the car into the drive of Sarah's large converted barn.

"Very nice," muttered Max, "crime certainly does pay!"

"This was Sarah's before she married Downs. Dad was a local builder and did well," said Brad in way of explanation still fuming at how easily they had all been duped by the man in question.

Climbing out of the car, Max was awed again at the open fields and panoramic views which were so different from his flat in the concrete canyons of Canary Wharf. The front door opened and Max was immediately struck by the woman now standing before him. Downs has done well was Max's first thought, she's beautiful.

"Mrs Downs. I am Detective Chief Inspector Stainmore and we're here about your husband's missing status."

Taking in the leather jacketed attire, confident stance, London accent and the air of authority Max always conveyed Imogen purposely ignored him and turned to Brad, "So glad it's you Brad because Sarah is rather worried as you can imagine. So with Covid are you allowed inside or should we meet on the back patio?"

"Back patio will be fine. Shall I lead the way?"

Nodding Imogen replied, "I'll get Sarah," as she closed the door. Inside the house Sarah was standing wringing her hands, trying hard not to appear nervous. She was dressed in a long sleeved long dress with a scarf to cover the bruises on her neck, that and clever makeup too.

"Ready? Right, there's three of them but Brad's

here too so remember what we've rehearsed and as Beth said, be as honest as possible ok?"

"I don't think I'll be able to get away with this Gen. I think I should just tell them what I've done!"

"NO! Listen to me, just stick to what we've rehearsed. There is no reason for this not to work if we all keep our nerve and stick to the story. Sarah you can do this! Please." Nodding, Sarah brushed away her tears and straightened her spine as she and Imogen made their way outside to join the three men waiting for them.

Max and Eddie were both struck by the same two things; how tiny and frail Sarah Downs was and how strong, almost protective her friend was beside her. Max was trying hard not to stare at Imogen, not because she was without a doubt stunningly beautiful but because he was still bristling at her dismissal of him and Imogen knew it and was already regretting it but opening the door to him had completely taken her aback hence the need to only engage with Brad.

"So Mrs Downs when was the last time you heard from your husband?" asked Max.

"He left for the airport Sunday to fly to Alicante."

"What was the purpose for the flight?"

"Business with my mother who lives there."

"You didn't go too? Not to see your mother?" queried Eddie.

"If you knew my mother you wouldn't ask. My mother and I do not exactly get along so there was no reason for me to go. Can't actually think of anything worse and I have my dogs to take care of too. Besides Grant, as usual, didn't invite me to join him."

"So when did you become concerned that your husband wasn't where he should have been?" asked Max.

"I'd been leaving him a couple of messages asking him when he hoped to be back as he is usually pretty good at letting me know his arrangements. His phone kept going to Voicemail so I rang my mother who hadn't seen him or even knew he was going to see her. The whole thing seems so strange so I rang Imogen who said I should ring the police and that's what I've done. I'm sorry, do you think I'm over reacting? Wasting your time? I know you must have loads on..."

"Not at all," said Eddie.

Turning those very icy eyes to Imogen Max said, "May I ask who you are and why you're here?"

Momentarily stunned at his directness that verged on the rude, Imogen replied, "I'm Imogen Holt and long- time friend of Sarah's. Sarah was worried and upset, so I thought we should form a support 'bubble' until Grant returns. It's quite isolated up here and as I live alone it seemed to make sense."

Imogen and Max were now openly staring at one another, trying to read each other. For some reason Max wasn't buying this and his gut was telling him something was not right and his gut was never wrong.

Coughing slightly Eddie brought back Max's attention and Max once again turned to Sarah. "May I ask how things are between you and your husband?"

Sarah looking confused turned to Brad who answering her unsaid query said, "It's procedure to enquire about the state of a person's relationship in cases such as these Sarah."

"In case all seven and a half stone of her managed to overpower all six feet something Grant, bludgeon him to death and hide him under the floorboards I take it?" queried Imogen rolling her eyes and folding her arms muttering, "For God's sake!"

"Something like that," nodded Max giving her a smile that didn't quite reach his eyes and which actually scared Imogen more than she would choose to admit. Sighing Sarah looked at the three men before her, saw Brad's total discomfort, saw how very sharp and on the ball the other two were and at that moment wanted to confess all. Then she looked at Imogen who nodded, something else that Max noted.

"My marriage is not in a good place Chief Inspector but if my husband has left me then I would think he would have taken his clothes too." Looking down, Sarah continued. "He married me for the family money and I was stupid enough to not see that. None of my friends liked him and I should have listened. Sad but true," and that was when Sarah broke down and Imogen was now afraid she would blow the whole thing.

"We can always come back if you're too upset Mrs Downs," said Max quietly.

"No. Sorry. I'm ok, really. My husband I may have our problems but I hope nothing has happened to him and if it has I'd like to know."

Nodding and seemingly to understand and accept this Max then asked the question he really wanted answering. "Have you ever met a man called Cameron Sheldon?"

"Yes. My husband does business with him I believe."

"What sort of business?"

"Building houses, we own a building business," Sarah now looking quizzically at the Police Officers.

"Have you ever met Mr Sheldon?"

"Yes and I didn't like him!" Looking at Max Sarah breathed very deeply then ploughed on. "I believe it was when Grant met Mr Sheldon that things really changed between us. He seemed to become more distant, colder," then touching her neck, "rougher." Sighing, then again looking at Imogen Sarah seemed to come to a decision. Slowly she removed her scarf revealing her bruised neck which brought looks of shock then understanding and then pity from the men before her.

Brad looked fit to burst. "Bloody hell Sarah! Why didn't you let me know?"

"I've already had this from Beth too Brad. I'm sorry I didn't tell anyone but I've been too ashamed," she sadly said whilst trying to smile as at least this was being truthful.

Max now spoke gently to Sarah. "We will try to find your husband Mrs Downs not only because you have reported him missing but because we would like him to help with other ongoing enquiries we are also pursuing. We will need access to your business premises and all monetary accounts too so have we your permission or do we need to get a warrant?"

"Certainly Chief Inspector, anything you need and a warrant won't be necessary as I've nothing to hide."

Nodding Max said, "Thank you and I'm sorry for what you've obviously been through." Looking at Max Imogen saw that he actually meant it.

Getting up Imogen led the way to the front of

the house leaving Sarah alone, whilst Brad still clearly upset as he said, “Look after her but bloody hell fire! How long has this been going on?”

Imogen smiled sadly saying, “I’m not entirely sure but a while I guess but I’m looking after her now Bear and she’s stronger than she looks.”

Nodding he turned towards the car where Eddie was getting in. Max turned to Imogen and said, “I’d like to say it’s been a pleasure but we both know I’d be lying but I suspect I will be seeing you again. Soon.”

With folded arms and a look of disdain on her face Imogen replied with deliberate surprise saying, “Really? Well I can’t think why Chief Inspector but if you deem it necessary I’ll be here supporting Sarah as long as it takes. It’s what we do up here.”

“Of that I am in no doubt Imogen Holt.” The way he spoke her full name seemed to issue a challenge of some sort that made Imogen nervous, very nervous and she was now thinking she may have over played the ‘tough cookie’ card. With that he turned and walked to the car, before stopping and looking at Imogen again and Imogen had no choice but to look back.

In the car Eddie was teasing Brad unmercifully. “What’s with this ‘Bear’ business then big lad?”

Blushing furiously Brad replied, “It’s what the

girls have always called me, ever since Beth and I first met."

Max looked at the two men, then made a decision asking, "Free for a drink later, after work? My place such as it is seeing as the pubs aren't opening yet."

"Wish they'd bloody hurry up, "muttered Eddie, "it's like bloody torture now!"

"Yeah sounds good," replied Brad grateful to prolong going back to his empty soulless flat he was now renting. Max wanted to know all there was to know about Sarah Downs and her friends but particularly the beautiful but enigmatically bolshie Imogen Holt who was clearly hiding something. There was more going on there than met the eye, of that he was certain.

Just as the three were leaving, a phone call was taking place that was informing Cameron Sheldon that Grant Downs was now officially missing. What chilled him to the bone was when he was told who the investigating officer was.

CHAPTER 13

Max had been allocated a rather swish penthouse apartment in Sheffield's S1 area overlooking the city centre. It had allegedly been the abode of a notorious drug dealer therefore now the property of the police for the foreseeable, hence a place for a visiting DCI during a global pandemic to rest his weary head.

Brad and Eddie were pointing out the various city landmarks of interest to Max from the vantage of a large balcony terrace, enjoying their Desperados and finally beginning to relax.

"So Brad or should I say Bear," grinned Max, "tell me about your wife's group of friends. Did you say there were four of them?"

"Particularly the lovely Imogen, heh Chief Inspector?" grinned Eddie saluting Max as he did so with Max merely saluting and grinning back.

"Yes, Beth, Sarah, Harriet although we all call her Harry and Imogen. Been glued at the hip since they were five or so when they first met at St James Infant School in Penton. You cross one and you've got the lot to contend with, trust me.

If we'd sent Lydia in today she would not have come out in one piece that's for sure if Imogen had met up with her again," grinned Brad, "I have seen Imogen reduce grown men to tears before now."

Brad then gave Max and Eddie a potted history of what he knew about the four friends, how none of them had wanted Sarah to marry and how they had nursed Imogen back to a life without her husband and unborn child. It was Imogen's story that never really failed to stun.

"Bloody hell," muttered Eddie, "poor lass. I don't know how you can completely recover from something so tragic," now thinking of his own wife and children whom he lived for.

"Imogen has had it rough but she is a tough cookie, good at her job as Deputy Head, will probably be the next Head at Grove South too. She's thrown herself into the job to be honest, but you'll not find one ounce of self- pity."

"Is she as tough as she appears today?" asked Max.

"Yes and no," said Brad, "but she's clearly very worried about Sarah. I suspect we would find more than a few bruises on her neck if truth be told but Imogen will also go where others wouldn't dare. Only yesterday she was delivering food to vulnerable families and taking on the local small time drug dealer. She's brave Max and a bloody good 'egg'."

"Well I don't think I made a very good first impression," mused Max.

"Well you are a bloody Londoner Sir. No offence," laughed Brad.

"None taken" grinned Max before asking, "no man in her life then?"

"Thinking of applying Sir?" grinned Eddie, "she is a bit of a looker!"

"She's a lot of a looker, but I think I'd have as much chance there as winning the Euro millions and how about you guys calling me Max when off duty?" The clink of bottles sealed the deal.

"No man," answered Brad after swigging his drink, "hasn't been anyone since Neil. I can't imagine Imogen with anyone else but Neil if I'm honest," and there was a sadness in Brad's voice as he made his point.

"So what do you make of Sarah's story?" asked Max.

Brad was unequivocal saying, "Sarah is sound and she will have told you all she knows and I suspect she didn't want me to know the half of it as well. Those bloody marks on her neck, I ask you!? What decent man lays hands on a woman in anger!? He'll get what's coming to him if I get hold of him!"

Max now looking serious asked the question

that was always going to be asked and he steeled himself for Brad's response, "He may have already Brad. How far would the friends go to cover for Sarah?"

Brad began to laugh then saw the look on Max's face then looked back totally incredulous. Brad now tried to control his temper and chose his words carefully. "The girls have something special. It's a real love between them and they would do anything for each other, absolutely anything, but would they cover up a murder? Are you seriously asking me Max, Eddie, if my wife, one of the best police officers, best women I have ever known, would collude to cover up a murder?!"

Max remained silent, watching him carefully as Brad continued, "I mean could they? Would they have the means? Would they know where to start?" shaking his head Brad shrugged his shoulders saying, "not possible."

Max spreading his hands before him replied, "You know as well as I do that a suspicious disappearance will invariably lead us to looking closely at family first so until we know better, then everything has to stay on the table." Brad and Eddie solemnly nodded as Max continued, "What I think and hope though is that Grant Downs has somehow upset Sheldon and that's where we need our investigation to lead us and I hope Sarah can help starting with her business premises. We need to go through it with a fine tooth comb starting tomorrow."

Looking down, Max was now wondering how best to approach his next concern. "About the rest of the team. How much do you trust Dan and Isiah?"

"With my life Max," said Eddie without hesitation, "and have done more than once."

"I know them both to be solid," this from Brad.

"That leaves Lydia. So is Lydia still in the Superintendent's pocket?"

"Why wouldn't she be?" said Eddie.

"I'm biased," answered Brad, remembering how devastating Lydia's betrayal had been for Beth and how in effect it was the catalyst for the rift now between them.

"Thanks guys, that's all I wanted to know. Eddie, tell Isiah to meet us at Greens tomorrow and only a handful of uniformed officers you would trust with the lives of your children."

Eddie putting down his drink looked at Max somewhat incredulously saying, "Are we talking 'bent' coppers on our patch?"

"Without a doubt. I do not want Sheldon to know what or who we are looking at or where or what we are searching?"

Both Brad and Eddie looked at Max then nodded both looking very troubled. "Bloody hell but it comes to something when you can't trust the men and women you work side by side with," said Eddie.

Touched by the man's naïve 'old school' attitude Max replied, "Men like Sheldon will find the weakness, the weakness we all have, whether we know it or not and he will exploit it without mercy. It is how he operates and is the crux of his success."

"How come you trust us?" said Brad, "I mean you could accuse me of being Grant Down's mate, being in his pocket. I mean I went to the shit's bloody wedding!"

"Who says I do? But I did see your reaction to Sarah's bruises and as for you Eddie? Let's just say there's something about you."

Both men looked down then looked at each other then they looked at Max. Brad standing first then said, "To bringing down Sheldon and Downs!" Eddie stood up too joining him as both men raised their bottles looking at Max to join them. "To bringing the evil that is Sheldon and his crew to their knees," he said as these three honourable men clinked their bottles in their common cause.

"Now are you ready for the trouncing Spurs will be giving Sheffield United on Saturday?" as Max deftly brought the conversation back onto safer normal ground for the remainder of the evening.

Later when his colleagues had left, looking out

over the city Max felt he had made real progress. He could smell Sheldon, knew he was getting a little closer. Brad had pointed out the direction of Penton and Max was now wondering if a beautiful woman with green eyes and black hair who clearly was hiding something was enjoying her view this evening too. A woman who had suffered more than most but there was definitely something about her that had piqued his interest, probably because she had been so dismissive of him and he wasn't used to that.

"Yes Imogen Holt, I believe we will be meeting again," and with that thought, Max raised his drink to her.

*

Meanwhile back in Penton, Sarah, Beth and Imogen were also discussing the day's events. Sarah was wringing her hands and berating herself. "I said too much! I showed them my neck! Christ I've given them a bloody motive!"

"You gave them the right amount of honesty," argued Imogen, "I was there and I felt you to be very credible. You had them feeling sympathy for your situation, I mean I thought Brad was going to blow his top at one point!"

Both now looked at her, "What?" asked Beth.

"To let a man like that go for just a second... well you need your bloody head looking at," said Sarah, who had been deeply moved by Brad's response to the injuries he had seen.

Beth merely looked at the floor then dismissing her friend's inference said, "So you think we've managed the first hurdle?"

"I do," concurred Imogen looking at Sarah.

"Yes I think so but the London Chief Inspector is no fool."

"But seriously hot!" said Beth now smiling conspiratorially, "he's causing more than a few hearts to flutter at the station."

"He couldn't take his eyes off you could he?" offered Sarah.

Not being able to meet either friends' eyes Imogen shrugged, reaching for the bottle of wine murmuring, "Wouldn't say that exactly."

Beth, relieved to no longer be discussing her marriage stated, "Brilliant. If he gets too close, we can always use you to steer him off course!"

"Are you talking about pimping me out? Thank you so much!"

"What a hard job that would be! Taking one for the team with the seriously sexy Detective Chief Inspector Max Stainmore who is the hottest thing to walk into Sheffield Police Central since, well me!" declared Beth dodging the cushion now being thrown her way.

“A bit of a cliché though? Leather jacket, black jeans, smoldering good looks for God’s sake. Who does he bloody think he is?!”

“So you do think he’s hot. Well, well, well Ms Holt!” teased Beth, again ducking the second cushion, “and about bloody time too!”

Looking on at her friends’ banter Sarah was quietly praying that all had gone well, as well as possible anyway.

Shaking her head, she began, “You don’t have to pretend, I know how much trouble I’m in but I need you both to understand something. If they find out the truth, that I stabbed him, then I alone will take the blame. The rest of you will not be implicated. My life is already ruined but yours won’t have to be.”

“It won’t come to that,” said Imogen with a confidence she did not feel. Chief Inspector Max Stainmore was clearly no fool and would not easily be duped and Imogen was now really afraid for her friend and indeed for them all. Yet she had started this and had no choice but to see it through to its end. She was now silently praying Malcolm Speight knew what he was doing.

“But it might,” said Sarah with emphatic certainty that was so out of character for her. “That monster has ruined my life but he will not ruin yours!”

CHAPTER 14

"So where is he?" screamed Cameron Sheldon, "he can't have just fucking disappeared?!" Pacing up and down in the palatial offices overlooking the City centre he was becoming seriously worried. "I make people fucking disappear! I fucking decide. No one else!"

Dave Richmond and Steve Richardson looked at each other then back at their boss. They too were worried, particularly when they were told who was looking into Grant's disappearance. Max Stainmore was one of the main reasons they had all left London and the fact that he had followed them here was a serious development.

"Perhaps his wife knows something?" offered Dave.

"That simpering fucking no mark! He was doing his best to get rid of her!"

"You don't think he could be...?"

"What! You think he would double cross me!" screamed Cameron as he took Dave by the scruff of his neck, throwing him across the room.

Steve stood up quickly now both arms out trying to placate his boss, "We have to look at all possibilities boss. He may have had an accident or I don't know, had a family issue back in the 'Smoke'!"

"He doesn't give a shit about his family," countered Cameron, "no something is very wrong here."

Dave was picking himself up from the floor and looking at his boss to see what he was about to do next. Looking at both of his men Cameron said, "Contact our people in the police and find out what they know so far. You," pointing at Dave, "get over to Penton. Make sure there's nothing that could look suspicious." Nodding Dave left the room, grateful to be out of his way.

Meanwhile in Penton Max and his team were already at Greens Builders Works and had been since before five am that morning. Sheldon's people in the police were unaware of this so hadn't been able to alert him of the impending raid.

On arrival Sheldon's Security were both shocked then belligerent. "You can't come here without a warrant," was the first line of defense from a particularly unhealthy looking specimen called Finn Jackson. He was very tall but clinically obese and with a complexion like sourdough. His smoker's breath also indicated more than one unhealthy lifestyle choice.

"We have the owner's permission," smiled Eddie.

"Mr Downs?"

"No the real owner Mrs Downs."

"So I suggest you move out of our way sunshine unless you'd like me to help you move?" said a smiling Isiah. Finn Jackson took one look at the man mountain that was Detective Constable Isiah Hanson and physically gulped.

Smiling Max said to Isiah, "Have him watched and he must not use a mobile or landline. Got it?" Nodding Isiah left the Security booth with a semi- belligerent grumbling Jackson leading the way.

"Right!" said Max, "leave nothing unturned!"

Despite the continued protestations of Jackson and other members of the Security team, the police began searching the premises but after two hours nothing seemed to be out of the ordinary.

"There must be something here," mused Max, "this is exactly the sort of place that would operate under the radar."

"I think you may be right Sir," said Isiah, "Jackson has gone from being very worried to wearing the biggest smirk this side of Lancashire." While the search was clearly going nowhere, Isiah had noted how less nervous Jackson was becoming. There was clearly something here but as yet they hadn't successfully detected anything out of the ordinary.

"Told you, you were all, wasting your time, bloody numpties," he sneered, "nowt better to do eh? Wasting tax payer's money! Should be a crime," he laughed finding his own sense of humour hilarious.

Before he did something he would regret later, Isiah had gone outside to get some well needed fresh air, well away from the various body odours emanating from Jackson.

"Morning. Bit early lad!" Looking around him Isiah looked down to see a flat capped, very diminutive gentleman, who was clearly getting on in years.

"Police business I'm afraid Sir, and we don't exactly work to a schedule," smiled Isiah.

"Thought you lot would be here sooner or later," came the response. Clearly interested in what this individual had to say Isiah asked, "Why would you think that Sir?"

"All comings and goings at all hours, day and night. Kept a log. Summat not reet if you ask me lad!"

Trying not to get overly excited Isiah said, "I'd like you to meet my Chief Inspector sir if that's ok? Possibly tell him what you have been observing?"

"Oh lead way lad. Lead way."

"Your name Sir?"

"Alec Dales," came the reply as they ventured inside to find Max and the others.

Now standing before him Max was looking at the complete parody of what he would have described a typical Yorkshire man from a certain era. Alec Dales looked like he had just stepped off the set of 'Last of the Summer Wine'. Isiah made his introductions smiling as he did so, at the look on Max's face. "This is Mr Alec Dales Sir, former Works Manager. He has some information."

"So are you gaffer then?" asked Alec Dales eyeing Max up and down with great suspicion.

"Yes, Detective Chief Inspector Stainmore. So you have information?"

"Aye lad I do," Alec Dales was now blatantly weighing up this leather jacketed man in front of him clearly thinking the police should look like the police looked like back in his day. Max could see what he was thinking so adopted a more deferential approach, knowing instinctively that it would be warranted if any information would be forthcoming.

"So sir, we would be very grateful for anything you may know as we're at a bit of a loss at the moment. So you used to work here?"

"Aye man and boy. First the old man, proper Mr Green who built this place from nowt. Then his son who was alreyt I suppose but then when he went that prat who married young 'un took over and well, nowt were't same like. I'd already long since retired by time he took over but my son worked here and he like most were given boot like. He told me new boss was a bit of a prat though. None of them liked him. Bit of a flash git by all accounts. Londoner too, no offence."

Max smiled and nodded, "None taken," as he was hearing such sentiments a lot since being in Yorkshire.

Alec continued, "Any road, shame as this used to be a good place to work back 'n day." Alec Dales was sadly shaking his head now, reminiscing and remembering better times.

Max was still trying really hard to follow what Alec Dales was saying and was grateful when Isiah took over.

"So, Mr Dales you were saying that you thought something dodgy was going on?"

"Yes, last Thursday in every month but occasionally a Tuesday an all. Being going on a while nah. Got dates and times written here," he announced producing a small notebook.

"May I?" asked Max gesturing towards the book which was handed over without hesitation. Alec continued, "Started about nine months ago I reckon. Saw lights on late one night and I thought that's not reyt. I only live up road like. Came and had a look but made sure I weren't spotted. Some rough 'uns work here nah. Didn't want no trouble. Loads of lorries coming in."

Max looking carefully at the dates and times meticulously kept turned to Alec and said, "So where would illegal contraband be hidden here Mr Dales? We've looked but everything seems in order."

"That because you don't know where to look lad," said Alec, smiling knowingly now touching his nose as he did so.

"Care to show us?" offered Isiah.

Smiling Alec said, "Aye lad, follow me."

What they were to find was beyond anything they had imagined. Veteran Green's worker Alec Dales took them to the edge of the property that bordered the railway station and indicated a padlocked door. Breaking it they found a shaft of some description, the like that would be used for coal mining in bygone times. Grinning at their shocked faces, Alec said, "Nowt to be afraid of lads. This was used as an Air Raid shelter for the town during the blitz when the Germans were bombing Sheffield, you know, when they were trying to take out steel works. Then old man Green worried about the Russians nuking us so he kept this just in case. Come on, it wain't hurt thee." Entering the shaft, Alec then pulled a lever whereby a cage came up from the depths. "I think down there is what you're looking for Inspector."

"I take it's safe to use?" asked Isiah who was now wondering if this was the time to confess his claustrophobia.

"Aye lad," smiled Alec who was clearly enjoying their collective discomfort, "shall I lead way then?"

Nodding, they all got inside the precarious cage that took them thirty feet below ground. With the exception of Alec, all were quietly terrified as they plunged further down into the darkness.

None were prepared for what they found.

Looking from an obscured vantage point Dave Richmond saw the police presence and was silently praying that they wouldn't find what he knew was there to be found. When the Armed Police Unit arrived quickly followed by the Forensics Unit, he realised that wasn't going to happen and dreaded the conversation he would be having back in the city. He was now praying that this particular messenger would not be shot or worse.

CHAPTER 15

Back above ground and sitting across from a badly shaken Alec Dales, Max felt real pity for the old man. For nearly eighty years he had lived a decent life in a beautiful place, raising a family whilst working hard to provide food and shelter for them. A man who never asked for anything he hadn't earned but wanting only to live in a place of shared values with those he had grown old with. All he thought he knew about the world, about his beloved Penton, had now been totally shattered. Max and the others were hardened police but they too had been shocked and disturbed at what lay beneath them.

Leaning forward Max touched the arm of the older man and said to him, "You coming forward Mr Dales, has helped us put a stop to this for the time being, at least here in Penton and bringing us closer to those who are responsible and I for one am very grateful for your vigilance bravery at coming forward sir."

Looking at Max with eyes of unshed tears Alec said, "How do you do it lad?"

"Do what?"

"Face that? Face men who do that daily? How do you sleep?"

Max looked at the floor and noticed that Eddie and Isiah were doing the same. Then he looked at Alec Dales and replied, "Because I have to, because I have to try and stop them even though at times it feels like trying to catch the wind and I also still believe there are more good people amongst us then bad. Look at yourself Mr Dales? You didn't have to come forward, could have just ignored this and got on with your own life but you did come forward because you knew something wasn't right. Today you Mr Dales, have made a significant difference to the lives of many."

"Call me Alec lad. You've earned that."

More touched than he knew what to do with Max stood up and when Alec offered his hand he took it despite the current restrictions on social contact. "Evil has walked amongst us and we didn't even know it," said Alec, shaking his head as he walked to the door adding, "you know where to find me if tha needs owt else Chief Inspector," and with that he made his short journey back to his home, his dog and his grandchildren, knowing he would never sleep as easily again for as long as he remained alive.

Eddie and Isiah looked after the old man then

back at their boss. "Poor old bugger, but I know just how he feels," said Isiah.

"How long do you think they've been using Greens then?" this from Eddie.

"A while from the looks of the underground system they have down there," replied Max. All fell silent again remembering what they had discovered. It was a huge, dark cavernous place of tunnels and underground caves. That is itself was the stuff of nightmares but the nightmares would truly begin when you realised what this place was now being used for. This was no longer a sanctuary against enemy aircraft or possible nuclear attack, but for something that was evil personified. Strewn across the cavernous space were an array of filthy mattresses, used needles, rotting food, used sanitary towels and general filth emanating from few toilet facilities that had not been cleaned or had been even functioning for decades. But it was the chains and manacles fixed to the walls and the signs of blood spilt and left to dry that told the real horror. People, most likely young women, girls, possibly those still classified as children in most countries, had clearly been held captive in this chamber of horrors. The stench was unbelievable but worse than anything else was the image of the one small child's toy stuffed animal, a kind of Gruffalo. It was this one item amidst all the rest that had made poor Alec Dales nearly collapse with the horror of it all.

"Jesus Christ!" Alec had muttered and grabbed the wall searching for a handkerchief in his pocket as he began to retch, then he had said, "That can't be a bairn's? Bloody hell fire. Not a little bairn down 'ere? Not like this?"

The three hardened police officers were just as much at a loss. Anyone being held for even five minutes in these conditions was bad enough but the thought of a child down there…was just unthinkable.

Eddie had whispered at that point, "The evil that men do."

Lost in their own thoughts it was a relief when one of the forensics team called up to Max. "Chief Inspector! You need to see this Sir?" All three went over to where the CSI teams were working. "So, what are we finding?"

Pointing behind him, the young forensics officer revealed the huge stash of what could only be drugs. "Heroin and Cocaine Sir. Tens of thousands worth of the stuff at the current street value."

"How much would you say?" asked Isiah.

"Probably up to half a million I'd say, give or take a couple of thousand."

"This is a loss that's going to hurt," smiled Max grimly, "so let's get this tagged and evidenced as soon as possible."

"May I do the honours regarding arresting our Mr Jackson sir?" asked Isiah relishing the thought of Jackson languishing in their cells for a while and wiping that smug smirk away.

"You may Detective Constable and Isiah? Good work today." Nodding Isiah went to break the bad news to Finn Jackson.

Now jumping into action, Max began the process of coordinating the various teams, documenting all DNA found would be vital and any other trace elements that would be useful when building their case. What he was praying for was anything that would connect what they had discovered to Cameron Sheldon. At the moment though, the finger was pointing firmly towards a missing Grant Downs.

As the others made their way to the waiting police vehicles Max told the others he would join them later. He was now walking on Penton's High Street, taking in the individual shops that ranged from high end fashion to the local greengrocers. He saw children skipping alongside their mothers without a care in the world whilst old men were 'chewing the fat', no doubt putting the world to rights, comfortably seated on the various benches that were scattered around. Coming to the canal bridge he saw the calm beauty and elegance that only the presence of swans gliding by could bring, all against the imposing back- drop of the Pennines, the backbone of England looking down on them all as they got on with their daily lives. Looking around this picturesque part of the world, Max knew that evil had walked here and when news broke of what they had discovered, this lovely little town would never be quite the same again.

Turning towards where he had left his vehicle, his attention was drawn to a figure approaching, her head down, clearly lost in thought. She had an elegant gait, moving with a fluidity that drew attention to her which then revealed she was beautiful to watch. As Imogen neared Max, he had to reluctantly admit to himself that he was indeed enjoying watching her. She was now only a few metres away, when she looked up to find him standing there clearly scrutinising her. When she saw him her expression changed to one of surprise then to one of suspicious wariness which was not lost on Max. Smiling now, Max greeted her with, "What an unexpectedly pleasant surprise Ms Holt."

"Good morning Chief Inspector." Imogen clearly had no intention of stopping or conversing and was making her way to cross over to the other side of the canal when Max approached her, blocking her progress.

"Taking your daily exercise then?"

"I am."

"Buying provisions too?"

"Correct and all within the boundaries of the law."

Imogen moved to leave when Max offered, "I do believe you and I may have got off on the wrong foot yesterday. I hope it wasn't something I said?"

"I'm aware you have a job to do Chief Inspector..."

"I certainly do Ms Holt."

"But to imply Sarah could be implicated seems to be rather crass and rather lazy policing. Well it does in my opinion but what do I know, so if you'll excuse me I ..."

Holding up his hands to stop her moving away Max immediately countered her argument by saying, "I can be accused of many things but "lazy policing" will never be one of them. All lines of enquiry will remain open regarding Mr Downs' disappearance until there is a reason to close them and that includes your friend and whoever may have helped her."

"Including me?" she challenged back.

"Why not you? Because you're beautiful?" Now completely thrown, Imogen found she had no response whereas Max now went in for the kill, "So Ms Holt, something to confess?"

Imogen felt she could feel the actual air around them now begin to crackle, her instinct to turn and run as far away from this man as she physically could. Instead she looked him squarely in the eye and said, "I don't think I like you very much Chief Inspector."

"I don't think you like me either," grinned back Max, "but people with something to hide generally don't".

"And," Imogen continued, as if he hadn't spoken, "making a personal comment regarding a 'suspect's' looks is more than inappropriate and …"

Max cut her off in mid –sentence, smiling broadly, now clearing enjoying their interaction, saying, "Totally inappropriate and worthy of an official complaint, that is until your 'mug' shot is shown to whoever and I would simply rest my case."

"Is this your idea of being amusing as well as time wasting?"

"Hey now," Max pretending mock offence, "I was being charming!"

"Really?! Well trust me Chief Inspector, but your idea of being charming needs serious work."

"Noted Miss! Must try harder at being charming." Max's grin was getting wider such was his enjoyment of this unexpected encounter which was allowing him a brief break from the horrors of the morning's discovery.

Completely thrown, Imogen now sighed dramatically, as if suddenly very tired saying, "May I continue with my day now Chief

Inspector? I'm sure you have real hardened criminals to pursue and incarcerate before this day is over and I would hate to keep you longer than is necessary?" Max merely nodded, still grinning.

Imogen crossed over to the other side of the canal, head high, her walk brisk, all too aware that Max Stainmore was watching her go. Turning onto Market Street she rounded the corner before leaning against the bricked wall of the Market Barn. "Bugger, bugger, bugger," she muttered, closing her eyes, willing her sense of panic to subside and not for the first time prayed that Malcolm Speight would be as good as his word.

CHAPTER 16

Back at Sheffield Central Max was greeted by a very excited DC Dan Devon. "Ah Chief Inspector, we've located Downs car in Zone B at Doncaster Airport. It's been there since Sunday evening."

"Well that ties in with Mrs Downs statement that he was flying to Alicante?" said Max.

"Yes Sir," said Lydia, "except that's not the only air ticket he purchased. One for George Town too."

"Where no doubt he has his offshore account or access to someone's," mused Max.

"Motive for Sheldon to take Grant out or teach him a lesson if he thought he was flying too close to the sun," said Eddie.

"Except, according to the flight records, he didn't board any plane to Spain or George Town," informed Lydia.

Max then brought the rest of the team up to speed with what had been discovered at Penton that morning.

"So we're dealing with some very dangerous

people who are commanding huge amounts of money and who will exploit the most vulnerable. We actually found a child's toy this morning in what can only be described as a hell on earth." Max now paused to let the implication of that piece of information to take root. Looking at his team's collective faces told him that it had as he continued. "God knows what it was doing there, or where the child it may have belonged to is now or even if the said child is still alive. The key to this is to find out where Grant Downs is or what has happened to him. Dan, I want you and Lydia to go to the airport and look at their CCTV. We know he didn't board any plane but we need to know where to start really looking."

"On it Sir," said Dan as the two young detectives left the room.

Meanwhile upstairs, South Yorkshire's Chief Constable Jim Haggerty had three very unhappy senior officers in his office. "I'm supposed to be his sodding line manager and he goes 'half cock' to God knows where with men I have not sanctioned, including a mountain of over-time, without one sodding word asking permission, or sharing any information if I'm brutally honest! Where does he think this is? The bloody wild west!" stated Detective Superintendent Tom Blakely who was very embarrassed and ill at ease for not knowing what was going on in the department he was allegedly in charge of.

"Exactly," agreed Superintendent Giles Baker, "he clearly thinks following protocols don't apply to him. I disliked his manner from the first moment I clapped eyes on him, so what are you going to do Chief Constable?"

"Do?" asked Jim Haggerty.

"Yes do? He cannot be allowed to continue keeping us out of the loop like this," stated Tom Blakely, his frustration palpable now.

Looking at the men before him Jim Haggerty was thinking hard. He had come up through the ranks with Ralph and Tom and still considered them as friends despite the position he now held. Giles Baker was another story, a man he could do without, yet all had valid points to make where DCI Max Stainmore was concerned.

Turning to his Deputy, Ralph Jones, he asked, "So Ralph, you've been quiet so far. What's your take?"

Looking at his colleagues then back to his boss Ralph Jones shrugged and said, "I think Max Stainmore should be congratulated[N2]."

"Bloody hell!" spluttered Tom, "Are you for real? The man is a sodding cowboy!"

"Oh I agree Tom and a cowboy that has discovered a human trafficking operation right on our doorstep and right under our very noses. I for one intend to buy him a drink."

Jim held up his hands at this point to bring the

debate to a conclusion. "Thank you gentlemen, I will take on board your comments. I am meeting the Chief Inspector in the next ten minutes so if you will excuse me."

"I'd like to stay Chief Constable," said Tom.

"I think we'd all like to," agreed Giles.

Looking at the trio Jim merely repeated, "So if you'll excuse me?" Looking like a collection of blood vessels were about to erupt all three stood and left, whilst Ralph looked back shrugging his shoulders.

Jim Haggerty listened gravely and without comment whilst Max relayed the day's discovery. He turned his chair to look out across the city, then turned back to look at Max. "So Chief Inspector, you were right and on my patch too. Bloody hell, evidence of a child, a small child?" Max solemnly nodded as Jim Haggerty, grandfather of three shook his head then asked, "So what are our next steps?"

"I'd like you to hold a press conference Sir, informing the public that a significant drug stash has been discovered in Penton and that we are looking for Grant Downs to help with our enquiries."

"Hoping to flush Downs and his people out?"

"That's the plan. I don't want to mention the human trafficking as we need to try to track and trace with some hope of rescue. We're liaising with Interpol regarding the registered missing and hope we can make some headway there with the DNA found at the scene although it will take some time to recover it all. It's a vast job and my team are making a list of possible outlets using their local intelligence."

Jim Haggerty leaned forward and said, "Did you run any of this past Superintendent Baker? Or Deputy Chief Constable Jones? Tom Blakely, who is your immediate superior?"

"No," said Max, "and I would rather it remain that way."

"What are you implying Chief Inspector?" now frowning and clearly not expecting to be happy with what Max was about to say.

Max looked at the man before him and saw a high ranking police officer but also a political animal too. Jim Haggerty saw Max silently wrestling with what his response should be. Staring at the man behind the desk, Max finally plumped for honesty and straight talking as the stakes were now so very high and he really believed he had nothing to lose at this point. Max needed to know who he could trust, what and who he was dealing with if he was to succeed in bringing Sheldon to his knees. "You know I believe Sheldon will have someone, some people in this force on his pay roll or in his power. For starters he belongs to the same funny handshake club that I'm aware Superintendent Baker belongs to although

I have no evidence that Superintendent Baker is an informer except that I've heard he has form when it comes to doing his Lodge friends favours. Until I know who they are then I want to keep as much information to as few trusted individuals as possible."

Jim now leaned forward nailing Max with a stern look saying, "I've had all three of your immediate superiors in here today and two want you stringing up for not keeping them in the loop. Only my Deputy is pleased with your work so far?"

"Really," said Max not sure how he was supposed to respond.

"You're actually admitting to me that you suspect any one or all three of my senior men could be 'in bed' with Sheldon?"

"Or not," replied Max, "the point is we don't know and favours have been in done in the past that have had consequences."

Jim Haggerty at this point in their discussion now looked very tired and very thoughtful, then finally admitted, "It was a regrettable business with Detective Constable Fairchild which in the era of 'Me Too' we would not get away with and to be honest we shouldn't have then. We need to put that right but Chief Inspector, how do you know you can trust me?" said with a challenge in his gaze that was not lost on Max.

Leaning back in his chair Max grinned then responded with his characteristic honesty, "I don't but we will soon find out won't we Sir?"

Jim Haggerty stared hard at Max then leaning back in his chair the Chief Constable of South Yorkshire shook his head then laughed out loud saying, "You really are a piece of work Max Stainmore!"

Max now looked at the Chief Constable with a certain respect that was possibly verging on trust, which was not an easy concept for him to acknowledge saying self- deprecatingly but without apology, "If you say so and my superior officers Sir?"

Jim continued, "I agree that we must keep our cards close to our chests therefore it's a need to know basis only, confined to as few as possible so I will deal with their egos and it won't be the first time. I have to say I'm impressed Max and can see why the NCA came calling." Nodding and accepting the well- meant compliment Max stood to leave and made his way to the door of Jim Haggerty's office, only turning when Jim said,

"And Max? Keep yourself safe. You are dealing with men who will not think twice about taking out anyone in their way and that includes a police officer." Max simply nodded, then left.

The local BBC News ran the story of the drug discovery in Penton on their six pm programme. The Chief Constable himself made the announcement with Max Standing at his side on the imposing steps of Sheffield Central:

"Today my officers have successfully uncovered a significant amount of illegal substance, namely heroin, which was destined for our streets to continue its destruction of so many lives. It is important that we now locate Grant Downs, a resident of Penton in order for him to assist us further in our continued enquiries in this matter and other incidents that have since come to our attention. If anyone has information, please call the number on your screens and feel safe in the knowledge that all information will be treated in the strictest of confidence and you can be assured that you will have our protection."

*

Imogen, Sarah, Beth and Harry all listened in their various locations.

"God but what have I got us mixed up in? I started all this," whispered Sarah, eyes glued to the screen before them.

Shaking her head Imogen replied, "No, I got us into this but we all made our choices and we're in it together ok Sarah? We just have to keep to the story until this ends." But what would the end look like was the unspoken thought sitting between them. Imogen also realised how her eyes were drawn to Max Stainmore as he solemnly stood next to the Chief Constable.

Beth was in her home feeling nauseous. My God but what if the truth comes out and where the bloody hell was Grant's body was her thought process as she listened to the Chief Constable?

Harry just felt numb but also guilty because she knew she had walked away from her friends for the first time since they'd been five years old.

*

Cameron Sheldon and his men were also listening. Cameron was still reeling from the past few days as it was less than a week since he last saw Grant and all was well, couldn't have been better. They'd had plans, huge plans and something beyond either of their control had happened but what? Who?

"It's obviously one of the competition?" ventured Steve, "who else would have the nerve or resources?"

"I agree," said Dave "but I thought we'd warned them off!"

Reaching for his phone Cameron said, "We did. Now it's time to reign fire on them again."

*

Malcolm Speight with his key men, Albert and

Eddie, were also listening to the Chief Constable.

"So boss. When are you proposing to get rid of his body?" asked Albert.

"Where it can do the most harm to that scum Sheldon because let's face it lads? The bloody 'key stone' cops aren't going to manage it on their own," was Malcolm Speight's reply as his trusted men nodded their agreement shaking their heads sadly at what they perceived was police naivety at best or incompetence or corruption at worst.

CHAPTER 17

Detective Constables Dan Devon and Lydia Smith had had a productive trip to Doncaster's Robin Hood Airport. Just an hour's drive away they had got what they had been looking for and were now returning with some valuable intelligence on Grant Downs' disappearance although they were now stuck on the M1 with its predictable congestion, even in a global pandemic.

"It's all been remarkably well thought out," said Lydia.

"Some real brains behind it that's for sure," agreed Dan as he maneuvered the car into the inside lane for the third time in ten minutes.

"You may as well stay put, none of the lanes are moving much," said Lydia slightly bemused at this point.

"Makes me feel better," smiled Dan looking over at her which at this point for some reason made Lydia blush.

Seeing her embarrassment and not understanding it Dan searched for something to say settling on the question, "What do you make of the DCI then?"

Not sure how to answer as Lydia was experiencing real trust issues these days, she replied, "Seems good at his job I suppose."

"Good," enthused Dan, "he's bloody brilliant! To discover the Penton connection so quickly. Man but that is ace!"

"Pity its July."

"Why?"

"You could have sent him a Valentine's card if we'd been in February!"

Looking at his colleague Dan really smiled and said, "Bloody hell but is that a joke? I never knew you had it in you."

Shrugging the jibe off she replied, "He was lucky with the Penton discovery that's all I'm saying. You're all so bloody hero worshiping though, even the Sarge whilst I'm persona non grata as bloody usual thanks to bloody Brad Fairchild."

Dan looked at her slumped shoulders and furrowed brow and looking closely, saw how badly bitten her nails were too. He knew she had not had an easy time since Beth had been demoted and he now realised she had hoped to make a fresh start with Max Stainmore. "You were the one today who spotted what was going on with Downs, spotting the tattoo. Your instinct all along was that he had not left the country and Max will see what a good copper you are. Ok?"

Dan was right. They had found Down's car in the designated car zone and its camera footage had shown a man that from a distance and through the grain of the footage available could have been Grant Downs. It was unusual however, that once inside the car it appeared to have been meticulously wiped clean, a strange concept for anyone to do when catching a plane. When in the actual airport they had contacted airport security and therefore were given access to the footage on the designated dates given by Sarah Downs. They had watched the man who looked like Downs enter the airport, check in his luggage, then making his way to Security but that was where they had lost him. They then began to look at other camera angles until they came across a man of similar height and build leaving the toilets. His clothes were different, he was also wearing a baseball cap which obscured his features even more, but Lydia had spotted the same tattoo on his neck that she had seen on the man they had presumed was Downs.

"Can you zoom closer onto his neck please?" Lydia had asked.

"What have you seen?" Dan had enquired.

"That!" Lydia now pointing to the tattoo now more visible. She had then turned to the technician and said, "Can we go back to the footage when he first arrived at the airport, getting out of his car please?" Complying all three had looked closely zooming in again at the man's neck.

"Bingo!" Dan had exclaimed, "Well spotted!"

Picking up more footage this man had then exited the airport through the Arrivals area and had been picked up by a car whose number plate had been deliberately obscured. Lydia nodded to Dan and was clearly pleased he felt she had done well. They sat silently for a while, still waiting for the traffic to begin its crawl again.

Eventually Lydia said, "You know if I could have the time back I would never have agreed to go against Beth. At first I thought it was what all good coppers should do and that is obey your superior officers." She glanced at Dan, who nodded his understanding, "but then when Beth kicked off like she did, well I thought perhaps I should support her. She was my partner but more than that, she was my friend."

Dan turning to look at her saw her infinite sadness and said, "So why didn't you?"

Shaking her head and now close to tears she answered, "Because bloody Giles Baker told me if I changed my statement and supported Beth's version of events, he would have me for gross misconduct, possible perjury and have me kicked off the force or even worse."

Clearly shocked Dan reached over to her and took her hand. “Bloody hell! Why didn’t you tell someone? Me or the Sarge? Isiah? Did the Super know?”

“Oh how I wanted to but the man was awful. I can’t begin to tell you how threatening he was, how vile and I felt you were all against me anyway at that point.”

Shaking his head Dan said with emphasis, “No! Absolutely not!”

“Oh yes. Don’t you think I knew how it was? Yes I was part of the ‘Cagney and Lacy’ of Sheffield Central CID but we all know who the star was? The one everyone couldn’t get enough of? Beth! I was just her ‘straight man’, her ‘prop’. All eyes always on Beth Fairchild, the blonde beauty that even had criminals wanting her to interrogate them for God’s sake, not the ‘plain Jane’ one!”

Dan looked at her saying quietly, “You sound jealous.”

Shaking her head, “But I wasn’t, I really wasn’t. I was proud to be her partner and it was ok taking a back seat as long as we got the perp.”

Sitting there in the silence of the car she said quietly, “I miss her so much. I miss you all because none of you feel the same about me now. You all believe I’m still in Baker’s pocket and don’t tell me any different.”

Nodding, Dan replied, “I won’t because you’re

right but there's a couple of things you're not right about. I agree that Beth used to breeze in with all the confidence in the world and yes she's a 'looker' albeit in a really obvious way if I'm honest, but you have a calmness and a thoroughness that made you two such a great team. We knew you were there, we know you are there and you would be missed if you weren't." Then looking towards the still unmoving vehicles he added, "I would really miss you and I wouldn't want you to be any different. You're also…," then he clammed up.

"Also what?"

Swallowing hard and now daring to look at her said, "No way a 'plain Jane' but rather lovely in your own right. Well I think so anyway for what it's worth." Dan was now staring out of the side window wondering if he had said too much. After a few moments of silence Dan heard the words, "It's worth everything," being Lydia's quiet response to such an unexpected admission.

There was now a very pregnant silence in the car only broken when Lydia reached for his hand and said, "Thanks Dan and I'm sorry I didn't trust you or the others to help me do what was right." Reaching over Dan stroked her cheek and realised he really wanted to kiss her at that moment. Lydia, looking at this man she had always secretly found so attractive thought she might die if he did or if he didn't. Suddenly a car horn blasted them back to the here and now as they realised the cars in front had moved and their journey could now continue. Putting the car into gear Dan began to drive, both of them silent but both aware that something had happened, something potentially fantastic or potentially terrifying which only time would tell. They looked at each other, then shyly smiled.

CHAPTER 18

Max and the team were impressed with the thorough findings of Dan and Lydia and were now fairly certain that Grant Downs would not be found alive. Lydia had ascertained from Sarah that although Grant Downs had tattoos on his torso, he did not have one on his neck.

“We need to understand why someone is going to so much trouble trying to make us believe he was out of the country and possibly trying to rip Sheldon off. It doesn’t sit easy with me,” said Max. Then looking at Brad said, “I can’t help thinking that all roads lead to Mrs Downs.”

“I know how it looks Sir, but really?” countered Brad.

Shaking his head Max said “Who is to gain in all of this?

“What about the competition boss” asked Eddie, “he’s by all accounts Sheldon’s right hand man? What better way would there be to rattle Sheldon’s cage?”

Lydia spoke up saying, “Then we could be

looking at an all-out war which will be hard to contain."

Max listening to his team nodded saying to Lydia, "You could be right and it certainly make sense to a point. Yet there's something missing that I can't quite make sense of but good work guys, particularly you two."

At this point Dan spoke up saying, "Actually Sir, Lyds, I mean Lydia needs to take credit for what was discovered at the airport. She alone spotted the tattoo. Just thought I'd say," as he noticed the looks of bemusement now evident amongst the others and a very blushing Lydia who looked as if she wanted the ground to open up.

Isiah was knowingly grinning at Dan now as Max smiled and said, "Thanks Dan. It's always good to give credit where it's deserved. Good work Lydia. So next steps? Max thought for a moment then said, "I want as many of your contacts, most trusted informants on this. We need to know what's going to happen before it does. Also, we need to find out where Sheldon is moving his people, the ones he's exploiting now that Penton's closed to him." Then Max turned to the window just before the team heard him say, "We need to find that child. We have the Gruffalo and he or she will be missing it won't they?

They all knew where he was coming from for that small child's toy epitomised what they were working so hard to achieve here. To stop the wicked becoming richer because they used people in poverty as if they were nothing more that goods to be bartered or used as they saw fit. As they all moved to their desks and contacts Dan went over to Lydia and quietly said, "Sorry if I embarrassed you but you deserved the credit."

"Not in it just for the credit Detective Constable," was the prim reply, "but thank you anyway," as she smiled up at him.

Dan lowered his voice further and said, "Still ok for later?"

Nodding Lydia said, "Very much looking forward to it Detective Constable."

Smiling as he moved from her desk Dan was confronted with a beckoning Isiah who was indicating the coffee area. Sighing Dan went over and waited, expecting what was coming next from his friend.

"Ok, now spill!"

"Spill what?" without looking at Isiah whilst busying himself with making the drinks.

"Don't even try to kid a kidder here mate! What gives with you and 'Lyds'?" making invisible air inverted commas as he asked the question, alluding to what clearly was a pet name Dan was now giving their colleague.

Sighing but looking seriously at Isiah Dan said, "She's been through a load of shite mate." Isiah now looking concerned but clearly waiting for more information, Dan continued. "She went back to Baker to tell him she had changed her mind and wanted to support Beth, but he threatened her with gross misconduct and possibly worse. She's been as much a victim to Giles 'bloody' Baker's bullying, no more than that, his bloody corruption as Beth has!"

"Bloody bastard! He wouldn't have dared try that on with a bloke!"

"I've been thinking the same, I mean this job is hard enough and particularly for women, let's be honest, but 'them' upstairs don't have to make it harder!"

"I wonder how many other times Baker has asked someone to change a report for one of his mates?" mused Isiah, asking rhetorically now.

Dan shrugged and said, "It's making me think a lot of things to be honest and I'm trying to persuade Lyds to go to the boss. He's new here and I think he would have no qualms at all to take the likes of Baker on but she wants to wait until we solve this case first. She's really dedicated Isiah and a bloody good copper."

Isiah nodded and then smiling said, "She is and ...?"

"Alright! Yes! I like her. I like her a lot but let's keep it quiet ok?"

"My lips are sealed mate," replied a smiling Isiah now pouring his coffee then looking at his friend added, “Good luck with it mate. I really hope it works out for you both.

CHAPTER 19

Max was a 'night owl' and loved the solitude walking at night time gave him, particularly when his days had been filled with the darkness and distress that only human beings were capable of inflicting, be it on animal or human. London was his home and his city and he loved it with a passion.

He had walked the streets of the capital in all weathers but he loved nothing more than being on Tower Bridge on a still dark night allowing himself to look over the stillness of the Thames. He loved seeing the lit dome of St Paul's in the distance or the lights of St Katherine's Docks, with the rest of London spread around him almost like a cloak, protecting him from the horrors or worries of his day. He felt so connected, feeling like the city almost belonged to him alone at such times.

Sheffield was very different and so small in comparison but it also had its share of beauty and tonight Max was standing in the large city square staring at the majesty of Sheffield's

City Hall. He had to admit it was impressive and would stand up well against any building London could offer.

"Evening," came a voice behind him as Max turned to see a police constable making his approach towards him.

"Evening officer. Lovely evening and pleasantly quiet," replied Max.

Hearing Max's accent he raised an eyebrow, "You sound a long way from home sir? Travelled far?"

Smiling Max said, "I'm here for work but yes I'm a long way from home. Beautiful building. Beautiful city."

"Aye it is that and on a normal night in a normal time this square would be full of people, enjoying the bars or sitting on the steps enjoying the evening. Well hopefully not too long before we can resume life as we knew it God willing. So what sort of business brings you to Sheffield?" queried the constable.

Reaching for his warrant card Max said, "Police business, I'm on the job Constable."

Looking at Max's warrant card and seeing his name and rank the police constable now looked closely at Max, then clicked his fingers saying, "You're the chap that's discovered that bad business over at Penton, right?"

Max surprised, raised his eyebrows saying, "Yes constable I am. You are?"

“Police Constable Philip Read. My son is also on the job, in Vice and he told me that a top London cop was here on the case.”

Running his fingers through his hair feeling slightly embarrassed Max replied, “Ok, but I’m not sure ‘top cop’ is an appropriate description.”

“His words not mine Sir.” Max was now smiling at this straight talking, typically Yorkshire, near to retirement, slightly curmudgeonly police officer.

“I’m Max Stainmore and I’d offer you my hand but I don’t think I’m allowed to at the moment. Been on the job long Constable Read?”

“Nigh on thirty- four years. Finish at the end of January.”

“Wow thirty- four years. Looking forward to retirement?”

“No not a bit. Keeping these streets safe has been my life Sir and to be honest I worry that some of young ‘uns coming into the job just haven’t got the wherewithal to do job properly in my opinion. You know they just seem to worry about paper work, or being seen to follow policy instead of bloody good old fashioned common sense. No offence meant Sir, just the way I think. No bugger takes any notice anyway.”

Nodding in agreement Max replied, “No offence taken Constable and I couldn’t agree with you more. So can you recommend any good city walks? I want to take in as much of Sheffield as I can whilst I'm here."

Smiling now at Max, Constable Read began his litany of suggestions. "The Botanical Gardens just up road are beautiful as is Endcliffe Park going up to Hunter's Bar. Then we have Hillsborough Park and its Walled Garden, the Peace Gardens and the Winter Gardens all in walking distance and worth a visit. If you fancy a drive then forty minutes that way you'll find yourself in the Peak District. Stunning countryside and if you want a bit of industrial history we have the Magna Centre over at Templeborough."

Now looking closely at Max and scrutinizing the same haunted look he often saw when he himself looked in the mirror, he then ventured, "I actually find walking along Victoria Quays on a night like this good for the soul Chief Inspector. Nothing like dark still water to stop the wheels turning, particularly when you do a job like ours, when you see the stuff we see." Max looked down still seeing the child's toy, the lorry in Dover, images never far from his mind if he was being truly honest.

"It's never easy Chief Inspector and it should never become easy. When it does, it's time to walk away," continued Constable Read looking at Max and nodding his head knowingly. Returning the scrutinizing gaze of this aging, wise police stalwart Max suddenly felt humbled but grateful for his wisdom. Moments of silence ticked by then smiling his gratitude he said, “Well I suggest you let the Sheffield Tourist industry hear about you. I suspect you’d make a fortune as a city guide.”

“Aye, no one knows or loves this city better. Now you take care Chief Inspector, you’re obviously doing a grand job,” and with that he took his leave with Max looking at his retreating figure

CHAPTER 20

It was exactly one week after Jim Haggerty's televised press conference and the Sheffield criminal underworld found itself ablaze and at war.

Cameron Sheldon was a brilliant strategist which was the key to his success in many respects. A week earlier he had Zoom conferenced the ones whom he considered his equals in terms of their 'war lord' status in cities across the UK. He needed their muscle as he intended to wage war on the Sheffield underworld the likes that had never been seen. Someone had taken and probably killed his main man, Grant Downs, and had therefore led the police to their Penton enterprise which had been crucial to his continued success in the north. For Sheldon that was a declaration of war and if they, whoever they were, wanted war, he would oblige ten- fold and he would win.

Looking at the screen he smiled at the faces before him. In truth these were the only people possibly on the whole planet he had any respect for and the only people he would consider his equals.

Smiling now he greeted the collection of images, "Morning Gentlemen and lady. So good to see you all alive and well in these extraordinary times my friends." The murmured acknowledgement echoed around his office.

"Let's hope these extraordinary times continue," responded Glasgow's Adam Leach in his thick Scottish burr, "business has never been as good this side of the border." Murmurs of concurrence were now in evidence as Manchester's Ryan Goodall asked the question all were thinking.

"So Cameron to what do we owe the pleasure?"

Smiling his legendary shark smile Cameron responded, "As always Ryan, straight to the point. It would appear some of the locals have forgotten who they are dealing with, are taking liberties, so I intend to reign fire like they've never seen and I would like to borrow some of your muscle to help me do so."

Silence then, "What sort of liberties?" asked Birmingham based Philip Sutcliffe. Cameron looked down anticipating this question and then breaking the habit of a lifetime opted for an honest answer. "Grant Downs is missing and I'm assuming he's been taken out."

"Who'd bloody dare?" asked Ryan Goodall.

"Not sure but I have three areas that need serious

intervention. The rest will topple like a house of cards if dealt with effectively," replied Cameron.

All were silent, digesting this information. Finally, the one person who made all those present think twice before action, made them visibly quake if the truth be known, such was the ferocity of response if ever crossed was the person who effectively ran London's Crime world, the undisputed boss, who now spoke for the first time since the Zoom call began.

Public school educated, the upper class vowels of Miriam Anderson could now be heard as she simply asked, "What do you need?"

Relieved but careful not to show it, Cameron replied, "The best you have. Grant was my main man and a hard lesson needs to be taught." The silent nods from those on his screen confirmed for Cameron that he had their support at least in principle.

Miriam Anderson eventually said, "You can have my Albanian contingent, so that should put the fear of God into those country bumpkins. They're bored stupid anyway so the exercise will do them good."

"I'm in. I'll send you what I can spare," agreed Birmingham with Glasgow and Manchester following suit quickly. Cameron knew now that he had an army of thuggery, the likes the North would not have seen or even dreamt existed.

They were about to descend on Sheffield's underworld, to execute fire and brimstone of epic proportions and he so wanted to fist pump the air but kept his expression impassive, remaining the consummate professional as would be expected.

"So," purred Miriam Anderson, "and what do we get in return?" Knowing this was the next part of the negotiation as all 'Pipers' had to be paid Cameron simply said, "Name it?!"

Smiling her deadly smile Miriam Anderson pretended to think then said, "I want to know that Detective Chief Inspector Max Stainmore will never step foot in London again. I hear he's in your neck of the woods and that's my price."

Breathing deeply Cameron nodded saying, "Consider it done," then without niceties the screen went blank.

Picking up a disposable burner phone he keyed in the contact and without preamble said, "I want Max Stainmore dead as soon as possible. Get it done."

CHAPTER 21

Life needed to still be lived, normality still seen to be done despite the cloud of horror and dread of discovery which were now constant companions for both Imogen and Sarah and it was taking its toll on both of them. Yet Imogen also had no choice but to return to school and get on with her job hence leaving Sarah alone and she needed to do so for her own sake too if she was being totally honest.

Now sitting alone in her car, Imogen was looking at and trying to make sense of what she had discovered on the floor behind the chair in Sarah's kitchen. She had been looking for her earring which she was notorious for constantly losing and as it had been the last gift from her husband Neil, finding it was crucial. She's found her earring and something else entirely. Closing her eyes, Imogen was now realising that she had come to certain decisions, jumped to certain conclusions, without knowing all there was to know and that perhaps she had actually got the whole thing completely wrong.

"Oh God. What have I done?" she whispered aloud to no one because this time she was very much on her own.

Imogen got out of her car slinging her bag over her shoulder, balancing her laptop case precariously as she attempted to lock her car. Entering the quiet mezzanine Reception area Imogen wryly reflected how she never thought she would miss the organised chaos and noise of a normal start to a school day. Unprecedented times indeed. "Morning", greeted Mrs. Mane whose polite greeting and middle aged disposition hid the fact that she was the one individual no one dare cross in the whole of the building. She ran the Admin team with military precision, brooking no nonsense from child, parent, teachers and anyone who insisted on being addressed by a title she felt was undeserved. "Glad to see you back Imogen. Hope you're ok? The older woman enquired.

Nodding Imogen replied, "Have we heard any more about Alice's condition?"

"No change as far as we know but," the older woman momentarily losing her composure, but blinking rapidly continued, "but it's looking bleak".

"Keep me posted and try not to worry," was Imogen's inadequate response because what can be said when confronted with such heartbreaking realities almost on a daily basis these days?

She continued to her office, hoping that the individual occupying the office further down the corridor would be too preoccupied by whatever he did to occupy himself, to require talking to her before the rest of the Leadership team arrived. Imogen proceeded to take off her coat, depositing her stuff, before turning round to see her colleague and other Deputy Head Peter Roberts and Personnel Director Ellie Simons entering her office.

Peter was not unpleasant looking and some even regarded him as handsome. The discerning eye however would always detect that there was something 'off' about him, something predatory and false that some, and it had to be said, mainly females, found to be almost threatening. He would stand too close and appraised anyone, man or woman openly as if you were a specimen in a test tube but without being openly inappropriate. However, it was the utter bullshit that spewed forth from his mouth that Imogen found so unforgiving and the fact that he would plagiarise and take credit when and where he could because being a strategic or creative thinker was clearly not a strength he possessed. She was still assessing what his actually strength was and could only come up with "Bull-shitter Extraordinaire"! And that was being kind!

"Nice to have you back Imogen. Feeling ok?"

Imogen knew it was barely 7.30am but remained silent wondering not for the first time why both of them always seemed to be in early since lockdown. It wasn't as if they were ready to confront the frontline like the rest of them. Glancing at her newly promoted colleague, who until recently had been a barely noticeable member of the Finance Team, but who was now, thanks to the Head, who was not always the best judge of character, the new Director of Personnel, Imogen thought, "Surely not?!" Pushing aside all rhetorical images, all completely stomach churning, Imogen summoned up the consummate professional she always was.

Before Imogen could reply he continued as to be honest he didn't give a stuff how Imogen was. "We're just discussing the Alice situation" said Peter Roberts, referring to the member of the Admin team who was now in the city's ICU having fallen victim to Covid.

"Yes Mrs Mane just indicated that's it's not looking good". Trying not to bristle at the term "Alice situation", Imogen proceeded to pour herself her first coffee of the day offering the others a cup too which they declined.

Imogen was the natural choice to be the next Head of Grove South Academy. Peter Roberts also thought he was the next natural choice as Peter Roberts planned to get to the pinnacle of his career by aged forty. In other words, to be an Executive Lead of a large Multi Academy Trust, paying himself an exorbitant salary and having no contact with students, teachers or their parents. So he was obsessed with image, self- promotion and results with no interest whatsoever in issues of Safeguarding or Staff welfare but instead surrounded himself with sycophants who did not question too closely certain questionable policies he was responsible for. Of course he had a huge 'thorn in his side' in the shape of Imogen because although a natural narcissist Peter was not stupid. He knew Imogen out performed him on every level, was indeed the popular choice but as most School Governors were usually completely clueless, their Chair of Governors was a particular buffoon for example, he still hoped to be successful. So he completely hated Imogen with a passion, didn't hide the fact he did so very well and was determined to win the Headship at all costs.

It was a relief when two of the other team members arrived. Strategically seated at least two metres apart Imogen smiled at her colleagues, Matt and Tina who were the new normal in today's teaching world. They were young and very ambitious to get to Headship as soon as possible and given time they could, should and would be excellent school leaders but she feared they were already looking at burn- out and that made her sad. The knock on her office door heralded the entry of the remaining two of her leadership colleagues namely Janet and Roy who chalked up a collective fifty -seven years between them and were both feared, loved and respected in equal measure by pupils, staff and parents, some of whom had been taught by them years earlier.

"How are you feeling Imogen? My word but you've lost weight you can't afford to lose. Did you get a test?" asked a very concerned motherly Janet.

Hating to lie but knowing she had no choice, "I was advised to self-isolate after being alerted by the 'Test and Trace' App but I'm fine. Everything ok here at this end?" All nodded as reply so Imogen continued, "Shall we begin with you then Janet?"

"Fine, so yes everything is ticking over as well as possible. Here is the staff Rota doing the face-to face in school for the key worker pupils," replied Janet as she handed the list to the team adding, "a few noticeable absences I'm afraid. More families of NHS front line workers in our local hospital are sadly having to self-isolate today too." An old timer of thirty plus years, Janet was solid as the Assistant Head for Raising Achievement after being a former SEN teacher and Head of Year no one was better when dealing with the most vulnerable and Imogen respected her with a passion.

Peter as would be expected felt her to be too old, too frumpy and not the demographic he wanted for his team were he to succeed in his ambitions and Janet knew this. He really had no time for 'bleeding hearts' and nearly yawned until a look from Imogen made him remember his manners.

"The online lessons are being uploaded and face to face digital lessons are timetabled and have been sent to Years 10, 11 and 13", stated Matt who received a vigorous nod of approval from everyone.

"I have to say Matt, you must be applauded for such excellent work on the digital front," said Peter, "speaking to some of our LT Colleagues on Zoom recently, whilst you've been MIA Imogen, some are having huge issues with distribution of devices and logging in. It's clearly the future of Teaching & Learning post Covid, got to be so well done. I do like Grove South to be ahead of the herd and thanks to you we are certainly heading that way."

Desperately trying not to roll her eyes or react to the 'MIA' jibe and only partially succeeding if Janet and Roy's smiles in her direction had anything to go by, Imogen interjected the impending monologue, "We have six staff absence today, four suggesting Covid symptoms which is worrying. Elise will you make sure all protocols are followed and make that your main priority today please?" Elise nodded and Imogen not for the first time wondered why she could never give Imogen eye contact.

"How are the food deliveries going Roy?" asked Imogen.

"They're going well but it's seeing what it's like out there as I'm sure you know Imogen. Actually Tina has been a huge help whilst you've been out of action."

"Don't you mean MIA?" smiled Imogen because she just couldn't help herself knowing full well Peter would take it as if she was laughing at him and that was the one thing he hated. Imogen continued before he could think of a come- back jibe saying, "Yes I know it's a tough gig doing the food deliveries only too well but thank you Tina for stepping into the breach."

"No problem but I have to say I had no idea, I mean the Cowden household looks to be in mayhem doesn't it Roy?"

Shaking his head Roy replied, "We do need to get Katie Cowden in school as a priority if it's possible to do so?"

"Not our problem if the parents don't want to," said Peter flatly still fuming.

"It's not that simple as well you know!" stated Janet angrily.

"Ok everyone," said Imogen, "I agree Katie Cowden is at risk as are many others but we will pursue her case as I believe we may have a significant Safeguarding issue there and Covid does not prevent our taking the necessary steps. So leave it with me? Janet can we meet later today to discuss a way forward?"

"Of course Imogen and it's so good to have you back," which Peter took as a direct criticism and if Janet was honest she meant it to be and smiled at him as pleasantly as possible. Various nods indicated to Imogen that harmony was briefly restored allowing her to draw the meeting to a close. "The Head hopes to be in later but until he appears I'm the Acting Head today. Ok?"

"Yes Brian ccd us all in the email," replied Peter through gritted teeth, "where is he anyway?" he being Brian Barnes who was their soon to be retiring Head who made it no secret that his successor should be Imogen.

"He didn't volunteer the information so I didn't ask," Imogen politely replied hoping that the gritting of her teeth this time wasn't evident at this point. Peter nodded looking furious, feeling usurped, whilst Roy and Matt tried not to grin. Janet looked pleased whilst Tina and Elise were busy looking at the floor.

"Excellent. So let's get at them," replied Imogen smiling her professional best thinking to herself how the world really did continue turning, with all of its petty jealousies and squabbles, even when murder, mayhem and betrayal were also part of the equation too, certainly where her life was concerned.

*

Back in Penton Sarah jumped at the knock on the door. She had had quite a morning so far as after Imogen had left the Scene of Crime Unit had turned up completely unannounced, a strategy designed to rattle any potential suspect. Detective Constable Isiah Hanson was the detective coordinating the search which was basically looking for any evidence that would indicate there had been 'foul play' on the premises.

As usual Isiah was professional, polite and as kind as possible under the circumstances. He had explained almost apologetically, "This is procedure as we must eliminate all persons who would have last seen Mr Downs and I am afraid that must include family members too."

Sarah saw the men in their white suits and gloved hands with their various instruments, saw the chemical luminal sprayed on the kitchen floor, the place Grant had laid dead, in a pool of blood, stabbed by her own hand and saw that it had detected nothing and she silently sent her thanks once again to Malcolm Speight. Finally satisfied that nothing was amiss they took their leave. "We are sorry to have bothered you today but I'm afraid there's not much I can do about that lot though," said Isiah as he pointed to the melee of journalists now on her driveway waiting to speak to her.

"Do I have to speak to them?" she'd asked Isiah.

"No Miss you don't and I would very much advise you not to," was his honest reply. Sarah was seriously appalled but nodded her thanks as she closed her door to the police, forming a barrier between herself and members of the press. Some of the reporters did not give up so easily though, aggressively banging on her door and peering through her windows, shouting such questions as, "Is your husband on the run Mrs Downs?" and "Did you know your husband was drug dealing?" and the rest. She had resorted to threatening to let the rescue dogs loose and only that threat had made them go away eventually. That had been well over two hours ago.

Hearing the knock Sarah tentatively opened the door to find someone else entirely unexpected, someone who simply took her breath away. "Hello Sarah."

Sarah just stared for more than a few seconds then seemingly snapping out of her shocked state declared, "My God! John is that you?"

Smiling at her he said, "Yes in the flesh. It's been some time hasn't it?"

"A lifetime." Now they were just stood looking at each other, until without warning Sarah simply broke down and cried. Then she was where she should be, should have always been, in the strong arms of this man she had loved since they'd been children of seventeen. Slowly steering them both towards the sofa John sat Sarah down before sitting next to her. "Bloody hell but how many years has it been and this is how I behave!?"

"Yes you were crying last time as I recall. Me too if I'm honest," replied John smiling, not being unkind but looking at her very much as he last did, with such infinite sadness.

Sarah was now really looking at John, remembering how the girls had always teased him about how much he looked and sounded like Sean Bean but now he really did. He had really bulked out too, looking like a piece of granite rock, but it was the long scar that reached from the corner of his eye, curving across his right cheek that drew her eye. Without thinking she reached up and touched it making John close his eyes before moving away from her. Embarrassed Sarah looked away then searching for normalcy looked at him and asked the usual question one asks someone they used to know, "So how have you been?"

"Busy. You know about my parents?"

"Yes, so sorry for your loss John. To lose your mum to Covid then for your dad to die from it too, well it's just too cruel."

"But they would have wanted it that way. They were never apart, not for over fifty years so one without the other would have been unthinkable for both of them. I saw you standing on their street when the funeral procession passed. Thank you for paying your respects."

Filling up again Sarah replied, "It was the least I could do. They were the best people and I... and I loved them," as I loved you were the unsaid words now between them and both Sarah and John knew it.

Pulling herself together she then said, "So coffee and then you're to tell me everything you've been up to in the past few years. Ok?"

"Really?" smiled John, "because if I did that, I'd have to kill you!" Smiling at each other Sarah reached for his hand saying, "But you will stay a while because I can't tell you how good it is to see you."

Smiling down at her, seeing how thin, how fragile, how damaged she was, made John Hilton want to have a serious word with this Grant Downs wherever he was. He also knew that he still loved her as much as he always had and probably always would. "Well it's good to be seen then and yes coffee would be great."

*

Meanwhile across the city of Sheffield Cameron Sheldon had just been informed that there had been a serious withdrawal of cash from one of his off shore accounts in the Cayman Islands, enough to make him hurt, over seven million euros. He was now thinking that maybe he had been played by Grant Downs after all; that he and his wife were planning a life together on his money and that Grant had just been pretending to be getting rid of her all along. His two henchmen Dave and Steve were now seriously worried because Cameron was as still as a statue, the calm before the storm. Someone was going to pay big for this, they knew that for certain. Finally, he balked, "Get the car! We need to pay a certain someone a visit!"

*

Meanwhile Sarah couldn't remember the last time she had felt so relaxed, so safe and yes actually happy for just a few hours. It was as if the years had melted away such was the ease of being in the company of John Hilton.

"Well as you know I joined the army and I'm still on active service."

"Wow for so many years?"

"Yes, well it's never seemed the right time to leave," he explained.

"So what is it you do in the army exactly? Do you have a trade? Are you still building?"

"I have a trade of sorts," and when she looked quizzically at him he continued with, "but I am not at liberty to say more I'm afraid."

Nodding that she understood, although in fairness she really didn't she then asked the burning question, badly needing to know the answer. "So I assume you're married?"

John looked at her and sadly smiled, shaking his head and answered, "No I've never married Sarah." Sarah rose from the sofa and walked to the large window of her barn conversion that looked so magnificently over Penton.

"I wish I hadn't, marrying Grant Downs has been the biggest mistake of my life." John said nothing, just looked at her. Looking back at him Sarah continued because she somehow felt that she owed him. He had come to see if she was ok, was offering her some form of support, perhaps only briefly and after what she had done to them both, yes Sarah knew she owed him the truth of what her life had been like without him in it.

"I think I always knew it was all a pretence, that it was the factory he wanted not me," she continued.

"And to think your dad thought I was the one after his money."

"He was wrong about most things to be fair although I think he suspected Grant towards the end."

"I still don't really understand why you married him though."

"Why not? He was as good as anyone." John

said nothing but just looked at her with such intensity that she had to look away before saying, "I hope you can one day find it in your heart to forgive me for what I did to us, to our baby."

John was now standing behind her and gently holding her by her shoulders said, "We both made mistakes Sarah and I behaved like a bloody tool. You had a right to make that decision and I was a fool to walk out like I did. We were kids and too young."

"We could have made it work."

"We'll never know and I think it's time to forgive yourself because I forgave you a long time ago. Do you forgive me?"

"For what?"

"For behaving like a Neanderthal. I'll lay money on Imogen or Beth calling me that!"

"And the rest and far worse." Looking at her he drew her into an embrace that was one of comfort tinged with sadness. "It's the past Sarah and we can't change it and we're different people now." Nodding Sarah stayed where she was, drinking in his smell, feeling safe for the first time in years until John finally said, "I have to go, but with all this coffee may I use your…" as he indicated where he should go.

"Of course, just through the double doors and first on your right."

As John used the facilities, Sarah was standing at the kitchen sink, washing the used cups and trying not to feel sad at the thought of John leaving, wondering how she could somehow suggest they meet again and how that might appear. She was concentrating so hard on what she could say that she did not hear the main door open or see the figure standing in the hall looking in at her.

Suddenly feeling the hairs stand up on the back of her neck Sarah realised someone unexpected was behind her. Turning slowly, her blood ran cold at the sight of Cameron Sheldon walking slowly towards her with his cold dead eyes and shark smile. "Well Sarah, it's been a while and I must say but you're looking much better than I was led to believe."

Feeling her bones turn to jelly such was her fear she asked the obvious, "What do you want?"

Feeding off her obvious terror Cameron swaggered towards her saying, "I want a lot of things but at this moment I want to know where your husband is and then I want my money back. All of it!"

"I don't know where my husband is or about any missing money but the police may..." but Sarah couldn't finish because Cameron Sheldon suddenly sprang like a cobra, grabbed her by her neck and pushed her up against the sink. Seconds later though, before she had actually registered what he had done, his grip released as he was bodily thrown across the room then lifted off his feet by his throat before being dropped like a lead weight to the ground. John Hilton had reappeared and Cameron Sheldon for once in his life had not got the upper hand.

Gasping for breath Cameron looked at this large hard granite of a man standing above him shouting, "You're a dead man. You don't know who you've just put your hands on!"

Nodding John Hilton looked at him with complete contempt saying, "Oh but I do know you. You've probably got goons outside because you're not a real man with real balls. You're the bully who no one will mourn when they're dead which will be very soon if you ever touch a hair on her head again!"

Cameron Sheldon was not a man who feared easily but he feared this man standing over him now. Climbing slowly to his feet he looked at Sarah and said with more bluster than he felt, "This isn't over!"

Cameron walked to the door, opened it then stepped out to get back into his car where his men were waiting. He turned to look at John then pointed his index finger as if it was a loaded gun at him, then got in his car which then screeched away at speed. John watched as the car drove away, then took out his phone.

"Hi it's me. I have a situation and I was wondering if you and a couple of the other lads fancied a trip to my neck of the woods? Yeah, got a friend who's in a bit of bother. Great, I'll send where I'll be. Thanks mate."

Replacing his phone in his pocket John looked at the retreating car then back at the house where a very frightened Sarah was waiting for him to return. What sort of man had come into her life that such men were now threatening her? What had she gotten into? He knew one thing though and that was he should never have left her in the first place.

CHAPTER 22

The night the Sheffield underworld burned, no one was spared. What's more the police were completely outnumbered, surprised and overwhelmed. At a time when all hospitals were dealing with the relentless onslaught of Covid, the hospitals of Sheffield and the rest of South Yorkshire now had casualties of this man made 'war' to deal with too. There were extreme burns victims, several life threatening gunshot wounds and many fractured skulls.

The Accident and Emergency Consultant Dr Lindon, strode up to Jim Haggerty the Chief Constable close to being outraged. "What in the hell has gone on? Isn't it enough we have Covid then for Sheffield to resemble bloody Syria!"

Shaking his head Jim Haggerty replied, "We do what we can and I'm aware that it's never enough, but this has now got personal doctor so please...he's a good lad." Nodding the doctor walked away to do the best he could as always for everyone and anyone despite what they had done or who they were.

Various sentences and comments such as "It felt like Sheffield was burning!" and "It resembled a war zone," could be heard intermittently as many uniformed officers and other police personnel mulled around the hospital's perimeter walls waiting on news of a much respected colleague.

The Travellers encampment on the edge of the city had been set alight first with all the emergency services converging to control what was so nearly out of control. News that three Irish pubs had also been set alight along with several taxi ranks that were owned by the Omar brothers were clear indications that this was an Underworld rout, undoubtedly orchestrated by someone with clout and vast resources. Any in Sheffield who were competition for Sheldon had been targeted and it was so obvious that it was almost laughable. Many paid very dearly that night with no one spared, not the very young nor the very old.

It was at the Traveller encampment when it happened. Men, women and children were trying to put out the fires and save what they could from their burning homes when Brad and his men arrived and began helping them. Out of nowhere gunfire opened up spraying all in its sights and many fell including the children. It was a miracle no one had been fatally killed on the spot. "Get down!" Brad had bellowed, before gathering as many children as he could, running them to the safe barricade of the police vehicles, then returning for more and more. The bullet went through his kevlar vest under the armpit, nestling close to his heart.

Max knew it was Sheldon's doing and was vociferously saying so to Chief Constable Jim Haggerty as they were standing apart from the others, "He is the only one who has the muscle, the means and the motive."

"I agree but we need the evidence too."

"But now he's really hurt one of our own Sir!"

"And he will live to regret that, don't you worry on that score," threatened Jim Haggerty. Nodding his agreement, Max turned to join the others. Dan and Lydia were standing apart from the rest and Lydia was very close to tears. "Beth won't survive anything happening to Brad," she whispered to Dan.

"I know, even though they're apart at the moment."

"They will never split permanently, it's what she's had to deal with that's driven them apart and I bloody helped," answered Lydia openly crying now. Steering her away from the others and finding a dark, quiet corner, Dan held her tightly and said, "Rubbish Lyds. She's a grown woman and makes her own mistakes. Not everything that's wrong in Beth's life is your fault so pack it in. Ok?"

Smiling up at him she whispered, "Ok. Thanks," offering up her face for the kiss she knew was coming and was grateful for.

Beth had been notified in the early hours of the morning and she was now sitting in the room designated to them with only Eddie at her side.

"He's strong Beth and he's got guts!" Beth merely nodded. She couldn't speak but was praying so hard making her deals, promising she would be better, that she would give anything, even her own life but the words please let my Brad live was all she could think of. The door opened and Harry stood there in all of her PPE glory. "Oh Beth, I've just heard." Harry looking at Eddie introduced herself, "I'm Harry a friend of Beth's."

"Ah the fourth one. I'm DS Sinclair and I believe I've met your friends recently."

Beth explained quickly, "Eddie is investigating Grant's disappearance."

Harry was now trying really hard to do something with her expression grateful for her mask until Beth said, "Harry please would you ring Imogen and tell her and ask her to go and tell my dad please. Also, see if you know what's happening with … Brad," then Beth's tears came like a torrent. Harry felt helpless knowing she couldn't physically comfort her friend so nodding she turned to leave and said, "He's in the best hands my friend but I'll see what I can find out."

Outside Harry leaned against the wall feeling physically sick. She had felt the police sergeant had been able to see right through her and perversely find her guilty. She now turned the corner and picked up her phone.

Imogen was in her car when Harry rang her. Using her hands free device Imogen answered and was pleased to hear it was Harry as she really needed to speak with her at the earliest opportunity.

"Gen, Harry here. It's bad news again because that's all I bloody do these days isn't it!? Give someone bloody God awful news!"

"What's happened? Please tell me it's not Alan or the kids?"

"No. Brad's been shot and it's not looking good." Harry let the silence continue as she knew how her friend would be processing what she had just uttered to her. "Beth wants you to tell her dad so can you do that please love?"

Finding her voice Imogen replied, "Of course I will. Oh Christ Harry."

"I don't know how much more I can take," whispered Harry, "it's bad enough here on a normal day but this with Brad and trying to keep quiet covering up what Sarah's done… I just don't know how much more I can take. I think I'd rather we just come clean and get it all over with because the police aren't idiots and if they come and question me I know I won't be able…"

"Harry! Harry! Shush! Stop it now! The police haven't even mentioned you and …"

"No, the detective with Beth just said to me that I'm the fourth one and..."

"Which detective? Did you get his name?"

"No but he…."

"What does he look like?" Imogen was now holding her breath, terrified that Max Stainmore was about to question Harry.

"He's in his fifties, rather plump, obviously from Barnsley…why?"

Breathing again and thanking God it wasn't Max Imogen continued, "Doesn't matter and it doesn't mean you are a suspect. He'll be looking after Beth not there to haul you in so listen to me Harry. All you have to do is stay calm, stay quiet and just get on with your very important job. You work on a bloody Covid ward for God's sake! What better alibi?" Harry remained silent. "Now come on Harry, you can do this! We can do this." Harry's continued silence made Imogen think she had already disconnected the call then, "Yes, you're right, you will get us through this I know you will but should I be worried?"

Imogen was now desperate to offload to Harry what she now suspected but knew she couldn't not yet so instead she heard herself saying, "No honey no, I really promise. Just kiss the gorgeous Alan and those wonderful bairns of yours from their Aunty Imogen ok? Stay safe too."

"I will and you stay safe too my friend."

*

Imogen knocked on Terry's front door and was surprised to hear laughter and female laughter at that. Although it was now after 4th July and more household mixing was allowed, people on the whole were still being ultra- cautious and she hadn't heard Beth say that Terry now had a lady friend, but good on him was Imogen's thought process whilst she waited for the door to open. The fact that it was Arlette her mother who was now standing before her was probably the last thing she expected to see.

"Imogen! What are you doing here?" asked a very flustered looking Arlette closely followed by an equally embarrassed Terry.

"Come in lass, come in," said Terry, " so er.. what brings you 'ere then?"

Imogen realised she was now standing with her mouth slightly open, but then found herself breaking into a genuine smile, a smile Imogen felt she would never truly do again then remembered why she had come.

"Sorry to have to tell you Terry but Brad's been shot. He's at the Hallamshire."

"Oh my word!" gasped Arlette whilst Terry just stared then jumping into action said, "I'd better go to Beth."

"You can't, Covid restrictions I'm afraid. She just wanted you to know and she will need you, she will need us all if... although I'm sure it won't come to that. They'll be doing everything possible for him but Beth wanted you to know."

"Thanks lass for coming to tell me." Imogen looked at these two lovely parents, one of hers and one of Beth's.

Smiling at them both she now said, "So I'll leave you both to it then. Right, so night then," as she closed the door behind her still reeling but smiling at what she now knew.

"Imogen," called Arlette walking on to the path outside to stand next to her daughter, "I hope you're not shocked or upset love?"

Shaking her head Imogen smiled at her mother saying, "Not at all mum."

"It's just we've been friends for such a long time and he's such a lovely man and we're not being disrespectful to Gill either. She was a lovely woman and my friend but it's good to have someone Imogen. Someone who is thoughtful and kind and decent."

Imogen looked at her mother, this woman who had endured so much for so many years and for most of it without a word of complaint or self

–pity. “Mum, he’s the dad I always wanted, the dad I should have had so better late than never eh?” as she hugged her mother tightly before remembering she shouldn’t, having been in school and in contact with others. The last thing she needed was Arlette and now Terry falling victim to Covid.

“I do hope Beth will see it like that?” murmured her mother looking anxious with worry.

“Beth has more to worry about at the moment mum. You deserve happiness, you both do and Beth will agree too, of that I’m sure”

“Thanks love, as do you,” as she hugged Imogen who was desperately trying to stop her.

“Mum! I’ve been in school today.” Arlette was unrepentant and reluctant to let her daughter go.

“As if you could or would hurt me?”

“Not intentionally mum but it’s not how this bloody Covid business works.”

Arlette smiled sadly saying, “I know love, just miss you that’s all.”

“Miss you too mum, so take care, both of you and I couldn’t be happier,” and with that Imogen left and for once felt she had something to feel good about. Closing the door Arlette returned to Terry and perched on the arm of the chair he was sitting in. “Are you ok love?” she asked tenderly.

Taking her hand, he said, “Aye love, but bloody

hell. Brad! Poor lad and poor Beth!"

"He's a bear of a man, that's what the girls call him isn't it? He's strong and a fighter."

"Lets' hope so love. So how has Imogen taken us?"

"As if all her birthdays and Christmases have come at once. She's always adored you Terry, you have been her hero since she was seven years old," replied Arlette looking at this strong, humble man whom she had silently and privately loved for years and years, ever since the night he warned Jake Taylor to leave them alone.

Blushing Terry drew her into his arms and onto his knee where they sat without words, watching the flame of the fire as they contemplated what the future would now hold for them all.

CHAPTER 23

The unmarked police car was in Sarah's drive when Imogen pulled in. Her heart once again in her mouth, dreading what she was to face next, she strode to the door and came face to face with Max Stainmore who was just leaving. Detective Constable Lydia Smith was behind him.

"Ms Holt!"

"Chief Inspector!" replied Imogen, then narrowed her eyes as Lydia Smith came into view. Looking down Lydia squeezed past making her way to the car, avoiding Imogen's steady gaze. "Certainly not with your usual calibre of personnel Chief Inspector. Clearly scraping the barrel I would say!"

"We've had a tough few hours," replied Max then lowering his voice added, "so play nice."

"Really when some don't even deserve to play in the same playground," replied Imogen loud enough for Lydia to hear, judging by the red flush of embarrassment creeping up her neck.

Max looked at Imogen with a glint of amusement

in his eyes, then shaking his head said, "You really don't take prisoners do you, but I think you'll find you're all wrong about Detective Constable Smith. I happen to think she is an excellent police officer."

"Perhaps Chief Inspector I don't care what you think. So Brad. How bad is it?"

Shaking his head, he asked, "And how, may I ask, do you already know about Sergeant Fairchild's injuries?"

"Harry told me," then seeing his confusion added, "she's a nurse at the Hallamshire and our friend."

Looking at her with a certain defeated exasperation Max replied nodding, "Ah yes, the fourth one, I remember now." When Imogen didn't reply but just continued to steadily look at Max he continued, "Well Brad's still in surgery last I heard as the bullet has lodged very close to his heart but they will be doing all they can."

Imogen looked away not wanting Max to see her eyes filling with tears as she thought of the possibility of another good decent man being taken too soon by those intent on doing harm. After a few moments as she composed herself she said, "His huge beautiful heart, I suppose it would be pretty hard to miss that I guess. And Beth?"

Seeing her pain and wanting to comfort her Max

simply said, "With Eddie. He's looking after her and I know you and your friends will want to be with her but we also take care of our own and both Brad and Beth are our own too. Ok?"

Nodding Imogen turned to go inside but then realised she hadn't asked why they were at Sarah's in the first place. "So Chief Inspector why are you here? Not just to tell us about Brad surely?"

"No, it would appear Cameron Sheldon, Grant Downs associate, paid Mrs Downs a visit today that could be classed as intimidation."

"Has he hurt her?" gasped Imogen feeling that Sarah really couldn't take much more. Shaking his head Max put up his hands indicating that all was well. "No she had a bit of a 'knight in shining armour' on hand, an old friend, someone called John Hilton who thoroughly dispatched our Mr Sheldon by all accounts."

Imogen's look of complete consternation changed her face completely as she declared, "John! John's back! That is insane and... wonderful." Her smile of relief was the first smile he had witnessed from her and he thought she was not just beautiful but breathtakingly so. Imogen's smile was now replaced with a somewhat perplexed look as she looked back at Max, who now realised he was openly staring at her. Recovering and somewhat embarrassed he said, "You know you should smile more often as it's so much nicer than your usual scowl."

"Another inappropriate remark Chief Inspector!"

"And grounds for another official complaint no doubt, so we must be in double figures by now." As he turned to leave Imogen called after him, "He won't return will he?"

Not wanting to alarm her but knowing the truth of the situation was warranted he replied, "Probably, but not tonight because that's not his MO. He will most likely let Sarah and her friend think the danger has passed but he will be back. We'll just have to be ready."

"How does he get away with it?"

"Because men are weak and greedy and also afraid," replied Max smiling sadly, "but we will get him and his friend Grant Downs, you have my word," and with that Max got into his car and drove away, leaving Imogen at the door looking after him long after he had left.

Sarah and John looked up as she entered the room. "Oh Gen," greeted Sarah, "you won't believe what's happened!"

"I've just spoken with the Chief Inspector so John! How fantastic to see you after all of this time and how brilliant you were here when you were!"

"Hi Imogen and yeah I'm just glad I was here too. So Sarah, I've got a few calls to make then I'll be back and I know you're staying here Imogen but

I'd like to stay too, just in case if that's ok with you Sarah?"

Both women just looked at John completely stunned. "Right then, I'll not be long," and with that he left the room.

"Bloody hell! What's happened to John Hilton?"

Looking like she had just discovered the Holy Grail for the second time in her life, Sarah said, "I can't believe what he did," as she quickly related the day's events. It was then Imogen's turn to explain the situation about Brad. Sarah sat in the chair and put her heads in her hands. "But don't you see this is all my fault. Sheldon is looking for Grant and I've killed him. If Brad dies his blood is on my hands! Beth will know this and she will never forgive me and why should she?" Sarah was now distraught, tearing at her hair, as she paced the room.

Looking towards the door fearful John would return and hear her, Imogen got hold of Sarah and gently shook her. "Stop it Sarah. Stop it! Stop it now!" Sarah did and for the second time that evening Imogen was once again making her friends stand firm. "Now listen to me. None of this is your fault. It is the fault of Grant and Sheldon and all men like them. Men that bring nothing but misery to others because they are greedy, power hungry and well downright bloody evil. Good people sometimes have to do bad things in order to stop the bad people. It really is as simple as that. Ok? I should bloody know so please Sarah this is not the time to lose it!"

Looking at her friend Sarah nodded and took a deep breath. "I'm sorry, I know I'm being weak and selfish. Sorry." They both looked up as John reentered the room carrying a bag. Looking at them both he waited for someone to explain so Imogen said, "I've just told Sarah that Brad Fairchild has been shot. Brad is Beth's husband who is also a police officer."

"I'm sorry to hear that but it happens in the line of duty I'm afraid," he replied as if discussing the weather and not the possible death of a dear friend. Imogen blinked and now really looked at John Hilton, taking in his obvious strength and fitness and the clear battle scars, at least the visible ones. She started to wonder who he had become exactly but instead she said, "You look like a man who is prepared for all eventualities," nodding at the bag in his hand.

"I'm on call so to speak and have to be ready at a moment's notice." Just then both women saw flashlight beams outside across the lawns. "Don't worry, that's three of my mates who have offered to join us, just in case. Is that ok?"

"Really? So I need to sort out where they will they sleep," said Sarah getting up and moving towards the hallway.

"Won't be necessary. They will remain outside keeping the perimeter safe whilst I'll kip on this sofa, with your permission that is?"

"Of course," she whispered faintly.

Imogen at this point also came to a decision. "Now I know you're safe Sarah, I'll get my things and go home for a while. I need stuff for work and I could do with my own space. Is that ok?"

"Of course my friend."

As Imogen turned to leave she smiled at John and said, "Guard her closely and keep her safe."

John smiled and quietly said, "With my life," and of that Imogen was in no doubt.

*

Sarah was now in a bit of a state. She was now alone with John Hilton who would be sleeping under the very same roof as she was. "So I'll say good night then."

"Good night and try not to worry." Smiling Sarah merely nodded and retreated to her room. She hadn't a hope of sleeping and was so aware of every house noise, wondering if John would come and join her, then castigating herself for thinking it because he was just too wonderful a man, too honourable a man to chance his arm in that way. He would consider it taking advantage of the situation but how she wished he would although she wondered if she would ever be intimate again with anyone. Sarah's physical injuries had far from healed and her body still bore the ugly scars from Grant's assault. Yet to be held whilst she slept by John would be enough for her of that she was sure. He'd made it clear that they were different people and maybe you only ever get the one chance to be with 'the one'?

Suddenly the bedroom door began to open. She realised she was holding her breath then yelped out when Scooby Doo followed by her pug Cyril jumped onto her bed to snuggle down with her. "Bloody hell you two, not what I hoped for at all. Come on then, snuggle in."

Feeling their softness and hearing their calming breaths Sarah finally found herself relaxing and heading for sleep, knowing that when she did awake, John would still be in her home and for now, still in her life.

CHAPTER 24

With news that Brad was out of surgery but that the next twenty four hours were critical, Max and his team had managed a couple of hours sleep before reconvening in their Incident room. As well as worrying about Brad and what had happened the previous night across the city, they had been informed of the incident at Sarah Down's and how Cameron Sheldon had assaulted Sarah but had been dealt with by someone calling themselves John Hilton.

One of the first things he had asked Dan to do was to find out all there was to know about John Hilton and Dan did not disappoint, in fact he was positively excited.

"It appears we have our very own Rambo here Sir," declared a triumphant Dan, "he is a Sergeant John Hilton but his file is sealed after his name and rank which my sources tell me means Special Forces including Black Ops. Isn't that something else?!" All were now looking very surprised as well as impressed.

"Bloody hell. One of the 'Who Dares Wins' lot?"

enthused Isiah.

"So one of our elite then," mused Max, "well, well."

Eddie was particularly ecstatic saying, "Is it just me but isn't it somewhat satisfying that a man like that, who puts his life on the line for Queen and country, puts a shite like Sheldon in his place!" the nods all round showed their shared agreement. Max looked at his team and felt as they did but knew it was sentiments that could not be allowed to take root. Knowing what he was about to say would not be very well received he said it anyway because it needed saying.

"But now we have a real motive," said Max, "and it saddens me to say this people but who better than to take Grant Downs out then a man like John Hilton? A man who has a history with Mrs Downs who has clearly been a victim of abuse by Mr Downs. That would not fit easy with a man such as Hilton if we are to believe what men like him stand for. Then there's the business of the money. Mrs Downs told us in her statement that Sheldon was demanding the whereabouts of Downs and his money. From what I know of Special Forces, Hilton will have the skills to orchestrate the disappearance of both with very few questions being asked."

Everyone was silent for the moment. Then Eddie spoke up saying, "So we're seriously now looking at Hilton and Sarah Downs Guv?"

Nodding Max replied, “We’ve to follow all leads, all possibilities and all lines of enquiries I’m afraid Sergeant. That’s just the way it works.”

“I know but isn’t there a poetic justice in all of this if indeed your theory is correct?” Eddie was now squaring up for an argument and Max knew it. He also knew the others weren’t far behind him.

“Are you suggesting we turn a blind eye Sergeant?”

Thinking but choosing his words carefully Eddie Sinclair shrugged his shoulders and said, “No Chief Inspector,” replied Eddie, using Max‘s full rank title for effect, “it’s just some crimes are more, let’s say righteous than others, more justified that’s all I’m saying. To pursue a man like Hilton just doesn’t sit that well with me.”

“Nor me Eddie. But righteous or justified or not, upholding the law is what we have because without it is chaos. Without it the likes of Sheldon win every time, so let’s do our jobs and go where the evidence will take us because at the end of the day that is all we’ve got. Let others do the judging. Ok?” The atmosphere had changed dramatically and Max knew he was in the minority of one when it came to thinking the worse of one of the country’s elite forces. Some of his team almost looked mutinous even Lydia although the furrowed brows now in evidence suggested that he had made a valid if somewhat, unpopular point.

So changing tack he turned to his Sergeant saying, “Right now though I think it’s time we paid Mr Sheldon a visit. What do you say Eddie, Isiah? Fancy visiting our resident scum bag who has a good deal to answer for and who can never be described as ‘righteous’?”

Nodding grimly Eddie replied, “Lead the way boss.”

Isiah nodded and got his coat.

CHAPTER 25

Very little surprised Cameron Sheldon but seeing Max Stainmore standing in his office had not been foreseen. He had thought he'd had Max Stainmore dealt with and he was not used to his orders not being followed to the letter so he was doubly unhappy. Now looking at the glacial eyes of his nemesis, Cameron began his usual dance.

"Long time no see Chief Inspector and what brings you to what I'm told is 'God's Own Country' then?"

"You!"

Raising his eyebrows in mock surprise Cameron continued, "Moi? I'm flattered Chief Inspector but I'm just a business man doing what all good business men do, so I am somewhat at a loss why such a distinguished officer such as yourself would leave the 'smoke' just for little ole me."

Cameron and his men were openly smiling, clearly enjoying themselves as they gazed upon Max, Eddie and Isiah with something close to disdain. "May I ask why you visited Mrs Downs earlier today?" asked Max keeping his eyes on

Cameron and his voice level.

"Mrs Downs? As in Mrs Grant Downs?" Max nodded. "Sorry Chief Inspector but I haven't had the pleasure of visiting the lovely Mrs Downs for some time."

Eddie growled, "Not what she and her friend had to say?"

Looking at Eddie with something akin to amusement he replied, "I've been here all day and every day, not left once have I boys?"

Dave Richmond and Steve Richardson still smirking nodded their heads with Steve saying, "Not moved from that desk hardly for days."

"Must be a case of mistaken identity," added Dave joining in.

"Or her being delusional. Grant did worry about her Chief Inspector. He thought she was having anxiety issues and did worry about her state of mind. Thought she might be going insane and it seems he was right if she is hallucinating about seeing me today," this from Cameron now clearly enjoying his little charade.

Isiah then in his soft deep measured tone simply said, "So you didn't get your arse kicked and handed back to you then?"

Suddenly it was if all the air had been sucked out of the room. Cameron and his men visibly stilled with his men watching him closely as their boss' infamous temper could erupt without warning.

This time it was Max and his men that were now smiling and nodding. Eddie now enjoying himself said, “Would have liked to have seen that boss. What about you Isiah?”

“Would have paid good money Sarge,” grinned Isiah winking at Cameron as he did so, making him quietly incandescent, he being a natural racist too.

Max continued saying, “I have to say I was surprised to hear it was actually you who had put his own hands on Mrs Downs. I mean Sheldon, you pay good money for the scum of the earth to do your dirty work for you. Sheffield is waking up to that very fact this morning. But I suppose a tiny little thing like Sarah Downs would just about be what you can handle on your own. Right? A big man like you? Yeah that would be right wouldn’t it? A tiny seven stone female is just about what you could manage.”

The ticking of a clock somewhere was the only noise to be heard as all six men kept their positions, each side waiting for the next move.

Finally, through gritted teeth Cameron said to Max, “As far as I am concerned it’s her word against mine. Now I would like you all to get the fuck out of my office as I am a busy man.”

“Busy looking for your mate Grant Downs? Your dirty money you think he may have, or new premises for your drug hauls and human cargo now that Greens of Penton is off limits? Or making open war on your competition that has hurt one of ours?" asked Max matter-of-factly as if discussing the latest football results but with an underlying menace that was palpable.

Sheldon and his men desperately wanted to crow about a police officer being hurt as a consequence of their actions but daren't, needing to bide their time. So voice dangerously low Cameron Sheldon rose from his seat allowing him to face Max eye to eye. "If you have anything to charge me with I suggest you do it and do it now Chief Inspector but you haven't, have you or you would have done it by now?"

"Not yet," said Max, "not yet but we will Sheldon, we will for that you can rely on because you will make a mistake. Men like you always do."

"I don't make mistakes," growled Cameron his face now puce with ill- concealed rage.

"Oh I'd say forty-three dead at Dover is as big a mistake can get," retorted Max, "as well as a good man fighting for his very life as we speak!"

"You couldn't prove I was involved then as you can't prove I am involved now."

Shaking his head Max replied, "Not yet, but I will Sheldon. I will. You know why? Because those poor sods deserved so much more and so does a real man like Police Sergeant Brad Fairchild. I will make it my life's mission Sheldon. You will never be rid of me until you're locked away never to see the light of day again, if it is the last thing I do." Cameron looked at Max, and saw a man who would never stop until he put to rest the incident in Dover and that meant bringing him, Cameron to his knees.

The seconds became minutes with the air of menace and potential violence permeating the room until finally he replied, "Well until then Detective Chief Inspector."

Max nodded to his colleagues and said, "Let's go and get some fresh air men as something or should I say someone, stinks in here."

As the men of law left, Dave and Steve looked at Cameron, then at each other. Cameron then picked up his phone and keyed in the contact. Then without preamble, explanation or introduction he merely said to the phone recipient, "Why isn't Stainmore out of the picture yet? Get it done and get it done now or you're finished but not before everyone you love is finished first and by that I mean in ways you can't imagine." Without waiting for a reply he finished the call.

Steve said, "Will he get it done?

"He has no choice. I own him," was Cameron Sheldon's grim reply.

CHAPTER 26

Beth did not at first see Brad's eyes flicker open. She had been at Brad's bedside praying like she'd never prayed before, making bargains and promises to whatever, whoever could possibly be listening. She would make it right between them, use a surrogate, adopt as many babies as he wants, anything just please let him live.

Deep in her thoughts she suddenly felt something change in the room. Looking at the face she loved more than her life, she gasped when she realised he was looking at her. Pressing the buzzer for assistance the room was suddenly full of experts and Beth now full of hope.

Waiting outside the room it felt like forever until Brad's surgeon Mr Asam Kapoor, came to speak to her. "He still has a way to go Beth, but I can now safely say that he will eventually make a full recovery. It's going to be a long process with a great deal of hard work..." the rest of his words were muffled as Beth flung herself into his arms as she sobbed her relief.

The news of Brad's survival was a welcome relief

for all. Beth rang the station, Brad's parents, her father then Imogen and Sarah. Each had their own way of dealing with the news. Brad's police family were now intent of finding the scum responsible for hurting their colleague, their friend. Brad's parents gave thanks and prepared their home so they could look after him properly as Beth was mentally doing the same. Terry and Arlette were delighted but now worried what Beth would say when she discovered they were together, but it was Imogen who now knew she had the hardest task. Imogen had some difficult questions to ask and difficult decisions to make and it would have to happen very soon. She still couldn't believe how stupid she had been and how easily she had been played.

*

Cameron Sheldon's men had staked out Sarah's place for seven days and nights and as yet had not detected any sign of a police presence. Sheldon and his kind knew the police were really being stretched with the Covid restrictions and the sheer stupidity of people so now was the time to strike in so many ways.

Sheldon was still smarting at the police remarks regarding what had happened when he had gone to Sarah's home that day. Some 'no mark' had laid hands on him and so that 'no mark' was now a walking dead man as far as he was concerned but his lieutenants felt he was rushing his revenge.

"Neither are going anywhere boss. We can get to her and whoever the new bloke is anytime so let things settle for a bit," was Dave Richmond's advice whilst his counterpart Steve nodded in agreement.

"Let them think they've won for a bit, drop their guard," he had added, "then make them pay. Who cares what a couple of rozzers think?"

Cameron turned his steely gaze onto them both, making them visibly shrink. "I fucking care. Whoever he is, he's going to die piece by piece but not before he watches me skin alive his little play mate. Let him hear her screams first then he can beg me, plead with me to finish him off by the time I'm done."

Cameron was now practically in a state of pure pleasure just thinking, dreaming and relishing what he was going to do to John Hilton and Sarah Downs. "No! We strike sooner because they won't expect us too. We will have the element of surprise so call the troops to meet here for the planning meeting. This is going to be epic."

No this was going to happen sooner rather than later because if he was brutally honest with himself, his psychopathy was such that he could no longer wait anyhow.

*

Meanwhile in the few days since Sheldon had

attacked Sarah, John and Sarah along with John's people, had fallen into an easy pattern with each other. She was glad that others were here on her property with them, grateful for their presence because she was now very afraid, terrified if she was honest. Her husband had clearly been nothing more than a criminal, a gangster and that was the sort of people who now had her in their sights.

John had refused using a spare room to sleep in but used the settee in her kitchen come living room if it wasn't his turn to keep watch outside. He and his friends, who were called Bud, Trey and Daz were on constant alert, taking it in turns to sleep and keep watch, guarding the perimeter of her property with military precision. Unlike Sarah they knew an attack was imminent. John could sense it, knew that somewhere, not far away dangerous, cruel men who had no pity and no honour were now plotting against them and they would show no mercy.

Sarah liked John's friends and was particularly taken with Trey because of his clear affinity with her dogs. He loved her dogs and they loved him back, particularly the four rescue dogs, two of them who had been abandoned and starved over the Covid period. Sarah often saw him stroking, hugging or feeding them, talking in a soothing kind tone that they had probably never experienced before. "Now then, need a stroke do you lad? Come here then," whilst he ruffled ears or stroked their backs. Even Scooby Doo and Cyril were completely smitten with Trey, briefly abandoning Sarah for once as they began to follow this gentle, kind man who seemed to understand and communicate with them so easily.

"You're good with them and they can sense that you love them," she had said to him.

"You can't beat dogs, better than most humans in my opinion," Trey had said adding, "Dogs aren't cruel just because they can be." Sarah had nodded her agreement, feeling sad at what this young kind man had most likely seen and dealt with.

Bud and Daz were far more laddish, constantly teasing each other. Today Daz had seen Bud using moisturiser and was teasing him mercilessly. "You'll be plucking your bloody eyebrows next!" he had jibed.

Bud had replied, "It's called grooming not that an ugly bugger like you would know anything about that!" It was all good natured whilst John was quietly in charge without it being said.

"Thank you so much for being here," she had said to Bud one morning.

"Pleasure to be here Miss," he had replied, "it makes a change to have a bit of comfort and a really good cuppa made."

"Beautiful green grass and fresh air," grinned

Daz, "what's not to love?!"

"Without the mud or dust in your teeth," agreed Trey.

John had joked, "Well don't get too used to it. Don't need you lot going soft on me."

The trio had grinned as they tucked into bacon butties, whilst Sarah, who had been an only child, often lonely except when with the girls, felt she had a band of brothers taking care of her and she basked in that feeling.

Later when alone with John she had said, "You are all very close aren't you?"

"They're my family, my brothers."

"You would do anything for each other, wouldn't you?"

"We'd die for each other."

"So where are their families? Their wives?"

John looked at her not knowing how to respond then said, "In our line of work it's better not to have wives or children so we in this team don't. Daz and Bud were brought up in care and to be honest the army has been the only family they've ever had. We have each other though," then smiling added, "for better or worse," then quietly said, "but always for Queen and country." Sarah nodded her understanding whilst realising how bleak and often lonely most people were, even this 'Band of Brothers'. Sarah was also aware how her heart would be destined to break again, once John Hilton went back to the life he had made without her.

As the days went by, Sarah learnt how the Hilton clan had grown in number with John showing her pictures on his phone of his numerous nephews and nieces and cousins' children and how well they were or weren't doing. "Do you remember our Milly? Steph's little 'un? Well she's just starting medical school."

"Oh that's fabulous," Sarah had exclaimed, "but I have to say Steph was seriously clever herself."

"Yes but she chose motherhood I suppose, but then again getting pregnant at seventeen didn't help exactly." An uncomfortable silence had followed then when Sarah changing the subject asked, "So what about your Martin?" referring to John's older brother.

"He's got his own local electrical business so he's doing alright, never been busier apparently. His lad Carl's been a bit of a disappointment though." Nodding Sarah smiled, happy that John and his family were still close- knit and once gain feeling sad at what she had given up.

It was one evening when John was based inside with her that Sarah suddenly looked at him and said, "Do you ever wonder who our child would have been? Wonder if it was a girl or a boy? How many we would have gone on to have?"

John didn't answer but instead looked away. A now heavy, pregnant pause was pervading the air, until in a voice close to breaking he replied, "All the time." Then she found herself in his arms, being held so tight until John cupped her face in his hands and kissed her.

"I forgave you a long time ago Sarah but didn't know how to come back and put things right between us. I know now that I should never have left you to them, your parents, but should have stayed and fought for you." Then she was crying and they were kissing and then John picked her up and carried her upstairs. It was then as he tenderly undressed her that John saw the marks still visible on her body and he could barely conceal his rage.

"I hope he is dead because if I get my hands on him..."

"Please let's not think about him, not now I'm finally where I've always belonged," then closing her eyes said, "but he did things to me John. Please don't ask me to tell you but I am not sure if I can ..."

He stopped her speaking and said, "Just holding you and keeping you safe is enough for me. It will all come right, you'll be well again. You'll see." Closing her eyes, drinking in his smell she prayed he was right.

As the days progressed they talked and

tentatively began to believe of a possible future together, despite what John had said only a few days earlier. John explained, "I have duties to fulfil for some time to come as the job isn't something I can just up and leave when I feel like it. These men, my brothers aren't people I can just walk away from either. We've been through so much together and I'm probably still alive because of them if I'm honest."

Sarah merely nodded and said, "I will take anything offered, just as long as you come back to me when you can."

Cradling her he had whispered, "Always my Sarah, always."

CHAPTER 27

Lydia waking from the best night's sleep she had experienced in ages, stretched whilst looking to her right and saw Dan smiling at her and holding a steaming cup of hot tea out for her to take from his grasp.

"You are just too good at knowing what I need Detective Constable Devon," she said smiling broadly and taking the steaming cup from him.

"Well that's why I'm a detective," as he leaned in for a morning kiss.

After a moment Lydia said, "This is nice but I'm not sure how allowed it is? You know work colleagues involved in a relationship of this nature."

Smiling at her he asked pretending to be confused, "And what would the nature of this be described as then Detective Constable Smith?"

Frowning at him she responded, "Are you making fun of me?" Laughing now Dan got back in bed beside her, being careful not to spill the made tea and said, "Not in the least, just love how 'proper' you talk. The nature of this? Well as far as I'm concerned this between us is bloody brilliant and I don't just mean bed either. I think we're good together."

Beaming back at him she said, "Me too, but we need to keep it a secret," then seeing his face she added, "Oh bloody hell. Who knows? Don't tell me Isiah. Well why am I not surprised?!"

"In my defense he guessed and he won't say owt, he wished me luck in fact." Frowning as he now worried what her response would be he then added, "Actually I told him about Baker too," holding up his hands in mock surrender when he saw her face change to one of anger, "and he's as bloody furious as I am and I know you're angry with me but you're going to have to put this right. So I want you to consider going to the boss with this sooner rather than later."

Lydia was now studying Dan's earnest face and realised how right he was and how lucky she was that he clearly cared about her so much. "So he wished you luck did he?"

Clearly relieved that a row of momentous proportions had been averted he smiled saying, "He did because I suspect he thinks I'm a lucky man this beautiful July morning," kissing her softly murmuring, "and he's not wrong."

*

A Molitov cocktail thrown into the rescue dog

kennels was the obligatory element of surprise, or it would have been if the perpetrator had not been summarily taken down with lightning speed.

The hulking figure had crept up to the kennels, threw the lit amateur explosive when almost immediately Trey took him down hard disarming and securing the perpetrator before he could call out a warning, knocking him out cold before trussing him up rendering him harmless. Although the kennels began to burn, all the dogs had been moved in to the main house for their protection but not knowing this, the remaining five thugs waiting in the shadows took the lit building as their agreed signal to attack so converged onto the property.

One by one they were taken down as men who faced down Isis, the Taliban, drug cartels and so much more, easily dealt with the thuggery before them with the whole business taking less than three minutes.

“Give the signal!” hissed John as he held Steve Richardson by the hair.

“Fuck you,” Steve had growled then howled in pain as John using his training and expertise made him do just as he’d asked with immediate effect.

Cameron as was his custom, was in his car until the hard work was done, waiting for the signal to his phone indicating to him that it was clear for him to join his men and begin his much anticipated revenge. He could barely wait. Taking the knife he intended to use from out of its sheath, he casually walked through the gates with his customary swagger and confidence. What he saw before him made his blood run cold as he gasped in complete surprise and horror at the unthinkable sight before him. Turning to run, he was hit by the butt of a gun and then he felt no more.

It took Max and his team with several squad cars, a fire engine and an Armed Police Response Unit approximately twenty seven minutes to arrive at the scene. Eddie would dine out for years on what they came upon.

Six of Sheldon's men were trussed up like the obligatory Christmas turkeys whilst Sheldon himself was out cold on the ground. Several of the trussed up thugs were shaking in terror, finally realising what it felt like to be at the other end of such extreme violence. Until the police had shown up, more than one of Sheldons's men had thought they were about to meet a gruesome end to what had been a life of making others wish they were dead.

Trey had been particularly angry with the one who had attempted to burn down the kennels thereby killing the defenseless dogs. "Do you know what you deserve? To knowingly burn to death defenseless animals? I'll bloody show you," he had said as he dragged the man by his hair to the still burning fire. "What about me leaving you here to burn to death instead? Hey? That would be justice you fucking scum!" It had taken both Bud and Daz to drag him away and pull the now hysterically blubbering cowed man away from the heat which had still delivered a modicum of first degree burns whilst singing his hair and blackening his face.

John's comrades were now in full professional mode with faces covered to obscure their identities, clearly carrying army issue weapons and in full army combat gear standing guard in the manner only such men can.

Max approached John who was standing over Sheldon, his face inscrutable. "Been busy I see Sergeant Hilton!"

John observed that Max had used his rank and replied, "Just glad we were here Chief Inspector."

Nodding Max replied, "So am I and I'm also pleased to know that you weren't in this country at the time of Mr Downs disappearance or I would be asking you some very difficult questions and I would have hated that." Nodding to his police colleagues Max added, "And you have no idea how unpopular that would have made me around here!"

"I would expect nothing less from you Chief

Inspector." Just then the whirring noise of a Chinook helicopter could be heard in the distance, coming into view to swoop down and land on the neighbouring field. "Like now", he said worriedly, "my orders have come and we must leave with immediate effect. I'm just relieved that piece of shit," as he pointed to Cameron Sheldon who was now fully conscious with an armed response police officer pointing his weapon at him, "chose to attack when he did."

Max nodded his understanding as Sarah came running out of the house, looking pale and so very frightened. John went over to her and said, "This is it Sarah. I've to go but I would stay if I could, you do know that don't you love?" As Sarah nodded he continued in earnest, willing her to understand, "Our orders came through earlier and I can't tell you when I'll be back."

Blinking away her tears she folded herself into his embrace and simply said, "Just stay alive and come back to me. Please, please, just stay alive, all of you." Easing her away he nodded to his men, who went to join the rest of their operatives waiting for them on the chinook.

John then stood over Cameron's prone body. "I know how to make a man's death take days even weeks. Look in her direction ever again and I will find you and you will wish you were dead. Make no mistake." Cameron nodded and looked away. John now looked hard at Max ominously saying,

"Take care of this scum Chief Inspector because I really don't want to have to do it again. Oh and we were never here, ok?" Both Max and Eddie nodded their understanding, taking the silent sub-text of John's words on board whilst Isiah looked on with something akin to hero worship.

"Good luck" said Max feeling words weren't enough for these men who were now going to face God knew what. As the helicopter left the ground John stood at its open door looking down at them all but really only seeing Sarah until it was out of sight.

"God bless 'em," whispered Eddie then said to Max, "I would not have missed that for anything," then turning to the men on the ground said, "See that?! And what's more they're going to God knows where, risking their lives to keep shite like you bloody safe in the streets you bloody terrorise. You know why? Because they're real men that's why! Men who believe in honour and respect, but I'm probably wasting my bloody breath. What would scum like you know about any of that eh?"

"Where do you think they're going Sir?" asked Isiah.

"To hell most probably," said Max quietly.

Cameron was very alert now and was demanding his rights, threatening law suits as was the way of his kind. "How fucking dare they.

All we were doing was to making sure a friend of mine's wife was safe whilst he remains missing. I'm bloody outraged and my Brief will be…"

"How fucking dare who?" asked Eddie wearing his most innocent and confused expression, "who do you think he's referring to Guv?"

Max happy to play along replied, "Must have banged his head when he tripped Sarge."

Cameron now almost apoplectic began, "If you think..."

Cutting him off before he could really begin Max stated firmly, fixing him with a stare that showed contempt and something close to disgust, "Just save your breath. You are trespassing on private property, brandishing a weapon with intent to cause grievous bodily harm for starters. Got you bang to rights for once Sheldon and we've only just started as well."

"Really!" Sheldon's swagger was back with a vengeance. "My Brief will have me out by lunch time particularly as no one was actually here Chief Inspector to say any different!"

"Get him in the van Sergeant," replied Max who was already worrying that would be so, such was the judicial system if you could afford it.

For her part Sarah stood there until the helicopter was nowhere in sight, now wondering if the life she had briefly glimpsed had also gone from her sight and if so, how she would never feel happy or safe again.

CHAPTER 28

Imogen was shocked and more than a little disturbed when she saw that Max Stainmore was standing outside her apartment complex, ringing her door bell. She saw that he was alone, so surmised that he hadn't come to arrest her, well at least not today.

Max has been surprised to learn that Imogen was no longer living with Sarah and relieved she hadn't been there when Sheldon's thugs had arrived but decided it would be only to be fair to inform her of recent incidents, all in the line of duty of course. At least that was what he was trying to convince himself he was doing so finding Imogen's address, he decided to pay a house call.

Opening her door, she proceeded to be as cool, formal and as straight to the point as possible. "What do you want Chief Inspector?"

"And good morning to you too Ms Holt. I thought I'd give you the courtesy of relaying recent events regarding Mrs Downs."

"Oh God, please tell me she's ok?"

Walking into her home, he replied, "Sarah is safe and Sheldon and his men are now under arrest so... I thought you deserved the courtesy of a house call."

"That's surprisingly...charming of you. Thank you."

"Well I took some advice and so I have been working on my 'charm' so to speak," Max now openly grinning at their 'in' joke.

"And progress has been clearly made although there's always room for improvement," was Imogen's prim but self- deprecatingly reply.

Max was now looking at his surroundings which constituted Imogen's home exclaiming, "What a place! Nice!" as he openly admired the high ceilings and beautiful furnishings, "And that is some view!"

"Thank you, bereavement can be very lucrative," replied Imogen.

No longer smiling, Max said, "Brad told me about your husband. That's a pretty tough break."

Blinking her surprise at his obvious empathy, Imogen merely nodded then, "So may I offer you a coffee Chief Inspector?"

"There it is! Finally!"

"Where is what?"

"That famous Northern hospitality I've been looking forward to. Coffee would be great thanks," following Imogen into her equally impressive kitchen, watching her move and she, keenly aware he was doing so.

"I imagine you are a 'no frills', strong, black coffee person Chief Inspector?"

"Max," as she raised her eyebrows as if asking a question, "I think coffee calls for less formality, so call me Max, and yes strong and black, thank you." Pouring the coffee, Imogen then motioned that they both go onto her balconied terrace, which was bathed in sunshine, making the Pennines look even more formidably beautiful. "Wow", said Max, "can any view anywhere better this? I must say it makes Canary Wharf look even more soulless."

"Is that your home?"

"For now it serves its purpose but it must have been pretty special growing up in a place like this."

"When you're young you don't see the beauty, its other things such as the people that you see, the ones who make your life worth living."

"Like your friends?" Imogen merely nodded.

"So, Brad told me you all met at First school?"

"Yes bonded when Billy Boyle hurt Sarah."

Grinning Max said, "Big mistake Billy boy."

"Huge," smiled Imogen, "and we've remained close ever since."

"What happened to Billy?"

"Probably locked up by your lot somewhere".

Laughing Max now deliberately changed the subject saying, "I was surprised to learn you had left Sarah's place."

"Why?"

"You appear to be worried and very protective of her and letting her out of your sight seems out of character for you." Imogen was now on alert and Max could see this by the renewed tension in her body language.

Shrugging she said, "John's there and I felt they needed their space if anything was to rekindle between them and to be honest I needed mine," now going on the defensive, "and how would you know what my 'out of character' is?"

"Because I'm good at reading people."

"Perhaps when it comes to me Chief Inspector, you're reading the wrong book!"

"Ah now come on Imogen? I thought we'd moved on, I'm Max, let's leave the rank for another day, okay and if I'm reading the 'wrong book' then I would really like to read the 'right' one." Max was now looking at Imogen with such intensity, the wry smile never leaving his face, but his eyes like ice probes that could almost see into her brain.

"Why?"

"Because I think I would find it a fascinating

read."

"I think you would become very bored very quickly. There's nothing fascinating about me."

"I'd like to be the judge of that." They continued to stare at each other, the atmosphere now electric, only interrupted by the ringing of Max's phone. Pressing the button, his eyes never leaving hers, Max listened before replying, "Ok. I'll be there in the next thirty minutes. So duty calls…unfortunately, just as we were getting better acquainted."

Trying to hide her relief but also acknowledging part of her, perversely, didn't want him to go Imogen said, "I'll see you out."

Walking to the door Max turned to her, smiled and said, "Well, enjoy the rest of your day."

Imogen just nodded, still unsure how to respond to this man who constantly wrong footed her. Closing her door, she felt she was in trouble though but for once did not know what to do about it or what sort of trouble it actually was.

CHAPTER 29

Malcolm Speight surveyed the room. The men before him, and they were only men present as expected in such company, did not look happy. Malcolm had a chequered history with all present but he knew he had been the catalyst for what they had suffered earlier in the week and he was now here to put things right as best he could, that is if they allowed him to.

Omar Mirza was the first to speak, his expensive public school educated vowels asking the obvious question, "So Speight why are we here?"

Malcolm surveyed the room and knew he had to tread carefully. All before him had been victims to Sheldon's viciousness, all had lost property and money. All had family and friends in hospital with conditions ranging from minor injuries to life threatening ones and he saw before him broken egos and a thirst for revenge. It was this last entity he hoped to exploit.

"I'm aware of what happened and I know who was to blame. We all do. Cameron Sheldon and his hired muscle," replied Malcolm keeping his voice firm and steady, "and I'm here because I believe it's now time we take our city back!"

"Jesus bloody Christ!" exclaimed Joseph O'Malley in his thick Irish brogue, "because it's that simple isn't it? Why didn't we think of that lads? Let's take our city back!"

Malcolm continued, "I feel your anger and I bloody share it but I do have information that will make a difference."

"So? Spill!" said Jack Smith, leader of the Tinker contingency and the encampment which had suffered the worst damage by far.

Taking a deep breath and realising he had no choice but to tell the truth, the whole truth and nothing but the truth, he continued, "I'm the reason the city went up in smoke."

The stunned silence was now speaking volumes until Joe O'Malley said with menace oozing out of every pore, "You'd better start explaining."

Nodding Malcolm continued. "Sheldon believes his competition, that means everyone in this room, is somehow responsible for the disappearance of his main lieutenant Grant Downs. I know that isn't the case."

"And how do you know this?" asked Jack Smith.

Swallowing hard and praying for the first time in years, Malcolm replied, "Because I am in the process of disposing his body for a third party. Yes, he's very dead and has been for a while now."

Omar Mirza's son Mohammed flew at Malcolm causing his minders Eddie and Dave to throw him across the room. Suddenly all were on their feet, knives appeared and fists became clenched and the prospect of total carnage became a possibility until Jack Smith yelled, "Enough! Omar, keep that boy on a leash. All of you, put away your weapons." Slowly all complied staring at each other, not trusting any one to behave with honour.

Omar was the first to speak next ominously saying, "My youngest son has suffered a fractured skull and two cousins are still missing. They were not men who attacked my businesses, my home, they were devils. Mohammad loves his family and his anger is justified."

"We've all suffered Omar," said Jack Smith.

"None of us deserved what those bastards dished out Jack especially when the one who should have had the fucking kicking is sitting over there!" shouted Jo O'Malley pointing to Malcolm, his anger palpable.

"And I want to put it right if you will agree to help me! Sheldon will get his, a hundred times over, but I can't do it alone. We can also send a message to that lot in London that this city is not for the taking! Not ever!"

The following silence went on undisturbed for several seconds. Malcolm even bizarrely thought in that time span, that Sergio Leone's famous signature theme would not have been out of place in this moment as there were some very bad and ugly characters here and no one remotely good.

Finally, Omar was the first to speak saying, "We must have vengeance that is a fact, so I will be interested in hearing what you have planned." Looking round the room, Malcolm saw the nods of heads that indicated he had got over the first hurdle.

"Okay. So Grant Downs body will soon be found and it will implicate Cameron Sheldon. We all know what a slippery bastard he is and his highly paid barrister will no doubt see a way out of a permanent conviction. What will happen though is that he will be held on remand and that's all we need, a window of opportunity." He had all their attention now as he continued. "We all have men we can trust on the inside in most of the prisons this side of Watford Gap. I'm hopeful that he will end up in Wakefield."

"Why Wakefield?" asked Jack Smith.

"Let's just say there is someone there who would be more than willing to ensure justice and vengeance is meted out in equal measure. I know we need a bit of luck in this unless someone here has access to the judiciary? I do think though that this could work very nicely for all of us." Looking around the room Malcolm knew he had them.

"So," ventured Jack Smith, "what about the rest? We may get Sheldon out of the way but what about the business end?"

"Yeah," agreed Joe O'Malley, "we've been shafted long enough in terms of revenue lost."

Nodding his agreement Malcolm said, "And that takes me to the next step in getting our city back."

Looking around the room he smiled knowingly at each man. "This is where we use our men on the inside and we all have 'em. By inside, I mean inside the police, those on our payrolls. We inform them where the premises are, they inform their 'snouts' so it looks legit. The police make their raids and arrest the rest of the London scum. Simples!"

Leaning back Malcolm waited for what he knew would be coming next, and it did. "What sort of cock –eyed bloody scheme is that? For a start since when did we help the bloody bastard law?" shouted Jo O'Malley.

"I'm suggesting we alert the authorities towards Sheldon's human cargo, not the drug or money laundering outlets. You lot can divide that lot between you."

"You're suggesting that we let go a lucrative market already in working order," said Jack Smith shaking his head, "not going to happen."

Leaning back in his chair Malcolm surveyed the room. Taking his time to reply he then leaned forward and said, "And here was I thinking I was in the company of men. Villains absolutely but men nonetheless." The atmosphere was once again charged. Omar's son Mohammed was about to move towards Malcolm who barely but noticeably gave him a warning to remain where he was. Malcolm continued, "In Penton, they discovered a dungeon of sorts. They found shackles and filth and they also found a child's toy. This London scum have been peddling all kinds of human misery including 'babbies'. So I repeat, I thought I was in the company of men not fucking nonces!" The use of the local dialect for small children was a deliberate use of language.

All leant back in their chairs digesting what Malcolm had said, what he had actually challenged them to think about. It was Omar who broke the silence. "I agree to this plan. We allow the police a small victory here and we do not deal in the buying or selling of women and their children."

Looking around the room Malcolm saw that they had an agreement and a solid way forward. "So," he began, "let's sort out the logistics."

"Before you do," interrupted Omar, "I need an assurance of one thing."

"I'm listening," said Malcolm.

"Promise me Sheldon will die slowly and in great pain and distress."

Smiling now at Omar Mirza and all the players around the table Malcolm Speight simply said, "On that you can be absolutely sure of my friend."

CHAPTER 30

Imogen was always the last to leave her school's premises, so was surprised to see another car parked next to her own mini. As she neared she saw a certain someone leaning casually against the car and realised it was Max.

Imogen had been in a state of alert and, she was alarmed to admit, something else since Max had called the previous Saturday, something that was reminding her what healthy women everywhere needed. There had been no one since Neil, no one coming even close and now the absolute last person on the planet, the one who could harm all she loved and cared about was the one she could not stop thinking about. She was at a complete lost at how he had somehow snuck under her radar and here he was leaning against his car with that infuriatingly relaxed smile of his.

"Hi and how are you this fine evening?"

"What are you doing here?"

"No "So pleased to see you too Max?"" Imogen remained silent. Shrugging, he continued, "Okay. I was hoping you would be public spirited enough to help me support the 'Eat Out to Help Out' scheme that our esteemed Chancellor of the Exchequer is suggesting we do? Even a busy woman has to eat?"

Recovering Imogen shook her head saying, "Thank you but no."

"Why?"

"I'd rather not."

"So take out back at yours then?"

"You have surely got to be kidding me? It wasn't that long ago you were suggesting I was under investigation and now you want to eat with me?!"

Shaking his head with mock sadness Max replied with, "And here I was thinking we'd made progress. I really thought that someone in your position would relish the idea of being public spirited and help the economy as well as showing kindness to a someone who is a long way from home!" Grinning now he added, "Come on. What are you afraid of?"

"I'm not afraid..." then sighing heavily Imogen replied, "You're really very persistent aren't you?"

Nodding and still smiling Max simply said, "It's why I'm good at what I do. So where do you suggest?" Standing there looking at him he could see how conflicted she was, wrestling with a variety of emotions, some he did not fully comprehend, but he was pleased when finally,

Imogen opened her car door saying, "You'd better follow me then."

Kelham Island was very up and coming and part of Sheffield's regeneration of its city centre, taking 'Brownfield' land and combining it with refurbished industrial buildings which represented Sheffield's Industrial heritage. It was a very trendy, well sought after place with a combination of restaurants and good old fashioned Sheffield pubs. The newly constructed apartments and houses that many students and newly qualified professionals lived in were popular and a good property investment and it was also where she and Neil had first lived when they had come to live in Sheffield after University.

As they entered an Italian restaurant, a particular favourite of Imogen's, the restaurant owner Lou Ferraro greeted her with his customary over the top warmth. "Bella Imogen! I want to embrace you but this stupid government forbids me. How can this be right? A beautiful woman must always be embraced!"

Imogen smiled her welcome knowing that he was playing to his restaurant audience replying, "Wonderful to see you too Lou. Table for two?"

"Always for you Bella"

Taking their seats Max suitably impressed asked, "So how come you know this place? Like the vibe, reminds me of the Borough Market back in the 'smoke'."

Nodding she said, "My husband and I first lived around here when we came back to Sheffield after University."

"Where did you study?"

"Imperial College in your neck of the woods."

"Didn't want to stay in the capital?"

"No, home beckoned me back. What about you?"

"London born and bred and I've never wanted to be anywhere else."

"So tell me how you're liking 'up North', seeing as you're a soft London lad?"

Smiling back at her and taking the jibe in his stride, Max countered, "Well now I'm beginning to break through the language barrier, I'm doing okay I think and I like it. Some of the natives are especially very interesting and particularly lovely to look at."

Looking at him, Imogen suddenly laughed out loud replying, "Oh smoothly done Chief Inspector, smoothly done. Infact positively charming." Imogen now realised she was relaxing, and actually enjoying this light banter and obvious flirtation. It felt good and it felt normal something Imogen hadn't felt in an awful long time. Their pasta arrived and the conversation turned to her friends and their closeness.

Max looking at her, said, "To be honest there's something that's always bothered me about this case where you and your friends are concerned?" Swallowing Imogen waited and hoped she didn't look as anxious as she was now feeling. "How on earth did a sweet lady like Sarah end up with the scum that is Grant Downs and what's more you girls let her?"

Breathing normally again Imogen answered honestly. "Believe me we tried to warn her but I think it was because Sarah's parents were very controlling to the point of abuse in many ways. I guess it's no secret and to give you more understanding you need to know that Sarah aborted John's baby when she was only nineteen because her parents were so insistent and John walked away, something he's also regretted too I believe from what Sarah has said. I can honestly say that I've never seen anyone so broken so when that piece of garbage that is Grant Downs came along, well she was easy pickings. Then it began." Max waited for her to continue. "The abuse Max. It's all a form of abuse isn't it and the evil that brings? Abuse has many faces and can be anyone and at first it pretends to care or even love you. Abuse will convince you that it is your fault because abuse cannot take responsibility or have empathy, is a narcissist, convincing you it's acting for the best but it will always be in its own self- interest. It then manifests itself as the deepest and most damaging bruises the ones that are unseen, remain hidden, whittling away all that possibility that can make you whole or make you happy and confident enough to walk away and find a future with someone who would, could love you. Because your Abuser makes you feel worthless, undermined and condemning you to a life not lived well." Imogen suddenly stopped, realising how passionate and angry she sounded and took a sip of her drink. Max remained silent watching her closely, waiting for her to continue. He sensed she had more to say. Looking at him, feeling his support she continued as if needing to say the words held long inside of her.

"That was Sarah's reality and it was also my mother's Max. Men like Grant and my father have no honour and no pity and they deserve to be put in a hell of their own narcissistic making where they should wither and die alone."

Max had stopped eating but was now looking mesmerized at the woman before him before quietly saying, "Sorry you had a father like that."

"He died when I was fourteen, apparently hit by a car whilst he drunkenly staggered home from the pub in the snow and we were glad when they came to tell us he was dead. Does that make me a bad person? Or my mother?"

"No it doesn't. It makes you both…human."

"You know you could say that this term abuse, which we throw around so easily actually accounts for the different forms of evil that can be found in the world and Sarah has a chance now, a real chance to be happy and have a family to love. Let's just hope John Hilton doesn't get himself killed before that can happen."

"Evil certainly walks amongst us, as a wise man recently told me, but what if Grant Downs rears his ugly head? We still can't account for his whereabouts."

Looking at her food, not able to meet his eye, she shook her head saying, "I suspect you may want to lock him up before he bothers Sarah again. Am I right?"

Max nodded then said, "What about you?"

Imogen raised her eyebrows in confusion wondering what Max was asking her. "Will you ever marry again, have a family?"

Shaking her head, "I was lucky to have loved and be loved by Neil Holt and we had ten wonderful years and in all honesty I don't expect to have that again. As for children, I lost that ability the night I lost Neil and our baby."

"Sorry Imogen I had no idea but never say never eh?"

"So what about you?" enquired Imogen wanting to change the subject, "how many former Mrs Stainmores are there out there? I assume there isn't a current one otherwise we wouldn't be here?"

Raising his eye-brows he asked, "Really? What makes you think that?"

"I suspect you're an honourable man Chief Inspector," and Max realised he liked the idea she thought so.

"Just the one and a couple of near misses. Vogue and I married too young and the job became more important than her if I'm honest."

"Vogue?" asked Imogen smiling.

"I know," laughed Max, "her name should have been warning enough. Her mother was a big Madonna fan apparently. Anyway she eventually found a footballer who has given her a lifestyle befitting her name and loads of kids so no harm done I guess. The only problem was that he elected to play for bloody Fulham!" shaking his head in mock disbelief.

Seriously looking at him now, Imogen quietly remarked, "Your job is everything to you isn't it?"

Seeing how serious she now was he answered with his customary honesty, "It can be I guess. There are so many bad people who want to do bad things, who enjoy it, who live to do the unspeakable."

"Like Grant? Sheldon?"

Nodding his agreement then adding in way of

explanation, "It's hard to un-see what should never be seen by any one because some things should never be allowed to happen. It's why I'm glad I never had kids because the world just isn't safe. Does that make sense?"

Imogen nodded her understanding saying, "Totally, but there are good men, good people," before adding, "I believe I'm having dinner with a good dedicated man now."

"As am I," answered Max and at that Imogen felt her heart begin to break just a little as she knew better as Max grinning at her continued, "Except I'm having dinner with a very beautiful woman who is quite the enigma."

"Enigma? Why would you say that?"

"Our first meeting, you weren't exactly friendly now were you? Positively bolshie I would say."

"Expect all women to fall at your feet then? All that leather jacketed smouldering good looks, tough 'cop' thing going on. I mean, really?"

Sitting back grinning, Max simply said, "So the lady thinks I'm good looking. Who knew?"

"Well I'm sorry I forgot to fall at your feet Chief Inspector, wowed by the Adonis before me," as Imogen now very coquettishly threw back, enjoying their banter.

Suddenly serious and now looking at Imogen with a look that would melt steel Max replied, "Well I am not too proud to say that when I first saw you I thought that crime did certainly pay, seeing as I believed you were Mrs Downs at the time. I think you're probably the most beautiful woman I've ever spent time with and I admit there's been a few," this now being said with such matter of fact honesty that an embarrassed Imogen found herself looking down at the tablecloth, grateful when the waitress came with the bill.

Both reaching for it, their hands touched and the thrill of that brief nanosecond connection wasn't lost on either of them. Recovering first Max said, "Mine I think."

"I don't think so!"

"I invited you so I Insist. Come on, let me, as way of my thanking you."

"For what?"

"For giving me the opportunity to eat food that hasn't seen a microwave." Smiling she acquiesced and realised she was sad the evening was coming to an end.

Making their way out of the restaurant, having said their goodbyes, Imogen and Max were now walking towards her car. It was a quiet, warm evening and all seemed well with the world although neither knew what to do or say next so Max began, "Thanks for this evening."

"It's been surprisingly pleasant and you've been almost charming, so thank you."

Smiling now Max ventured, “Oh well I’m full of surprises and I’ve really been working on the charm so perhaps we can do this again? You know, doing our civic duty and helping the economy.”

Smiling back Imogen found herself saying, “Perhaps.”

Max nodded then quietly said, “Goodnight Imogen Holt and drive carefully.” Neither made a move to touch the other although both were thinking about it but instead Max began to cross the road.

It happened in seconds but that’s life isn’t it. All’s well in the moment then seconds later life is no longer as it was. Out of nowhere came the car with its screeching tyres, accelerating straight towards Max with no intention to avoid the imminent collision of metal against skin, bone and blood. Imogen heard a scream and later when remembering, realised it had come from her, as the car hit Max throwing him onto its bonnet before he dropped to the ground.

Without hesitation she ran to his prone body, still screaming his name not realising the car was now reversing back towards both of them. Out of nowhere, from the side street opposite, another car zoomed forward to purposefully collide with the car set on reversing over the two now static on the road, hitting it hard as it swerved into a parked vehicle rendering it motionless but activating its screeching alarm system. Two masked hooded men stumbled out of the car that had been used with the intent of committing murder and ran for their lives, as far away from the scene as they humanly could.

Detective Constable Isiah Hanson scrambled out of his car, the car that essentially had just saved two lives and raced towards Max and Imogen speaking on his phone as he did so. Lou and his other customers had now left the Italian restaurant, flocking around the figures still in the middle of the road, screaming their horror, asking unanswerable questions whilst filming everything on their mobile phones to post at the earliest possibility, mostly being horrified but thrilled in equal measure that they had witnessed and captured such an event.

All this happening as if in slow motion, with Imogen again at the scene of a road traffic accident, terrified at what lay ahead or what she was again about to lose before she'd barely recognised what she may have actually once again found.

CHAPTER 31

Eddie and Isiah found themselves waiting at the Hallamshire's Accident & Emergency department and once again waiting to hear the fate of one of their own. Eddie had immediately dispatched Dan and Lydia to the scene of the crime, wanting their own to begin collecting any available evidence.

"Jesus Christ Isiah now take me through it again lad," said Eddie.

Isiah, wearing a neck brace due to possible whiplash whilst having his third cup of sweetened tea at his nurse's insistence began. "It's like I said Sarge, I was on my way home and had just picked up a take-away when I saw the boss across the road with Ms Holt. I heard the car tyres screeching before I actually saw the car hit the boss. No attempt to avoid him whatsoever so I drove to get to him to see how bad he was when I realised the car was coming back for a second go and at that point Ms Holt was by his body in the road." Running his hands across his shaved head he continued, "I can't remember thinking, just knew I had to stop that car so I drove into it."

"And you deserve a bloody medal lad because we would be looking at two murder victims if you hadn't! Jesus bloody Christ! It was a hit then and we all know who will have bloody sanctioned it." At that moment the duty doctor appeared as Eddie and Isiah stood, looking at the doctor and fearing the worse.

Putting his hands up to allay their worst fears the doctor began, "Right, you have one extremely lucky colleague in there who is remarkably unscathed to say he's been hit by a car! He's sustained a serious concussion, a couple of broken ribs, a dislocated shoulder and a severely sprained ankle. We're keeping him in overnight, although we'd rather not with Covid, but I'm still concerned about his concussion so we need to monitor it carefully for the next twenty- four hours. I've ordered a CT scan to check there is no bruising or bleeding in his brain and when I'm happy with his balance, coordination, memory and reflexes, we hopefully can get him home the day after tomorrow." Then turning to Isiah he said, "He was very lucky you were there Detective otherwise I dread to think." Nodding both Eddie and Isiah thanked the doctor as they made their way to the exit.

Sitting on the wall outside was Imogen and a WPC. Eddie and Isiah made their way to her with Eddie saying, "I thought I told you to get yourself home Miss."

"Just tell me he's alive," was Imogen's flat emotionless response.

Sighing Eddie nodded saying, "He is and he's remarkably unscathed according to the doctor. He has to stay here tonight but should be allowed home in the next day or two." Imogen's shoulders slumped as the wave of relief washed over her. Looking at Isiah Imogen said, "I believe the Chief Inspector and I owe you our lives Detective. Thank you," and it was at this point Imogen began to shake and the tears came, then just as suddenly she swiped her eyes and stood up saying, "My apologies gentlemen."

"Hey lass, you've had a bit of a shock, a reaction is to be expected," said Eddie as he sat at a respectful distance beside her.

"It would appear I don't have a lot of luck when it comes to accidents involving cars does it?" then sensing their unease she added, "except this wasn't an accident was it Sergeant?"

Eddie just looked steadily at her and said, "I'm not at liberty to comment but I would like you to now allow one of our delightful WPCs to get you home."

When Isiah nudged him Eddie said, "What? Aren't I allowed to call anyone delightful these days either? Bloody hell, what is the world coming to!" Everyone was now smiling, the tension now relieved which was exactly what Eddie had hoped to do at his own expense.

Getting up she nodded and said to Isiah, "Thank you again Detective except it seems such an inadequate thing to say."

Isiah brushed her thanks away saying, "I'm just happy I was there and I'm sorry you had to deal with it. Don't worry, we'll find the low lives."

At that Imogen allowed herself to be taken home.

*

As Imogen was making her way back to Penton, Dan and Lydia had been at the crime scene with a forensic unit, going over the wrecked car with a fine tooth comb. Now back at the station they had learnt that the car had been stolen from the large retail park that resided on the outskirts of Sheffield and would have most probably been set on fire if the perpetrators driving the car had managed to escape in it. CCTV had shown the theft but the thieves had covered their faces making identification impossible.

"With luck they may have been injured because they were going at speed," suggested Lydia.

Nodding his agreement Dan said, "But they won't risk going for medical attention in Sheffield, so let's send uniforms to Rotherham and Barnsley hospitals to see if they've gone there."

"OK. Let's get these phones over to the lab too to see if there's anything on them. Who knows? We could get lucky," said Lydia. All phones from the public who had gathered had been confiscated as potential evidence, much to a certain few members of the public's annoyance. It would be painstaking work but who knew what it could offer in terms of clues to who may have done such a heinous act to one of their own.

It was a relief to see Eddie and Isiah walk into their area, Isiah to the applause of those just beginning the night shift but also to those who had come into work to offer their help and support. Isiah's embarrassment was profound particularly when Lydia hugged him.

"Come on! Enough already," he quipped, thoroughly embarrassed, "let's just find the bastards!"

"Aye lad let's do just that!" agreed Eddie.

CHAPTER 32

Max gradually woke up to the unfamiliar sounds and surroundings of the hospital, with an unbelievable pounding in his head and pain in his chest that made it hard to breath. Blinking hard he was trying to remember what had happened and how he had got here.

An Image of Imogen came into his head and he felt panic now as he wanted to know what had happened, where she was and if she was in one piece. His drawn curtain moved aside to reveal a PPE clad nurse whose nameplate had the name Clare in bold black letters. "Ah finally Chief Inspector, you're awake. Let's see about your vitals then as you've had a good many people worried about you."

"Imogen. Is she hurt?"

"No, she's absolutely fine now she knows you are. I imagine you won't remember much about what happened last night?" Shaking his head but then wishing he hadn't Clare took his hand saying, "Lie still Chief Inspector and I will get the doctor."

“I will need my phone please. I need to call the station.”

At that moment Dr Fraser arrived shaking his head. “Oh no you don’t Chief Inspector. I’m still worried about the state of your concussion so complete rest at least whilst you’re here. Clare, make him do as he’s told as only you can.” The nurse nodded as Max closed his eyes, allowing the natural healing process his body was now demanding, begin to take over.

*

The banging on his back door startled soon to be retired Constable Philip Read out of his deep slumber. Looking at the clock on his bedside table he saw the time to be around 11.30 pm. Raising himself from his bed, he made his way cautiously down the stairs when the banging began again. Now hurrying he went to his back door and peered through the small pane of glass and saw a dark hooded figure leant again the door.

“Who is it?” barked out Philip, now ready to deal with a possible intrusion.

“Dad it’s me, Phil. Let me in.”

“Phil?” Philip exclaimed, totally alarmed now as he began to unbolt the door, taking off the security chain and turning the main door key. His son Phil Read Junior, practically fell into his father’s arms as he lurched forward as the door opened.

“Bloody hell lad! What’s happened? Are you hurt?!”

Nodding Philip’s son allowed his father to help him sit on the nearest kitchen chair, holding his side and dragging his left leg as he did do. His father was now looking at his son and took in what was before him. There was blood coming from some injured part of his body and he was clearly in a great deal of pain.

“What’s happened and why aren’t you going to hospital?”

Shaking his head his son simply said, “Can’t. The hospitals will be the first place they’ll look.”

Now dreading what he may be witnessing, his father said, “Who exactly are ‘they’?”

Grimacing in pain Phil could not look or directly answer his father instead saying, “I need painkillers dad. What have you got?” Philip continued to look at his son, seeing a man in trouble, a man in pain and a man clearly with a great deal to hide. A cold creeping dread began to seep into the pit of his stomach. “What aren’t you telling me Phil. Look at me?!”

Phil found he couldn’t look at his father, couldn’t let his father look back at him. Philip Read took hold of his son’s chin and forced him to look at him. “I repeat! What aren’t you telling me?!”

His son’s face crumpled as his put his head in

his hands. After what seemed like an age he lifted his head and said, "The Police. They'll look at the hospitals first. They'll be looking for two men who were seen running away from a car accident, who may have sustained injuries. That's why we can't go to a hospital because they are looking for me and Ian, my partner."

Philip was processing what his son was now saying but could not fully understand why his son was saying what he was hearing. "What the bloody hell are you talking about? If you've been in an accident, you go through the correct procedure for Christ's sake! You can't just pretend nothing..."

Interrupting his father young Phil, his father's pride and joy now proceeded to destroy all his father had always held dear. Wild eyed with his voice at fever pitch his son was now hysterical. "For Christ sake's dad, don't you get it!? I'm in trouble! I've messed up big time! If they find me they'll throw the sodding key away which is why I'm here. You've got to help me dad because I don't know what to do," as he began to sob.

Philip his father then went on autopilot and proceeded to fetch water and paracetamol, two whisky tumblers and a bottle of his finest Glenallachie single malt whiskey. Then sitting down his father looked at him and quietly ordered, "Tell me exactly what you've done son. What you have exactly got yourself into and leave nothing out ok?"

Nodding Detective Constable Phil Read currently working in the Vice Division took several of the pills now offered and drank deeply from the glass of water. He downed the poured whisky in one gulp and then he began.

"It started about eighteen months ago. It was just the odd bit of cash from the drug hauls to begin with, then accepting the odd 'gift' here and there from a few of our regulars to turn a blind eye."

Seeing his father's face Phil was now growing angry saying, "For fuck's sake dad! How did you think I was paying for Laura's sodding lifestyle eh? The house, the holidays? The kids' bloody private schools?! On my salary? Where did you think the bloody money was coming from eh?!"

Looking at his father's granite like features, he sighed heavily, then continued. "Then we got approached by the big guy and now we're in such deep shit. There's no way out," as he poured himself more whisky drinking it down in one once again.

"Big guy?" queried his father.

"Don't ask dad because he's the last man you need to get on the wrong side of."

Shaking his head Philip growled, "No two bit thug scares me lad!"

Shaking his head Phil his son sadly said, "Dad please, I'm not talking about a criminal!"

"Who then?" then the answer now started to dawn. "Jesus." Neither spoke for some time, both looking for different answers to what was essentially the same problem. For Philip Read Senior though, it was as if all he knew or thought he knew and believed no longer existed. Looking at his son Philip now asked the question uppermost on his mind. "So what happened tonight? How come you're so injured?"

Looking down and to his credit, looking ashamed Phil simply replied, "Was ordered to take out someone but it didn't go as planned."

The silence in the kitchen was almost eerie as Philip Read Senior looked at his son with a look close to horror on his face. Then standing up, he towered over his now quaking son who knew what that look meant, knew how devastated he had made his father. "Are you telling me you were ordered to kill someone and you attempted to do it? Are you telling me that my son, my pride and joy is nothing better than a bloody scum of the earth murdering gangster? Is that what you're telling me?" His father's voice was no more than a whisper but its effect on Phil was palpable and he had no answer, no response. "So which poor sod were you ordered to kill then?"

Sighing heavily then wincing in pain his son simply said, "The London cop I told you about. Max Stainmore."

Philip slumped down on the chair he had

moments earlier vacated. "Oh no lad, not another copper, not one of our own."

"I didn't want to do it dad I swear, neither of us did but we were given no choice. You've no idea what they're capable of, what 'G Man' is capable of."

"'G Man'?" repeated Philip now finding he could barely breathe.

"Once they get you, once they have something on you then they show no mercy dad. You just have to go along with whatever they ask no matter how terrible."

Shaking his head Philip replied angrily, "Well, when you lie with dogs what do you bloody expect? A police officer? One of our own? I don't bloody believe this." Philip was now pacing the room, his anger such that he really didn't know what to do next. His son was now looking at his father and pleading with him, pleading for his life in many respects. "Dad I know how badly I've fucked up. I know how disappointed you are..."

"Disappointed!" exploded his father, "this is not me reading you could work harder on your bloody school report! You have attempted to murder someone, another human being despite who he is. Who the bloody hell are you?"

Looking down before slugging down his third shot of whiskey Phil simply said, "Think about the kids dad, your grandkids. They need their dad and I can't do time either dad, you know what happens to coppers in prison. I am your son and I need your help."

Sighing heavily as he slumped onto his chair, his father replied, "Yes you are and yes you do. I'm just glad your mother's not alive to see this." Looking at his son now, Philip could see the effect the whisky, paracetamol and the evening's adrenaline was having on him. Rising from his seat he gently pulled his son up and held him close before steering him into the living room and onto the sofa. Phil was now out for the count as his father covered him with a throw, making sure he was warm as all parents do when dealing with their young.

He then looked around the room his gaze falling on the selection of pictures he and his late wife had displayed with such pride. His son in his first uniform, each holding their grandchildren, their wedding photographs, christenings, wonderful Christmas days. All of it seemed like a sham now. He picked up a photograph of his deceased wife Linda and found he was crying.

"We never really liked her did we lass?" referencing his daughter in law with her blonde hair extensions, fake tan and desire for a lifestyle that had tempted his son to perform criminal acts, although that was no excuse. We all have choices to make in life, choices that must always be owned. Philip senior understood this and he knew his son now only had one choice and he would make it for him.

Moving back to the kitchen Philip Read picked up his phone and went into his contacts then waited for the connection. "Eddie? Philip Read here. You and your people need to get to my house as soon as possible. I have who you're looking for, one of them any road and he needs an ambulance too."

CHAPTER 33

Max had been finally allowed home. His broken ribs were gradually knitting together, his dislocated shoulder painfully put back in place but the fact his doctor was now happy that he had not sustained a serious brain injury had allowed him to be discharged. Eddie, Dan, Isiah and Lydia had been to the apartment, making sure he had food and all the pain meds he needed within easy access. They had also apprised him of recent developments, namely the arrest of Detective Constables Phil Read and Ian Wharton, both of the Vice Squad. Eddie relayed the events of the night Max had been injured. "My old mucker Philip Read Senior rang me and told me that his son and partner were basically who we were looking for. His boy had gone to his dad's as he was badly injured and hoped his dad would somehow help him get away with it, but he should have known better. They don't get much straighter or better than Constable Read."

Remembering meeting him only a few weeks ago on his solitary late night walk in the City centre

Max asked, “So what have they said?”

“Not a bloody dicky bird,” answered Isiah, “they’re scared, that’s for sure. IPCC involved now.”

“Where are they now?” asked Max.

“The Northern General under police guard whilst their injuries are dealt with,” answered Lydia, “before being transferred to a nick in Nottingham.” They had all been fairly shaken when they had discovered fellow police officers had been involved in the attempted murder of their boss and the protectiveness they felt towards him was now palpable. They didn’t want to leave him alone and they had made this very clear.

“Are you sure you’re going to be ok?” asked Eddie.

“We can take it in shifts?” Dan had offered.

“I’m happy to stay,” said Isiah.

They had not wanted to leave him but Max had insisted. Although touched at their concern he was itching for them to get back to the investigation. If he couldn’t physically do so himself, he wanted his team there as this had just got even more personal for him. “Thanks but no because I really want you all back on the job. I’m fine thanks to Isiah here but although we have the scum who did this we need the even bigger scum who ordered it. Ok?” So it was with real reluctance that they had eventually left.

It wasn't long after they had left the apartment that he heard his doorbell go. Scowling because he really did need to sleep, he made his way to his door, looked through the peephole only to see the last person he expected. Opening the door Imogen stood there before him. She took in his grazed bruised face, the stick he needed to walk with, the obvious pain he was in and she found herself walking forward and wrapping her arms around him without saying a word. Max dropped his stick automatically folding his arms around her, breathing in her scent and closing his eyes, only letting his hold loosen when the pain in his ribs made him wince and pull away.

Smiling through his obvious pain Max smiled saying, "So now you decide to throw yourself into my arms and I'm in this state." Imogen tried to smile back but found she couldn't. Looking away she felt his hand take her chin as he gently forced her to meet his eyes as he said, "Hey, I'm ok. It looks worse than it is honest. I've had worse, much worse."

They had managed to get back to the sofa, with Imogen saying "Someone tried to kill you Max. How much worse can that get?"

"It's the job and I'm clearly upsetting the people I'm trying to upset." He then drew her into his arms, as it seemed the most natural thing to do as Imogen gingerly allowed herself to rest her head on his uninjured shoulder, both lost in their own thoughts for a while each reliving what had happened with Max knowing it was bringing back painful memories for her and that made him feel inexplicably guilty. Looking at him she said, "Stop it."

"Stop what?"

"Feeling guilty that I was there. How were you to know?"

Smiling at her perceptiveness he said, "You're pretty smart aren't you?"

"Perhaps you're just too easy a book to read. Now do you need anything?"

"Oh I can think of one or two things that would do me the world of good," grinning as he said so.

Smiling she said wryly, "As if with your injuries, but I was thinking pain meds or food?"

Touching her hair and placing one loose strand behind her ear Max answered, "I've got everything I need thanks, especially this very moment." Looking at him and seeing his tenderness as well as his vulnerability, Imogen leaned forward and very gently kissed him. As the kiss deepened, it was with reluctance she moved away whilst she still could. "I need to go."

"Must you?"

"You know I do and I'm not sure if this should be happening considering the circumstances Max. Aren't there rules about this sort of thing?"

"Yes and ask me if I care," as he found her lips again. The sudden mutual explosion of passion surprised them both. Imogen had not been thoroughly kissed for a very long time and for Max's part, he hadn't really wanted or needed to thoroughly kiss anyone in a very long time too. As their kiss deepened Imogen's arms, as if by their own volition found their way around his neck, clutching his hair, soft moans escaping from her mouth. As electric moments passed Max was the first to speak, "Well, who knew that was on the cards?"

Shaking, Imogen pulled back only for Max to pull her again into his arms but Imogen was now shaking her head saying, "No Max, this can't happen."

"Why? It's clearly what we both want," as Max pulled her forward, kissing her again, this time with more passion until the pain in his ribs and shoulder made him pull back allowing Imogen to move away from him.

"You have just been hit by a car if you remember so with the greatest respect you're not up to misbehaving any further," smiled Imogen, attempting at levity although to be fair, she felt as shaken by their mutual passion too. So she now retrieved a blanket, fetched more water and gave him the pain medication he was in such obvious need of, plumping up cushions, making him as comfortable as possible. It struck

Max then. "You're good at this, helping others I mean."

Nodding Imogen shrugged then looked at him softly saying, "It's what I do Max, what I've always done."

"Promise me we can resume this when I'm less broken?"

Walking to the door, she turned to look at him, smiled sadly and said, "This can't happen again Max," and with that she left. Max felt the apartment was suddenly very empty and he was surprised that he found himself missing her already. He also knew that his initial instincts had always been right where Imogen and her friends were concerned. Imogen cared and protected those she loved and he was now hoping upon hope that her natural instincts had not been misplaced or at worse, been taken advantage of.

Walking to her car Imogen acknowledged how seeing him so badly hurt had affected her and that after all her time alone, she was actually being drawn to the one man who could actually take away her very own freedom. What was it that Shakespeare wrote about "tangled webs being weaved"? They didn't get much more tangled than this she surmised sadly as she drove away.

CHAPTER 34

As the days passed Cameron Sheldon was becoming a very unhappy man. He had learnt that Max had been injured but not actually dead and heads were now going to roll but especially one.

"When I issue an order I expect it to be successfully carried out," he was saying into his phone then listening to the excuses he merely uttered, "then sort it! You have twenty- four hours!"

He still had no idea where Grant was or why he had disappeared along with his money but he was hoping he was dead though, as he clearly had betrayed him and no one did that, not ever.

Unbeknownst to Sheldon however, his day would be going from bad to worse because at the moment he was issuing his latest threat, his septic tank was being emptied. However, the septic tank company had encountered a very unpleasant surprise that morning, the discovery of a very badly decomposing body. They had rung the police immediately who had arrived within thirty minutes of the call.

Eddie was already there at Sheldon's house when a limping Max arrived, complete with his walking stick and a body pumped full of pain medication. "What the bloody hell do you think you're doing and how the bloody hell did you know to be here? You should still be recuperating! The doctor ordered bed rest! I was there!"

Max waved away Eddie's concerns smilingly saying, "I'm okay dad, honest. Isiah told me and don't shoot the messenger. So, do you think it's Downs?"

"We can hope," said Eddie still exasperated with Max's appearance at the crime scene as they moved towards the body that was being zipped up. Max really did look like hell and Eddie was simultaneously worried about him whilst being secretly pleased to have him back on the job.

"It appears the[N3] Medical Examiner has discovered evidence of stab wounds and something else that had been lodged in the body's mouth. A Cayman Islands bank receipt for over seven million Euros payable to a Mr Grant Downs," announced Eddie to a very surprised Max.

Max whistled softly.

"Can today get any better boss? Could it be this easy?"

Shaking his head, Max said, "When something

looks too good to be true it usually is. Come on let's get back to Central but let's ruin Sheldon's day and have him picked up."

As Dan and Isiah approached Max said, "You two. Take some officers and go through the house and any out buildings with a fine tooth comb. Let's see what else our Mr Sheldon could be hiding whilst we're here."

Grinning Isiah said, "Would be rude not to and it's great to have you back Sir."

*

Across the city Malcolm Speight was being informed of Sheldon's imminent arrest. Eddie and Albert were well pleased and said so. "Worked like a charm boss. They must have him bang to rights now!" crowed Eddie.

"We can hope so although I'm worried that it might look a little too smooth, too good to be true for the London cop. From all accounts he's no fool," frowned Malcolm, "despite his recent bang to the head."

"He's lucky to be alive by all accounts," said Eddie adding, "and I'm glad our little lady was unscathed because that would have been a shame."

"Aye you're not wrong there," replied Malcolm who had been more than upset to hear our close Imogen had come to experiencing another fatal road accident.

"Won't matter how smooth it looks if the rest of the plan works though boss," said Albert always the optimist even in his line of work. He looked at his two men, his stalwarts whose opinions he valued.

"No Albert it won't so fingers crossed for just a bit longer then eh lads."

*

The only way to identify Grant Downs had been via his dental records such had been the three weeks of decomposition and the amount of time his body had been immersed in the septic tank. His injuries had been identified as excessive stabs wounds plus certain minor amputations, an obvious signature of a one Cameron Sheldon. So cause of death was pronounced as the fatal stabbing of key organs plus an excessive loss of blood. It was at this stage hard to ascertain just exactly how long he had been dead.

Dan and Isiah with Beth as support went to see Sarah to break the news to her that his body had been found and identified. "We're very sorry Mrs Downs but I think you were already aware that it was a remote chance that we would find your husband alive," said Isiah.

"Do you know how he died?"

"We believe he was stabbed." Sarah paled and Beth quickly interjected, "Try not to think of the details Sarah. You've already been through so much," as Beth was now worried Sarah would confess all.

"Beth's right, so it may be time to put all of this behind you," said Dan.

"It feels like a long dreadful nightmare," whispered Sarah, "and I seem to spend the whole of my life crying these days."

"You've had plenty to cry about but better days are ahead my friend. At least you know now love." Looking at her colleagues Beth then added, "I suggest we leave Sarah to it chaps if that's ok?"

Nodding Isiah said, "Agreed. Take care and we will let you know when the body can be released and you can then make the necessary arrangements." After they had left, Sarah rang Imogen.

"Imogen? It's me Sarah. Apparently Grant's body has been found. No they didn't say where just that I would be able to make arrangements very soon. No I'm ok. I'll let Harry know. Ok. See you soon."

As she disconnected she then left a message for Harry. She had missed Harry but understood the reason she had had to stay away and keep her distance. Now Sarah finally felt she had a way forward, a future even if she didn't really deserve one. After all she was responsible for killing someone, albeit a monstrous someone, but a living breathing human being nonetheless. Can that ever be right? Can that ever be forgiven?

*

Sheldon smirked as Max limped into the interview room. "Been in the wars I see Chief Inspector," he had laughed.

Ignoring him Max began, "Seems your septic tank held more than the usual filth even by your standards Sheldon."

"Oh yeah. Pray tell me more?" was the sneering response.

"A body. A body we believe to be that of a Mr Grant Downs," finished Eddie.

Sheldon's complete surprise and consternation at what they had just said to him were not lost on either Max or Eddie. "You have got to be kidding me! Grant's body in my septic tank?!" Sitting back in the chair clearly shocked, he soon recovered and his habitual sneer came back with a vengeance.

"So which one's Ant and which one's Dec then eh? Because if you think you can make this stick then you're bigger bloody comedians than I took you for. As if I'd be that fucking stupid! Muppets!"

At this point his very expensive Barrister spoke, "My client is stipulating Chief Inspector that he has no knowledge what the contents of his septic tank were and that others would have access to it."

Max then produced the off shore account cheque and moved it across the table. “For the purpose of this tape, Mr Sheldon is being shown an off shore banker’s cheque found on the deceased for a significant amount of money. We believe the account to be yours.”

“Believe all you want, try proving it!”

“Again my client has no knowledge of such a transaction. Have you any actual evidence Chief Inspector?”

Max was always amazed at the continual dance played out in Interview rooms across every police station in the country and for once wished the cards were stacked differently. “We have enough to hold you whilst we continue with our enquiries Mr Sheldon and we intend to exercise that right particularly given your trespass on Mrs Downs property and your clear intent to cause her bodily harm.”

“Again prove it!” was the snarled response.

This time it was Eddie turn to smirk saying, “Your own ‘Muppets’ didn’t enjoy a taste of their own medicine and some are singing like the proverbial canaries, so no worries on that front mate.”

Sheldon looked at his Barrister who shook his head. “I wonder why I bloody bother,” was his exasperated comment. Looking at Max now Sheldon began, despite his Barrister indicating that he should be quiet.

“Why would I do Grant Downs? We were business partners and business is good gentlemen, better than good, positively booming!”

“And what business would that be?”

“My business Chief Inspector. I am being set up and I hope you find out who is doing it before I do!”

“Are you making threats now Cameron?” asked Eddie.

“No I’m making promises Detective Sergeant and I am Mr Sheldon to you and don’t you ever forget it MATE!”

CHAPTER 34

Former Police Constable Phil Read of the Vice Division was in the process of leaving the Northern General hospital. He still was reeling from the fact his father had turned him in and he now feared what the future would hold for not just himself, but for his family too. He was currently being visited by Sergeant Eddie Sinclair, the officer who had arrested him and who was also an old friend of his father's whose complete disgust for the man lying in the bed was not being disguised in the least.

"We need to know who ordered the hit so if there's any decency left in you, then I suggest you begin to spill your guts now!"

"You have no idea who you're dealing with," Phil had countered.

"I know I'm dealing with a corrupt piece of rubbish that has just broken his father's heart."

"Oh yeah, the same father that betrayed me," was Phil's response, "although what should I have expected. Bloody too good to be true, holier than thow..."

"Don't you bloody dare! Don't you bloody dare speak ill of your father because there's not a better man walking and you know it! We need answers from you or from your mate, I don't care which one turns first but answers we need and answers I intend to get one way or another!" Eddie sat back in the hospital visitor's chair waiting.

Phil didn't respond for some time, then eventually said, "I have conditions. If they are met, then I will tell you everything. Its dynamite so my family, including my father will need to be in witness protection and I will need protection. Sort that and I will tell you everything but not until I know they are all safe."

Nodding Eddie got up to leave only turning back to the injured man in the bed when he said, "Why did dad stay on the beat? Everyone says he could have gone up in the ranks as far as anyone. Was practically bloody begged to or so I've been told, but instead he chooses to walk the beat for all these years, even before I was born. Why?"

Eddie thought for moment, then simply replied, "Because your father is incorruptible and because he chose to be in a place where he felt he would do the most good, where he thought he would be most needed. He was right and I wish there were more like him and it's a sodding crying shame you even had to ask," and with that, sadly shaking his head Eddie left the room.

*

Meanwhile, Malcolm Speight was looking at the man he had crossed over to West Yorkshire to see. Anthony Dolan was a man who looked like he had visited a place called Hell and had been unable to find his way home. Now a resident of Wakefield High Security Prison he was looking at Malcolm with great suspicion.

"Thanks for agreeing to see me Mr Dolan."

Anthony Dolan was naturally and immediately suspicious. He had earned respect in prison the hard way and was unused to politeness unless it was forced. Eyeing the man before him he took in the loud pinstriped suit, the overpowering aftershave and the slicked back greying hair. "What do you want?"

"I have a proposition for you."

"Not interested."

"Oh but you will be. How badly do you want to make Sheldon pay for what he did to your grandson?"

Anthony Dolan changed before his very eyes at the mere mention of Sheldon's name. He nor Malcolm spoke for several minutes with neither man breaking eye contact with the other. Finally, he said, "Sheldon is a fucking monster. I would give my life to make him pay."

"I'm hoping that won't be necessary, as if all goes as it should Cameron Sheldon will very soon be on remand in this nick. My associates and I have our people in here who will make sure you get some alone time with Sheldon for a significant amount of time. I have been asked that he suffers an immense amount of pain and eventually he will need to die but only when he is totally broken and prepared to do as he's told. Can I be assured you can offer this service?"

Smiling now Anthony Dolan merely nodded saying, "How can I ever repay you?"

Malcolm leaned back in his chair and smiling benignly said, "My pleasure Mr Dolan, my pleasure."

CHAPTER 36

Chief Constable Jim Haggerty looked at the assembled colleagues before him and knew what was coming. Max was flanked by Detective Constable Lydia Smith and Police Constable Beth Fletcher with the Police Federation representative Bob Smeaton seated on their left. Superintendent Giles Baker was seated on the right of his desk with his customary supercilious sneer firmly in place. Looking at him Max couldn't wait to wipe the sneer metaphorically off his arrogant self- entitled face.

"So Chief Inspector," began Jim Haggerty, "you have requested this meeting as a matter of urgency. Would you like to begin?"

Before Max could speak Giles Baker jumped in saying, "May I say and may I have it put on record Chief Constable that I am extremely unhappy that I have been summarily called to a meeting without prior knowledge to what the content or purpose of this meeting could possibly be about thereby being unprepared."

Max leaned back in his chair, folded his arms

then said, "Finished?"

Giles Baker looking surprised at Max replied, "Well yes but I'm very unimpressed with the manner in which you seem to think is appropriate towards a senior officer Chief Inspector!"

"And I'm more than unimpressed but downright disgusted that a senior officer has taken it upon himself to bully and threaten junior officers to change a legitimate report in order for that senior officer to curry favour. Then for that same officer to throw a junior officer under the proverbial bus, whilst threatening a second junior officer who wished to come forward with the truth, when his actions and his actions alone resulted in not one but two fatalities."

The stunned silence that followed went on for seemingly forever but was less than a minute in reality. Max's gaze of utter contempt was pinning Giles Baker to his very chair and the man for once looked completely poleaxed. Then recovering he began to splutter, "This is outrageous. Chief Constable I…"

Waving his hand Jim Haggerty turned to Lydia Smith asking, "I've read your statement Detective Constable Smith. Is this a true and accurate account of the facts pertaining to the deaths of Mr Richard Black and his daughter Mrs Helen Spencer?"

Taking a huge breath Lydia nodded and began. "I approached Superintendent Baker to withdraw my statement pertaining to my disagreement with Detective Constable Fletcher's version of events. I had initially allowed myself to be swayed by the Superintendent's rank and thought agreeing to change my statement would not be harmful. My colleague Detective Constable Fletcher was rightly upset with me and understandably angry but I had thought the Superintendent was probably in possession of facts I was unaware of. When the fatalities occurred and it was then evident that Beth, sorry Detective Constable Fletcher was going to be blamed I approached Superintendent Baker to change my statement but he refused, telling me, no threatening me with dismissal, even criminal prosecution. I am ashamed to say that I allowed myself to be bullied, thus allowing my colleague and my friend to take full blame for something she had worked so hard to avoid. I am ashamed and I want it on the record that I wish to fully and unreservedly apologise to her for my cowardice in this matter and that now it is timely that I put the record straight and take on board any disciplinary consequences for my actions."

Giles Baker was now practically apoplectic shouting, "This is completely preposterous. How dare you suggest that I..."

Jim Haggerty held up his hand and said, "Thank you Detective Smith. I fully appreciate what it must have taken for you to come here today and saying what you have clearly needed to say for a very long time. Bob may I thank you for your presence and we can perhaps meet later on to finalise where we will be going next?" as Bob Smeaton nodded Jim Haggerty continued, "Constable Fletcher may I extend to you my personal apologies that you have been so unfairly treated by those who should have known better. I can assure you that all records will now be put straight expunging any suggestion of your culpability in the Black/ Spencer case. That will be all. Chief Inspector please remain."

Beth had not spoken a word but was clearly in a profound state of shock as Lydia touched her shoulder gesturing that they were to leave. As they made their way down the top floor corridor Beth turned to Lydia. "What the bloody hell just happened in there?"

"Something that should have happened a long time ago. I'm so sorry I wasn't braver, so sorry I let you down."

"Well I think you may have just made up for it mate!"

Lydia blinked then said, "Am I? Can I be again? Your mate that is because God knows how much I've missed you."

Beth stood there looking at Lydia and said, "You are a bloody goody two shoes and I'm always the bloody bull in the proverbial china shop but we both could have done better and I for one have missed you too. So Covid or not come here," and at that Beth threw her arms around a relieved Lydia who hugged her right back.

Back in Jim Haggerty's office Giles Baker was now a very silent and very worried man. Jim was also silent instead reading a number of papers that were on his desk. Eventually he looked up and began, "So would you like to know what I'm reading?" Giles slowly nodded as Jim continued, "more than one suggestion that you have on occasions asked junior officers, or should I say, junior female officers to change reports that you have found, what's the word, inconvenient."

When Giles did not respond Jim looked at him with something close to contempt. Turning to Max Jim asked, "So Chief Inspector I believe you have something else on your mind for Superintendent Baker to ponder. Over to you."

Giles Baker could not look at Max but head down he was now waiting for what, he dare not think. Max began, "So soon not to be Superintendent Giles, because even you won't be stupid enough to think you will get away with this kind of out dated abuse of power. Men like you will always give the rest of us an uphill struggle to fully have the public trust and for what? What is it you gained? Money? No I bet you just needed to lord it over the rest of the sycophants who believe it's who you know not what hard graft can achieve. Eh? Am I right?"

Giles remained silent but now looking at Max with undisguised loathing. Max now leaned forward, "Someone in this building was told by Cameron Sheldon to take me out and my money is on you. So am I right or am I right?"

All colour drained for Giles Baker's face as he now shaking his head said, "You're right about how I have abused my position, about the Black/ Spencer debacle, how I liked to make the odd speeding ticket disappear. Yes guilty as charged, but to collude in the killing of a police officer, even one I can't stand the sight of? No. I'm not that stupid or that brave. You need to look elsewhere because I am not your man."

Jim Haggerty nodded his head and said, "Have your resignation on my desk by the end of the day. Understood? I will be discussing the nature of criminal proceedings which are to be presented to the CPS in due course. You will of course be allowed access to Federation and legal representation as is your right but if I have my way you will lose your pension and never be able to work in Law Enforcement again or even step foot inside a police station unless it is to lock you up and throw away the key. Now get out!"

Nodding Giles Baker, now a broken shadow of the

man he was when he had first entered the Chief Constable's office only an hour earlier, merely nodded as he stood up and made his way out to enter the office he had always been so proud to occupy, for what would be his very last time.

Watching his departure Jim turned to Max and said, "Do you believe him?"

Max nodded and replied, "Unfortunately I do. He's not brave enough or the type to get into 'bed' with the likes of Sheldon.

Nodding grimly Jim concurred saying, "Which means we still have a 'fox in our very own hen house' and he or she needs flushing out pronto!"

"A rattled fox who will be even more dangerous now," concurred Max.

Sighing heavily Jim said, "Watch yourself! For God's sake be careful and watch yourself."

CHAPTER 37

Sarah was sitting wondering what to do next. She had just been informed that Grant's body could now be released for his funeral and she was at a loss. She wanted nothing to do with it, didn't want to attend it herself if she was honest. Who would apart from the low- lives and gangsters that it appeared were Grant's basic associates? She was thinking what would happen if she refused to take responsibility for the body? Surely that must happen? What happened to the homeless or the missing? Those who had no families to claim them? Grant was not her family and she just didn't want him, not after everything he had brought to her door and into her life.

Her thought process was interrupted by the ringing of her door bell. Scooby and Cecil did their customary warning welcome barks, as she made her way to her front door, wondering who it could be with that little dread of worry she always had these days settling in the pit of her stomach.

Sarah took in the dark haired, well dressed, middle aged, very attractive but slightly familiar woman standing on her doorstep. Sarah waited for the woman to speak, but the older woman just stared at Sarah saying nothing. Eventually Sarah broke the silence. "Can I help you?"

Still staring at Sarah the woman replied, "I've come for my boy."

Sarah knew immediately that she was looking at Grant's mother. As the two women stared at each other Sarah was the first to make a move. "Mrs Downs, you'd better come in."

"Thornton," replied the other woman who had still not moved despite Sarah's invitation, "my name is Thornton. My son was Samuel Thornton and I've come to take him home."

Shaking her head sadly Sarah said, "So even my name is a lie like everything else since the first day I met your son." Lorraine Thornton just continued to stare, her stance tall, her body language proud then as if a switch had been flicked she simply crumpled and would have collapsed if Sarah hadn't caught her in her arms. Manoeuvring them both towards the nearest seating, Sarah sat this stranger down, then sitting beside her took her hands saying gently, "Hello Mrs Thornton, my name is Sarah and I believe I was married to your son. I'm very sorry for your loss."

Lorraine Thornton blinked at Sarah then said, "After all he would have done to you and you have the grace to say such a thing." Then the deluge, the torrent of grief and regret and yes shame poured out of this woman, this stranger who was now sobbing uncontrollably in Sarah's arms. After what seemed an age the sobbing subsided allowing Sarah to fetch Lorraine Thornton a hefty measure of brandy.

Sipping the soothing liquid amber she began to speak. "He was the most beautiful baby. I couldn't go anywhere without people being wowed at his face. It was the same as he got older, even the teenage years when others had acne or had 'puppy fat' my Sam always looked like he was ready to be photographed for a magazine. But from an early age I knew he was different, I knew what his looks were hiding. He was cruel but I bet you know this already." As Sarah nodded, she continued, "He was cruel and he enjoyed the pain cruelty would give to a small animal or a small child. When other parents would beat a path to our door with their accusations, me and my husband Ken just dismissed it, saying it wasn't possible. I mean just look at him I would say as Sam would be stood looking like an angel with a tear sliding down his beautiful face as if on cue. His sisters knew though, had seen it and suffered it too. Then the trouble with the police began, running with gangs, Young Offenders then proper Prison. It was a relief when he left us."

Sarah took her hand, "But he was your son and you are now in mourning, despite what he became."

Lorraine shook her head saying, "I believe he was born bad, it was in him from his first breath because there's no other explanation. But you're right, he was my baby, my beautiful little boy and I loved him with every beat of my heart despite everything he did but be happy you never had his child. His wickedness needed to die with him." Then looking at Sarah she asked, "Did he tell you we were dead?"

When Sarah nodded Lorraine laughed without humour saying, "Boating accident in the South of France or the skiing accident in the Italian Alps?"

"Boating accident," whispered Sarah whose heart was slowly breaking for this poor woman sitting beside her.

"Yes and those good looks got you didn't they?"

"Got my parents. Grant, sorry, your son was everything they thought they wanted for me. My dad was eventually getting his measure but died before he could do anything and then ... well he just took over and well... I was scared of him in the end."

"Are you glad he's dead?"

Sarah couldn't look at her, at this mother but then she heard Lorraine Thornton whisper, "Because may God forgive me but I'm glad he's dead. He nigh on killed his dad, my Ken, died of a broken heart or shame or both. Do we know how he died?"

"Death by stabbing but the police don't as yet know who's responsible," was Sarah's reply now unable to look at her.

Then both women were holding each other and Sarah at this point felt such an overwhelming sadness for both of them, for what both of them had suffered at the hands of the same man. "So," ventured Sarah, "his funeral?"

"Which is why I'm here. With your permission I would like to take him home. I gave birth to him and I think it is fitting that I lay him to rest."

Nodding Sarah said, "Thank you Mrs Thornton."

Lorraine Thornton looked at Sarah and was now smiling kindly saying, "You're a pretty little thing aren't you and look at this place? Very different from the poky East London flat we all lived in when the kids were small until we managed to move out as the kids grew older. Got a small place in Kent now."

Sarah nodded but Lorraine hadn't finished, "You're good too, I can tell and Sam would have sensed that. He could spot a good soul a mile away and he would then exploit that goodness until it was sapped out of a person leaving nothing but an empty shell. I'm glad that hasn't happened to you."

"It nearly did."

"Then you've had a lucky escape." Getting up to leave she said, "So will you arrange for me to have the body?"

"Of course and again, I am very sorry for your loss." Nodding, Loraine Thornton got to her feet and began to take her leave then looking at Sarah said with sadness in her voice, "I would have loved to have had you as my son's wife, a daughter- in- law. I think we would have been friends."

Nodding Sarah embraced Lorraine Thornton for a final time saying, "I think so too. Goodbye Mrs Thornton and take care."

"Goodbye Mrs Thornton. Please have a good life now."

When Sarah closed her door she found herself feeling unbearably sad and once again unbearable guilty.

CHAPTER 38

Cameron Sheldon was a man who knew the score. He knew they had him for the attempt on Sarah but Grant's body found on his property could be explained away as circumstantial and most juries were gullible enough to find reasonable doubt wherever. He always found it amusing how the ordinary man or woman in the street would prefer to think the best of people and they of course made up juries and he could always find a way in with a couple of those on a jury too if necessary.

He also paid enough in Barrister fees to ensure he received as minimum a sentence as possible and he could get lucky with the presiding judge as he had a few of those in his pocket too. He knew he would have to lay low for a while, do a little time, but he had enough people on his payroll to weather this and enough people on the inside to make his life as comfortable as possible. So Cameron Sheldon became the latest on remand at HMP Wakefield until the date of his trial. It was the day Anthony Dolan, another Wakefield inmate, had been hoping and praying for ever since Malcolm Speight had come visiting.

There are many things a man may survive, but the guilt you feel every day, that your actions, your decisions maimed your only grandchild is one that eats away at your very soul to the point that life becomes meaningless. Anthony Dolan knew the Dover transport from Zeebrugge had illegal contraband but never in all of his wildest nightmares did he believe his cargo to be human and dead human cargo at that. He was prepared to do his time but Sheldon needed to pay too and he had made that clear. What Sheldon had personally done to his three- year old grandson was something that kept Dolan awake, something that was sending him slowly insane. So when Anthony Dolan was visited by Malcolm Speight it was like he had won the lottery.

Sheldon had been on remand three days and was feeling his feet. His cell door was open as were all cell doors so he wasn't particularly surprised when a man he did not know entered the small room.

Looking up Cameron took in the size of the man and snarled, "So who the fuck are you and who said you could come in here?"

"Message for you."

"Who from?"

"Someone who matters."

His interest now piqued Cameron got to his feet and sauntered towards the man who when closer he had to look up significantly, such was the height and width of the man. Not wanting to show any sign of intimidation Cameron belligerently repeated, "I said who from?"

Ignoring him the messenger said, "Be in the laundry room in fifteen minutes. It's in your best interests," and with that he left.

Cameron did not know what to think but knew he had enough kudos to know he would not be in any particular danger but sensed a possible business opportunity. Intrigued Cameron made his way to the designated place, surprised how quiet it was and how few people were around. Walking round a corner, he heard the door behind him close and then the unmistakable sound of the door being locked. Cameron Sheldon was not a man accustomed to feeling vulnerable but he instinctively knew he was and also that he was not alone.

"Long time no see," said a voice.

"Who's there?"

"No one to bother about, just someone who used to work for you. Someone who did your shitty dirty work for you, just one of many," said Anthony Dolan as he came round the corner and into view. It took a moment for Sheldon to register who the man before him was. Anthony

Dolan had bulked up whilst being inside, taking his impotent fury and rage out of the machines and weights available to him. He now had scars, tattoos and a hardness in his eyes and jaw that suggested a barely concealed rage, no longer being the mild mannered driver who used to work for him. Then it hit Cameron why he was here and he had some idea what was going to happen but at this point was still not particularly worried replying, "Long time no see Dolan and I see prison has changed you somewhat."

"Is that the best you've got?"

"What do you want me to say? What is this? Do you think you're going to extract some sort of revenge? On me?" Cameron laughed still confident in his superiority, his perceived sense of importance.

Anthony Dolan remained silent, staring unblinkingly at the man, this monster disguising himself as a man before him. The silence was now making Cameron uncomfortable so as always he took the initiative.

"You know you were to blame for what I had to do? I'm a business man and you were about to spill your guts so you left me no choice but you have a choice now because I'm a reasonable man. Whatever it is you're planning you need to think. Really think. Walk away and I will forget this ever happened. Ok? I mean I wouldn't want to have to order another visit to your daughter and her son would I?"

"Are you threatening me?"

"No just saving you and your family from yourself."

Anthony pretended to consider this proposition, then shook his head. "Actually, I've had a much better offer from, how can I put it? A kind benefactor who will ensure my grandson and my daughter never want for anything for the rest of their lives and will be in a place you and your thugs can never find them. No, I've been thinking about this for a very long time. What would be the best form of revenge to take out on a man such as yourself? A man who enjoys hurting others, who never feels pity or shame? A man who believes he can do whatever he wants to anyone he wants sometimes just because he can." At this point Anthony Dolan revealed the very sharp, and very deadly shiv that he was holding behind him.

Eyeing the weapon Sheldon suddenly realised he was actually in trouble and that the man before him was not a man he could reason with. "Killing me won't be the answer."

Anthony began to laugh saying, "Oh dear me Mr Sheldon, I'm not going to kill you, not at all," as he slowly but deliberately moved forward. Cameron swung at Dolan, giving him the opportunity to grab his arm and forcing it up his back forcing Cameron to his knees, screaming in pain as he did so. Grabbing him by the neck Dolan deftly tied his hands in front of him then stuffed a cloth rag in his mouth. "I'm going to take some time now and I'm fairly certain you're going to be in excruciating pain made worse as you'll not be able to scream or so I've read. I really hope that you let my little Ollie scream because as you will remember when you did what you did, he was barely three years old bless him. You know I can sometimes hear his screams particularly when I sleep so I don't sleep any more. Perhaps I will after today? What do you think? Ah but you can't answer me can you? Don't matter as I'm not much fussed what you think if I'm honest oh and I've been asked to make sure that your pain is, what was the word my kind benefactor used? Ah immense, that's the word and I'm more than happy to oblige because you and I both know how much you've had this coming." Cameron was now shaking with fear as he now realised he was in the grip and at the mercy of a completely insane man, a man by his own cruel and wicked actions he had himself created.

CHAPTER 39

Phil Read knew he had no choice but to cooperate with Max Stainmore, the man he had tried to kill. He knew he was never going to survive prison but he also knew he had to put the safety of his family first. He felt safe for the moment, was in segregation and as far as he knew only the prison officers knew who he was and what his police status had been. He knew that would not stay as such for long so needed to make his statement and deal for Witness Protection as soon as possible. So he was relieved when he was informed that Chief Superintendent Max Stainmore and Detective Sergeant Eddie 'pain in the arse' Sinclair were due to interview him within the hour.

Lying on his bunk he was again wondering where it had all started and how had it come to this? He was now remembering the first time he had set eyes on his wife Laura. She was standing at the bar at the latest trendy nightclub in the City Centre aptly named 'The Pick 'n' Mix' and he thought she was the loveliest woman he had ever seen and knew straight away that she was the one for him although Laura did need a great deal of persuading at the time. Laura who worked as a hairdresser and part time lingerie model, had made it clear from the beginning that she wanted the good things in life and by that she meant anything that had a designer name tag attached to it, so being a police officer's wife had not been in her plans. He had worked hard to give her all she wanted though and looked where it had landed him.

His partner Ian and he had been good officers once upon a time, doing their job well but gradually it became apparent that they were fighting a losing battle when it came to the moneyed men behind the drug industry. The money they made, the lifestyle they lived was beyond imagination and certainly beyond anything he or Ian could ever hope to earn, not even in several life times. After the first bribe, after the first helping themselves, it became easy and when 'G man' came calling, even easier because it almost made it seem legitimate. He'd been a fool and what's more he had broken his father's heart. He needed to protect his dad from 'G man' too because he only had his dad to make sure Laura and the kids would be okay now that he was out of the picture for God knew how long. Phil was so lost in his own thoughts he did not hear his cell door slowly opening. Looking up from his bunk, seeing the approaching shadows, he knew with certainty his time had run out.

*

Max and Eddie were through the prison security checks and making their way to the Prison Governor's office to meet Phil Read when it seemed like all hell had broken loose. Sirens were ringing out with prisoners being herded back into their cells which were then closed and bolted and several prison officers calling for medical assistance. Max and Eddie looked at each other with Eddie muttering, "Please don't let this be what I think it could be for pity's sake!"

Max with a face akin to thunder strode up to the Prison's Governor and said, "Tell me now it isn't Read!?"

Red faced and clearly devastated Prison Warden Gordons said, "He's just been found hanging in his cell. Looks like suicide."

"You mean it's been made to look like suicide!" stated Eddie.

"By that you're suggesting that someone on my staff could be involved Detective Sergeant!"

"I am that!" was Eddie's response as his eyes bored into the officious but embarrassed man.

"Take me!" demanded Max as they strode towards the cacophony of activity.

Pushing through the collection of officers and

medics Max and Eddie saw the prone lifeless body of Phil Read with the knotted white prison bed sheet still knotted around his neck.

"Who found him?" barked Max.

"I did Sir," responded Prison Officer Glen Fairham, "I was coming to get the prisoner to take to the Governor's office as was my orders. Found him hanging from the window bars with the bed sheet knotted as a noose."

Looking at Phil Read and the garotte markings around his neck Max said, "You'll find that injury and consequent fatality wasn't made by the sheet but by a home- made garotting device, probably shoe laces which means someone had access and on your watch Governor. So we're now looking at a murder enquiry. No one and I mean no one leaves this building!"

*

Hours later and now sitting outside Constable Philip Read Senior's house knowing what they now had to do was something both Max and Eddie dreaded so it was with both heavy hearts that they made their way to his front door. Philip answered on the first knock, took one look at their faces and knew.

"You'd better come in," as he opened his door wider for them to walk through. The hallway showed a collection of children's shoes, coats and school bags strewn as only children can when let out of school after a long day. Now Children's Tea time television could be heard from the lounge as they made their way through to the kitchen where a tired looking, very thin woman was facing the kitchen window, dealing with dishes. Looking round she saw the three men, looked at the expressions on their faces, put her hands to her mouth as her legs buckled beneath her. Philip rushed to catch her as he gathered her in his arms and allowed her to quietly sob the tears of the broken hearted. The door from the side opened and a little voice whispered, "Why is my mummy crying Grandpa?"

Philip said, "She's just a little upset sweetheart but she will be alright in a minute, won't you mummy?"

Eddie then did what he excelled at by saying jovially, "Is that 'Dora the Explorer' that I can hear? That's my favourite! Is it the one about the giant and the lion?"

"No its Sparky the horse. That's my favourite," replied five -year old Alice, who was now looking at Eddie as if she'd found a kindred spirit, "do you want to watch with me?"

"Oh I would like that very much," as he quietly ushered her through to join her seven- year old brother.

Max with Philip and Laura sat down at the kitchen table where Max began by saying,

"There's no easy way to say this Constable Read, Mrs Read, but your son, your husband was found dead in his cell earlier today."

Nodding Philip Read Senior held the hands of his daughter-in- law whose devastation was absolute. Finally, blinking back his own tears of utter anguish Philip asked, "How?"

Knowing this question would be forthcoming Max answered with honesty, "They're saying suicide."

Shaking his head Philip said, "But we know different don't we?"

Nodding Max replied, "I have my suspicions."

Laura Read looked up and said, "What's going to happen to us now?"

Summing up his customary calmness and inner strength he replied, "You and the kids will stay here with me for the foreseeable, that's a given. It will be one day at a time but we will get through this and I will make sure that you and the children will want for nothing. Okay?" Nodding Laura broke down again. Philip got up at this point and said, "So thank you for taking the time Chief Inspector, I very much appreciate the courtesy."

Understanding that he and Eddie were now being asked to leave he retrieved his Sergeant then made their way to their car closely followed by Philip.

"So was Phil able to give you any useful information before his his...." Finding he couldn't say the words Philip Read very nearly lost his composure as Eddie immediately answered, "No Phil, we got there too late. Can't tell you how sorry we are mate."

Shaking his head with eyes now burning with unshed tears and something else, something both Max and Eddie recognized, a need to know and a need for answers. Instead he said, "He'd lost his way and has disgraced the badge, the service, our family but my lad didn't deserve this." Both Max and Eddie nodded their agreement whilst remaining silent because there are times when there are no words that a devastated father wanted or needed to hear. Nodding Philip turned back to his house and the devastated lives within it.

CHAPTER 40

As Imogen opened her door, Max was holding the door jamb with both hands looking down, then slowly raised his eyes to hers. Without a word being said he walked towards her and then she was in his arms, responding to his kiss with as much passion as he was offering.

Suddenly Imogen pulled away, stepping back and Max then followed her gaze as it fell onto the smiling face of Neil's photograph situated on the table next to the window. He saw her conflict, her turmoil and felt her indecision. Running his hands through his short silvery hair he murmured, "Sorry Imogen, it's been a tough day and for some reason I found myself coming to see you and..." Looking down, he turned to leave only to feel her take his hand and then without a word she led the way to her bedroom.

Turning to him she whispered her fears saying, "It's been so long Max. There's been no one since Neil and I don't know if..."

"It's ok Imogen, everything will be ok." Smiling now, bending to kiss her neck, he began to unbutton her blouse, uttering endearments and gentle words, coaxing her to relax before his kiss deepened and Imogen found herself lost in his arms whilst her basic instincts gave way to the needs of her body, needs she had neglected for so long.

Later Imogen would marvel at how easy being with Max had been and how wonderful being intimate again was. Now looking at his relaxed face with both eyes closed she traced his jaw with her finger as he opened one eye and smiled. “What are you thinking?”

“Oh just how much I’ve missed this and that you really have the most handsome classical profile Chief Inspector.”

“Why thank you Ms Holt,” smiled Max as he began another exploration of her naked form, touching her scars.

“That one is where my spleen was taken,” she explained, “this where they performed the emergency caesarian and here on my leg, where they put the pins in. A testimony to medical skill on ensuring one’s survival whether at the time you wanted to survive or not.” Max said nothing, just looked at this beautiful, courageous woman who had dealt with so much. As if reading his thoughts, she touched the scar just above his hip and asked, “And this?”

Shrugging off the scar near his kidney as if

it was nothing he replied, "Years ago when I first started on the job. Knife wound because I made a rookie mistake, turned my back on the wrong suspect. Nicked my kidney but the Docs managed to save it so... nothing really except that it just adds to my manly torso and to the glamour of the job," he said self- deprecatingly.

Smiling at him she asked, "What brought you here tonight, not that I'm complaining?"

"I didn't intend to come over but found myself driving here. I think I just wanted to be with someone who would make me forget and make me remember how good the world can feel." Looking down at her, he saw how sad she looked. "Don't be sad Imogen, it's the life I've chosen".

Shaking her head, she said, "The world you inhabit just seems so harsh, so cruel, always seeing or thinking the worse of people."

"Don't think about it, not tonight" he whispered, kissing her as they came together again but this time so much more slowly with so much more tenderness, taking their time, enjoying each moment.

In the early hours of the morning lying in each other's arms they talked, really talked. "What was your husband like?" asked Max.

Imogen was silent for a while then said, "He was really very wonderful, the kindest of the kind, that's the best word to describe him and really thoughtful with just about everyone. He hated cheating of any kind and inconsiderate driving too and he would not allow anyone to queue jump." Now smiling she continued, "Neil was also such a practical joker, I mean he would drive me and his mother and sisters insane with what he considered funny, but he was also ruthless when pursuing the truth too particularly when in court. That's what made him so good at his job and so well respected by all who knew him." She then said something she had never shared with another living person, but here in her bed she felt safe enough to be truly honest, to be herself with this man she barely knew. "I really didn't want to live when they told me he had gone, couldn't bear the thought of life without him. When they told me my baby was gone too… it was just too much. I actually seriously thought about it if I'm honest, thought of the different ways I could do it just so I could be where they'd gone. I guess grief can make you pretty crazy for a while."

"What changed your mind?"

"My friends I guess. Suddenly they were there in shifts all the time. Feeding me, bathing me, sleeping with me, occasionally yelling at me or swearing at me when it was warranted, until I woke up one day, took a deep breath and thought that I'd better get on with it."

They lay quietly for a while until Max said, "Just like now with Sarah." Imogen remained silent as Max bent his head so he could look into her eyes before saying, "Thank you for sharing that Imogen. Takes guts."

Embarrassed she replied, "Actually it takes guts to keep on living Max and thousands face that choice daily, especially these days."

"Yes they do."

"Actually I'm pretty sure you and Neil would have liked each other, been on the same team."

"I'd have been as jealous as hell of him because he would have had you on his arm giving me no chance but he sounds like he was one of the good guys."

Smiling at him in the darkness she said, "He was. He'd have made a wonderful father and I like to think that somewhere they are both safe together, our son and him."

Squeezing her closer he kissed her hair whispering, "I like the thought of that too. It's good to feel there's still beauty and tenderness to be found and that people are basically good and can still speak the truth. I don't want to think the worst of everyone, be that sort of copper." Turning into him Imogen found she had no response because she knew better and hoped upon hope that Max never discovered what she too was capable of, what she too had done. He would never understand or forgive her and she realised that would be another loss and one she hoped upon hope she could avoid.

Watching his now sleeping face she also knew she was looking at a man she could feel deeply for, something Imogen never believed would happen for her again. If only she was who he thought she was. If only.

CHAPTER 41

The following morning a very chipper Max walked into Sheffield Central. Waking up next to Imogen had been something special and he was realising it was something he really could get used to. The drive into Sheffield from Penton was equally as pleasant too, with stunning scenery and half the traffic London would offer. Yes, Max Stainmore was beginning to understand why Yorkshire was called 'God's Own Country'.

Walking into the squad's briefing room he sensed something major had occurred. Looking at the sombre faces of his team he simply asked, "Ok. Hit me with it!"

It was Eddie who began saying, "Would appear our Mr Sheldon has been involved in a major incident which has resulted in him being admitted to hospital. The Hallamshire."

Max asked, "I assume he has been seriously injured then if the prison hospital wing won't do? Do we know the extent of his injuries and who may be involved?"

Dan replied solemnly, "He was found in a

pool of his own blood minus all ten of his fingers including his thumbs, down to the very knuckles. We have no suspects as yet."

Max sat down was silent and clearly shocked. They were all shocked by the barbarity of what had been reported to them and also aware that another gang related war could again be sparked by this. Having just survived the last one they knew their resources would be stretched to their limit. Running his fingers through his hair Max began, "Just when you think you've seen it all. Right. Has he been interviewed yet? Is he able to be interviewed?" The other detectives in the room glanced at each other, saying nothing, "What?" asked Max clearly at a loss.

Eddie shook his head saying, "Well that's the other thing boss. He apparently wishes to make a statement but only to you."

*

The man he was looking at in the hospital bed was unrecognisable from the man he had dealt with so many times before, the man who was responsible for the deaths and maiming of so many. The man he believed had ordered the attempt on his own life and although he felt no real pity for the man, his appearance was nonetheless shocking. It wasn't just the fact that his heavily bandaged hands had crippled him beyond repair, but it was if he finally understood something really important. He was diminished, finished and he knew it.

Max and Eddie silently stood by his bed until Cameron eventually looked at them both and began to summon up some of his old swagger. "Gentlemen, thank you for your prompt appearance."

Max replied with his customary officiousness when dealing with hardened criminals, "I've been informed you have a statement to make but only to be taken by myself so, I'm all ears and I haven't got all day."

Cameron smiled sadly, "Ah to be a busy man, whereas I now appear to be a man of leisure who will be waited on hand and foot from now on." At this point he turned to Eddie who had looked away from him, not wanting to show the pity he was feeling for the man saying, "Don't you fucking dare feel sorry for me Sergeant. I'm still more than a match for you!"

Eddie looked him in the eye and replied, "Before or after someone wipes your arse for you?" The cold fury evaporated from Cameron's eyes as he looked away.

Max now intervening said, "You asked to see me and I'm here. Can you identify your assailant?"

"No."

"The nature of your injuries suggest that you have been given a taste of your own medicine so I will ask you again. Who is responsible for this?"

Cameron smiled, "I have nothing to say on the matter and it isn't why I asked you here."

Confused Max asked, "So why are we here?"

Cameron smiled and said, "I wish to confess that I was the one who executed Grant Downs as I believed he had stolen from me and was attempting to leave the country so I killed him."

Staring at him both Max and Eddie shook their heads. "Treating us as fools to the last eh Sheldon?" growled Eddie.

"Cleansing my conscience Sergeant."

Max shook his head. "You're a monster and you've clearly been taught a lesson but we're not in the business of pinning a murder on just anyone, even you. So why admit it now? What was your motive? Wasn't he good for business?"

Cameron looked at both men then said, "And here was I thinking you'd be grateful to my finally doing the right thing. I suggest you tape my confession Chief Inspector, as my autographing days are behind me."

Eddie took out his phone, put it on record then placed it beside the shadow of the man he and his boss had come to hate so much. Max began ensuring interview protocols were followed, knowing that all that would be recorded would be scutinised and picked over by barristers, a jury and a judge. "The time is 10.23 am, the date 29th August 2020. Present are

Detective Sergeant Eddie Sinclair, Detective Chief Inspector Max Stainmore and remand prisoner Cameron Sheldon. Cameron Sheldon you have requested to give a statement in regard to the unlawful death of Grant Downs. Please speak clearly for the recording."

Cameron looked just above the heads of the men situated beside his bed then began:

"I received an anonymous tip that money had been sequestered from one of my overseas investment banks. I was reliably informed that the person responsible was Grant Downs. Of course Grant denied this when first challenged by myself but his subsequent actions resulted in his death."

Eddie then asked, "Can you further explain the term "subsequent actions" which resulted in the aforementioned person's death?"

Cameron continued explaining, "When challenged he became very aggressive and a fight broke out which resulted in my stabbing Grant Downs several times until he was dead. I admit the attack was a frenzied one such was my anger, my disappointment in a man I had come to trust. I made him suffer before he died as is my way. I then had his body put in my septic tank until he rotted away as I believed he didn't deserve to be treated with any decency such was his betrayal."

Silence ticked by for several seconds until Max

asked, “Have you anything else to add to this statement?”

Cameron shook his head prompting Max to say, “For the benefit of the tape please answer my question?”

Cameron replied, “No. I have nothing else to add except...”

“Except what?” prompted Max.

“Except perhaps Grant had realised that I had feelings for him, feelings he wasn’t interested in which is why he did what he did and steal from me.”

“Anything else?” asked Max.

“No.”

“Interview suspended at 14.22pm.”

As Eddie stopped the recording on his device he said, “You’ve learnt your lines well Sheldon. Are we supposed to believe that load of shite?”

Cameron remained silent as Eddie continued, “Seriously? What the bloody hell do you take us for?”

“I expect you to take the win Sergeant and now I would appreciate it if you’d both just piss off and let me get some sleep.”

Nodding their agreement, they moved to leave when Max said, “Still no idea who could be responsible for your injuries?”

Cameron smiled slyly and said, “What do you

think?"

Max shook his head and said, "Sheldon, I for one don't have a clue what to think anymore," and with that they left the room, more bewildered than when they had first entered it.

*

He felt her presence in the room before he saw her. "So when can I get it done? I've done as I was told, told them everything I was told to tell them. He promised me I would be able to get it done as soon as possible."

The nurse merely said, "It will be done in good time Mr Sheldon but only when our mutual friend is satisfied ok? He is a man of his word."

Nodding with tears of frustration running down his cheeks, Cameron Sheldon, the man who brought terror and butchery, blackmail and sleaze, a man who had blatant disregard for those he considered expendable, now understood what it felt to actually be completely expendable.

Outside in the hospital car park Max and Eddie were contemplating what had just occurred. "I'm buggered if I know what's going on?" said Eddie whilst Max nodded in agreement.

"Someone is playing us that's for sure."

"But aren't we getting the right result boss?"

Max shook his head and said, "But are we?

Someone is pulling our strings and I for one intend to find out who?!"

CHAPTER 42

Philip Read was a patient man, a man who knew how to bide his time. As he waited for the man who he blamed for his only child's death he felt the weight of the world on his shoulders. Looking down at the dark swirling waters of the River Don he was asking himself not for the first time, if he too was also to blame.

It was a beautifully warm night, the sort that he and his late wife Linda used to love as they would walk along the water's edge. He could hear the revellers from the various restaurants and bars that had sprung up over the years and envied the obvious joy and laughter that he could hear from afar. Would he ever laugh again he wondered? Dealing with Linda's premature death had been hard enough and he had felt grief like no other, but this? The death of his son Philip Read Junior whilst on remand was beyond anything he had had to endure in the whole of his lifetime. It was the manner of his death too that made him want to rage and rant at the world. Christ but he hoped his boy had gone as quickly as possible despite what he'd been involved in.

He felt rather than heard or saw the movement from his left as he was joined by the man he had arranged to meet, a man he used to regard as his friend, a brother even. Both men stood side by side looking down at the dark murky water. "Been years since I've found myself down here. Did a fair bit of courting here back in the day."

Philip remained silent, looking at the water then quietly replied, "Is that all you've got to say to me? After everything that's happened? After what you've had done to my boy?" Deputy Chief Constable Ralph Jones did not answer but instead said, "So I would appreciate it if you would hand me your telephone and I will also need to search you before we continue to speak frankly as I'm sure you understand." Philip nodded then handed over his device whilst raising his arms in order to be frisked. When Ralph Jones came across the loaded pistol found in Philip's pocket he whistled. "Really Phil? Really?" as he threw the weapon into the dark river.

Shaking his head Philip replied, "Why not? Do you think you deserve to live after what you've done and probably will continue to do? What for? Money? Women?"

Ralph looked at the man he regarded as his oldest friend and replied, "Both but the money mainly. Gambled more than I should and to be honest

Sheldon saw me coming. In it up to my neck. Taking Stainmore out was supposed to pay off my debts."

Nodding as if understanding Philip said, "So why my boy? Why choose Phil to do your dirty work?"

Shaking his head Ralph simply said, "He was dirty before I got to him mate and I thought I could rely on him with my being his Godfather. He used to look up to me you know, said he wanted to do as well as me. I should have known he would spill his guts to you."

"Aye he did look up to you and look where it got him. He could never understand why I didn't want to go up the ranks. Why can't you be more like 'G man' dad he would say? Do you want to know what I use to say to that?" Ralph waited, "I'd say because I want to be able to sleep straight in bed at night."

Chuckling mirthlessly Ralph turned to Philip. "Was it the night we found the 'drag' queen dead in the cells and covered it up that has made you such a sanctimonious holier than thou bastard? You stayed schtum like the rest of us! Hid behind the 'blue wall' just as me and Baker did. It was over thirty years ago for God's sake and who missed that bloody freak at the end of the day!?"

Sighing sadly, looking at the dark swirling waters Philip simply replied, "His mother. His poor heartbroken mother if memory serves me well."

Shaking his head Ralph Jones looked pityingly at his former friend. "It's still a dog eat dog world out there, survival of the fittest and you know something Phil, I sleep just fine, straight or not."

Still staring at the dark swirling water's edge Philip quietly replied, "Some things aren't easy to forgive or forget making sleep impossible. Ordering the death of my son should be one of them and I will have my vengeance if not today but one day Ralph. I think about it all the time."

Seconds of silence turned into minutes. Finally, Ralph looked at his old friend and said, "I'm sorry it's all gone down as it has and I'm prepared to help out financially with Laura and the kids, well as much as I can, but your son knew the chance he was taking and he made his bed."

Shaking his head Philip looked at his former friend with something akin to complete disgust. "He was my boy, my son, your Godson. You were his G man and my friend. We go back years for God's sake but instead you turned his head, offering him the world. Did you give the order to have him taken out? Let me hear you admit it? Let me hear you tell the truth for once in your sorry life!"

Ralph Jones looked down at the water and said, "He gave me no choice. He was going to make a statement to Stainmore and Sinclair and I couldn't have that. I've come too far down this road for your boy to find a conscience that would implicate me. With Sheldon now out of the picture, I'm actually home and dry mate. Even got a shot of becoming the next Chief Constable when that idiot Haggerty finally buggers off. I was always meant for the top job Phil even though you were always the 'one to watch' at Hendon, remember? Yeah well they got that wrong didn't they?!"

Nodding Philip replied, "Yes I remember and your future certainly did look bright Ralph but you must understand, I had no choice either old friend. Did you get all that Chief Inspector?"

Startled Ralph turned to see Max and Eddie with several police officers, some armed emerge from the various points of camouflage situated on the water's edge. "Loud and clear Constable Read," came Max's reply as Chief Superintendent Ralph Jones was unceremoniously handcuffed but the sneer remained in place as he uttered, "Why am I surprised, always by the sodding book eh Philip? Didn't even have the balls to shoot me yourself eh?"

Philip now went up close to Ralph jabbing him in the chest as he said with quiet fury blazing in his eyes, "I want to know you will be in prison for the next decade or so. We both know what happens to cops 'Inside' and I want you to feel fear, real fear, real pain, real regret and real loss every day for the rest of your miserable corrupt life for everything you hold dear and for a future you can never have. Like my lad did the night I had no choice but to turn him in."

"But you did have a choice, you sanctimonious bloody bastard. You could have looked after your precious son and the reason he is dead is down to you. You!" spitting the words out with such anger that the police officer restraining him felt the need to forcefully pull him back.

Max now stepped forward, putting his body between the two men, issuing his orders as he did so. "Read him his rights Sergeant Sinclair and get him processed as soon as possible and as public as you like, in fact radio ahead. Let the good hard working officers see for themselves what greed and corruption look like. Get the scum that is former Deputy Chief Constable Jones out of our sight now."

Watching as they marched their once superior officer away Max now turning to Philip said, "The gun? Tell me that was just for effect?"

Shaking his head Philip replied, "No I wanted to use it and possibly would have under different circumstances." Looking at Ralph Jones' retreating figure he added, "I wish I had. Perhaps that would have been real justice."

Running his fingers through his hair Max replied, "Well I'm glad you didn't because I think you've suffered enough and your grandchildren will need you now more than ever. I hate the idea of you being banged up too for that piece of work."

Philip turned world weary eyes onto Max and said, "You don't have children do you?"

Shaking his head Max replied, "No but I can imagine wanting to shoot and kill the bastard that caused my son harm."

Philip leant forward on the rails overlooking the river and appeared to age before Max's eyes. "I'm tired Chief Inspector, I'm very tired. I've already resigned from the job, the job I have loved and given my life to as of today in fact. Can't stand the looks of pity or sneers," then standing up he added, "but I want to thank you for tonight, for having the guts to go after the top brass. For seeking justice for my boy despite what he tried to do to you."

Max looked away embarrassed then held out his hand and said, "It has been an honour to know you Police Constable Read." Former Police Officer Read took the offered hand saying, "I imagine your father is very proud of his son Chief Inspector and I envy him," before slowly turning to begin his long lonely walk home; a home where two children were beginning to learn to live without a father as he was learning to live without a son.

Looking at the broken retreating figure Max

knew there was only one place he wished to be, needed to be.

Speaking into his phone he said, “Imogen. Max here. Have you eaten already?”

CHAPTER 43

Sarah looked at her friend as Imogen disconnected her phone conversation with Max. She saw how Imogen was smiling, looking quietly excited and pleased and how she had not looked like this for such a long time.

"Max?" asked Sarah.

Blushing and unable to meet Sarah's eyes, Imogen nodded then said, "I know I'm being stupid, I know it can't go anywhere and I know I'm playing with fire."

"But?" asked Sarah.

Shaking her head Imogen shook her head and said, "I can't seem to keep my distance from him. He's just so..."

"Right?" offered Sarah.

Imogen nodded then looking at her friend said, "I can't believe that after all this time after Neil, the one man that has made me feel like this has to be a man who could harm all I love and hold dear."

Shaking her head Sarah countered, "Like I've said before I will 'fess up to what I've done."

Imogen held up her hand saying, "It's too late for that now. We have to see it through and Max will return to London when this case closes and I'll have been just a pleasant interlude he had whilst 'up north'."

Shaking her head sadly Sarah said, "But he is so much more for you which is why you perhaps should stop it now before more damage can be done. You've suffered enough and it makes us all vulnerable."

Imogen went quiet, feeling suddenly angry with her friend. "I know you're right but perhaps I'm tired of always having to sacrifice my needs for other people albeit the people I love."

Sarah now looked close to tears, "I've said I'll own up."

"We both know that's out of the question, we're all in too deep and have been from the beginning." Imogen rose from her seat and stared out over the darkening skies. "If I'd never gone out to dinner with him that night and then seen him hit by a bloody car we wouldn't be in this mess. I guess we both stopped pretending who we were after that as he lost his swagger and I stopped pretending to be so tough. So my friend, being with him is something I seem to need to do for the time we have left together. Does that make sense? I'm also constantly scared he'll somehow find out the truth too."

Sarah now thinking of John Hilton and wondering not for the first time what she would do if he never came back or if he too discovered what she had done said, “Absolute sense but just be careful for all our sakes.”

*

Later that evening whilst looking out at the setting sun that made the view from Imogen’s balcony even more spectacular, Max found himself finally relaxing for what seemed like the first time in days. Looking at Imogen he smiled at her compelling Imogen to ask, “So what are you smiling at?”

“Oh I’m smiling at you Imogen Holt,” replied Max, “you and pepperoni pizza are enough to make me a happy man. Who knew?”

Coming to sit beside him Max drew her into his side where she with her head on his shoulder also drank in the view, feeling safe and content in the moment.

“What was it like growing up in such a beautiful place?”

Imogen thought for a moment before replying, “I don’t think I realised how beautiful it was until I left it. I loved London but it made me realise I’m a semi country girl at heart which is why I wanted to return so badly.”

Max sensed her sadness, the memory of loss that was never far away from her surface as he said,

"Accidents happen Imogen and few of us are masters or mistresses of our own fate. I guess it was a pretty grim fate that actually brought you and me together in the first place but I'm glad it did."

Nodding and reaching up for him Imogen whispered, "I'm glad we met too although I so wish it had been a different 'fate' Max, one that wasn't filled with so much misery and awfulness." Their kiss was long, slow and deep, filled with so much longing and feelings that Imogen was finding impossible to ignore.

Eventually Max said, "So how would you have liked us to have met?"

Imogen thought before replying, "I would be buying take-out coffee and you would be standing behind me, too close, I might add and as I turned I would accidentally spill it on you. I would be mortified and offer to have your jacket dry cleaned."

"I would then give you my number."

"And that would be it!"

"Except you would have probably detected that I would have been standing too close in the first place, challenged me and told me to get my own jacket cleaned. That would have been more like it," laughed Max.

"And you would have followed me out and convinced me that I needed to give you my number just in case the dry cleaning was an issue," added Imogen.

"You would have said, 'In your dreams',"

Laughing now Imogen continued, "Then you would have staked out the coffee house in order to 'bump' into me again."

Smiling down at her Max replied, "Oh yes!"

Sadly, Imogen found herself saying, "If only." Imogen suddenly felt unbearably sad at this point and disentangled herself from Max's embrace, picking up their finished plates, taking them to the sink as Max followed her with their finished glasses of wine. Coming up behind her, he placed his arms around her waist nestling into her neck and whispered, "I could get used to coming home to you." Imogen nodded unable to speak as there they stood for several minutes before Max, realising what he was implying, cleared his throat saying, "I suppose I should consider making tracks back into Sheffield."

Looking up at him Imogen thought for a moment then said, "Oh I think you could consider making something else Chief Inspector? I mean you make the best coffee especially first thing in the morning, and that's something I could get used to."

Gathering her to him Max smiled, saying, "So it's only my coffee making skills you're interested in not my..." Imogen's kiss took away his words as she began to slowly unbutton his shirt, dipping her mouth to kiss the hollow of his throat. Groaning Max, could only whisper, "You're killing me Imogen, do you know that? And I'm loving every second."

CHAPTER 44

The news of the attack on Sheldon spread like wildfire across the underworld and like a deck of cards Cameron Sheldon's enterprises began to fold. Without his leadership and psychopathy there was no direction, just chaos. His lieutenants, Dave Richmond and Steve Richardson did not have the acumen to control the various local factions who were determined to have their revenge as well as take their city back plus the police were suddenly all over their outlets in the region, closing down a number of fake massage parlours, tanning shops, nail bars that were fronts for enforced prostitution and money laundering courtesy of some very accurate anonymous information received.

Max, Eddie, Dan, Lydia, Isiah and Beth were all sitting in a surveillance van outside an alleged tanning shop in the city's Attercliffe area. They had been reliably informed via one of Eddie's Confidential Informants that activity around people trafficking was taking place in the building. An Armed Response Unit was going in first to secure the premises then Max and his team would enter when it was deemed safe.

"So tell me again how we have come in possession of all this information?" asked Max feeling very skeptical.

Eddie replied, "My snout has been sound for years. Since Sheldon's fate his organisation has been leaking like a sieve. Right Dan? Isiah?"

"Absolutely Sarge," answered Dan, "coming out of the woodwork like the cockroaches they are."

Max remained silent thinking not for the first time how easily everything seemed to be falling into place. Almost as if someone somewhere was pulling everyone's collective strings and he didn't like it! He didn't like or trust it one bit for one second!

Their van was approached by the Sergeant of the ARU saying, "Premises secured Sir. You're free to enter."

"Thank you Sergeant. Right let's go and see what is to be found this time."

*

The premises looked as expected from the entrance but it was when you walked through into the back spaces that the multitude of rooms appeared almost like a maze. Each room were varied in size but all had the required beds and the obligatory sex aids, condoms, lubricants and all other manner of paraphernalia. As they ventured further into the building they were led by the officers who had gone before them down steep narrow steps into what could only be described as a large dormitory, full of small cot beds with little else in terms of comfort. On each bed were an assortment of young women, some mere children in some cases, all now shivering with fear and drug withdrawal, wondering what would become of them all next. It was heartbreaking. However, it was when they came upon the final bed in the room that Max felt something break inside of him; something which made both Beth and Lydia cry out. There huddled in the corner, with fear and bewilderment etched across his tiny features was a very small child, a boy not quite four years old.

"Jesus Christ!" muttered Eddie, "could this be our 'Gruffalo' little fella?"

Beth stepped forward and held out her arms saying, "Hello my sweet and what's your name then?"

The child remained where he was, cowering further into the corner until a young girl, barely fifteen came up and gathered the child to her, whispering words none could understand except the two of them.

"I've told him not to be afraid, that you are good people who are here to save us," said the young girl in a heavy Eastern European accent.

"And you are Pet?" asked Eddie.

"Ksenia."

"And the boy?" asked Max.

"We don't know his name as he hasn't been here long? I call him Mieloji. It means 'Dear' and he likes it."

"His mother?" asked Lydia.

"Was taken by the tall one. We know not where. We never know," answered Ksenia.

"How long have you been here Ksenia and where are you from?"

Shaking her head, she answered as truthfully as she could, "Who knows? Time becomes meaningless here. I am from Minsk in Belarus. I came with my mother. They told us there were jobs here for us."

"Your mother?" asked Max already dreading the answer. The child called Ksenia then crumbled before them unable to now speak. Eventually she shook her head saying, "She was taken as soon as we arrived. She was screaming they were criminals, animals and that she demanded we be allowed to leave and then... and then... she was gone."

Both Lydia and Beth approached where the now both sobbing children were. Beth said, "You're safe now love. Nothing bad will happen from now on."

Ksenia turned large tear filled eyes up to meet Beth's and whispered, "The worse has already happened, every day and all day for so many days," as her sobs worsened.

Max turned to the sick, saddened faces of both Dan and Isiah and issued his orders saying, "We need Social Services teams and medics for these people. It won't be easy with Covid restrictions but we must do the best we can for these poor souls so we need to remove them from this hell hole as soon as possible. Get moving."

"On it," muttered Isiah, "come on Dan."

The ARU Sergeant appeared and said to Max, "We think we've found the woman in charge. She was hiding upstairs then pretended she was a victim but far from it from the way the others have reacted to her so far."

Behind the uniformed officer stood a woman, much older than the others in the room but still barely thirty years old. She was better dressed and clearly fed well without the gauntness of a drug addict unlike the rest of the poor souls found there. What defined her however, was the harshness of her features and the brittleness of her stance and demeanor.

Suddenly a young woman leapt from the bed and began clawing at the woman's face screaming in a language others knew and were shouting back, urging her to continue her assault. Pulling her away Max held the young woman firmly, felt her thinness, saw her hatred for the other woman and more than anything else felt her fear and loathing emanating from her frail body. Ksenia pointed to the woman and said, "She is a bad woman but the man is far worse. Please make sure you get the man, the man who likes to hurt us, to leave his mark on us."

"Please be assured that the man who brought you here is already in prison," said Max quietly assuring her.

"Thank God," whispered Ksenia, "when I first saw him I thought he would save me as he was so handsome, like... like as you say James Bond."

"Do you remember what this man was called?" asked Eddie, already knowing the answer.

"Grant, but we learned to call him 'Diablo'."

The woman who had been attacked began to laugh saying, "As if? You're all trash. Who'd bloody bother to save the likes of you?!"

Pointing to the woman now laughing defiantly Max issued his orders, "Get her out of here and straight to Central. She has some questions to answer that's for certain." The young woman in his arms was now deflated and sobbing her anger out as she too was helped by some of the others as they waited to leave this hell on earth they had lived in too long.

"Bloody hell boss but if I live to be a hundred

I will never understand the depths of depravity that men and women are prepared to stoop to," said Eddie shaking his head in bewildered sadness and utter horror.

"Me neither Eddie, me neither," said an equally shaken Max. He would never understand any of it and hoped the day never came when such things ceased to shock and disgust him. He actually feared that more if he was honest as he remembered Alec Dales's words "When evil walks amongst us" now seemingly more apt than ever because evil had most definitely walked here.

*

Hours later back at Central Station Sheffield Lydia and Beth were sitting facing the woman they were now certain operated as the 'Madam' of the place they had raided that day.

"Name?" asked Beth somewhat unceremoniously.

When the woman before them just stared back at them both defiantly Lydia took over saying, "Your name is Ruth Hill and you have quite an impressive record for possession with the intent to supply, two counts of GBH, prostitution, benefit fraud, credit card scamming and shoplifting although you were a juvenile when that occurred. Have I missed anything?"

Still no response from Ruth Hill as Beth now took

over. "Of course all the above will dwindle into obscurity when the charge of People Trafficking and Smuggling are on your charge sheet. Then you will be looking at a life sentence so you're now what twenty- nine? You'll be coming up to fifty when you get out that's if you survive prison. You do know what happens to people in prison who hurt children don't you?"

Ruth Hill now sighed heavily and said, "Yes I do and it won't be anything I haven't already received one way or another. So are we finished?"

"Nope," replied Beth, "we're just getting started. We want names, dates, times and other contact sources. If you co-operate fully we can help when it comes to your sentence. Even where you do the time."

"Nothing to say," was the reply.

"Sheldon's already banged up and you've heard what's happened to him? The man can't harm you or anybody else."

For the first time Ruth looked upset but what shocked Beth and Lydia was that it wasn't for herself but for Cameron Sheldon. "He bloody didn't deserve what some animal did to him in prison but I bet you're not knocking yourself out finding who did that are you?"

"We're making our enquiries but Mr Sheldon is refusing to cooperate at this moment in time," replied Lydia, "but why are you so upset over a man like him?"

Leaning back in her chair Ruth replied, "He was bloody good to me, got me off the streets. It's where he picked me up to be exact as he was new to Sheffield and he liked what I could do for him. Thought me very talented, not that you'd understand that," then turning to Beth asked, "I bet she's still a bloody virgin right?" gesturing towards Lydia.

Lydia was now blood red but remaining calm replied, "So your reward for being so 'talented' was to put you in charge of victims of human trafficking. Correct?"

"No brainer. First time I'm not on my back since I was thirteen years old when dear old dad decided to pass me round his mates to pay off his gambling debts. I've been on and off the streets ever since until Cam found me."

Seeing how the women before her were now looking at her Ruth looked towards the two- way mirror where Max and the rest of the team were listening and smiled broadly.

"You've clearly had it tough but we need to know the extent of the operation. We found a child in your place Ruth, practically a baby for God's sake. Where's the mother?" asked Beth.

Ruth now looking chastened replied, "I told Grant and Cam that we could not, that I would not deal with the kids. Why do you think the little bugger was still there and unharmed? I held my ground for him."

Nodding Beth said, "And that will be taken into consideration but what happened to the mother?"

"Grant Downs. You know he was far worse than anything Cam did. Anyway she was picked out by him when this batch arrived and that was that."

When both Police Officers looked at her blankly she continued with, "Well she was so badly beaten and traumatised when he'd finished, that she overdosed, leaving her bloody babbie as well stupid cow. Now that's what I call bloody selfish! I mean I know that Grant was important to the business an' all but when he'd finished with the girls they were fit for nothing. I tried complaining to Cam but he wouldn't hear a word against Grant and I often wondered if he had a thing for him. He was so bloody gorgeous he could turn anyone to be fair. You know I bet he would even have persuaded you to 'pop' your cherry!"

Outside the Interview room Max and Eddie and the other two detectives were listening until Max felt his two officers doing the interview needed a break. He certainly felt he had heard more than enough for one day.

"Get our girls out of there Eddie, I think they've done enough for today." Max then looked at Dan and Isiah and asked, "You guys ok?"

Dan nodded but Isiah asked, "Does this shit get any easier boss?"

Shaking his head Max replied, "No Isiah it doesn't and the day it does is the day I walk away."

It was then that Max heard Lydia ask again the key question, one they all were desperate to know the answer to. "So Ruth it's important we get to the source if we want to stop the human misery we found at the place of your work. We need to know which port the lorries arrive and when the next delivery is due. We would then be able to interview the drivers to track down the country or countries of origin where possible. So what can you tell us?"

Ruth looked somewhat aghast then burst out laughing saying, "And why the fuck should I help you with that?"

Without missing a beat Lydia replied, "To perhaps help, even save that thirteen year old, who has been badly betrayed and used by the very people who should love and protect her but now finds herself fighting for her very own survival in a world that is bleak, terrifying and devoid of any sort of kindness."

Ruth had stopped laughing but now sat back in the chair blinking hard at the two women sitting across from her.

Finally, she could be heard saying, "Belfast

in lorries then into private cars with faked passports from there, to get the merchandise into Liverpool. They change their arrival points constantly to avoid getting caught since the raid on Penton. Often the drivers don't speak English although one of the girls thinks the regular one is from Belarus. She understood his swearing last time he was here."

"That would be Ksenia?" asked Beth. Ruth nodded once, now looking at the table top.

"Thank you Ruth. Interview suspended at 19.27pm," said Lydia.

As Lydia and Beth joined the rest of the team Dan surreptitiously squeezed Lydia's hand as Max said, "Good job! Very good job! Now get some rest because all those found tonight have to be interviewed thoroughly. We need as much information to give the Immigration and Customs people as possible as well as Interpol." Max turned to Lydia who was still watching the interviewed woman through the glass. "You Ok?"

Lydia shrugged before replying, "Yes sir, just... well, the poor cow never stood a chance did she?"

Max nodded his understanding saying, "We've made a real difference to the lives of many today, so home now people because we've got more tough days to come."

*

Malcolm was now happily surveying the room

and knew all was now well. Order had been restored and revenge had been metered out, with Omar and Mohammed Mirza, Jack Smith and Joseph O' Malley all in agreement that the status quo was as it should be with their collective powers left in- tact and beyond question.

"So," Malcolm began, "with your permission gentlemen I'd like to now fulfill my bargain with Sheldon. He has done as I requested and I don't believe his staying alive will be of any benefit to anyone in this room. I gave him my word and I like to keep my word even to scum like him."

Omar grinned at Malcolm and said, "I have to say I think your methods have been suitably cruel and somewhat inventive for such a man. We are impressed are we not Mohammed?" His son Mohammed merely nodded.

"Yes," this from Jack Smith, "put the bastard out of his misery."

Nodding Malcolm said, "Thank you gentlemen and may I say, it has been a pleasure doing business with you all," as the main leaders of Sheffield's Underworld took their leave from each other and left to continue what they all did best.

CHAPTER 45

It was a grim Jim Haggerty who was looking at the two men before him. Max was seated next to Detective Superintendent Tom Blakely his supposed line manager but who in effect Max had had little to do with whilst being in Sheffield. Finally, Jim began to speak saying, "Well where do we start gentlemen?"

Tom Blakely said, "Well can I start by saying that I wish to congratulate the Chief Inspector here for uncovering the 'nest of vipers' we had in our midst and of course for the subsequent arrests made that have effectively terminated the criminal practices of Cameron Sheldon."

Max nodded his thanks whilst the Chief Constable looked on. Tom had more to say. "I am aware how little I have been involved in any of the work undertaken and I am also aware that it has been an issue of trust too and who can blame the Chief Inspector. Therefore, I think it better all round that I tender my resignation forthwith."

Jim and Max just stared at the man not expecting such a turn of events. Jim was the first to speak saying, “Tom I don’t understand. Why?”

Tom now visibly relaxed and smiled at his old friend. “I’m just so bloody tired of it and gutted if I’m honest. We both knew Baker was a pompous little pillock but Ralph? Corrupt! Not just a corrupt copper but a murdering bastard to boot? No Jim, I’ve had enough mate.”

Max said, “Not once were you ever under suspicion Superintendent.”

Smiling Tom replied, “I’m bloody glad to hear it but I think it best that there is a clean sweep at this level, to not just restore public confidence but also to our lads and lasses on the beat. They need to feel we have their backs and that we’re cleaner than clean. No, it’s my time to go gentlemen and as soon as I can Jim if at all possible.”

Jim slowly nodded then rose to his feet as Tom had done. Max stood too as hands were shaken all round as Detective Superintendent Tom Blakely smiling sadly, left the room.

“Bloody hell,” muttered Jim, “does this happen every time you sweep into town, turning it on its head before you sweep out again?!”

Max shaking his head said, “I did not see that coming.”

“No,” agreed Jim, “but I see his point.” Then Jim stood to look out of his office window before continuing saying, “It’s been quite a few months since you arrived and what you've managed to uncover is simply extraordinary."

Max looking at the floor now considering his next words carefully. "Yes Sir, too extraordinary."

Jim Haggerty returning to his seat raised his eyebrows saying, "Explain."

Max shaking his head said, "Just all too neat Sir, as if orchestrated almost. The way we found Downs' body, the subsequent attack on Sheldon, the Confidential Informant intelligence we were spoon- fed almost. I'm telling you it's just too... too convenient almost."

Jim thinking hard before replying to the troubled man before him said, "Interpol have already managed to place a good many young women we've found in Sheldon's various premises and who are now gratefully returning home. We estimate we have managed to rescue over fifty young women, some barely in their teens and this is hopefully just the beginning." Jim Haggerty now smiled at Max at this point, before turning his computer screen to allow Max a view of what he wanted him to see. On the screen was a photograph of the child they had rescued from the raid, the one whose mother had died after Grant Downs had violated her beyond her sanity.

"This Max, is Pavel Kuzsack from a little place just outside of Krakow. His eventual destination would have been a pedophile ring if not for your intervention. He's now safely going back to the custody of his grandparents."

"The owner of the Gruffalo," said Max sadly, still looking at the screen, "but we couldn't save his mother could we? God knows how scarred for life he will be."

Jim Haggerty shook his head saying "But let's take the win. I mean, bloody good show Detective Chief Inspector."

Max still shook his head, convinced he was missing something, something vital and he couldn't help thinking he was being played somehow. Jim Haggerty allayed Max's fears repeating again, "Take the win because today is a good day and we still have plenty of clearing out to do too. You were right about Sheldon having officers on his payroll but not just Sheldon either so several members of our Drug Squad are now finding themselves on the wrong side of a jail cell. It would appear Phil Read and his partner weren't the only ones dirty there." Now smiling Jim conceded, "You've been quite the whirlwind, not to mention what your team uncovered whilst searching Sheldon's house."

Looking sad now Jim Haggerty continued, "We have evidence of at least three members of the city planning department being filmed taking bribes as well as sniffing cocaine and getting involved in some very dubious activities of a sexual nature, not to mention my wife's favourite BBC weatherman! Loads of what we could laughably be described as this city's finest citizens, not being very fine at all! It beggars bloody belief and as for that actor chap!?"

"Always a pleasure to be of service Sir," smiled Max being somewhat amused at his boss' outrage and touched also that this man who had been in the job for so long, still felt shock, horror and disappointment of those who should know better, who should not have been turned by money, illegal substances and forbidden sex.

"Yes, you're a piece of work alright and you'll do for me, which is why I want you to consider making your position here in Sheffield permanent."

Looking at Max's stunned face Jim held up both hands saying, "Please I'm not asking for an answer today as I know leaving London will be a big deal for you, but you're really highly regarded by all who've met you and worked with you and let's be fair, you've not been here five minutes. I will be needing a Detective Chief Superintendent and a Chief Superintendent. Your choice but I'd like you here permanently." Jim Haggerty stopped for a moment before continuing, "Also, we won't be the only city in the North dealing with the sort of human misery you've uncovered here because, let's be honest, it's like a bloody epidemic and if I was in the NCA I would want one of my best operatives based up here.

You being here on a permanent basis could be beneficial all round."

Max leaned back into his chair feeling flattered and surprised in equal measure but he did think the Chief Constable was making sense. "I need to give this some thought sir, but I thank you for the offer."

Nodding Jim Haggerty stood and offered his hand saying, "That's all I'm asking. You'll do for me Max Stainmore. You'll do for me just fine.

CHAPTER 46

Sitting in Sarah's large comfortable kitchen come sitting room, Max was once again struck by the solidarity of the women before him. Sarah was flanked by both Imogen and Harry whilst Beth was standing at their side, on duty but her position being very clear.

Max and Eddie were sitting opposite the women before them, here to officially inform Sarah about the outcome of their investigations into her husband's death. Max began, "So we now have a full and signed confession from an associate of your late husband, a Mr Cameron Sheldon, that he did in fact kill your husband as he believed he had stolen a significant amount of money from him."

Nodding Sarah whispered, "So what does this mean?"

Imogen answered for Max saying, "I think it means this nightmare is finally over. Is that correct Max?"

Max smiled and agreed, "Yes it's over. Mr Sheldon was already in custody but will remain there now for some considerable time."

Eddie added, "Let's hope he'll never bloody get out!"

Sarah looked at all assembled then simply burst into heavy tears as all three friends now gathered around her, making soothing noises of comfort. Sarah finally pulling herself together said, "God but I'm so bloody pathetic! So it's really finished with? No more thugs threatening or journalists appearing on my doorstep?"

Eddie answered saying, "The papers may still bother you for a story but it's up to you if you want to speak with them but it's now time to put this all behind you and start to look forward."

Harry said, "Well put Sergeant and you're the least pathetic person I know Sarah. After everything you've been through I think you're bloody amazing and I for one am proud of you!"

"I for two!" agreed Imogen.

"I for three even though I'm officially on duty!" laughed Beth. Max was watching the dynamics of the group closely and not for the first time felt he was really missing something, something important. Imogen saw him watching them all and again felt vulnerable, very much like the first time they had met all those months ago. He really was a man who was not easily fooled and she once again found herself wishing they had met under very different circumstances. Despite their obvious feelings for each other, Imogen knew she would have to let him go and soon, whilst she could.

Getting up to leave Max said to Sarah, "Take care Mrs Downs and I hope all works out for you and your Sergeant Hilton. Ladies."

As they all stood Sarah extended her hand to Max then to Eddie saying, "Thank you so much for all you have done and my name is Sarah. Are we allowed to shake hands?"

"No but I'm passed caring," said Eddie accepting the hand offered as Max did the same both now smiling as Harry intervening quickly dispensed liquid sanitizer to the three of them.

Briskly saying, "Come on, we're not getting through all this just for you three to get bloody Covid. We're not out of the woods yet you know?"

Smiling Imogen led the police officers to the door. Max held back as the others left whispering to Imogen, "Can we meet later? Dinner at the Italian?"

Imogen whispered back, "I think I'll be needed here tonight. Sarah is still very vulnerable but tomorrow?"

Max was disappointed but nodded his understanding, then surreptitiously squeezed her hand before joining his colleagues in the waiting squad car. As he pulled on his seat belt he was aware of the two grinning faces now looking at him. Embarrassed Max merely growled, "Just drive Constable Fairchild, just drive," as he heard Eddie's quiet chuckle coming from the backseat behind him.

Back in the house Sarah was sitting back in her couch seat with closed eyes and a face of such relief that it spoke volumes. "I can't believe that it's finally over. After all these months, after everything that has happened. It's finally over."

Harry agreed saying, "Finally, perhaps we can all now sleep soundly. What say you Imogen?"

Imogen was still watching the police squad car pulling out of the drive before agreeing with her friends, "Yes a dreamless sleep. It's what we all need."

Except Imogen knew it wasn't over. Far from it and possibly the worst was still yet to come.

*

Cameron Sheldon had had a bit of a day. A day when he was talked to about prosthetics, rehabilitation, physiotherapy and previous success stories of injured veterans who had survived IEDs in some godforsaken part of the globe. He just wished they'd leave him be as he knew none of it would be necessary and he wished they'd just hurry up and put him out of his misery like the injured animal he was. He hoped to God, if indeed one existed, that the

'Fixer' character kept his word. If not, he would have to orchestrate a Plan B if he needed to come up with one. After everything he had recently suffered it was his feelings of utter helplessness that made life so insufferable, so impossible to take. He wasn't a naturally patient man and he was so eager for death, wanting it more than he could remember wanting anything else.

He'd had a lot to think about whilst lying in this hospital bed, a lot to remember and plenty to forget. He was now remembering the squalor of his childhood, the smell of filth and how as a child he used to sometimes eat from dustbins if he wanted to eat at all. He remembered being taken from that poor excuse of a mother and how she hadn't given a shit, just glad he was finally off her hands. He was now wondering what had happened to her, if she was even still alive but realised even now lying waiting to die himself, he didn't actually care.

Grant. He was remembering Grant and was now acknowledging if he had ever loved anyone in the whole of his violent life, the nearest one was Grant Downs, whose disappearance and death had started his own demise. For the life of him he still couldn't figure out who had had the balls to kill him either. Surely not that simpering wife of his although the British Army had been known to do have done worse if the news was to be believed. Shaking his head now Cameron felt John Hilton wasn't the answer either. Grant. Handsome, witty, clever, sadistic Grant Downs aka Samuel Thornton was undoubtedly the unspoken love of his life. What they could have gone on to achieve would have become the stuff of legends. If only. Cameron was so deep in thought that he hadn't heard the door open and a solitary silent, shadowy figure appear at his side. The voice he now heard was soft almost soothing as the woman said, "So are you ready Mr Sheldon?"

The reverence in her voice pleased him and made him feel...valued. That's the word, like his life mattered.

Cameron nodded unable to speak as she produced the vial that would give him eternal sleep, preparing to insert it into his intravenous saline drip. "I am happy to take your Confession Mr Sheldon, before you meet your Maker?"

Cameron laughed replying, "You mean the Devil?"

"Is that where you believe you're going? To Hell Mr Sheldon?"

Nodding emphatically Cameron replied, "Most definitely."

The voice remained silent for a few seconds before saying, "Are you afraid to die then? To burn for eternity if the Bible is to be believed. What do you think your Hell will be like?"

Cameron shook his head and replied, "I'm more afraid of living, living like half a human being, like half a man. This is Hell, a real living Hell. What Death can offer can't be worse than this."

"Men live with worse."

"Not men like me. Please let me go. Let me go now. Please," which were the final pleading words of the former gangland boss called Cameron Sheldon, the man whose very name initiated terror to so many, as the cocktail of a barbiturate paralytic combined with a pure potassium solution entered his blood stream swiftly travelling to his black and wicked, ultimately soulless heart making it stop forever.

Heavily gowned and in full PPE the woman who had administered to Cameron Sheldon in his final minutes on Planet Earth waved to colleagues as she made her way out of the hospital building and into her waiting car, shedding her gown and PPE as she went. Running her fingers through her hair, before picking up her phone and saying to the person who answered just the two words he was waiting for, "It's done." Then putting her car into gear she began her drive home to Penton, back to her lovely husband and adorable children singing softly as she did so, to the sound of the radio's sad song of love and loss that was quietly playing on her car's sound system. For Harry of the charmed life, would always be there for her friends when it mattered.

CHAPTER 47

Anthony Dolan was the chief suspect for the injuries sustained by Sheldon but the prison authorities had no evidence as the prison laundry room CCTV had mysteriously not worked that day and he himself had now been fully admitted to the Prison's Psychiatric Unit since the morning he was found rocking happily and constantly singing 'Row Row Row Your Boat.'

Max was sitting across from the Prison Governor, Darryl Cross who was explaining what he believed had occurred on the day Sheldon had been attacked and permanently maimed. "You need to understand that we run a tight ship here which is why we house some of the worst offenders this country has ever seen."

Nodding his agreement Max asked, "So what do you think happened?"

Shaking his head Darryl Cross replied, "As far as our investigations have shown, the electrical fault that brought down our cameras temporarily was activated remotely approximately fifteen miles away. I mean who knew that could happen?"

Max shook his head saying, "Technology helps criminals that's a given but surely he had inside help if it was Dolan?"

Nodding his agreement Darryl Cross agreed saying, "Absolutely but I do not have a shred of evidence or indeed any clue who to start looking at. Dolan is to be moved to a suitable facility for his obvious condition as soon as possible. The medics believe he is now in a permanent state of psychosis and will need specialist treatment probably for the rest of his life. You know how he got here don't you?"

"I do. Infact I was the first officer to interview him after the Dover incident so you could say I actually helped put him here."

"What happened to his grandson was beyond evil," flatly stated the man now looking hard at Max which made Max very uncomfortable and not for the first time, knowing what he was now thinking.

"Yes it was and it will always weigh heavy on me Governor, probably for the rest of my life."

The silence now hung uncomfortably between them before Darryl Cross said, "Sheldon was a cocky bastard when he got here and I expected plenty of trouble if I'm honest but never this so I don't think I can help you."

Getting up to leave Max said, "Thank you for your time but would it be possible to look at the list of visitors Dolan has had over the past couple of months?"

Picking up his phone Darryl Cross said, "I'll have it emailed over to you directly although if I'm honest I don't know why you're wasting your time on a piece of human garbage that is essentially Cameron Sheldon."

"I know, you and everyone else," replied Max sighing heavily.

*

It was this list he was perusing when Eddie joined him at his desk.

"So you'll be leaving us I take it? Back to London with its poor excuse for ale and lack of clean air eh?"

"Got a few loose ends to clear up but I suppose I'll be required back to London soon I guess," said Max frowning as the idea of leaving didn't make him very happy although staying was a huge decision. Leaving Imogen was not making him happy at all. She wasn't just beautiful, it wasn't just great sex, although that was pretty sensational, it was that she herself was so much more. It was the feeling he was where he should be whenever he was near her that Max was so rattled by and for once didn't know what to do with. He had the chance to stay here and have a life, a life he thought he was destined to be without. A life he realised he did want after all.

As if reading Max's thoughts Eddie nodded understandingly saying, "I've heard long distance relationships can work although I've heard on the grapevine that you've been asked to stay?"

Shaking his head with bemusement he replied, "Is there nothing sacred in this place? Yes, and I'm thinking about it."

Smiling Eddie said, "Be great to make this permanent boss. We've loved having you here, a bloody breath of fresh air even though you're a soft southern lad!"

Nodding Max took the compliment before saying, "So this list. Anyone on it that perhaps shouldn't be? Might help us find out who's behind all this violence for starters."

Eddie scanned the list saying, "Just family, the odd mate and… oh now he's interesting. Malcolm Speight. Hmm, surprised to see him on this list."

"So who is he?" asked Max.

"A local 'fixer'. Was a boxer back in the day, quite tasty too if memory serves me well. Actually the nearest we got to him was when he upset a couple of mates of Superintendent Baker but his case was dismissed when his brief uncovered blatant evidence planting." Eddie was now frowning and stood up to leave.

"What is it?"

"Nothing," replied Eddie.

"What aren't you telling me?"

"It's probably totally irrelevant," replied Eddie who was reluctant to continue the conversation.

Max now really interested merely looked at Eddie, waiting. Sighing and with a heavy heart Eddie simply said, "I remember the name of the Brief, his Barrister that's all."

"And?" asked Max, clearly puzzled at Eddie's obvious reluctance.

Finally, Eddie said it. "It was Neil Holt."

"Neil Holt," repeated Max, "as in Imogen Holt's deceased husband?" Eddie nodded looking at the floor, not meeting Max's steady gaze.

Max leaned back in his chair and closed his eyes because there it was, the missing piece, the piece that put this whole business together making it make complete sense.

At that moment Isiah rushed over. "Boss. We've just been alerted that Cameron Sheldon has just been found dead in his hospital bed."

"Cause of death?" asked Max although he already knew what that would be.

"Massive heart attack brought on by..."

"Overdose of barbiturates and potassium. In other words, by Lethal Injection."

"In this case lethal intravenous input," finished Isiah.

And there it is thought Max, all bases covered.

CHAPTER 48

Malcolm Speight was looking around the tacky opulence of his office situated in the City Centre. It was large and expensively furnished in the worst possible taste, as if Liberace had joined forces with Laurence Llewelyn- Bowen and they had come up with a design after having drunk several bottles of alcohol. Gold leaf and animal print were everywhere with the odd piece of diamante or crystal thrown in for good measure and Malcolm loved it.

Now he was waiting for his visitor an unexpected one at that. Eddie and Albert had voiced their concerns but Malcolm had squashed their fears. "Like I told the Chief Inspector boys, I am more than happy to help the boys in blue with their enquiries although I am somewhat at a loss of how I can be of service." Smiling at the worried expressions on the faces of his loyal men he then added, "Relax lads, its nowt, nowt we can't handle any road."

Max was now sitting opposite Malcolm who smiling benignly began, "So Chief Inspector how can I be of help this fine day?"

Max was not sitting across from Malcolm Speight to play games so skipped any expected social pleasantries and abruptly asked, "How well do you know Imogen Holt?"

The directness of the question momentarily surprised Malcolm but recovering quickly he said, "I don't know Ms Holt. Her deceased husband was my Barrister, and an excellent one too. It was a very sad day when he was killed. Why is it the good ones go too soon eh?"

Ignoring his question and Malcolm's attempt to engage him in a conversation, Max continued, "So you've never met Ms Holt?"

Looking at Max directly, eye to eye he replied, "I never said that and yes I have. Her husband's funeral and again at the Inquest but I wouldn't say I knew her. Now, may I ask why you want to know?"

"No other time?"

"Again Chief Inspector, may I ask why I am being questioned about my association with Ms Holt or how many times we may have met?"

Malcolm was now realising how tough the man before him was and that he had underestimated how difficult fobbing him off would be. Unbeknown to both men however was how much each one of them cared about Imogen, how important she had become to these two very different men who had very different agendas where she was concerned.

Max looking at Malcolm realised he was the sort of man he had always had to deal with. A diamond in the rough, a man who would always look like he was wearing a cheap suit or too much cheap aftershave despite how much he may have paid. Yet he would be loyal and if he has pledged his loyalty to Imogen then Max would not get the answers he was looking for. This he knew with certainty as he knew that Imogen would be so easy to pledge to. She was a woman most men would die for.

"Perhaps I'm trying to join certain dots together."

Malcolm looked at Max and too also recognised the man before him, a man conflicted, but also a man who lived by the truth, a man of integrity and a man he knew would always go by the book.

Changing tack Malcolm said, "From what the news outlets are saying you're the man of the moment, the 'top London cop', the toast of the National Crime Agency who brought down a huge network of human misery in sleepy pretty little Penton?"

"But am I?" said Max leaning forward and nailing Malcolm with very cold ice blue eyes.

Malcolm started shaking his head, tutting as he did so saying, "Are you telling me the papers are telling fibs Chief Inspector?! Never! Lads can you hear what the Chief Inspector is suggesting? Beggar's belief. What is the world coming to?" Malcolm now displaying a heavy sarcastic fake mock horror with Albert and Eddie following their boss's lead shaking their heads too.

Max very nearly losing the little restraint he felt he still had snarled, "I'm telling you that I don't like being played," as his fists were clenching and unclenching as if by their own volition. Albert looked ready to pounce if not for Malcolm's almost imperceptible shake of his head. Instead Malcolm leaned back in his chair and smiled almost piteously at the now angry Max.

"So what is it that's troubling you exactly?" Max remained silent whilst Malcolm continued, "Or is it your ego that's hurting you, that it? Is that all?" shaking his head.

Max rose from his chair, placed his hands on the gold leafed desk and leaned forward. "It's about the truth! A lie doesn't become the truth and wrong doesn't become right because it's convenient. In my world the truth, and nothing but the truth matters." Malcolm rose from his seat and placed his hands on his desk and like Max he too leaned forward to the degree that just another two inches and their noses would touch. Eddie and Albert were now seriously worried where this would end.

"It's about more than truth or honour or some bloody social code. It's about what is right and righteousness and justice has many faces. You've been around, you've seen enough and you know the score. Justice is not always about the law because if it was there would be no need for the likes of me."

Malcolm then stood up and walked towards the floor to ceiling window that looked out across the city, a city he had grown up in and thought of a beautiful, good woman who had only wanted to protect her friend. A beautiful good woman who had reached out and trusted him to help her. "What is that famous quote now? You know the one about good men and evil?"

Max watching Malcolm replied, "'Evil triumphs when good men do nothing'," Max then laughed without humour asking, "Are you seriously telling me you're a good man?"

Malcolm turned to look at the man before him, this protagonist whom he envied not because of his looks, his stance, but because he had seen how Imogen looked at him. What he'd give for her, a woman like her, to look at him the same way? Quite simply all he had and the rest.

"Not one bit, I know what I am but I also know a good woman when I meet one. A woman who has dealt with more heartbreak and misery then most do in a lifetime but never looks for pity or gives excuses. A woman who does understand loyalty and friendship. A woman most men would give all they had to just have her smile only for him." Then sadly shaking his head he added, "Yet she smiles only for you."

Max now felt the hairs stand up on the back of his neck asking, "And how would you know how she smiles at me?"

Malcolm looked at Max and merely smiled back at him saying nothing, but silently saying everything.

Max now saw a man who lived by his word once it was given. Max knew there was no fighting that but Max also knew how dangerous such men were and he was now seriously worried because Imogen would have no idea what this man stood before him would be capable of. Max knew. Max had seen it before. Too many times before.

"I think we're done!" announced Malcolm with a finality that brokered no argument.

Nodding Max got up to leave then said, "Sheldon's dead by the way."

Malcolm keeping eye contact said, "Everyone dies and it was obviously his turn." Shaking his head with pure disgust and with eyes full of loathing for the man before him, Max walked out.

Staring at his receding back Malcolm, picked up his phone waited for the connection before saying, "I'm sorry, but it's obvious he knows."

Disconnecting the call, he accepted the large

brandy Eddie had poured for him as he walked towards his large floor to ceiling window, showing the panoramic view of the city he loved. He'd tried so hard to protect her from more hurt, more heartache and had failed. Drinking the liquid in one he looked at the expensive crystal before throwing it against the reinforced glass, watching the splinters fly and hoping against hope Imogen's heart would not be shattered into a thousand pieces again.

CHAPTER 49

Beth was so happy. Brad was coming home, back to their home and back to her. They had talked, really talked and a whole fresh new page was now opening up for them. "There's loads of ways for us to have a house full of kids. We meet enough in this job to give some of them a decent start."

"We will have loads of little buggers running around and driving us mad."

Yes, there would be babies in their future, ones they would love as much as if they had made them themselves. Yes, life would be back on track again and she would be where she was always meant to be with her 'bear'.

Brad had made a remarkable recovery, lesser mortals would have died and Beth would be forever grateful that they had been given this second chance. She had behaved badly, had done wrong, but she would now live an exemplary life. This she vowed.

She was due at the hospital within the next hour and was about to leave when suddenly she needed to vomit. Rushing to the toilet she did so, then sat on the seat wondering what she must have eaten. Actually, hadn't she been sick yesterday too? Thinking now she started to count weeks. So she hadn't had a period in a while but then again, she's had enough stress recently to never have one ever again! She was now searching the cabinet for a Pregnancy test kit, a remnant from their 'trying for a baby' days. She couldn't be but it wouldn't hurt to check was her thinking process. Now she was looking at the thin blue line with a kind of wonder. A baby. She was having a baby. She was having a baby but not Brad's baby. Closing her eyes, she knew and wondered why? Why did it have to be him?

*

Max and Imogen were facing each other across the vast expanse of her lounge. Neither had spoken, each waiting for the other to begin. It was Max who finally broke the impasse.

"I met an acquaintance of yours today, a Malcolm Speight and what a piece of work he is," when Imogen didn't react he continued, "but you will already know that won't you because you're always one step ahead eh Imogen?" Again Imogen said nothing, did nothing but continued to look directly at Max, prepared for whatever he chose to do or say. Max walked over standing directly before her as if to gather her in an embrace and for the briefest moment she hoped that nothing had changed. Instead he softly asked, "So are you fucking him as well as me?"

Imogen's poker face, now changed to one of disbelief and then fury as she raised her hand and slapped Max as hard across his face as she possibly could. The impact sound of flesh on flesh echoed around the room as Max now held her by her arms as she prepared to strike him again, staring into her eyes that were now full of anger before taking her into an embrace, holding her tightly as she pummelled him with her fists. Shoving him hard she attempted to escape his hold only for Max to pull her back with more force than necessary.

"Get your hands off me you bastard..." but the rest of her words were cut off as Max grabbed her head pulling his mouth to hers, both now kissing with fury, ripping at each other's clothes with anger before Max turned her back to him and roughly bending her over the chair arm, entered her hard, making her cry out and for once not from passion. When he slumped against her, Max felt nothing but shame, whilst Imogen began to silently weep. The humiliation felt would stay with them both for a long time as they straightened clothes, not looking at each other, the silence of regret already taking root. They both knew that they would never return from this moment.

"God I'm sorry," muttered Max.

"Worried what I'm going to accuse you of? Don't worry on that score."

Shaking his head Max felt an overwhelming sadness uttering, "Christ Almighty, but who the fuck are you?"

As she turned to silently face him he continued, "What I will never understand is how you could possibly trust a man like him, but not me." As Imogen remained pale and silent Max continued, "But before I go you need to understand something. He is a bad business and he will make you pay!"

"Like I just have you mean?" Imogen knew that her words, quietly spoken would hurt. Max visibly flinched as if she had violently struck him again and he now looked at her with such utter contempt that she felt something actually break inside of her but outwardly remained looking resolute. With nothing more left to say Max now turned towards the door and walked out without looking back or saying another word.

CHAPTER 50

Many of Sheffield's finest were frequenting the local 'Frog and Prince' pub across from the station giving Max a send -off as he prepared to leave Sheffield, returning to London and the National Crime Agency Headquarters. Even the Chief Constable Jim Haggerty had called in for a single drink, not wanting to put a damper on proceedings by being present.

He and many colleagues had tried for well over a week to persuade Max to stay. "Are you sure we can't entice you away from the Metropolis then?"

"Thank you Chief Constable but I think I'm better off where I am."

"Well if you ever change your mind, there's a senior position for you here. Good luck and thank you again, oh and the next round is on me everyone," leaving a tab open behind the bar for the next round for all there which earned him significant 'brownie' points.

"Bloody hell," announced Eddie, "but I never thought I'd live to see the day when one of the top corridor brigade dug deep into his pockets and buy a round. It's a bloody miracle! You're nothing short of a bloody miracle worker Max!"

All were also really happy that the pubs were open again, even under the pretence of selling food. "I tell you," announced Dan, "that a scotch egg is regarded as a meal. It was on Jeremy Vine! Lyds tell the Sarge."

Laughing Lydia replied, "Leave me out of this one."

"Ah well lad, bring it on that's all I can say, as long as the ale is flowing," said Eddie, balancing the tray of drinks as he made his way over to Max who was being hailed as hero of the decade, with many asking him to stay on or at least stay in touch.

Isiah was saying, "It won't be the same boss so please reconsider? I mean look what you're going back to? Beer like piss, shite football teams and all those American tourists? Don't do it boss!"

Dan interjected saying, "Leave the man alone Isaiah but seriously boss how can you abandon us? I mean who will stop Eddie eating all the donuts on a morning?" as he ducked Eddie's pretend head swipe.

Laughing the young police officers headed for the bar as Eddie smiled, "It looks like you'll be missed boss," as he handed Max his pint and whisky chaser. Nodding Max merely smiled saying, "They're good people, good coppers that's for sure."

At that point Beth came over and looked Max very squarely and somewhat defiantly in the eye saying, "I would just like to say thank you Chief Inspector and hope all goes well for you back in London."

Max looked at Beth and nodded saying, "Give Brad my best and I hope he makes a full recovery. We need good men like him in the force." Nodding Beth began to move away before turning back and said, "You will be missed Sir, and not only by the squad."

Max looked her squarely in the eye then merely nodded and remained silent as Beth continued towards the exit.

Eddie looked at him and at Beth's departure and said, "So now you're leaving, may I frankly be honest and perhaps forget our ranks for a while?"

Sighing Max answered, "Just depends," because he didn't want to hear what he knew this good Yorkshire man, good family man wanted to say to him.

Lowering his voice Eddie continued as if Max hadn't spoken. "We would have never nailed Sheldon if you hadn't been here." As Max attempted to interrupt him Eddie said forcefully, "No hear me out. Downs would have been another missing person and Sheldon wasn't even on our radar because you put him there! We can only surmise the rest of it but you know isn't it time that occasionally the 'good guys' get a break? Get a little helping hand from an unexpected source?"

Shaking his head Eddie took a long drink from his pint of beer before continuing, "How many times has a bastard Barrister made one of us look like an idiot or even worse a liar? How many times has a legal loophole allowed some low life to leave court laughing at us? How many times has a young woman or man stood up to a rapist only for the courts to verbally rape him or her again?" Shaking his head Eddie said sadly, "I believe that for once the cards fell in our favour and I don't care how it happened if I'm honest!"

Then Eddie looked down and took a deep breath saying, "I also believe that good people, decent people can be driven to do what we in the law business would constitute as a crime, when in reality they have merely fought back and for once bloody won. For once gave back as good as they were being given."

Max looked at Eddie and at that moment envied the simplicity in which Eddie was viewing their world.

"You've met Speight?"

Nodding Eddie said, "More than once. Why?"

"Well how could she trust such a man like him but not me?"

"You sound jealous and that's unworthy of you lad!" Then shaking his head Eddie looked at this man he respected more than most, trusted and admired like no other if he was being brutally honest with himself.

"We aren't privy to what actually happened to Downs, it's all supposition. Who knows what that poor lass Sarah suffered, I mean will you ever forget that bloody dungeon we found? Or what that poor cow Ruth told us what he liked to get up to?"

Max shook his head, "We have a process and no I will never forget the lorry at Dover or what we discovered in Penton or Attercliffe but…"

"But what Max? The world's a safer place without those low lives in it and let's face it, there's plenty more where they came from! This victory won't last long."

Nodding Max looked at the man before him whom he now regarded as a friend and who had not yet finished. "I also remember when you first laid eyes on Imogen Holt. I remember the look on your face and it was the same for her. I also remember her face the night we thought we might lose you too. It was like ...anguish, real anguish and the relief she felt was bloody real."

Sighing Max ran his hand through his hair then leaning back in his chair he asked, "And your point?"

Smiling sadly Eddie replied, "Only to let such a woman go because a person believed she had managed to hide something important from him all for the right reasons I might add, would make that someone a bit of a self-righteous pillock now don't you think? Or a bloody self-righteous fool at the very least, or a very proud fool and we all know that's what goes before the proverbial fall? Particularly if what was being hidden was to protect a friend, a vulnerable abused friend at that. Never forget, to quote our old mate Alec Dales, how evil walks amongst us every sodding day."

Clearly surprised at Eddie's choice of words Max merely nodded and looked down then after a heavy pause said, "I know you're right but I think I've truly blown it where Imogen is concerned."

"So put it right!"

Sighing heavily whilst scrubbing his hands through his hair and over his face Max replied, "I don't think I can. I don't think she'll ever want to see me again after... after how I... behaved and I wouldn't blame her either. I behaved like everything I bloody hate." They remained silent, both lost in their own thoughts until Max seemed to pull himself together saying, "You know I was going to stay. I felt I'd finally found where I belonged here with this team, in this city..."

"With the right woman too eh?" Smiling

his wry smile, Max merely nodded as the silence lengthened between them before Max, seemingly pulling himself together said, “I believe this is my round so same again?”

Nodding sadly Eddie merely answered, “Aye lad and make it a bloody double!”

Max got up then looked down at Eddie, this man he had instinctively trusted from the moment they had first met and whom he personally liked enormously, this man who he now regarded as a friend. “Will you promise me something?”

“If I can. Name it?”

“Keep an eye on her and Speight. Don’t let him get too close to her, just in case?”

Nodding his agreement Eddie shrugged replying, “I will do my best but we both know whose job that should be?”

Nodding his understanding of the point Eddie was making, Max merely answered, “I’ll make it treble then ok?”

CHAPTER 51

Whilst Max was saying his goodbyes, Imogen was sat looking at her two friends, listening to their voices and wondering how she would get through this next much needed conversation. She couldn't remember a time without the four of them being in each other's lives. What would life be like if this was the end of them? She'd already lost Max, so what more was she about to lose? She was about to find out.

"Sorry I'm late, just called in on the Chief Inspector's leaving do," began Beth giving Imogen a look that spoke volumes, "but I thought we were due at Sarah's anyway. Why the summons?"

"Is Sarah ok?" asked Harry, worrying that more bad news was on the horizon.

"She's fine as long as John Hilton remains alive and well," replied Imogen.

"Who would have credited quiet John Hilton from Grimsdale to have ended up as, well one of the 'Who Dares Wins' lot? Just incredible," remarked Beth.

"Not everyone is as they seem are they?" said Imogen.

Harry looked at her and said, "What is it? What's wrong?"

Taking a deep breath Imogen began, knowing now that there would be no going back. "Harry, the night you came across Sarah and finding Grant dead, did you make Sarah change her clothes?"

"What? Of course not, I rang you guys and waited. Why are you asking such…?"

"We all saw the blood, the blood splatter. It was everywhere so I need to ask both of you for both of your opinions professionally speaking. Why was Sarah not splattered by his blood? Covered even?" Silence.

"Because Sarah wasn't the one who actually plunged the knife into Grant Downs was she Beth?" continued Imogen.

Beth remained silent but Harry was incredulous. "Imogen! Have you lost your mind?" Imogen did not answer but merely placed on the coffee table what she had found the day she was looking for her lost earing. There in its silver shiny glory was the metal police identification number with part of the torn cloth epaulette still partially attached.

"I assume this was torn off by Grant in the struggle? I mean I assume he didn't just stand there and be stabbed?!" Beth was now staring at her identification insignia as if she was seeing something completely alien. No one spoke for several minutes.

Then Beth replied, "No I suspect it was torn off when he tried to rape me, not that he thought he was raping me. He thought, no he knew I liked it rough, really rough with him, the rougher, the more violent the better in fact."

Harry gasped, her hands over her mouth but Imogen merely rose to her feet, walked over to the kitchen island and brought back the glasses and wine she now placed before them. Pouring generous quantities, she quietly and without anger said, "We need to know it all, you know we do and you owe it to us." Nodding to her friends Beth began the sorry story of her brief affair with Grant Downs.

"It began in May, just after we had noticed Sarah's bruises and I went to tell him that I would arrest him if he ever touched her violently again. The bastard, well he just laughed at me and that was when I lost it and actually went to physically hurt him, which somehow ignited into sex."

Harry now interrupted, completely incredulous saying, "You mean you had sex with one of our husbands as if it was nothing?"

Almost defiant, Beth shrugged and replied, "Yes and it was great sex, incredible even because it was brutal, devoid of any real feeling except for self- loathing I suppose."

"So just the once?" asked Imogen.

Laughing mirthlessly Beth shook her head saying, "The next time was in the back of his car, the time after that in the cheapest dirtiest doss house Sheffield had to offer, hating him so much, but hating myself more but unable to stop. The day he died, ok... the day I stabbed him dead, I had come to tell him that we were done, that I would never go near him again and if necessary tell Sarah and encourage her to leave, even if it meant our friendship would be over and no reconciliation with Brad. The bastard just laughed, saying how much I loved the sex too much and the self- loathing. To be honest he wasn't far wrong."

The room fell silent with each of the women dealing with this new reality until Harry asked, "But you've still not explained how he ended up with a knife in him?"

With eyes shining with unshed tears Beth found herself now reliving those minutes which in effect had changed all their lives forever, to a point of no return. "Like I said, he laughed, wasn't taking me seriously but started tearing at my clothes, thinking I was still playing the game because as far as he was concerned the rougher the sex, the better we both liked it. The more I fought back the more aggressive, the more turned on he became to the point I thought he may actually kill me this time. Trying to get away, I found myself backed up to the unit where the Knife Stand was. I remember reaching for the first knife I could find and plunging it in his back which made him stagger backwards. I can still see the look on his face, how baffled he was and he actually smiled at me, almost amused then I couldn't stop. I just kept on plunging the knife in, again and again and again until he wasn't smiling or moving anymore. I can't remember leaving, I just remember arriving home, then Harry ringing. You were there for the rest."

Beth looked up to see Harry quietly crying but Imogen was just staring at her.

"Were you ever going to tell Sarah that she had not murdered her husband?" asked Harry. Beth did not answer. "Beth?"

Eventually she replied, "No, I thought I'd got away with it. I thought we had all got the best possible outcome. I thought I'd lost my identification insignia in the Sheffield pub fight I'd dealt with earlier and I actually was beginning to believe our lives would be as they should be except better because Sarah was rid of that scum!" Then looking at Imogen she shouted, "For Christ's sake will you say something?!"

Shaking her head Imogen said, "How can you possibly believe that this would just allow us all to go back to normal? Do you want to know the first thing Sarah said when she knew about Brad being shot? She blamed herself. She immediately believed that she had inadvertently started a chain of events that had led to a man she has grown to love like a brother, as we all have, to be so badly injured that he could possibly die! You, knowing the truth, let us all conspire to hide a dead body, thinking we were protecting Sarah who had clearly been so savagely attacked! Who was obviously a victim of the most awful abuse!"

Looking at her friends with something nearing consternation Beth spluttered, "But you would have done the same for me wouldn't you? Protect me like you did Sarah?"

Shaking her head Imogen was now at a loss. "Protect you, a serving police officer who was actually shagging the husband of one of her closest friends and then killed him when she'd had enough? Had sex with the victim more than once! Had actually gone back for more, again and again! Why would we feel a need to? Were you vulnerable? A victim of domestic abuse so badly damaged that we wondered if you would survive the trauma if not physically but mentally or emotionally as we did Sarah? No your reasons were that for once in your life things were not falling into place. For once what you wanted wasn't happening. For once you were expected to take it on the chin like the rest of us, to be a bloody grown up! For once!"

"And you!" spat out Beth, "so ready to jump in and save the sodding day eh? Imogen the fucking protector, when all you wanted to do was lay your own guilt on the rest of us for you killing the low life that was your own father!"

Imogen then for the second time in her life slapped hard the person standing before her with Harry shouting, "No Imogen don't," as she pulled her away, looking at her with horror and concern. Never had she seen her friend so close to losing her self- control. Shaking with anger borne out of disgust and pain, Imogen moved away from her friends, picking up her half full glass and emptying its contents in one.

Beth said nothing because there was nothing for her to say as she rubbed her cheek knowing Imogen's mark would be there. She also knew she had that coming, that everything Imogen was accusing her of was the truth. Her wanting to hurt Imogen and somehow justify her actions was something she was already regretting. No one had anything to say for several minutes and it was an ashen faced Harry who broke the silence first. "The thing is Beth, as a police officer you could have explained it away, an act of self – defence when you confronted a violent thug who was hurting a tiny defenseless woman. One look at Sarah's injuries would have been enough so why didn't you?"

Shaking her head Beth shrugged saying, "I can't

answer that. Looking back, it's like it was happening to someone else." The silence was now hanging heavily in the room, as each one of them looked into the abyss of this new reality. Beth was the first to speak, now holding her breath, terrified of the answer as she asked, "Do you want me to hand myself in?"

Imogen looked at Beth with such intensity that Beth was now afraid of her when she quietly asked, "What is the penalty for perverting the course of Justice Beth? Surely you know? I looked it up. Life imprisonment! Life! Knowing what you had done you let us do just that, have a life sentence hanging over each one of us, for the rest of our lives."

"Oh my God!" whispered Harry now putting her head in her hands.

Imogen looked at Beth, saw the fear also the shame and regret then shaking her head said, "No the police are never to know, not officially anyhow," as her thoughts briefly flickered to Max, "but Sarah deserves to know the truth." Harry nodded her agreement.

"So you're going to tell her," said a defeated Beth tears welling, now fearing what would happen next.

Imogen looked at Beth and shook her head replying, "No, you are. You for once in your spoilt self -indulgent life, can take some responsibility and tell her yourself!"

CHAPTER 52

Sarah opened the door holding a bottle of Bollinger in one hand and a brimming crystal champagne flute in the other and she had clearly started without them.

"At last, where have you been? I've actually started without you guys for once! Actually managed the cork on my own too!" She looked so much better, so much like the Sarah of old, the Sarah of pre Grant Downs days, the Sarah who was happily in love with John Hilton as she had been since she was seventeen years old. As her friends came in she was struck at how subdued they were.

"So," she said, "there have obviously been developments but before you tell me there is something I have to say first." She was now standing on the spot Grant Downs had died and although that was clearly a coincidence, it was not lost on the others. "I want to thank you all from the bottom of my heart for looking after me. No listen," as Beth tried to interrupt, "I have to say this. I know what I did was a shocking thing, to stab someone to death, no matter how wicked that person is, no matter what that person had done to me and I suspect many more but ... and please don't be shocked by this, but I actually now realise that it is something I had to do. Like you Imogen, I somehow found the strength to fight back for once, to not allow myself to be this...this ...victim! I, petite, pathetic dog loving Sarah, found the strength to say to the beast that was Grant Downs, no! I will not be your victim! I said no, you will not continue to hurt me or anybody else! Imogen we are survivors. We are... are... warriors! We all are in all of our different ways and we are fabulous with it! There. Said it! Now what's happened? Hit me with it, I mean how much worse could it be?"

Beth began to speak, "Sarah there's something you need to know."

"It's about the fall out regarding Grant's criminal activities, isn't it Beth?" said Imogen, holding Beth's eye contact, slightly shaking her head.

"Yes Beth, what was it you were going to tell us?" agreed Harry, nodding at Imogen her unspoken agreement that this was for the best. No one was going to take Sarah's newly acquired self -empowerment away from her, not after everything she had endured.

As Beth did have news, very unpleasant news at that, she continued, "Cameron Sheldon has been found dead from a huge drug overdose allegedly.

They found him dead in his hospital bed this morning."

"How could that happen?" gasped Sarah, "with his injuries?"

"Clearly paid someone to do the deed," replied Beth. They were all silent for a moment, thinking about the cruellest of men who had suffered the cruellest of ends.

"Wow," breathed Sarah, "so it really is over. A toast then, to better days, days without having such awful people in our lives."

"To better days," muttered her three friends. "Also," because Sarah was now drunkenly on a roll, "to being women! Because only truly strong, brilliant women really understand the power of friendship and sisterhood and that's what we are, what we have! To sisterhood!"

"To sisterhood!" Harry spied Beth not touching her drink when both toasts were declared.

"Not drinking Beth?" queried Harry.

Taking a deep breath Beth replied, "I've always understood that drinking alcohol was not to be recommended if you're pregnant."

Stunned silence followed then, "What?" exploded Sarah, "Oh my God Beth but that's fantastic! Brad must be over the moon!"

Beth did not know where to look but decided she now needed to be as honest as possible to these women whom she owed so much to. "He doesn't know and I don't know how he'll take it. The baby isn't Brad's."

The silence was heavy and prolonged until Sarah ventured, "So who is the father?"

"A one-night stand, couldn't even begin to tell you who, just some random when I was off my head. Sorry to be such a disappointment," replied Beth realising how quick and easy the lies came when they needed to.

"Are you intending to have the baby?" asked Imogen very quietly.

Beth nodded saying, "Yes, I have to as it may be my only chance and if I have to do it alone, well so be it."

"You won't be alone though will she?" said Sarah, shaking her head with tears in her eyes as she came to hug her friend.

"No," agreed Harry, "and I think Brad will understand."

"A baby," said Sarah, "we're having another baby, how wonderful. What a lucky baby to have the two of you and the rest of us because Harry's right, Brad will forgive how this happened and love this little one. You know I'm so relieved I didn't fall pregnant with Grant's baby. To have a child that would have his DNA, his genes to pass on would have been truly awful. Even his mum said that and that must have been so hard for her.

No the world is a better, safer place without that so another toast, but for you mum-to-be, with water!"

Beth smiled but Sarah's words had hit their mark. To be having Grant's child was not what she would have wanted either but it was what she was having and looking at Harry and Imogen she knew that they had also connected the dots too.

CHAPTER 53

Life goes on and the world continued to turn even in the bleak days of 2020. The summer had gone and autumn was now bringing its own challenges as Covid 19 renewed its energy and came back with a deadlier force that had been unforeseen since it had first begun back in March. Harry knew how bad it was and how bad it was predicted to become and she despaired. Imogen too, now the newly appointed Head of Grove South knew how another full National lockdown would be inevitable and she feared for her more vulnerable pupils and the burn out rate of her staff.

"So it looks like we're back in lockdown next week," said Beth looking at her friends.

"Well at least we won't have to worry about which bloody Tier we're in, I couldn't keep up," muttered Sarah, "although the Construction Business work can still go ahead thank God."

Sarah had successfully revived the family building business that her late husband had exploited and almost destroyed, bringing back to

Penton much needed local work. Old timer Alec Dales and his son had been an invaluable help to her and finally Greens reputation for quality housing and home improvements was slowly being restored.

"Who would have thought that we would live in such times? Hope it's over before this one decides to be born," said Beth rubbing her baby bump that was coming into its sixth month of gestation.

"Who knows but Alan thinks a vaccine will be ready by Christmas but we've got a way to go yet although there's at least a glimmer of light at the end of the bloody tunnel now," was Harry's informed reply.

The girls had accurately predicted Brad's reaction to her pregnancy. At first he had been so hurt, so disappointed to the point that he had left their home to go to his parents to think. That had lasted the whole of three days and Beth would never forget Brad's words on his return to her and to what they now regarded as their baby.

"It's not the way I wanted us to have a baby but it is what it is. I wanted to go down the surrogacy route and that's how I intend to see this from now on. I love you and I think I've already started to love your baby too so with your permission, I'd like to regard this baby as mine as well as yours."

Beth had burst into tears and flung herself into

his arms, temporarily forgetting he was still in convalescence.

"How lucky is this baby and how lucky am I to have you, the best man I ever known to be my baby's father. I love you my Bear."

Folding her into his arms Brad said, "I love you too but bloody hell Beth, but you don't make it easy!"

"I'll do better," she smiled, "promise," and she meant every word.

All were quiet now worrying what was ahead of them. "Just hope the 'oldies' get through this ok," said Beth adding, "I mean Arlette and my dad and your mum Harry? I'm not ready to lose any of them yet."

Sarah nodded smiling saying, "It's just too lovely that your mum and your dad have got together. Do you remember how we all used to pretend we were actual sisters? You two can be now of sorts."

Harry was now looking at both girls whilst an unaware Sarah was continuing to smile happily believing all was as it should be and had always been. "The wicked step- sisters," mused Imogen, "so who's Cinders then?"

"That will be me," said Harry desperate to keep the conversation light, "in inadequate PPE gear if they don't get their bloody act together before the next onslaught!" The girls smiled at her feeling her frustration and sharing her worries for what was to come.

Beth said, “I couldn’t be happier that Dad has found happiness again and I know mum would be happy too.” So looking at Imogen Beth said, “So let’s raise a glass to Terry and Arlette.”

As they clinked their glasses Beth looked at Imogen with such sadness that Imogen found she had to look away.

Sarah was now talking about John and when they would be able to meet again. “Lord knows where he is but it looked incredibly cold,” she was saying telling the girls about their last FaceTime.

Now having what would probably be their last meal together for the foreseeable future Beth decided to tell the girls her other news. “Looks like I’m heading back to CID. Was asked if I was interested today in being a permanent member of the team as it would appear I’ve been missed.”

Murmurs of congratulations came forth with Imogen quietly saying, “Everything has worked out well for you Beth. Baby, Brad and now the job.”

Beth looked at Imogen and then looked away, not quite able to meet her friend’s eye because it was true. Despite everything she had done, she had all she ever wanted.

“Well that’s great Beth,” gushed Harry anxious to move the subject on before Sarah questioned the sudden drop in temperature. Harry as was her way had moved forward with Beth, putting the past events behind her but Imogen was a very different persona entirely. She and Beth were still very much estranged and this situation was unlikely to change in the near future.

Beth had more though. "Looks like I have a new CID boss too. He's been recently promoted and well he's worked with us in Sheffield before."

"Who?" asked Harry, but looking at Imogen as she was beginning to guess what Beth was about to say.

"Now Detective Chief Superintendent Max Stainmore," said Beth as all eyes now turned to Imogen.

"Max is returning. For how long?" this from Sarah.

"Permanently as far as I know but I suspect it's not just the job he's back for."

Imogen remained silent and outwardly unaffected by this unexpected news. There hadn't been a day since Max had left that she hadn't thought of him, missed him, wished him well, hoped he was safe but knew there would never be any future for them, the circumstances being as they were. Knowing he was back, was going to be hard though, and she hoped that the county, that the area, that the city of Sheffield would be large enough for them to permanently avoid each other.

"Do you think he'll get in touch Gen?" asked Sarah.

"He has no reason to," was her definitive reply.

"Yeah right," scoffed Beth but allowed the matter to drop when Imogen clearly gave her a look that meant she wasn't prepared to discuss Max's return particularly with her.

Later as they walked back to their respective homes they said their good nights to Harry and Sarah and Imogen and Beth found themselves alone for the first time in a long time.

Beth with her head down said, "Will you ever forgive me? For Max? For what you lost with Max?"

Shaking her head Imogen looked at Beth saying, "It was a fling, nothing more."

"It was more than that," argued Beth, "and I took it away from you one way or another."

"No you didn't, I did that all by myself."

Beth shrugged as they continued to walk in silence until Beth said, "But you'll never really forgive me, not the way Harry has and I have to live with that because I know I've lost you, the part of you I've always needed and relied on and I want it back. I need, no we," pointing to her ever -growing abdomen, "need it back!"

Beth was stroking her baby bump then asked Imogen, "What do you believe is the stronger?

Nature or nurture?" Imogen shook her head remaining silent as Beth continued, almost as if speaking to herself. "Sarah is relieved to think Grant's DNA died with him but we know different don't we? By all accounts even his mother thought he was born to be bad, an 'evil' seed. I mean could that even be a thing?"

Shaking her head Imogen replied, "Stop it. This child will have the best parents and the rest of us."

"Including you? Even with you still so bloody angry with me her mother?"

"You're having a girl, a daughter? You never said," whispered Imogen as Imogen's eyes rested on Beth's baby bump, again wistfully wishing for something she could never ever have.

"We never speak, not really so why would I tell you?"

Imogen shaking her head began to walk away then stopped turning back to Beth asking something that had bothered her ever since she had discovered Max was back. "Max has his suspicions about who was to blame for Grant's murder and the cover up afterwards. You're included in that too so how are you going to work for a man who deep down suspects you?"

Beth was emphatic saying, "He can be as suspicious as hell but he has no proof and a signed confession from a man who had killed before and who is also dead. So for us, the authorities, the case is closed, a 'slam dunk'! I can live with it and he clearly can too so the only one who can't around here, seems to be you."

Slowly nodding Imogen turned to walk away when an exasperated Beth indicated a bench and said, "Wait! Just sit here and listen to me." Imogen stopped, sighed heavily because to be honest she was bone tired and just wanted to be alone, but did as Beth asked.

"So?"

Looking at this woman, this unforgiving good woman she had always regarded as family and loved like a sister Beth began. She knew what she needed to say and knew she would only get the one chance to actually say it. "You and I have both taken a life, the lives of two bad men. How bad they were I know, is no excuse, certainly not in the eyes of the justice system but we were both operating within a context that made the situation such that in the end we had no choice. Your father could have gone on to kill your mother and I believe Grant would have seriously hurt me and Sarah would not be here today if Grant Downs was still alive. He was drugging her and slowly driving her insane and eventually to her death and that's before we even mention what he actually inflicted on her, the rape and the rest. Do you think John Hilton would have allowed Grant to continue to live if he had somehow found out what he'd been doing to her? I for one would have held his coat because Downs had it coming! Most people would agree so why is it so different that I was the one to do it? Because I'm a woman?"

Shaking her Imogen said, "What are you saying? Seriously? That it's ok to be judge, jury and executioner? No police? No courts? You're an officer of the law for God's sake!"

Shaking her head Beth continued as if Imogen had not spoken saying, "There are hundreds of people but mainly women and children who are not being exploited, living a life of misery, wishing they were dead because Downs and Sheldon are dead instead. What they found at Greens was something out of a nightmare. Some of the police officers who worked that crime scene are still receiving counselling. When Lydia and I interviewed some of the women we rescued, the things they told us about Grant! What he regarded as his right, his perk of the job so to speak! The younger the better. My God but the man was a sodding monster." Blinking back tears of frustration, Beth leaned back into the cold hard bench sighing heavily.

"My reasons may have been selfish at the time and yes I was thinking of my own self-preservation. If I'm being totally honest I think I was just about on the right side of insanity too."

The moon came out of shadow and Imogen saw

Beth eyes shining bright with unshed tears and a profound sadness. “But,” she continued, “the outcome is Just Imogen, righteous even and you bloody know it.”

Shaking her head Beth continued now with her usual bravado and bluster, “Max Stainmore is back and he’s back for you and what’s more you want him back so get over yourself, stop the sodding martyrdom because it’s seriously tedious now and go and bloody get him.”

Looking at her with something close to astonishment, Imogen found herself without a response so they sat there quietly digesting what had been spoken between them.

“So anything else?” asked Imogen eventually.

“Nope,” replied Beth as they both got up and silently walked the remaining distance home.

*

It was a very cold, still, crisp night that was perfect for walking and for thinking and Imogen was thinking hard about her past choices and not for the first time.

When she’d hit her father with the poker that night all those years ago, it was to make him stop, to make the violence he brought with him stop. Her mother immediately wanted to take the blame but Imogen was afraid she would go to prison whilst Arlette did not want her child to be known as the girl who killed her father and end up in care. So they did what they did to survive and they got away with it.

When she believed Sarah had killed Grant, again Imogen did not trust society, the police, the men in the police, the judiciary, the men in the judiciary to treat her friend with compassion and understanding. Certain institutions were still full of misogyny and sexism and operated as such via a relentless media and of this Imogen was in no doubt. Sarah was wealthy, attractive and outwardly looking like she lived a life most would envy and the gossips and tabloids would have judged her, look at poor Caroline Flack? No one would have believed she was oblivious to who Grant Downs really was either and she would have been completely vilified despite being so innocent. Society treated outwardly successful women harshly not allowing them to have problems or issues. So she'd had to protect Sarah from all that and she had done, completely unaware how victimised and innocent Sarah really was and how duped they all had been by someone who should have known better, who had betrayed their love and trust. Yet Beth's argument this evening had been persuasive and to be honest Imogen was tired of being angry with one of her oldest friends. This next few months were going to be hard enough so perhaps it was time to 'let it go' as the song went, move on and enjoy the baby, that little innocent who had no idea as yet what life had in store.

She was also admitting to herself that thanks to her father Jake Taylor she had real trust issues. She did not deep down really trust men and she knew she was being unreasonable and unfair, acknowledging how much damage her father had in reality, actually done to her. Her late husband Neil had been a wonderful man, yet she had never told him about what had really happened that night when she was only fourteen years old. Did not trust not to be judged by him if she was being brutally honest with herself. Yet her mother had found a good man in Terry and she loved the good and honest man that made up Max Stainmore and he was back. But why was the question?

As Imogen walked the rest of her way home, she was at a loss at what to really think about Max's return but knew for the preservation of all she loved he could not come back into her life. She'd been more than foolish to have allowed him to get so close in the first place. Beth didn't know him like she did and having this between them would eat away until there was nothing left of what could have been something quite wonderful and that would be heartbreak all over again. She missed him though and realised she probably always would and that was the price she would have to pay for the choices she had made.

She was so deep in thought, she did not at first see the shadow waiting for her as she neared her gate. Max watched her as she approached, lost in her thoughts and was reminded of the first time he had laid eyes on her just a few months ago. She had that same serious, worried, wary expression and he suspected he was probably the reason for it this cold, crisp evening. He knew she would be startled when he approached and he knew she may be afraid too, afraid of why he had returned, what he had returned to do. That hurt and he was at a loss what to do about it but hoped he could find the words. What he knew he couldn't do, was walk away from her again because she was his home and he now just had to convince her of that, convince her that he had been a fool and that he did understand and probably always had done. As Eddie had so astutely said, his ego had taken a hit and to allow this woman to no longer be in his life because of it was just too stupid for words.

Stepping from the shadows he quietly said, "Hello Imogen."

Imogen jumped from her reverie and stopped in her tracks, then recovering she continued walking towards her gate and towards Max. "I didn't expect to see you so soon."

"But you expected to see me?" Max smiled, shrugging his shoulders, "of course you did because you're always one step ahead aren't you?" Max was now standing before her, silently looking at her, looking handsomely disheveled and very cold.

Imogen stared silently back at him and then asked, "Cold?"

"Bloody freezing, it must be at least twenty degrees colder up here!"

Shaking her head as she opened the locked gate she replied, "Well if you're here for a while you will need a bigger coat with you being such a soft London lad. Winters here can be harsh and unforgiving."

Smiling and shaking his head Max replied, "I suspect not only the winters can be harsh an unforgiving around here and I'm not here for a while, I'm here to stay."

Imogen knew what he was trying to say but merely added, "We're expecting snow and you'll feel cold like no other. Snow and Covid will be hard to take."

Shaking his head as if dismissing her dismissal, Max continued, "I was hoping we could find that coffee shop, have coffee sometime." Looking away from her now with a look of embarrassed shame he continued, "I behaved like everything I hate the last time I was here. If I'm honest, even I can't begin to ..."

Shaking her head Imogen cut him off with a finality that brooked no argument. "It was sex, rough sex but nothing happened that I didn't want or...", as she now looked away, unable to finish.

Max finished for her. "Or what? Deserve?" Imogen remained silent but looked as if she was carrying the world's woes and would never smile again and Max desperately wanted to take her in his arms to reassure her that all would now be well. "It was sex that wasn't us and no woman deserves how I treated you and I behaved like a... like a brute. I'm better than that." Then shaking his head added, "No, we're better than that. So I'm sorry and I'm back and I'm back for us because we deserve to see what we can become given a different set of circumstance. We can't change how we met but we did so... let's just find that coffee shop eh?"

Shaking her head, she closed her gate, now watching Max as he walked towards her through the iron bars, an ironic physical metaphor that was not loss on either of them. "We should never have begun because we never stood a chance, so go home Max because there's nothing for you here. Not then, not now, not ever."

Max's smile was grim as he watched her stubborn retreating figure. He knew before he had made his journey back north that he would have his work cut out, to win her back, to win her trust but this was only the beginning because he was going nowhere. "Well I'm back for good so get used to it because I am not giving up on us!"

"There is no us," was the call back from over her shoulder. Yes, thought Max, it was never going to be easy but she was worth the fight, despite the bloody cold. Turning up his collar as he hunched his shoulders against the biting chill, Max was thinking how he really did need a 'big' coat when suddenly he felt himself being violently knocked towards the railings with a sudden pain exploding in his chest, only then acknowledging the loud noise that seemed to be all around him. Then there was another piercing pain but this time he also heard her voice, screaming his name as he felt her arms around him. "Max! Max! Oh my God Max!"

As the darkness began to close in Max smiled, drinking in her scent, thinking that he was exactly where he wanted to be, what he'd come back for. Back in the arms of the woman he loved whilst she called out his name asking him to stay.

****

ACKNOWLEDGEMENT

When you write a novel, it is a solitary experience, easy to get lost in a world you create out of your own imagination. For me sharing what I have created has been more difficult than the actual writing in many respects so I have certain people to thank from the bottom of my heart for their relentless support and enthusiasm and for encouraging me to publish and be 'damned'.

Thank you so much to Graham Saunders and Phil Sokell who have done the hard mechanics of publishing for me. Graham, your personal support for my writing has been a constant for a long time now and I can't tell you how much I appreciate it. To my friend Milly Johnson, thank you for sending me the wonderful Scott Pack who tells you the truth, as painful as it is, steering a writer in the right direction. Scott, you are worth your weight in gold.

Thank you to my beautiful sister Denise Thackray, my dear friend Susan Harding and her lovely husband Ian who loved my second draft

and said I needed to be published and to Jane Booker, it's a very different book now Jane but you encouraged me to continue.
Finally, to my husband Nick for putting up with me when I'm in the writing 'zone'. Thank you for your encouragement, your patience and your unquestioning love.
Best wishes,
Chrissie Yates.

ABOUT THE AUTHOR

Chrissie Yates

Chrissie Yates is a retired English teacher and is happily married to her husband Nick and living in the beautiful Market Town of Penistone, South Yorkshire. When she is not writing, she is travelling, shopping or looking after her grandchildren.

COMING SOON

The Sequel

'When the Devil is Owed',
book 2 in the Penton Series

Printed in Great Britain
by Amazon

33339785R00258